PRAISE FOR *STATE OF SHOCK*

"You don't have to be a lawyer from Chicago to enjoy this gripping story, but it doesn't hurt. It sails along nicely before suddenly really hitting you between the eyes. Then it's a race to the dramatic finish line! I now eagerly await the next in the series."

—Randy E. Barnett, Patrick Hotung Professor of Constitutional Law, Georgetown Law

PRAISE FOR *MENTAL STATE*

"The Professor's murder mystery delivers the rough and tumble goods, and it will leave readers wanting more."

—Kurt Schlichter, lawyer and bestselling author

"A pure page-turner. A must-read if you love the country, the Supreme Court, or just a book that will keep you up at night."

—Ben Shapiro, public intellectual, talk-show host, and bestselling author

"Try as I might, I could not put *Mental State* down. It's terrific. At times hilarious, always interesting, and in parts truly disturbing. I loved it."

—Michael Seidman, Professor of Law at Georgetown University Law Center

"Henderson's debut novel had me white-knuckling it from chapter to chapter in this heady, emotional, suspenseful and expertly-crafted page-turner."

—Mark Feuerstein, film and television actor

STATE OF SHOCK

9 Mar 21

Stephen,

Enjoy!

VTY,

TODD

BOOKS BY M. TODD HENDERSON

Mental State
State of Shock

M. TODD HENDERSON

STATE OF SHOCK

Copyright © 2021 by M. Todd Henderson

All rights reserved. No part of the book may be reproduced in any form or by any electronic or mechanical means, including information storage and retrieval systems, without permission in writing from the publisher, except by a reviewer who may quote brief passages in a review.

Down & Out Books
3959 Van Dyke Road, Suite 265
Lutz, FL 33558
DownAndOutBooks.com

The characters and events in this book are fictitious. Any similarity to real persons, living or dead, is coincidental and not intended by the author.

Cover design by Zach McCain

ISBN: 1-64396-151-9
ISBN-13: 978-1-64396-151-4

For Charlotte, Grover, and Maeve

Stars, hide your fires:
Let not light see my black and deep desires...
—Shakespeare, *Macbeth*

Then every thing includes itself in power,
Power into will, will into appetite;
And appetite, an universal wolf,
So doubly seconded with will and power,
Must make perforce an universal prey,
And last eat up himself.
—Shakespeare, *Troilus and Cressida*

PROLOGUE

Holding a newspaper in his hands felt strange. His mom still subscribed, out of interest or habit he wasn't certain, and so the paper sat there lifeless on the counter every morning while he sipped his coffee and looked out the window at the brick wall of the apartment building next door. He was used to reading the news—sports, the *Chicago Defender*, the *Daily Law Journal*—on his phone. Never once had he pulled the morning paper out of its blue plastic bag. But today was different; today was a paper day.

Unsheathed and unfolded, he set it down on the kitchen table, then eyed his fingertips. He wiped them with a napkin, still soggy from soaking up a bit of milk that bounced off his Honeycomb and splashed on the table. The ink stains lingered, and for someone who liked everything just the way he liked everything, that fact stuck in his mind like a pine needle in a shoe. But there was a story he wanted to read—to see on the printed page. He'd survive the old-fashionedness and the inkiness.

There it was, right column, above the fold: "Ex-FBI Agent that Brought Down President, Chief Justice to Be Released." He blinked. Deep breath through his nose like he was preparing to bench press some serious weight, he read.

> Petersburg, Va.—Royce Johnson, the former FBI special agent whose investigation of his brother's

murder led to the resignation of a president and the impeachment of a chief justice, will be released Thursday from the Petersburg Federal Penitentiary after serving a sentence of a year and a day.

FBI Spokesperson Sam Wicklegreen declined to comment on the release, noting that “Royce Johnson is no longer an employee of the Federal Bureau of Investigation.” Several former colleagues spoke on the record to criticize Johnson’s tactics, but off the record, others praised his unauthorized investigation as one of the most important things ever done by the Bureau.

Royce Johnson’s brother, Alex, a law professor at Rockefeller University, was found dead of a suspected suicide in his home in 2014. Believing otherwise but without jurisdiction, Agent Johnson launched an investigation on false pretenses. His investigation focused on Marcus Jones, 28, of Chicago, a former student of his brother. A failing grade, an incriminating email, and a receipt from a local gun range were enough to convict Jones of first-degree murder.

With Jones facing the death penalty, Agent Johnson discovered new evidence—a letter written by his brother, accusing the president’s pick to be the next Chief Justice of the United States, Duc Pham, of rape.

After restarting his investigation, the trail led to a covert team, headed by Bob Gerhardt, a former Navy SEAL turned Washington lawyer, that was unofficially handling the Pham nomination. Coming on the heels of several failed nominations and withdrawals, and with the ideological balance on the Supreme Court about to swing from conservative to liberal for the first time in several generations, Agent Johnson accused Gerhardt's team of killing his brother to prevent him from coming forward and derailing Pham's nomination.

During the process of trying to make the case against the president and her team, Johnson broke numerous laws and violated a host of FBI rules. The charges against him, which he pleaded guilty to in exchange for the minimum felony sentence, included weapons charges, breaking and entering, assault, and attempted murder. Several of Gerhardt's team were assaulted by Johnson, and at least two bystanders, a shopper at a suburban Virginia mall and an Arlington-based priest, were injured as well.

Then-Chief Justice Pham denied any involvement in the plot, any knowledge of Gerhardt's team, and any ill will toward Alex Johnson, whom he regarded as "a dear and long-standing friend." But in the wake of reporting by the *New York Times*, eleven boys came forward, alleging they were sexually assaulted by Pham over a period spanning thirty years.

Johnson faces an uncertain future upon his release. He is a felon and disgraced former federal agent, but also a national hero to many. His family could not be reached for comment, and it is unclear where he will go or what he will do next.

Pham is facing rape and other charges in three states. He is out on $5 million bond. The first trial is scheduled for December 1 in state court in Illinois.

Bob Gerhardt is serving a life sentence at an undisclosed federal prison. Several of his team are serving sentences ranging from five to fifteen

> years for their involvement in the conspiracy to kill Alex Johnson.

The man put down the paper, exhaled, then picked it up and read it through again. When he'd finished, it fell onto the table, draping his cereal bowl like a tarp.

"National hero?" he muttered to himself. "Not to me, he ain't," he spat.

Picking up his phone, he checked his schedule.

"Thursday? Hmmm," he said aloud, flipping through the meetings he'd set to drum up business for his new law firm—Jones & Associates—even though he had no associates and, as yet, no clients. Then he typed "Petersburg, Virginia" into Google Maps.

"I'll see you soon, Royce, old pal," he said, as he looked down at the paper. A picture of a smiling Royce Johnson, an American flag behind him in his official FBI portrait, stared back. "We'll see how heroic you are."

CHAPTER 1

Mike Church eased his kayak into the water, holding on to it with a line attached to a hook on the back. Turning the kayak sideways, he stepped into the cockpit with a middle-aged wobble, and settled back in the mesh chair. Short and stocky, with sandy hair and wide-set eyes, Church looked younger than forty-one. But he could feel the years and the lack of exercise brought on by the coldest Chicago winter in a generation.

The cool wind off the water made him glad for his wetsuit and wool hat. A few seat adjustments, his water bottle and waterproof pouch in their spots, and he was ready to go. As he pushed off the dock with his paddle, he couldn't help but admire the new boathouse, with its sleek Scandinavian design and roof-line of sharp, sequential triangles. The dark gray brick and oversized glass windows gave it a slightly sinister look. From the waterline, it looked like a face, eyebrows raised, scowling through wide-glass eyes that reflected the bright spring sun. The towers of the city behind him, he dipped the paddle into the water and headed west on the South Branch of the Chicago River. As soon as he was a foot from the dock, his blood pressure dropped and his heart rate slowed. He felt transported. Twelve inches made a new world.

The Eleanor, as the boathouse was known, was proof of the Chicago Park District's ambition, both in architectural design and as leading edge of the mayor's plans for urban renewal on the South Side. Long the side of Chicago that was ignored, that was underfunded, that was bereft of opportunity, the South Side was going to have its day. The Eleanor's home was a splotch of green space in a miles-long industrial corridor flanking both sides of the Chicago River on the outskirts of downtown. Called "Park No. 571"—naming things after people had long since grown too fraught—it was three hundred square yards of hope.

The South Branch of the Chicago River ran south from the main branch of the river, then turned west after cutting Chinatown (to the east) off from Pilsen (to the west). Headed southwest toward the Mississippi and eventually New Orleans, it paralleled the Stevenson Expressway for miles, all of which was lined with warehouses, industrial yards, concrete plants, manufacturing facilities, power stations, junk yards, and every other kind of operation that can blight a landscape but makes modern life possible. Despite the grit, millennials had flocked to the Pilsen neighborhood, given its proximity to downtown, its cheap rents, and its "authentic" vibe. Authenticity was as fickle as political correctness, but for now, Pilsen had it. Once the home of German immigrants—some thirty of whom were murdered by the 22nd US Infantry during the great railroad strike of 1877 —and more recently Hispanic immigrants from across Latin America. Revitalizing Pilsen and the surrounding neighborhoods was at the top of the mayor's to do list, as he bid for a third term in charge of the Second City. The Eleanor was both a beachhead of gentrification and a sop to the hipsters, whom he needed in order to maintain his grip on the city council.

At the point where the Eleanor stood, a small, mile-long capillary of the South Branch went off at a nearly ninety-degree angle, headed due south. In the process, it dissected two other up-and-coming blue-collar neighborhoods, McKinley Park and Bridgeport. Former home of the Great Chicago Stockyards, these neighborhoods had produced the political machine that had ruled Chicago for decades. It was to this day the hardscrabble heart of political power in the city and thus the entire Midwest. The mayor's family home—an unassuming tan brick ranch where knees were bent and whispers made or broke fortunes—was just ten blocks away. Easily accessible to transportation into and out of the city and filled with great characters and eclectic architecture, Bridgeport's vacant parcels were being gobbled up by developers and drooled over by aldermen looking to expand the tax rolls and their own opportunities for shaking the tree. Even the mayor's dull-witted nephew, the newly elected alderman for the Bridgeport ward and the next link in the dynastic chain of Doherty power, could see the possibilities. If he were to own the city one day, as he and everyone else drinking Old Styles at Ricobene's before a Sox game thought inevitable, he'd need to show the developers he knew the score.

On a map, this mile-long offshoot—really just a pinkie finger—was called the South Fork of the Chicago River, but everyone called it "Bubbly Creek." Among all the streams, brooks, channels, tributaries, and creeks that drained the vast American continent into the Gulf of Mexico, Bubbly Creek was easily the most famous per mile. At least at a time. The creek was the dumping ground for animal parts and industrial waste from the Chicago Stockyards for four generations. More than three feet of fetid remains of cows, pigs, and sheep were at the bottom of the creek, lining the bed from the Eleanor all the way to where it petered out into an industrial park near Pershing Road. More than ten million cubic feet of rotten animal waste—enough to fill one hundred fifty Olympic-sized swimming pools—that didn't make it into Swift sausages dwelt below the now-placid waters of the creek. Then as now, the methane produced by the rot bubbled up through the waters like a fart in the tub. This gave the creek its nickname and infamy. But weekend kayakers were oblivious. To them, history was charming.

Church paddled hard on his right, causing the kayak's nose to turn left and head down Bubbly Creek. An avid outdoorsman, Church studied engineering at Princeton and worked for five years as an environmental consultant before going to Yale Law School. After a stint at the EPA in Washington and work for various environmental groups in San Francisco, Church came to Chicago to launch an ambitious new environmental law clinic at Rockefeller Law. Although it had been up and running for only a few years, he'd already brought several high-profile suits against the refineries that sulked along the southern tip of Lake Michigan like bullies on the playground leaning against the wall smoking disdainfully.

Neither environmentalism nor law brought Church to the creek; on this day, he was just looking to sweat. But, truth be told, sweating here, where so much environmental progress had been made, was way better than doing so in an air-conditioned gym surrounded by AirPod-clad investment bankers. Eighty years ago, one could walk across the creek on the animal remains and other waste that floated on the surface—now, an environmentalist could imagine it never happened.

The waters were calm and Church was eager to raise his heart rate, so he quickened his pace. The Stevenson Expressway overpass roared and shook as he passed beneath, his eyes focused on the shape the leading edge of the kayak cut into the water. Trying to ignore the loading docks of the mattress shops and fast food joints and nail salons that lined this part of the creek, he dug the oar deeper into the water and pulled it back and forth with increased intensity. He could almost pretend he was somewhere he wanted to be.

Ahead, the creek narrowed. The shops were gone. On his left, a vast, nearly mile-long open space was overgrown with brush and remnants of its former life. He drew the paddle out and let the kayak coast. The trees were budding, some leaves already starting to create the inklings of a canopy. Come back in summer, Church thought. Then, he could hide his eyes from the scars of commercialism he'd dedicated his life to undoing.

Just as he felt a blanket of relaxation fall over him, he felt a jolt. *Greeeeeeech*, the plastic of the kayak groaned its disagreement, as it collided with a submerged rock or industrial fossil. Church lurched forward, and then flipped into the water. His wet suit provided some relief, but within seconds, the creek's forty-degree water sent him into near shock. Enveloped in cold, Church lunged toward the shoreline like a lungfish making its first moves onto land. He half swam, half ran to shore, collapsing in a lump on a rocky shore of broken concrete, garbage, and riprap.

For a moment, he felt like a castaway, but then realized that he was just a hundred yards from city streets and a quick Uber ride home. Church pulled the kayak to shore and retrieved his smartphone from a waterproof bag. Three bars. He opened the Uber app and requested a car. He set his location as the intersection of 31st and Benson Street. Gabriella was on her way in a silver Toyota Rav4. There was a time getting a cab on the South Side of Chicago would have been nearly impossible, but technology had beaten racism, at least in this small part of the world. Flipping over the kayak revealed a deep gash. A total loss. He pushed it aside and let it float downstream. It'd be collected by the men in overladen pickup trucks who stalked city streets for recyclables like hyenas on the savannah picking at the bones of others' kills.

Waterproof bag in tow, Church scrambled up the steep slope of broken rock and concrete. He needed to get out of the wetsuit, at least get into the sun. Emerging from the tree line, he slipped on a moss-covered rock, his waterproof bag spilling out onto the concrete slab of a now-demolished factory or industrial site of some sort. He rolled over awkwardly, and a piece of rebar poked into his ribs. Rising to his knees, the smell hit him. Hit him like Mike Tyson—square between the eyes, sending him reeling and wishing he could roll back time. The acrid sting watered his eyes and forced up a dry heave.

Church looked down at his feet. An orangish-brown ooze bubbled between two pieces of broken concrete. He was in a small clearing of large oak trees, about ten feet from the shore, and still nearly a hundred yards from the public street. He looked around. Empty concrete foundation for as far as the eye could see. Tufts of grass peaked ambitiously through cracks here and there, and two cardinals danced on top of broken pieces of concrete that had the appearance of sofas, strewn about a disheveled living room. Rebar poked up in spots, bent and twisted like so many worms sticking up out of the mud in the garden plot he shared on the roof of his downtown loft. On all sides, except the shoreline, the area was ringed by ten-foot-high fence. Acres and acres of a past that had not yet been made into a future. Back on his knees, he poked his face at the sludge, the odor searing the lining of his nose and making his skin shudder.

The yin-yang of the moment struck him. Disgust. The bit of ooze was a sign of a potential sea of toxic waste under hundreds of acres of prime, riverfront real estate. Bubbly Creek wasn't coming back to life, but to death. His environmentalist heart ached. For a while, he sat staring at it like a toddler frozen by the blue glow of an iPad.

Then, he leaned in. The environmental lawyer in him was overjoyed. If the sludge was toxic, his career just got made. Tenure was certain. Much more than that, though. A new federal law permitted individuals to sue landowners to force them to pay for cleanups. It was an attempt to mobilize an army of Mike Churches to take on the polluters. Lawyers who prosecuted environmental crimes got a bonus of ten percent of the total cleanup cost for their work. That ooze was gold, and this was his Sutter's Mill. It would be front-page news—not just the *Trib*, but maybe even an above-the-fold story on the *New York Times*. Church and his clinic would be on the map, part of the scene. And to be in the scene was to be everywhere.

Church rose to his feet and scanned the horizon. From the looks of it, this area didn't get any foot traffic. He saw no stray beer cans or food wrappers, no used condoms or signs of vagrancy. These were common along the river and the lake shore in areas of high traffic. No, he was pretty sure not many humans exited Bubbly Creek and headed up a steep, slippery embankment to an abandoned industrial site inaccessible by any other means.

He walked on. Fifty yards further inland, the trees gave way and the concrete slab was intact. There were outlines where buildings used to be, discolorations and half walls, but Church was certain the site had been unused for decades. It was a moonscape. Looking back over his shoulder, the river was out of sight, and so was his claim. Hidden by the trees and the brush and the slope, it was safe.

At the gate on Benson Street, there was a giant padlock and a sign he could only see the back of. Looking right and left, he saw the fence was intact. Church went back the way he came. On the slope of crumbling concrete falling toward Bubbly Creek, he scanned in vain for other signs of the ooze. There was just a pocket. *His* pocket.

As he stood over the small spot that would make his career, doubt rang the bell. Maybe he should just call the Spill Line. Get the Metropolitan Water Reclamation District of Greater Chicago or the IEPA involved. This would be a Superfund site in a matter of weeks, and remediation could start immediately. The feds would sort out later who owed what to whom. Easier, no doubt, but he'd be forgotten, like a kid who stumbles over a dinosaur bone on a hike, gets a pat on the head and a special museum tour someday, while the gal with the PhD who answers the phone gets the glory. He wanted to be the paleontologist, not the kid. This was his find. He'd still welcome federal involvement, of course, but only after he broke the case, took it far enough to get famous and get paid. They could bring their scientists and their lawyers and their clean-up crews, but only after Mike Church became what he always wanted to become. He was the main character in his imaginings of what was going to unfold here, not the extra.

Church picked up some sticks and underbrush and covered

his pocket, just about ten inches on a side. Then he scrambled down the hill and along the shoreline until the fence ringing the property hit the shoreline. He went back into the water, ankle deep, to get around the fence. Up the slope, he traipsed through a sparse forest, then found himself in a cul-de-sac, surrounded by recently renovated townhomes. Two middle schoolers, their moppy hairdos covered by Sox caps, tossed a baseball. Church ignored them, walking down the middle of the street in a wet suit, a look of immense satisfaction on his face.

CHAPTER 2

Marcus Jones checked his watch: 8:59 a.m. The second hand of his Seiko Presage swept toward twelve. He looked up toward the gate of the electrified fence that separated him and a gaggle of reporters from the outer yard of the Petersburg Federal Corrections Center. He eavesdropped on attractive young women in too-tight skirts breaking the news. The soundbites that would crackle across TV screens and trend on Twitter were a gut punch. It hurt even though he could see it coming and knew it would hurt. He'd underestimated just how much. He knew seeing the prisoner freed would surface memories he wished would stay buried, but hearing the words come out of their made-up faces made him spin. The reporters stood side by side, high heels dug into the gravel, retelling the story that ruined Marcus's life.

"Any minute now, ex-FBI Special Agent Royce Johnson will walk out of the gate of the Petersburg Federal Penitentiary behind me..." said one into a camera held by a chubby man in an Iron Maiden T-shirt.

"...Johnson conducted an off-the-books investigation of the apparent suicide of his law professor brother, Alex..." intoned another. They all talked over each other, telling the same story in slightly different words.

"...the murder was initially pinned on Marcus Jones, a one-time student of the dead professor. Jones was convicted and sentenced to death, but with his appeals pending, Johnson reversed his accusation, sniffing out a trail of conspiracy to cover up sexual abuse allegations against a Supreme Court nominee that led all the way to the White House…"

As Marcus heard his name, he pulled his Homestead Grays hat down to the top of his eyebrows.

"…the chief justice of the United States and the president resigned in disgrace, and high-powered lawyer and former Navy SEAL Bob Gerhardt, who led the team that killed the professor, was sentenced to life in prison…"

Marcus had heard enough. He'd lived it. He didn't need to hear failed beauty queens read it back to him. He slid down the hood of his Impala, landing softly in the gravel parking lot. He crumpled the McDonalds wrapper that had held his Egg McMuffin, tossing it over his shoulder in the direction of the driver's side door. Settling on the balls of his feet, eleven months of anticipation appeared as a smile in the corner of his mouth.

The chain-link gate started to inch across at precisely nine, a red light flashing and a weak siren sounding. The reporters turned in unison to face the way Marcus was already facing, waiting expectantly for Royce Johnson to emerge. The scene reminded Marcus of the baggage claim at O'Hare, as the reporters jockeyed for position, eyes fixed on the chute that would spit men back into the world.

When the gate slammed into its place on the far side of the driveway, an inner door in a tall brick wall opened. Pale-faced guards in matching blue uniforms led a two-line procession of about a dozen men, walking in lockstep. It was the prisoners' last act of obedience, and with freedom not yet theirs, they were all on their best behavior. Eyes straight, shoulder width apart, they looked like the 82nd Airborne.

Shutters clicked and flashes flashed. Marcus bit his upper lip with his bottom teeth. He couldn't wait.

As the men crossed into freedom, they ran into the arms of loved ones like babes. Marcus felt his four hundred twenty-two days behind bars—the last few dozen on death row hoping against hope—well up inside him and push out through his ears. The day he walked out to freedom, his lawyer had to hold him up as he walked. His mamma's eyes wet with glee made him melt.

Then, as if popped by a pin, the mood of anticipation deflated and the cameras dropped to the cameramen's sides. A muffled murmur arose from the reporters. The prisoner everyone had come to see wasn't among them. Everyone scanned the ex-prisoners again and again, but no Royce Johnson. Marcus cocked his head to one side and sniffed loudly. The reporters between him and the gates were then all on their phones, sending off texts to producers about the story that wasn't.

The inner door slammed shut, announcing to the remaining residents of Petersburg that things were back to normal. But the fence gate stayed opened. Noticing this diversion from protocol, an alert and eager reporter waddled like a penguin toward the guardhouse, her stilettos stabbing into the gravel. As she got within shouting distance, a windowless van sped out of the gate. A single blue siren on the roof groaned into the distance.

The reporters took the bait. Cameras swung along sides as news crews raced for vans. Doors slammed. Marcus leaned back on the grill of his car and turned his head to watch the show. News vans large and small, fancy and antiquated, vied for position, all hoping to get a glimpse of the most famous ex-con in America. They threw up stones and were off in pursuit, east on Route 645 headed toward the town of Hopewell.

When the last news van disappeared over the last visible hump of the two-lane country road, Marcus turned back toward the gate. He knew a diversion when he saw one, having participated in his fair share over the years. The conspicuous van with "FCI Petersburg Low" written on the side, the siren, the timing—it was a package. A package perfectly designed for gullible, thirty-something reporters who overly romanticized the idea of a chase. It was just missing a bow.

Looking over his shoulders, Marcus realized he was the last

one left in the parking lot. This meant there was no family, no friends. No one to meet the hero. Marcus wasn't the kind of guy who took delight in other people's misfortunes, but in this case, he'd make an exception. Settling in behind the wheel, he turned the key halfway, and searched the radio for an R&B station. As country station gave way to religious station, he wished he'd gone for the satellite radio option. His regret began to snowball. He should be behind the wheel of a Benz and have all the music in the world at his voice command. He should be practicing law in an office tower in the Loop, not slumming it in a converted three-flat in Englewood. The loss was palpable. And Royce Johnson was to blame. In that moment, Marcus was glad to be the only member of his welcoming committee.

Marcus let his shoulders fall into the seat and strummed his fingers on the steering wheel to a country diva warbling about a breakup. He figured he wouldn't have to wait long. A handful of minutes later, he was proven right. A black Ford Crown Victoria with tinted windows eased out of the gate, opened just enough for it to fit, and turned out into traffic like a student driver. The car headed south on Route 645, the opposite direction from the absurd news chase he'd just watched. The prisoner wasn't visible, but Marcus trusted his instincts. He eased the Impala into gear and headed south in gentle pursuit.

The Crown Vic obeyed the speed limit, which meant it went far too slow as it drove along River Road. Marcus dialed back the Impala, but he could hardly stand it. The tree-lined stretch, passing a Korean Baptist Church and a few nondescript housing developments, was deserted this time of day, and they could easily be traveling twice as fast. But he idled along, not wanting to spook his prey. The Impala growled its disagreement.

One after the other, they turned west on a divided highway, and soon rose up over the Appomattox River. Then, just as they crossed, the Crown Vic turned off into the parking lot complex of a local mall. At the first stop sign, Marcus turned right as his mark turned left. But then he quickly took a left down a parking row, and another left in front of the mall to loop back around in time to see the Crown Vic come to a stop in front of a Walmart Supercenter. Marcus passed them, resisting the urge to crane his neck to stare. He then hooked two more quick lefts into an available parking spot the other side of a shopping cart return. He eyed them, waiting again for the prisoner to emerge. This time there were no sirens or flashes of cameras, just a lanky, balding man dressed in a plain gray sweat suit emerging from the back seat of an average American car. The prisoner shut the door behind him, and the Crown Vic sped off.

Marcus squinted, unsure and hoping to extend his visual range. It was him. *Goddamn it, it was really him.* A bit leaner and gaunter, less of himself than the last time he'd seen him. A man who'd been taken down a peg or three. Yet, Royce Johnson was still much higher up on the board than he should be. Fingering his Smith & Wesson, Marcus planned to change that.

CHAPTER 3

Royce Johnson scanned the parking lot with nervous eyes. A green garbage bag he held with two hands dangled in front of him like the pendulum on a grandfather clock. Time served, he should have been feeling electric, but like that feeling after feasting on a Big Mac and fries, the letdown came hard. He was a hero, he changed everything, yet he felt like a loser. He stood frozen watching as the morning shoppers opened car doors and bribed kids with promises of sweets. Life as it should be lived. He was ready to get restarted. His shoulders relaxed for the first time in over three hundred days, as the garbage bag kept time. But there was no sign of Jenny. He raised his left wrist to check the time, but he'd left the Omega Seamaster his dad got him when he joined the Bureau, with his wife on the day he reported to Petersburg.

"Excuse me," he said to a woman pushing a cart laden with kids, "do you know the time?"

She eyed him suspiciously, his sweat suit and garbage bag giving off strange vibes.

"Nine forty-five."

"Thank you. Have a great day!" It was too eager. *Pump the brakes.*

Jenny wasn't due for fifteen minutes. He had time to take the first step back into life. He turned and headed toward the entrance to the Walmart. As his eyes scanned the parking lot for threats—a year inside taught him the importance of this—he thought he saw something odd. Focusing on an Impala about thirty feet away, he saw a man slunk down in the driver's seat watching him like prey. For a second, Royce thought it looked like the man he sent to death row for a murder he didn't commit. But that made no sense, and he chalked it up to paranoia, something else he learned in prison.

A quarter of an hour later, Royce emerged. Sporting new khakis and a plain blue polo shirt, New Balance 990s, and a Nationals backpack, he felt more Royce-like. He put his arms through the straps and donned a pair of sunglasses. As he strode off the sidewalk confidently, a feeling of euphoria overcame him at the thought of soon seeing Jenny.

Their eyes met as soon as Marcus opened his door and stood tall. *It was him. What is he doing here?* Royce flinched in shock. Instinctively, his right hand reached for the fanny pack that held his Glock 9 mm service weapon. His training was still with him. But although he felt the pack tight against his waist and could sense the metal shape of the weapon snug in place, there was nothing there. A phantom limb.

Royce was exposed but not in danger. No one with a brain—and he knew Marcus had a big one—would pick a Walmart parking lot for a murder. Even if Marcus had reason to kill him, which Royce doubted, he wouldn't do it here. *And why would he want me dead?* There was little reason for revenge. After all, Royce had initially fingered Marcus for his brother's murder only because the government wanted him to—Marcus the patsy set up to shield a pedophile recently confirmed as the chief justice of the United States. Although Royce got Marcus arrested, it was also Royce who discovered the truth and his own mistake, freeing him from death row for a murder he didn't commit. If Marcus suffered—and yes, he did suffer, not only months in jail but a life of hard work taken away when he was tossed from one of America's elite law schools—it was because of the president, her minions, and the Rockefeller University administrators who enabled the plot. Without him, Marcus would have still gone down. And without him, he would have stayed down.

Royce breathed a deep sigh of relief. *I'm a hero. Perhaps he's here to thank me.* It wasn't very convincing, even to himself. *Why would Marcus come all this way for that?*

They were ten yards apart, tensed like gunfighters.

A man, arm full of groceries, passed between them. The tension broke. Royce looked away. He reached into his pocket and pulled out a prepaid flip phone, encased in a shrink-wrapped cocoon. Standing in the road, he unwrapped it and powered it up. He need a distraction. He also needed a ride. *Where is Jenny?* A recording intoned that her cell phone number was no longer in service. Looking up again, he caught Marcus's glare, fixed on him, unblinking. Royce turned his back and started walking toward the Walmart. He tried the landline at home. No answer. *She'd promised to be here to pick me up!* Royce started to panic but calmed himself with the thought that she must be back at the prison, that she didn't get the message about the location change. *But why would her phone be out of service?* He had to go back. He needed a taxi, but he didn't have a number. Someone at Walmart could help him. He quickened his step in the opposite direction of his former foe.

Royce emerged ten minutes later, cab en route; Marcus was still standing by his car, eyes locked on the entrance to the store, then on Royce, like he was dinner. *There is no avoiding it.* Plus, Royce was curious and, frankly, relieved to see a familiar face, even one with so much baggage. Royce started towards him, ready for what might come. Images of how their lives intersected flashed in his mind's eye like the slideshows his father had subjected them to after every family vacation. Royce could hear the roar of the fan and the flick and slap of old slide projector. Marcus stepped out from behind the cart rack and strode towards him. Images of their confrontations—in the alley behind a Thai restaurant, at a Starbucks downtown, in a Chicago courtroom—

projected on the white bedsheet in his head.

Royce extended his arm as he approached, but Marcus shook his head and pursed his lips.

"Marcus!" Royce barked. "It's good to see a..." Stumbling over what to say, he reached out for him. "Prison sucks. I'm..." Marcus strode toward him, arms swinging.

"Spare me the pleasantries, motherfucker." Marcus scowled, lips on the verge of spitting. Royce braced for an impact that never came. "I'm not here to welcome you with hugs and flowers. I'm here to see you swinging in the wind like the brothers they used to string up on these magnolia trees." There weren't any magnolia trees in sight, but Royce got the point.

"I'm out. I'm moving on, and I suggest you do the same." Royce backed up as he pleaded. He half wondered if Marcus had anything to do with Jenny's absence.

"Move on?" Marcus snorted. "Bitch, you have no idea what you did to me. You ruined my life. I had the brass ring." He held up his hands, palms to the sky. "The six-figure salary, the life I worked for and my family deserves. You have no idea how hard it was for me to get out of Bronzeville. No one goes from there to the Gold Coast." He paused and stared, slant-eyed, at Royce. "You took it. All of it."

"I'm not going to argue with you, especially not today and not here." Royce motioned around the parking lot, as shoppers came and went. "We'll just have to agree to disagree about what happened. We're both victims. My brother was murdered by the same people that set you up, er...set us up. That dean and that chief of staff, they struck a deal long before I came on the scene. They kicked you out. They sicced Gerhardt on both of us...all of us." Just saying it all out loud again made Royce tired and sad. The image of Alex's contorted body, blood matting his hair, seared his mind's eye. The taste of prison food still on his lips.

"Tell yourself whatever you need to, man. You and I both know the only reason their plan worked is because they knew you were a racist cracker who would jump at the chance of blaming it on a brother. That you got set up so easy is the whole point, man. Don't you see that?"

Staring blankly at him, he didn't. He shook his head slightly.

"Bait works because fish are stupid. They want to believe that shiny metal is food. You were just the racist they were looking for, Agent Johnson." Marcus sighed, closing his eyes as he shook his head. "Why do you think they picked me? A poor black kid—not just black, but dark skin, from a bad neighborhood. I was the lure designed to attract the likes of you. I was the bait you were looking for."

Royce eyed him, seeing a story he'd replayed in his mind a million times in that six-by-eight-foot cell. For the first time, he saw it in an entirely new way. It was a revelation. Sobering and disconcerting, but fascinating. Royce didn't think of himself as racially motivated in any way, but Marcus certainly had a good point. *Why did I jump so enthusiastically to pin it on the poor black kid from the South Side? Would I have done so if it were a white kid from the suburbs?* Royce felt sick.

He looked up, hoping Marcus would see the recognition in his eyes, see his contrition and his pain at what he'd done. That he'd find forgiveness there, and that this would be a stepping-stone back to his life. But in Marcus's dilated pupils he saw only pain, only rage. The sight scared him. He scanned Marcus's belt line for a bulge.

"I'm sorry, Marcus. I was...a fool." He stepped forward, arms down and palms extended, his backpack sliding down off his shoulder awkwardly. "He was my brother. My baby brother, and I was blinded by that. I rushed headlong, not thinking. And, you're right. I fell into a trap that maybe only someone who thinks black guys are more likely to be bad guys would fall into. I get it now. I guess...well, I guess I need to look at that and figure it out."

Royce looked down at the asphalt parking lot. When he looked back up, he saw Marcus relax a bit. The moment, if there was one, passed. His eyes drooped and a smile peeked out and then was gone. His look said the twelve-hour drive had been worth it. That he'd won. Marcus turned to leave. Then he stopped, flatfooted. He turned his head back over his shoulder.

"You're alone, aren't you?" he asked.

"It seems that way," Royce whispered, embarrassed of the fact his family wasn't there to meet him. "They were supposed to..."

"Don't sweat it, man. Prison makes everyone crazy. Give 'em time. They'll come around."

They eyed each other over a moment of silence. Royce could see a crack of empathy in Marcus's exoskeleton—the one that the streets made him build over the years to protect his caring heart underneath. Just as he saw it open, it widened into a fissure.

Marcus stepped toward Royce, who flinched. He stretched out an arm—stuck in his fingers, a business card. "In case you need a lawyer."

Royce watched him open the door to his car and back out. Marcus remained a mystery to him. A Go-playing genius who intermixed his sentences with five-dollar words and two-bit cusses. A lawyer versed in philosophy with a posse of friends and hangers-on that would embarrass anyone. A guy you couldn't help but like the first time you met him, but someone you understood less the more you learned about him.

As the Impala headed out of the parking lot, Royce felt a wave of loneliness wash over him. In Petersburg, he longed to be alone, even for a minute to take a crap. But now, cast free into a Walmart parking lot with nothing but a backpack full of belongings, Royce wished for the company of the thugs and outlaws who had given him companionship over the past year. Humans, he'd come to realize, need family around them. Any family will do.

CHAPTER 4

"Here? Are you sure?" The cab driver eyed him in the rearview mirror, his square acetate frames holding thick glass smudged to the point of opacity. There wasn't a driveway in sight. The cabbie spun around on his hips as far as his paunch would let him. A raised eyebrow and a peer under his frames asked the question again.

"Yup. Right here is perfect." Royce counted out a stack of singles from a narrow tan envelope the prison gave him as he was released. "Fifteen, sixteen, seventeen...twenty-two...twenty-five. Keep the change."

He got out and stood alone in a forested lane just wide enough for two cars to pass, mirrors just missing. There were no houses in sight. The Checker cab lingered. When Royce flipped his backpack onto his shoulder and headed into the woods, it sped away.

There wasn't much of a trail. Tall pines blocked out most sunlight, making the ground easily traversable, even for a guy who hadn't stepped on anything other than cement for a year. In his excitement, he tripped over a few roots that stuck out of the ground but caught himself before falling. The ground rose up to a peak that looked out over his children's school to the east and led down steeply to the ravine behind his house. He paused at the top, sucking on a water from the tap in a gas-station bathroom he'd poured into a Fiji water bottle in Breezewood, Pennsylvania. The laughter and screams of the children on the playground behind the school rose up to meet him, and his heart beat faster. He could feel the hugs, even from a hundred yards away.

At the bottom of the hill, he leapt from stone to log, traversing the creek behind his house in a few strides. There was no time to stop and look for crawfish or see if the beaver family had shored up the dam that had given way in a storm a few years back. His own family—just up the hill but so far incommunicado—needed shoring up too.

Royce approached the edge of the woods cautiously, hunched over and using the abundant cover of the forest. Unable to reach anyone for the almost two days it took him to get here from outside Richmond on a series of Greyhound buses, Royce was growing increasingly concerned about his family's safety. Her parents weren't answering his calls either. *It could be nothing*, he reassured himself as he took a knee.

The architect of his demise, Navy SEAL commander turned political fixer, Bob Gerhardt, was in jail, but his loyalists, of which there had to be dozens—people who owed Gerhardt their lives many times over—had to be out there looking for revenge. Jenny and the girls were an easy pressure point. But the frogmen turned political mercenaries were just the tip of the iceberg floating in the sea of Royce's troubles. A president disgraced and impeached; a chief of staff in jail; seventy million Democratic voters outraged that their chance to control the Supreme Court was taken from them. A conservative majority on the court again and for the foreseeable future. And Royce to blame for it all. He gulped. Of course, they were coming for him. *For them.*

Royce took out a cheap set of binoculars from his backpack, sweeping his backyard looking for anything askance. The grass needed cut (that's how real Pittsburghers say it, and Royce prided himself on being an authentic yinzer), and Jenny's minivan wasn't in the driveway. But he didn't see anyone scouting the place. It looked like a typical suburban afternoon.

Exiting the cover of the forest, Royce darted forward a dozen yards to the cover of an old playset that he'd built from a kit with his father-in-law when their second daughter was born. He turned sideways, using the wooden structure as a shield. He raised the binoculars again and saw nothing. He took a deep breath and walked toward the back deck. Instinctively, his left shoulder led the way, his right hand nearby his belt. There was no weapon at the ready. It was just muscle memory.

He walked slowly up the back stairs, and once up on the deck, peeked into the family room and kitchen. Nothing. Dark, empty, quiet. The grill—*his* grill, a ceramic furnace his father-in-law got him in Japan—was missing too. The burn marks on the deck from stray coals formed a rough outline of where it used to be. A chalk outline of memory like ones Royce had seen at crimes scenes dozens of times, tracing the place where something amazing used to be.

The family room furniture appeared unchanged, at least what he could glimpse through the plantation shutters that covered the French doors and windows that looked out over the cedar deck. But the room seemed staged for a house-flipping show on HGTV—no toys, no cushions askance, no coasters, no signs of life.

Royce walked cautiously around the side of the house toward the front yard. Again, he peered around the corner, seeing only some neighbor kids scooting down the middle of the street and Dick Jacobs cutting his grass.

The bell chimed. No answer. The turtle statue with the false bottom for hiding a key was missing. It was odd, at the least. *At the least.* Maybe it was worse. Royce peered through the vertical windows that flanked the red door, but the house was dark and deserted.

He walked again to the back porch, seeking some privacy where he could collect his thoughts. Panic welled up in his throat and adrenaline surged toward his extremities. Royce scanned the yards right and left, but they contained just an occasional bird.

No killers. No vanquished foes filled with vengeance. At least none the naked eye could see.

The thought of breaking in crossed his mind, but as he put his hand inside his sweatshirt sleeve and raised it to break a window, he remembered he owed his parole officer a call, and that calling him from the back of a Fox Chapel Police Department squad car was probably not a good idea. He was an ex-con now, and that meant he was going to have to change his tactics.

Royce took a seat on the top stair of his porch. The dream of a life gone, or, not yet gone but astray, washed over him. He worked hard to build a family life he felt comfortable bragging about, that people envied. It was evaporating, and he couldn't catch the steam and put it back into the pot. Fear. *Who am I without them?*

He'd sat in that spot countless times, nursing an Iron City Beer while his girls played in the grass yard he'd worked so hard to get for them. He could see their couple-friends milling about in his mind's eye as he grilled steaks and burgers; he could hear the laughs and the occasional cries. He could recite from memory the talk about the Steelers. He could taste the beer and his grandmother's famous baked beans, the ones he made for every backyard BBQ. He could hear himself shouting at the de Jong boys to get off the shed. A tear rolled down his cheek and landed on the deck.

Where the hell is my family? The tension in his muscles went out. He collapsed onto the deck. Sobs arrested the urge to retch. He couldn't form words; thoughts of the future and memories of the past swirled in his mind. Images of his daughters being born and scenes at their future weddings made him dizzy. His legs buckled, and ex-FBI agent Royce Johnson, who'd collared drug kingpins, chased killers through darkened alleys, and uncovered America's greatest political conspiracy, passed out.

Two hours later, Royce stood up from a wheelchair in St.

Margaret's Hospital. He had no idea who found him or how he got there or what a vasovagal syncope was. Leaving felt good though.

"Someone picking you up," the orderly asked without looking up from his smartphone.

"No, I'll get an Uber. I'm good." He wasn't. On any level. He was down to a few bucks in cash and didn't know whom he could trust. No job, no prospects, and powerful people who wanted him dead, or at least to suffer some more. He could feel himself starting to faint again.

He steadied himself with thoughts of walking on the beach with Jenny. Of sipping margaritas in Playa del Carmen, while the kids laughed and wrestled in the pool.

Realizing he had only a Walmart flip phone and that Uber wasn't an option, he turned over his shoulder to the orderly.

"Can you call me…or can someone at the reception desk call me a cab?"

Five minutes later, Royce folded himself into the back of a dilapidated cab painted in Pittsburgh black and gold. Ten minutes after that, he was back in front of his house. There was nowhere else to go. He sat on the rocking chair made from recycled milk jugs that they bought in Vermont one summer. He called Jenny's mom knowing she wouldn't pick up an unknown number and left a message with the new cell digits. Ten minutes later, his burner buzzed.

"Hello?" It came out as a scream.

"Royce—it's me." Her voice was aloe on Scottish skin baked in the Mexican sun.

"Thank God! Where are you? I'm at the house."

"You shouldn't be there."

"Where are you?" he said, ignoring her warning.

"You need to leave. Walk away. Now!"

"Relax, there's no one here."

"They've been watching us. A van, a car that looked like a cop car, strange guys ringing our bell. We've gotten threats—

they put a dead rabbit in our mailbox, Royce. Caroline couldn't stop crying."

His heart sank. This was his fault. Putting them in this position was a cost he was willing to bear, but now that the bill was coming due, it made him wish he never bought this mess.

"Are you okay? How are the girls?" It leaked out.

"My dad told me not to come...there...for you. I wanted to. I even bought a disguise. But he talked me out of it. Said it was just too risky. I needed to be there for the girls just, well, just in case."

Tears rolled off his cheeks.

"You did the right thing. Your dad is a smart guy. That was good advice. I'm just glad you're okay."

"Come to the cabin. Come here, now!"

He wanted it more than anything. To feel her touch, to hold his girls and hear their giggles. But it was impossible. If Jenny was right, they might be watching him. The last thing he wanted to do was give away the location of his Alamo.

"You know I want to, but I can't. It's too risky."

"Can't you..."

"No. Not yet. I need to figure this out first. I just got...well, you know. Can you give me a few days to get things straight?"

"I've waited this long."

"It might be longer. I don't know..."

"I love you."

"I love you too, Jen." He felt the tears stream down his face. He could smell her hair and feel her touch through the phone.

"We need you, Royce."

"I'll make it right. I'll get to you. Soon." He didn't believe it. Or, at least he didn't know yet how he would.

"But where will you go? You can't stay at the house; you can't come here. We can't risk you going to my parents'."

"There's always Chicago."

CHAPTER 5

A week after the ooze stung his nostrils, Mike Church steered a rented Boston Whaler down Bubbly Creek in search of his meaning. Three second-year law students, known as 2Ls, shivered in the back, wrapped against the wind in a Neapolitan-ice-cream-colored throw his grandmother had knitted him as a dorm-warming gift when he left for college. He was embarrassed by the look on his Princeton roommate's face when they saw him under it on the couch watching *The Simpsons*. For the first but not last time on those sacred grounds he felt like an imposter—the kid they needed from West Virginia so they could say the class of '93 had students from all fifty states. His distinctive talent was the accident of being born on this side versus that side of the Ohio River. It was worse than being a running back or even a legacy—at least they had skills or connections to fund raising prospects or job networks. But he'd showed them that a geographic accident could matter more than quick feet or a last name. The athletes and legacies were now all working for their daddy's golfing buddies, making spreadsheets to turn money into more money. Church was making a difference.

He fingered the steering wheel and throttled down as he eyed the shoreline looking for the spot where he'd gone ashore in his kayak. Idling in, just past the narrows, the metal bottom of the boat screeched against the rocky shore. One of the 2Ls inhaled loudly, more dramatically than the situation required, but Church didn't turn around. His mind was on the pocket, on the case, not on a neurotic law student. He jumped out, splashing his Dockers with cold water. Grabbing the bow line, he pulled the boat and the frightened law students ashore. Boat tied to a tree, the four of them ascended the slope shoulder width apart. From afar, they looked like the Scooby-Doo gang—only the Mystery Machine and the punch-drunk Great Dane were missing.

"Professor! Here, I found it." Becca Goodman, his most eager student, stood tall, one hand raised, the other pointed down at a pile of sticks. Her toothy smile was a lighthouse among the trees. Seeing it, Church turned heel and bounded toward her.

He met her proud eyes. As the professor walked toward her, the eager look in her eyes delighted him but also set off some alarm bells. He knew Becca, or, Ms. Goodman, as he preferred in order to maintain some distance, was trouble. She was a mediocre student dragging her family money around like an anchor. He'd been told by her on occasions too many to recall that she'd come to law school because her parents wanted her to go to medical school—psychiatry was both the family business and its pastime. Her father's work was published on every continent and her mother was the can't-do-without therapist of the Hamptons set. Their only child was a test subject that had been mentally poked and prodded but didn't warrant even a nod in the acknowledgements. Hence law school. Smart but not insightful, maybe on purpose, Becca's round face and wide-set eyes gave her the kind of look that if she was a few pounds lighter and grew up in a different family would have gotten her on the cover of *Teen Vogue*. As it happened, it got her into a boat on Bubbly Creek, where Church knew she was just another lost student who fell into law school and hoped that Church's environmental justice clinic would be the thing she was looking for all along. The something that would justify a rebellious choice.

It wasn't just this that worried Church. He knew Becca wasn't traipsing around a toxic waste site just to spite her parents—it was obvious even to him that she'd been infatuated with him from the minute they met at orientation. Or, that is what bounced around in his mind on lonely nights staring at Netflix. It wasn't unfounded. She told him—over coffee at the "Pastries with Professors" events on Wednesday mornings and over beers at the "Barristers Bar" events in same spot on Thursday afternoons—that it was his lecture on environmental justice that made her want a career at an NGO. Saving whales or creeks or poor kids from getting asthma, it didn't matter. Every class he had taught, every lecture he had given, Becca had been there. And when he'd asked for volunteers for a special project one day, her hand jabbed the ceiling before he'd even described the project.

Church patted her on the back, and soon the others were huddled around, staring down at the ground. The spot was marked with branches set across it, just as Church left it.

"Okay, good. Now, let's take some photos," he spouted off like a drill sergeant. "Sam, get that measuring tape and let's get our location relative to the shoreline and the property line. Devon, try to get GPS coordinates. I want every detail recorded. Anything you see or observe. Write it down. We are making a case here."

They scribbled in their Moleskin notebooks.

"These will be admissible as evidence in our case. Lawyers' notes are often the crucial bits that make or break a lawsuit." This wasn't just a field trip.

The students took to their tasks. ISTJ-personality-types all, they were the perfect helpers. Diligent, organized, analytical, dogged. Church had high hopes for them and his clinic. It—no, he—was going to remake the Great Lakes Basin in the image of economic production in harmony with nature he'd had his mind since he picked daisies in right field for the Junior Pirates in Wheeling. He was no environut, and he enjoyed the joys of red meat and the internal combustion engine as much as the next guy. To him, environmental law and activism was about making capitalism work better by making sure businesses were charged the full costs of their activities. Environmental cheaters were just that, cheaters. And Mike Church hated cheaters. He confronted line jumpers at amusement parks and at the merge onto the Eisenhower from the Dan Ryan.

Measurements taken and locations mapped, it was time to find out what they were dealing with. Church donned a Tyvek hazmat suit, thick rubber gloves, and a breathing mask. At the sight of it, the students backed up casually, tripping over each other to put some distance between them and the professor. One handed him a Styrofoam cooler, lined with thick plastic sheeting. He took the top off and leaned it up against a piece of broken rebar. Then, Church grabbed a scoop from his bag. The scooping bit was about the size of a softball, set on the end of a long, extendable handle like those used to roast marshmallows in a fire. He dipped it into the pocket, plopped two scoops of ooze into the container, and put the lid tightly on with bungee straps.

Church put one foot on top of the cooler, like he was striking a pose at a tailgate party on a Saturday morning during football season. He propped his mask on his forehead. He felt like Indiana Jones, but he could see in the students' eyes, he looked more like Walter White. It was not just a generational thing, he feared.

"Time to rock and roll," the professor chirped. It was a lame dadism, and the kids didn't buy it. But despite this, they looked at Church with the adoration that children have for their father, even when he makes stupid jokes. Becca stepped forward to help, lifting one edge of the cooler and thrusting her hip toward it to signal for help.

Church and Becca carried the container at arms' length down the slope toward the waiting Whaler, while the other students kept their distance. The team had covered their tracks, and none of the students asked the professor why they were being so secretive. The leverage of grades compelled surprising levels of obedience.

Then, they were gone. In a swirling wake, the Whaler and its passengers disappeared up Bubbly Creek. The contents of the container eventually headed for the lab of Mike Church's college roommate, now a chemist at the Illinois Institute of Technology. The law students headed for an afternoon of research on the property and the potential legal actions that could be filed. There was a long memo to be written on the Resource Conservation and Recovery Act and the applicability of section 6972 of the United States Code to matters like Church had discovered on Bubbly Creek. There were records to pull at the Cook County Property Records Office. It wasn't sexy, but it was how big cases were won. At some point, every legal entrepreneur, from Clarence Darrow to Thurgood Marshall to Ruth Bader Ginsberg, had to spend countless hours poring over statutes and cases to find the way in, to find the arguments that would win the day for justice.

Stepping out into the shallow water to watch the group depart, a man in waders and a camouflage jacket raised his smartphone to his ear. Tall and angular, topped by a flattop, he cut a figure not to be trifled with.

"Four people in total," he reported without salutations. "Looked like the professor and three students. They were on the property for about thirty minutes. They took a sample, put it in a Styrofoam cooler. Took some measurements, too. I didn't see anyone with video or such. I got names."

On the other end, a man simply said, "Good job," and hung up.

The man put his cell phone face down on the massive oak table that dominated his luxurious office. He kicked his feet up on his desk and stared up at the ceiling. Photos of his daughter and his grandchildren caught his eye. He looked away, trying to hide his shame. There was no choice. The stakes were too high. *Four people.* Regret washed over him. *I have to find another way.* He closed his eyes, clear in his mind what he had to do.

CHAPTER 6

In the years after the Columbian Exposition of 1893, the Hyde Park and Kenwood neighborhoods of Chicago—situated right on Lake Michigan about five miles south of the Loop—experienced a boom. Frank Lloyd Wright built several properties in the neighborhood, including the famed Robie House at 58th and Woodlawn. A preeminent example of Wright's Prairie Style, thousands of tourists came each year to walk its halls and marvel at its simplicity.

The same year the Robie House went up but a few blocks north, an architect lost to history built a three-story house with a broad front porch framed by brick columns for a prominent Chicago lawyer. The house, around the corner from the former home of Muhammad Ali, just down the street from the compound of the Nation of Islam, and nearby the home of former members of the terrorist group, the Weathermen, is unremarkable. Made of red Illinois brick, its rectangular shape and flat roof would be easily reproduceable in Legos. But it blended into the other more aesthetically pleasing mansions of the neighborhood, shielded as it was from the street by ageless oaks standing guard in front. Several prominent families lived in the sixteen-room house over the years, including the judge who oversaw the trial of Leopold & Loeb—who lived, as did their victim, in the neighborhood—and a doctor who patented a drug that turned the tide in the war against leukemia.

When Alex Johnson bought the house upon joining the faculty at the Rockefeller Law School, he knew nothing of this history. His wife, Claire, wanted an old house with crown moldings and pocket doors and a yard for their growing family, and there weren't many properties on the market that ticked all her boxes. When she trailed the real estate agent in through the entryway on a frozen March morning a decade and a half ago, Alex knew it would be home. The subtle release of tension in her shoulders was everything he needed to see. He'd find the money somewhere, make it work somehow.

They made it work, for a while at least, their children marking their growth on door frames like prisoners in old movies counting the years to freedom. But suddenly the children stopped growing. Or, at least the doors would tell you that. The divorce froze everyone in place, most of all Alex. The children went on to leave their marks on other doors, in other houses, but Alex never left his Lego house. He was carried out in a plastic bag with a hole in his skull and brains leaking out as he bounced on a gurney down the cement stairs he'd bounded up so many times. And now, although tourists don't traipse through it, it is the most famous house in Chicago, if not the country. It was in its front room, where Alex's children had parked their scooters, that the president's men killed him in order to salvage a takeover of the Supreme Court. It was in the house they made a home that a nation came to grief.

Royce Johnson felt the weight of this history as he pushed a silver key into the lock and pushed open the door. The stress of the past two years pinched at his temples. He squinted to make it go away or maybe to get up the nerve to walk back in—back to the place where the life ran out of his brother and soaked into the hardwood floors picked out by that Chicago attorney a century earlier. When he opened the door, it swung in like an ancient vault. The musty smell overwhelmed him. Dust covered every surface and junk mail, indifferent to the fact Alex wasn't coming back, was strewn in the entry way like paper covering the bottom of a bird cage.

The alarm beeped. Claire gave him the passcode when he'd called her from the bus station and begged her for a redoubt. Claire being Claire, she kicked her empathy drive into high gear, dropping her work and picking him up on a moment's notice. He resisted a trip to Macy's and the salon in the Gold Coast, but she insisted. The hero wasn't going to suffer anymore, she told him. The house was his for a while, until he could straighten things out and get home to Jenny and the girls. It wasn't a hiding place, but at least if they came for him, it would just be him they were coming for.

Royce stood on piles of catalogs and looked at the spot where it happened. He willed his legs, but they declined his offer. Beyond the place where Gerhardt's men put a bullet through Alex's brain was the kitchen, where he'd sat at Alex's table and drunk his whiskey, and beyond that was the backyard, with the tree that had led him to Marcus and ultimately to 1600 Pennsylvania Avenue. He wanted to make it to that table and taste that whiskey and look out on that tree. He stood on his toes and felt the rush of their life together, from beginning to end, and beyond. Maybe one day he'd make it further than five feet inside. He set down his backpack and looked around the foyer, as if he was looking for a comfy place in case he needed to sleep there. Maybe after some food and a beer or three, he'd find his courage.

"Claire—it's Royce." She picked up on the first ring.

"Did you get in?"

"Yeah. Well, more or less. Honestly, I didn't get very far. I guess prison…well, I guess I'm not the same as I was."

"He was your brother, Royce. You can't expect this case to have been like the others." Her voice soothed him, her logic impeccable.

"Right, of course. I know that. I just figured that, after all this time, I'd be—" he sighed deeply, "—ready to move on."

"Let's meet. We'll talk about it. About Alex, but mostly

about moving on. Give me half an hour. I'll buy you lunch."

"Thanks, Claire—the usual?"

"Alex's usual. See you soon."

CHAPTER 7

At lunch—burgers at Medici, the kind of diner with graffiti names on all the tables and walls one finds on every college campus in America—Claire slid a Tiffany's gift box across the table. Royce fingered it like it was an IED or an engagement ring from his dead brother's ex-wife, then pulled the ribbon and revealed the business card of Leslie Musgrove, PhD, the Richard & Eileen Cooksy Professor of Classics. It was Claire's gift to him. From her and from Alex.

"What's this?" he played dumb.

"I figured while you're hiding out you could use a distraction. Get back to normal. You know, exercise some old muscles. Make a buck or two."

A lead on a freelance surveillance job. Royce guessed the obvious—a philandering wife of a nerd in a tweed jacket. But Royce wasn't licensed for legitimate PI work. Plus, Chicago was supposed to be a brief redoubt, not long term. Alex's old house was a prison without bars.

"Is this a hint?" he said with a mouthful of cheeseburger. Royce fished if this was about the rent.

"I told you I can loan you some money until you sell the house—I meant it."

"Thanks," he wiped mustard off his chin.

"And the proceeds from the sale are all yours."

"I couldn't."

"You could, and you will. The insurance payout was enough to take care of the kids. The university pays for their college, and I make enough to pay the day-to-day. The house was Alex's after the divorce, and he'd want you to have it. For what you did for him." She stared down at an untouched patty with lettuce playing the role of the bun and a sad piece of avocado on top looking like a garrison cap.

"That's mighty generous of you, Claire. I...well, we'll see, I guess. I don't want to..."

"We won't see anything. You lost your job, you've been in prison for us, and Jenny and the girls need it more than we do. Sell the house and go home to them."

"I can't. The media. Gerhardt's men. I can't expose them to anymore risk. They've...we've all suffered enough."

She paused while she munched on some ice from her Diet Coke.

"I don't think you need to worry."

"Easy for you to say. I'm worried. Jenny's so afraid, she's been holed up at the cabin for nine months."

"Look, I'm not saying I don't understand. But the media is going to lose interest. The Royce Johnson story isn't playing well for the agenda of the *New York Times*—it reminds everyone of what happened. Everyone who voted for her wants to forget. In a week, everyone will be on to something that fits the narrative. That, or a Kardashian wedding."

She made some sense. Fox News might want him on the crawl every day, but they weren't going to stalk him. And he could manage that situation with a competent PR person. An appearance or three, and America would be on to the next thing.

"And Gerhardt?" He gulped at the thought, almost choking on a fry.

"He's rotting in jail, and you've proven to be a formidable opponent. I bet his minions are moving on to easier targets.

Plus, short of getting plastic surgery, you aren't going to be able to hide."

"Do you know someone?"

They shared a laugh and some moments of silence as they ate together. Then, her pager interrupted the moment. She excused herself.

Surprised that doctors still used pagers, Royce got up too and went to the bathroom. He relieved himself, then splashed water on his face. The cold, fresh lake water jolted him. In the mirror, he saw himself in his eyes—the person he knew and wanted to be—but his face was unrecognizable. The sunken eyes, the half beard—the stare of a prisoner, not a man. He knew what he had to do. Sell the house as quickly as possible and wire the money to Jenny. Start to rebuild the life he'd left behind to find Alex's killer. In the meantime, he'd find out what Professor Musgrove wanted. He needed a way to pass the time, and getting back in the game was better than binging on all the shows he'd missed on Netflix.

Back at the table, Claire was putting two twenties on the table.

"Hey."

"Hey." She turned. In that moment, Royce saw the beauty in her that Alex had. In the way she carried herself, in her choice of skirt and tasteful jewelry, he saw that duality of intensity and softness he heard Alex tell him about after their first date. The joy and excitement in Alex's voice in that phone call echoed across the decades.

"What?" she asked, picking up her bag.

"Nothing. I…I just see why my baby brother loved you."

He saw her face flush.

"He didn't love me enough."

"Yeah, I know. He was like that. But I see why he fell for you. You're something, Claire. I'm glad Alex found you, even if it ended like this. I'm glad he lives on in your kids. I just…"

She put her index finger on his lips.

"It's time to get to work, Royce. Alex is gone. I'll miss him, but we need to let him go."

"But..."

"No buts. Go see about that classics professor. Sell that old place. Then go home to your family. They need you."

Royce followed her out on to 57th Street. A stream of students headed to nosh between classes diverted around them as they stood eyeing each other for a moment. He hugged his sister-in-law, breathed in the sunshine, and headed for campus.

CHAPTER 8

"Good morning, Professor."

"Morning, Ralph."

The woman looked up from tightening the laces on her New Balance running shoes. She looked into his eyes, waited a beat, then went back to work. The doorman didn't realize she was practicing.

"Oh, wait, I guess I need to call you 'Dean.'"

"You heard? Not yet, Ralph, not yet. I'm waiting on final word from the provost. Until then, I'm just a simple environmental law teacher." She switched feet.

"Everybody is rooting for you." His voice was calm with a bit of airs fitting the posh lobby of the Powhatan apartments. Situated on the lakefront, Charles Murray's Art Deco masterpiece had long been the residence of choice for muckety mucks at Rockefeller University.

The woman raised her leg up on to a radiator, stretching forward to touch her toes. Her nose brushed the skin of her knee. She leaned in, feeling the delightful pain as her hamstring stretched. Looking up, she saw the doorman admiring her. She checked her watch. It was 6:02 a.m. Two minutes behind schedule.

The woman stood tall, then lifted back and grabbed each foot in turn, bringing heel to butt. Her eyes scanned the lobby, famous for its Native American murals and the only twenty-four-hour manned elevator in Chicago. She breathed it in, trying to imagine the white-gloved attendant jobs as opportunities for South Side men, instead of leftovers from of a shameful legacy of racial subordination. The twenty-two apartments in this building used to have covenants in their deeds banning sales to people that looked like her; now, this black woman was not only living in an apartment near the top, she was about to become the dean of one of the best law schools in the world. She let a smile creep into the side of her mouth. The theme song to *The Jeffersons* played briefly in her head—"Movin' On Up" indeed.

She put in her earbuds and pressed play on her iPhone. An NPR podcast she'd stopped listening to on the ride home last night picked up in mid-sentence. It was something about mantis shrimp. Exactly the kind of cocktail party ammunition every dean needed in bulk. But she wasn't feeling like learning this morning. She scrolled through her iTunes library and found "Running Mix 12," the one with Beyoncé's latest. She turned the volume up and raced out into the morning.

Turning south, she was soon striding above the early morning rush on Lake Shore Drive. The pedestrian bridge was crumbling on the edges and its handrails were rusting, but she ignored the decay. She looked to her left as she ran her regular route, watching the sunrise glint off the skyscrapers in the Loop. Even though the windows of her apartment had this same view, she never tired of it. Chicago was a strange and bitter fruit for her, like it was for most of its African-American residents, but boy was it beautiful.

At the end of the bridge, she accelerated down the hill and merged onto the jogging trail. She was headed south toward Promontory Point, where she'd do three laps around the park before heading back. She found her groove, staring straight ahead, her neon green shoe tips flashing into her field of vision. The music spurred her on, but her mind was on the weeks ahead—her first meeting as dean, her first speech to the faculty, her first email to the entire school. She composed each of them in her head as her feet pounded the pavement.

Her predecessor was a legend. He'd raised over twenty million dollars in the past year. All of it was going toward scholarships that would make Rockefeller accessible to anyone with the intellectual chops to get in. He'd also expanded the faculty and moved the school up two places—to third—in the coveted *U.S. News* rankings. Finally, Harvard and Yale were in striking distance for the Second City's best law school. His were big shoes to fill.

The woman dazzled in her interviews with the former dean, provost, and university president—all white men. The time was at hand for Rockefeller to have an African-American dean, and that she had top-drawer paper credentials—Harvard, Cambridge, Stanford—and was a respected scholar and teacher, made it impossible for them to hire anyone else. She'd earned it, and as she rounded the Point for the second time, she felt the accomplishment wash over her like the waves of Lake Michigan rushing over the riprap along the shore. But she never let such feelings last long. Quickly they receded back out to the depths and were replaced by anxiety.

Am I up to it? She was an easy choice, but because of that, her ideas for the school weren't put through the fire. She mentioned expanding student and faculty diversity—of course she had—and she'd talked about creating new clinics to work for underserved communities on the South Side and beyond. Time to give back. These were good ideas, but they were also vague clichés. They were not a plan for action. Plus, she was taking over what was widely regarded as one of the most conservative law schools in the country, famous for law and economics, not social justice or serving the indigent. No doubt some of the faculty and many of the students were going to see her as an imposter from day one.

A furtive email from her predecessor—"Go to Church, be penitent, and keep your head down."—stuck in her head like corn in her teeth. *What did it mean?* The question bounced in her mind as she ran along. The capitalization of "church" was odd but could have been a typo. If it wasn't, and he wasn't known for being sloppy, was it about a house of worship or something else? The dean wasn't a religious man, so the metaphor, if that is what it was, fell flat. It was even a bit offensive to her, since she was a person of faith. And then there was the curious fact that the name of one of her new colleagues was Mike Church. They hadn't met, but he ran the environmental law clinic, an area close to her own scholarship and teaching. *Could this be a warning about him? Or a message to go see him?* She'd planned to meet with all the faculty, Church included, in the first few months. *Perhaps, he should be at the top of the list.*

As the thoughts raced, her mind seized her body, bringing her to a halt. She stood, alone in the middle of the path along the south shore of the Point, panting. She checked her Garmin watch—one hundred beats per second. She breathed in through her nose and out through her mouth deliberately, letting the tension ease. She popped her earbuds out and listened as the waves crashed on the sea wall and the chickadees sang. *Good morning.* The paths would soon be full of joggers, and she hated crowds. It was time to head home, to get to work.

After a few minutes back on the trail, she cleared her head and felt the relaxation return as endorphins surged through her body. She let her mind wander, imagining the world that would soon be open to her—yes, the life she had dreamed of, that her mother promised was hers for the taking, was finally within grasp. She'd been raised blocks away from Rockefeller, but to kids like her, it might as well have been the moon—you could look at it and dream about going, but that was it. She flew away from home, found herself, and impressed the world, and now was flying back. Feeling elated, she hated to stop, as she did every morning, at the restrooms along the trail. But routine was routine, and she was a routine girl. Plus, she had to pee.

She pushed open the steel door to the little brick hut decorated with murals reflecting the diversity of her neighborhood and flipped on the lights. *First one in this morning.* She checked her watch—6:18. *Not bad, not bad at all.* She pushed open the door to the only stall, John Legend serenading her at running-speed volume.

She didn't hear the shot, but felt it sting right above her left breast. It was like someone put a flaming hot poker right through her. Her eyes met the shooter's. Piercing blue. He was standing on the toilet, squinting at her, pistol still pointed right at her heart. She felt the warm blood running down her sweat-stained Lululemon running top. She thought for a second that it would be ruined, then realized the hole in the shirt was the least of her problems.

The woman who would be dean reached up with her right hand to feel the wound, but before she could, she fell straight to her knees. In that instant, the look on the man's face turned from cold indifference to satisfaction. She gasped, then fell onto her side. The right side of her head smashed against the toilet, but it didn't hurt like it should have. Then she fell forward, crashing into the hollow steel frame of the stall, causing her earbud to fall out onto the ground. She could hear the distant sound of singing coming up from it. The strange white shape floated in a sea of red.

The shooter got down from the toilet, unscrewed the silencer, and stepped over her, out of the stall. In a second, before she even knew what was going on, he was gone. *How rude!*, she thought, but couldn't even laugh at the absurdity.

The lawyer in her tried to record what happened: *What did he look like? What was he was wearing? What was the weapon he used?* But as the questions were asked, as the facts were recorded on a yellow pad in her mind, she realized that she might never get to tell her story. No, she had to save herself first.

The life was seeping out of her. She looked down at her hand, and it was covered in deep red blood. The blood—*her* blood—was now sopping into her shorts. She felt it now against her thighs and seeping into her underwear. The coldness enveloped her.

She tried to stand up, but that was impossible. Nothing worked. She turned her head but saw only her blood, running toward the low point in the floor, a drain at the center of the room. The thought of her life running into the lake made her vomit. It wasn't much—just a bit of the orange juice she chugged before setting out—but it embarrassed her.

Her breathing quickened and her mind raced at how to fix this. She was a problem solver, and there was a solution. Every problem had a solution. She'd overcome too much to die in a public restroom. The anger and frustration and fear swelled inside. All the while, John Legend sang to her.

That's it, my phone!

She wiped the blood on her hands off on her shorts, unstrapped the phone from her arm, and pushed her thumb against the home key. It buzzed in her hand. No go. The mix of sweat and blood on her thumb clouded the print, making the phone inaccessible. Her heart sank—*every second counts*, she thought, and *I don't have time to*...She typed in her passcode, and the home screen appeared. She pressed the phone icon, but it didn't respond. *Damn. Damn!* She wiped her fingers on her shorts again, trying to dry them off. But she'd now fallen completely on to her side and was soaked in her own blood. There was no part of her shorts or shirt that were not drenched in sweat and blood and vomit.

Her body ran cold and she started to gasp and convulse. Her phone slipped out of her hand and fell facedown into the growing puddle of her blood filling in the grout lines in the tile floor. Her head was resting on the floor now, and blood soaked into her hair. She reached for the phone, but it slipped out of her hand again. She flipped it over and over as she tried to grasp it with her two forefingers, but the increasing slipperiness of the phone and her decreasing dexterity made it a lost cause. As her eyes began to fail and the phone case, once a bright yellow like the sun, blended in with the blood, she gave up. Her only hope now was another jogger. She tried to call out but could make no sound. She rolled onto her back and stared up at the water-stained ceiling. It was the last thing she saw before she closed her eyes.

Three hours later, Royce Johnson sat on a park bench, panting heavily, staring at the concrete building that served as restrooms along the lakefront trail. His Suunto watch said he'd finished six miles just this side of an hour. Not the old Royce—the one his FBI team assigned the toughest stretch of the Annual Baker-to-Vegas Law Enforcement road race—but better than the squatter he was trying to kick to the curb. The scene in front of him was familiar. Uniforms keeping the perimeter, detectives in surgical gloves collecting evidence, flashing red-and-blue lights, yellow tape, a stretcher, and a floppy black body bag waiting to be filled. The investigator's itch covered his whole body, and he had to talk himself out of walking over, ducking under the tape—as he'd done a million times—and asserting federal jurisdiction. Flash the badge, see the resigned look on the cops' faces. *Royce Johnson, FBI.* Saying the words made him feel like Batman. Every time. Now, he wasn't even Robin.

Feeling his muscles starting to seize up, he stood and reached unsuccessfully for his toes. Nearly. *A few more weeks.* Reaching, he felt the strain, the work, the progress. There was more to do, but the gap between the internal image of himself and the external reality was getting smaller every day.

Striding down the hill toward the rear of the small brick building, Royce eyed the body bag. Now full and bulging like an anaconda after a big meal, two men wheeled it away toward an ambulance, flashing silent sirens. The moment always stunned him. That morning, someone set off expecting to return home. They imagined a life ahead; they could never, ever have imagined being in that bag. If you'd told them it was possible, they would have scoffed and dismissed the idea out of hand. But there they were. All zipped up and headed for nowhere.

CHAPTER 9

Twenty-four hours later, while the medical examiners were processing the murdered dean-to-be, officials from across the university set out across campus toward Steinlauf Hall, where the provost, a hot-tempered physicist named Uri Valanov, had called an emergency meeting. Rockefeller University had created the first provost position a century earlier to run the academic affairs of the university, leaving the president free to set the vision and shake the trees. This meant it fell to Valanov to deal with the murder of the first African-American woman ever tapped to be a dean of a top five law school, not to mention Rockefeller's first ever black dean in any department. That she was a black woman murdered on the South Side of Chicago, where race relations were plagued by a history of exclusion and where violence was endemic, made the situation combustible. But unlike the provost's work on quantum mechanics and nuclear fusion, this was a problem that couldn't be solved on a blackboard.

The various deans came from across campus, like emissaries from the far-flung reaches of the Roman Empire, dreading having to leave their realm of power and autonomy to bend knee to Caesar. Six men—they were embarrassingly all men—from the university's major departments all left their offices about 9:45 a.m. to ensure they wouldn't be late for the ten o'clock meeting. It didn't take fifteen minutes to walk from any part of the campus to any other, but this was one time when punctuality mattered to them. The deans, like the propraetors of Gaul or Palestine, were as obsequious when they were called to the capital as they were imperially minded and aloof when on their home territory. Every prince became a vassal when the king called. And, in this world, Valanov was king.

Steinlauf Hall, like Rome itself, sat at the center of the Rockefeller empire, a twenty-four-square-block campus surrounded by urban blight. From the north, near the border of the crime-ridden neighborhood of Woodlawn, came the head of the Divinity School; from the south came the lords of the Graduate School of Management and the Public Policy School; coming in from the east were the bosses of the Humanities Division and the Graduate School; and from the west, the president and CEO of the hospital. The last was the only person on campus with that illustrious abbreviation before his or her title, and for good reason. Medicine was where the federal grants were, and thus the chief of the Biological Sciences Division was the most important person on campus. Also the highest paid. He could run the meeting and pick the new head of the Law School if he'd so wished. It would be merely an application of the Golden Rule—he with the gold makes the rule. But the doctor couldn't have cared less about the Law School, or any other department for that matter.

The Law School was the seventh separate college of the university, but its leader had been by the provost's side all morning. It was his pick decaying in a basement freezer downtown, and he wanted to be sure he picked her replacement, as well.

The six deans carried backpacks and dressed in jeans or khaki pants, making them look more like retirees taking advantage of adult education than the dons of Cambridge or Oxford in Hollywood's imagination. Most were shaven and had combed hair, but some had not bothered. This was not remarkable on the Rockefeller campus, where sartorial standards were as low as every other place in American life. But it was somewhat surprising since they were attending a high-profile meeting in the one building on campus where suits were de rigueur. Sloppy dress was usually a sign of laziness or about signaling that ideas mattered more than appearances, but in this case, it was an act of rebellion by the colonies.

The men arrived almost in unison and took their seats in Valanov's outer office. A mousey assistant begged their patience, offering them bottled water with subtle fruit flavors. Each man took out a laptop, connected to the ubiquitous, high-speed Wi-Fi network, and got to work. Rockefeller demanded deans continue their scholarly pursuits, so spreadsheets were opened and grant applications were restarted. Then, at the crack of ten, Valanov opened his door and beckoned them inside.

The room could have been in any office park in America—the provost didn't collect knickknacks or display his trophies. There was a map of a nebula on one wall and what appeared to be an abstract portrait of Neils Bohr on the other. In the center of the room, across from a small, stand-up desk, was a large oval table surrounded by eleven chairs. Three were occupied—the outgoing dean of the Law School, the head of public relations, and the general counsel of the university. The provost took the spot next to the GC and asked the others to find a space. He dispatched his assistant to bring coffee and water, then urged her to shut the door and deflect all inquiries.

"Thanks for coming," Valanov started, as he inched in his chair.

Unnaturally lean and angular, with a shaved head and bushy eyebrows, Valanov hid his narrow blue eyes behind wire-rimmed glasses a Bond villain would pick out. He'd only been on the job for a few months and was already feeling the pressure of the loss of two Nobel-contending economists and the lack of a donor for a five-hundred-million-dollar hospital building and research complex that he could see out of the floor-to-ceiling window of his office.

The general counsel spoke first. Laptops opened.

"Obviously, this is a tragic day. We are working closely with the authorities—I've spoken with the Chicago Police, as well as the FBI." At the mention of the feds, a few eyes came up from screens—the federal link was not obvious, unless it was being viewed as a hate crime. The GC ignored the eyes and the issue. "They are confident the killer or killers will be found. We are doing everything we can on that front. The initial view is that this was...well...a hit. She had nothing valuable on her while jogging, other than her phone, which wasn't taken. It wasn't a sexual crime. The police tell me the shot was precise and there were no obvious traces at the scene. It looks, ah, professional."

"Good gracious," the head of the Divinity School gasped. "Who would do such a thing?" Then, after a long pause, asked a doozy—"*Who* was she?" The question, implying that the victim might have brought disrepute on the university, hung over the table like a bomb falling from the sky.

"We don't know anything about the whys here," the GC hoped to defuse it before impact. "The detective I spoke with—" she checked her notes, "—a Lieutenant Simms, told me that it..."

Valanov cleared his throat. "Let's stay on point, here, okay?" There was a mild irritation in his voice. "We aren't the police. Let them do their work. I met Jante—she was—" he gulped, "—a delightful person. Charming, kind, brilliant. She isn't...she didn't do anything. This was not her fault. I'm one hundred percent confident about that. Okay?" He paused and made eye contact with the group. "Okay. Moving on."

"As for the students," the outgoing dean of the Law School chimed in, "we are setting up crisis centers and offering free counseling and supports of various kinds. I'll tell you, there is a lot of fear and shock among the students, faculty, and staff. That Jante was...well...the murder of such an historic figure...and it being a woman and such a brutal...we are all quite shaken." He trailed off.

The provost stood and walked over to the windows looking out on Ellis Avenue. He let the silence that hung in the air grow roots and take hold.

"Do you see that?" He looked back over his shoulder to make sure the eyes of his deans were off their screens. "Normally, I look out on dozens of food trucks ready to feed our community." He turned back toward them, his hands on his hips. "This morning there was an ABC News van in the spot where I get my morning croissant and Americano. Look."

The deans all half stood. When they did, the scene matched the provost's stress. Satellite trucks and news vans jockeyed for position, blocking Ellis Avenue and spilling onto the sidewalks, through the arch under Steinlauf Hall, and out into the Quad.

The provost took his seat.

"Our public relations chief will coordinate our media strategy, and she will be available to meet with each of you and your teams. But the reason we are here is to discuss the next dean of the Law School."

"We simply cannot afford another mistake in this position," the GC interjected.

The word "mistake" sounded like a tray of falling dishes. Valanov cast a sideways glance at the lawyer, then tried to save her again.

"Choosing Jante was not a mistake, so that was a poor choice of words. No one here wants to diminish her loss. But we have to move on. We have to be pragmatic. Our dean before Andy was disgraced and took her own life—of course, you all know that. And with the murder of a Law School professor and then that, and the attention we got from the impeachment of the chief justice and the..." Valanov saw the look of exhaustion in the eyes of the department chairs. He knew they knew this, and he felt he was losing them.

"What I think Uri is trying to say," the PR guru offered a buoy, "is that we'd like your input into the selection process for the next dean of the Law School. It is important that the university make this decision as a whole. The stakes couldn't be higher. For all of us."

The coffee arrived in the nick of time, and as it was poured and prepared, the group got down to work.

The dean of the Graduate School of Management stated the obvious—"It's got to be a black woman, right?" Heads nodded. He continued. "This is now a missed opportunity, and if we don't seize it again, the story won't just be another murder near our campus, it will be about the backsliding. We have to give them the closest facsimile possible to neutralize this."

The rotund and thickly bearded head of the Public Policy School, stood and paced to the windows to look out at the news trucks and reporters using Steinlauf Hall as a backdrop. He rubbed his beard as he spoke.

"I hear what you're saying, and I agree with the goal. But I see it differently. This isn't just a stunt. The Law School has had ten white male deans in a row—"

"And one woman," the B-school boss interjected.

"Well, sure, and a woman before Jante, but we'd all like to forget her, right?" He turned back toward the group. They were eyeing him like a professor. "My point is that this was a historic decision we made. That the president and trustees made. Rockefeller has always been at the front of the pack on issues of women and minorities in terms of admissions and the like. We never had quotas for Jewish students like our Ivy League friends. But we, like them, have not seen minorities rise to the positions of leadership. This was our chance to be the leader here too. And this chance was taken from us. Taken from everyone who would have benefited from it, from our students to little black girls on the South Side who would have seen her as a role model."

"Who's the next best female African-American, Andy?" the provost put a point on it.

All eyes turned toward Andrew Saland, the outgoing dean of the Law School. He swallowed and bit his lip.

"There isn't an obvious. We looked and looked, but Jante was our best option. I'm not sure. We could look into it." His squirming spread around the table like the wave at a soccer game—everyone wiggled or shrugged their shoulders as if to work out a knot. "I want to say, however, that I completely agree with the sentiment expressed by my friend from the Policy School."

"We have to work harder," the provost implored. "We need to look for talent in places we don't normally look. I get it. There aren't many obvious candidates for a variety of reasons, not the least of which is the lack of access to educational resources and workplace discrimination. I get it, trust me, I get it. But that doesn't mean there aren't people out there capable of doing the job—they just aren't in the typical places. Let's raid a law firm or a government department or a business. Let's get creative."

"Does it have to be a woman? Wouldn't any African-American scholar work? That should deepen the pool enough to get us some names—right?" The general counsel tried to move the discussion forward.

"Sure," Saland answered, "but we didn't set out to pick a woman necessarily—our original list included several prominent African-American men."

"Okay," the dean of the Policy School urged him on, "let's see the list."

"We came down to Jante."

"We know that, Andy." Valanov was growing impatient. "But who was your second choice?"

"There wasn't one. She was the only person the faculty felt comfortable with. We...I think we'd have to go back to the drawing board. Regather names and do our due diligence. It will take time. I'll need to get faculty support, and there isn't any for the other names on that particular list. Right now, I'm afraid all our candidates would be unacceptable."

"We don't have time for due diligence." Valanov pounded the table. "And stop playing word games. I need a goddamn name. Today! This week. There are news trucks reporting on the murder of one of my deans. A historic choice for Rockefeller shot. In the fucking toilet! Are you kidding me? You need *faculty support.*" His tone mocked. "We all got shot in the fucking heart yesterday and we are all dying. I need to staunch the bleeding, and you are talking about faculty politics. This is a goddamn shit show and you want to stroke some egos. No way!"

The head of PR put her hand on Valanov's shoulder, rose from her chair, and stepped around to the head of the table. It was time for her to help him.

"I'm afraid Uri is right. The situation is dire. We need to come out with something sooner rather than later. I've advised the president and the Board of Trustees that we should hold off on naming a selection until after the funeral, maybe a good bit after, but that the process should be finalized and in the can. The sooner we can get the person picked, the sooner we can get to work on the messaging. We have one shot at this."

"What about an LGBTQ or trans person?" It was head of the Humanities Division.

"That's interesting," the PR maven interjected, looking toward the provost to see if she was out over her skis.

"Or a Hispanic for that matter," another dean added. "Once we open it up a bit, the list has to grow to include more people, right?"

"Latinx, please," someone chirped.

Valanov looked toward Dean Saland. "What about it, Andy? Do you have any names?"

"Does it have to be a woman?" The outgoing dean of the Law School opened a file on his laptop as he asked.

"What do you think?" Valanov asked looking back at his PR point. "Would a gay man or a Latino man be enough to short-circuit this?"

Saland scanned his file.

"Does South American count? I have a possibility."

Everyone looked at him, but Valanov answered. "We have guidelines on what counts as Hispanic for various scholarships and such, and my recollection is that we don't think of South Americans that way. As Hispanics, I mean. I'm pretty sure you've got to be Mexican or Puerto Rican to count as Hispanic. Is that right, Sue?" He leaned over toward the general counsel, who nodded. "Right, so no South Americans. Although maybe a Venezuelan woman might count? We might be able to sell that."

"I'd prioritize a woman over a gay man or Hispanic man from a PR perspective," the PR lead chimed in. "I think it will be more impactful."

"But my predecessor was a woman," the law dean noted, "and we know how that...well, I mean to say that that barrier was broken already. I think getting a real minority is what we're after."

"What about picking the best person for the job?" The head of the hospital tossed his comment like a grenade into the center of the table without looking up from a spreadsheet summarizing operating room utilization rates.

"I see your point, Doctor, but we are talking about the best person for the job, all things considered." Valanov moved quickly to placate his most important faculty member and to avoid derailing what he thought was a productive session. "The stakeholders of the university, public and private, demand we do our part to remedy the historical injustices that undergird our society. We are not immune to this, having benefited from it and being the best positioned to be able to help remedy it. So, I agree with you. We should pick the best person. But, at this time in our history, and at this exact fucking moment when our savior is in a fucking meat locker, the best person is a black, gay woman if we can find her."

"I see your point, Uri." The doctor went back to his spreadsheet, his face full of indifference.

The ever-pragmatic dean of the Business School came to the aid of his Caesar. "McDonalds did not tie itself in knots thinking about what its customers *should* want, it just met in rooms like this to hear reports about what they *did* want, and then to figure out the best way to get that to them at the lowest possible cost. The Big Mac was an act of satisfaction, not leadership."

The analogy was not tight, but the point was made, even if it made Valanov bristle a bit at the comparison.

"So, can you have your search committee shift into high gear and get me five names as soon as possible? End of the week?" Valanov asked the outgoing head of the Law School.

Saland nodded his agreement and set to his keys to fire off an email.

"Make sure the list includes a few internal candidates as well," the provost added as footnote. "And make them white guys."

"Good idea," the PR person added. "That way it doesn't seem…"

"Like we're doing what we're doing," the head of the Business School chirped sarcastically.

"Exactly," blurted out the general counsel. "And, speaking of that, this conversation never happened. This isn't exactly…well, let's just say that I don't want a visit from the Justice Department."

"I have a strong internal candidate we can reject—Scott Miller. He is the most likely of my faculty to being willing to talk to strangers and the least likely to spill on himself or others while doing so."

The group shared a laugh. They all knew and liked Professor Miller.

"I'd add Tim Benton to this list," said the dean of the Humanities. Benton was a famous historian of ancient China. He had distinguished himself as a prolific fundraiser for Rockefeller's new Beijing Campus, and was known to harbor ambitions that if not satisfied locally might make him leave for a competitor. "Giving him a look might be enough to tide him over. Plus, it will be good political cover."

"Good," Dean Saland typed and added him to the list.

Valanov liked these names, but he knew that white men were as desirable on college campuses these days as rotavirus in a salad bar. As he thought this, Valanov felt his whiteness. It was like a winter coat he couldn't take off as he sweated in a sauna. For the first time in his life, he felt what it was like to be uncomfortable in his own skin.

At that, the meeting adjourned and after some small talk, the potentates headed off in all directions back to their fiefdoms.

CHAPTER 10

Max Klepp traced his finger along the path Bubbly Creek cut through the South Side of Chicago. His index finger was plump and his knuckles hairy, but a seventy-five-dollar manicure set off the nail as a point of sophistication, like a monkey wearing a tuxedo. After four decades in real estate development, he could perfectly visualize the completed project from the blueprints, the buildings rising and the people shopping and dining and walking their dogs. The thrill was still with him. At his command, steel and concrete rising out of the ground like corn stalks from seeds he'd planted. His imagination, played out in Tinker Toys when he was a boy, now at scale. Dead land brought to life. He knew no greater joy than creation—to be God, at least for a few acres of vacant Chicago riverfront.

"Mr. Klepp," a voice beckoning from the outer office interrupted his daydream.

"Yup?" he grunted in the general direction, eyes still on the two-dimensional renderings of his creations soon to rise from the soil.

"Line one for you. A Mr. Steinlauf. Should I tell him you're out?"

"Nah, I'm here. Hold on a sec."

Klepp unfolded himself from the high-back chair, cracking and creaking his way to vertical, feeling his seven decades suffering under Earth's gravity. He shuffled over to his oversized oak desk, modeled after the Resolute Desk he saw in person when he visited President Reagan in the Oval Office during his time as the deputy undersecretary of Treasury.

"Ruby, my boy, how are you?" Klepp held the phone between his shoulder and ear as he used his hands to pour four fingers of Talisker into a Bohemian cut highball.

"She's dead, Max. Hasn't hit the news yet." His tone was khaki brown.

"Who's dead?" Klepp sat down and took a swig of scotch.

"Professor Turner. The dean. Or, dean-elect, I guess."

"Hmmm," he moaned as the scotch swirled and burned in his mouth. "Interesting. What's the play, Ruby?"

"Play? What's our play? You seem pretty nonchalant about this, Max. I'll tell you what our play is—we get as far from this as we possibly can. If someone—"

"I understand your concern, Ruben," Klepp barked, rising out of his chair on instinct. He paced over to the windows that looked out from the sixty-fourth floor of the Hancock Building onto Lake Michigan stretching out to the horizon full of possibility. Three white-sailed boats cut across the frame. "This is a tragic loss for Rockefeller, and we should offer to support our friends there in their time of need." There was no need to say what was understood. He hoped Steinlauf took the hint.

"Right. Of course. What do you suggest? To support them, I mean."

"Who knows? This is your turf."

"Sure, I'll figure out something."

"More importantly," Klepp said, "this is an opportunity for us. Professor Turner wasn't going to stop that nut case from making outrageous allegations about our site. That was abundantly clear, right? So, we use her unfortunate demise as a do-over."

"Do-over?"

"Yeah. We didn't pick her, but we can pick her successor. A

successor of our choosing to do our bidding. Or, at least to pick a thorn out of our paw. Rockefeller installs a dean with a head on his shoulders. Someone who will do the right thing and put an end to a bunch of hippies traipsing all over our site trying to dig up problems and stand in the way of progress."

"You've always had a way with words, old buddy."

"Well thank you, Mr. Steinlauf. I love you too."

They shared a laugh.

"Are you sure this is a good idea?" His doubt seeped through the line and poured out onto Klepp's leather floor.

"Of course I think it is a good idea—it's my fucking idea, and my fucking ideas are always good ideas. Haven't you learned that after so many years?"

"You know I trust your judgment, Maxy, but..."

"Don't be a pussy, Ruben," he spat.

"That's a first. It sounds like you have someone in mind?" Steinlauf fished.

"Well, as a matter of fact, I do. My son-in-law."

"Really?"

Klepp didn't like his incredulity or the lack of trust.

"Really. He is the perfect choice. Good kid. Smart and capable. I think he is looking for the next challenge. He'd be good with alumni and donors, seeing as he makes eye contact when he talks to you, something that can't be said about most of his colleagues. A bunch of spaz cases, Ruby. I don't know how you deal with these people."

"They only send me the ones who wear deodorant."

Another shared laugh, and this time they let it linger, appreciating each other's friendship over the years. Klepp raised a glass in silence to his old friend, fairly confident that across town he was doing the same.

"So, we are agreed. We get him in. I assume that is just an ask for you, since you've funded the whole damn place practically."

"Well, I don't know about that, but yes, my munificence has earned me some goodwill on campus, if that is what you are saying."

"Don't be coy, you old fart. If a few hundred million bucks doesn't buy you the ability to pick the occasional dean, what good is it, right?"

"You really think this is a good idea, Max? It tightens our connection."

"Yes, but if done correctly, it seals the deal. He gets in, throws up some roadblocks. We just need to get the approvals and get the foundation poured."

"And the professor? The tree hugger. He's not going to give up." Klepp could hear his fear. This was unusual for his friend, one of the richest and boldest men he knew, and he knew a few. Talking about murder did that to people.

"I'm working on it, Ruby, I'm working on it. You just get our man in the dean's suite. I'll take care of the rest."

Klepp didn't wait for a response. He hung up the receiver and downed the rest of his Talisker in a gulp.

CHAPTER 11

Ruben Steinlauf gripped the cell phone in his right hand like he was trying to choke the life out of it. Distracted by his rage, he caught the eye of his assistant, standing a few feet away and holding another phone with a victim waiting. After three more minutes of verbal machine-gun fire, Steinlauf hung up, signaled to his assistant, and swapped phones without missing a beat. The tone and speed of dialogue didn't let up. Nor did the torrent of profanity.

Steinlauf was a real Horatio Alger story, something that he told everyone he met. He grew up in Alphabet City in Manhattan during the postwar boom. His father was a furrier, which was the family business but on his mother's side. The Kushnirs were from the Pale of Settlement; they came, like millions of others from the Ukraine and Belarus and Poland to America, through the turnstiles of Ellis Island. They didn't have the means or connections to make it very far, or very far up. When his grandmother, Marina Kushnir, married Oscar Steinlauf, a line worker at a cash register factory in the Bronx, the family prospects did not improve considerably.

When he was not yet forty, Oscar died, along with fifty-nine others, in a fire that ripped through the factory where he worked. It raged for two days and it looms large in the lore of Bronx fire stations to this day. Ruben was told the fire was set deliberately by the managers of the Sussman Register Company in an attempt to hide their embezzlement from the company's owners. This made a big impression on Ruben's father, Abner, who for this reason decided to choose the business of Marina's family instead. So, it happened that Ruben spent his formative years doing his homework under long tables piled high with dead animal skins in his father's workshop in the East Village. The bits of flesh and fat that hung off the unrefined skins and the metallic smell of blood that permeated his clothes for days turned Ruben into a vegetarian and, when it became a thing, a vegan. It had been six decades since he'd eaten any meat.

Ruben took quickly to math, and by the time he was ten, he was helping make sense of his dad's books—they were a mess. He graduated at the top of his class at Stuyvesant High School, then The City College of New York, and finally, the Rockefeller Law School. He excelled in his legal studies but no one suspected he'd be a lawyer. His tiny frame packed too big a punch for even the biggest case in the grandest courtroom. No, all of Ruben's classmates and teachers suspected he was headed for a bigger stage. Those who didn't like his particular flavor of politics took to calling him "Nappy," as in diminutive for "Napoleon."

Finding that finance, not law, was his passion, Ruben went to Wall Street, where, in the course of two decades, he earned a vast fortune in private equity investments. He decamped for Chicago mid-career, building a trading empire in derivatives, trading everything from Yellow Corn #2 to wind farm credits. Although now into his seventies, Ruben worked fifteen-hour days, never took vacation, and had long lost count of how many billions he had made for himself and others. There were only two causes that Ruben cared about—breast cancer, which took his daughter a few years back, and the Rockefeller Law School, which gave him the full ride that set him up for success. He gave generously and was viewed as indispensable to both. It was for this reason that he was able to convene a meeting with the provost of the university at a time of his choosing on less than a day's notice.

His assistant held up her Carl F. Bucherer ScubaTec watch—a gift from her boss for a job well done—into Ruben's field of vision and pointed at it with her index finger. She mouthed, *Let's go.* She and his wife of fifty-two years Sunday were the only ones that could get away with this.

They were standing on a gray flagstone patio in front of Steinlauf Hall in a courtyard that had been recently refurbished through a donation of the Kushnir Family Foundation—Steinlauf had given so much money to Rockefeller he had converted to using other family names to make it seem like there was more widespread support among rich alumni. As he stood shouting into his phone, twirling around like a ballet dancer during warmups, he got more than a few stares from earnest college students who, when passing by, heard the little bald man use words they probably figured were forbidden these days.

"I've got to go, Mort. Listen, you tell those sons of bitches that we are in for a hundred million, no more, no less. If they don't like it, they can pound sand. Okay? Okay. I'm off."

Steinlauf handed his assistant the phone and marched away. She dropped the phone in her large tote and ran after him. Despite the fact she had five inches on him, his normal gait was double hers. His legs turned over so fast they seemed to blur together like the cartoon Roadrunner. Especially when he was late. He hated nothing more than to be late.

The provost rose when Steinlauf burst through his door with a knock that was more of an afterthought. Valanov was reviewing the tenure file of a classicist. He was happy for the distraction Steinlauf offered. He dropped the manila file on his desk, set his readers on top, and rose to greet the most important person in his world.

"Uri, sorry I'm late. These Slovenian bastards are trying to screw me." He shook the provost's hand, then took a seat and put his feet up on Valanov's desk. "Wait, you aren't Slovenian, are you?" Before he could answer, Steinlauf changed the subject.

"Who cares. You know it's not personal. With me, it's never personal. You know I love you, right?" Again, he didn't wait for a response. "So, let me tell you why I'm here."

The provost smiled. He pushed a pewter bowl of chocolate-covered espresso beans toward Steinlauf.

"No thanks, my doctor told me I need to cut back on caffeine. He's got a point, right?" Steinlauf paused, but it was more like reloading.

"What can I do for you, Ruben?"

"The dead lady—I've got a name for you."

Steinlauf pulled a folded piece of paper from the inner pocket of his double-breasted Armani suit. He slid it across the desk. Valanov eyed it suspiciously, squinting through his rimless frames.

"Don't get too excited, Uri," Steinlauf pushed it further toward him. "I don't know who did it."

Steinlauf studied the look on his face—a mix of relief and disappointment. He guessed: relieved that his biggest donor was not knowledgeable about a murder of one of his deans; disappointed at the prospect of the case remaining unsolved.

Valanov reached for the paper and unfolded it carefully.

"What's this?" Valanov squinted aggressively.

"The name of the next dean of the Law School," Steinlauf said matter-of-factly, as only a man whose name was on the building could. He downed a handful of the beans, smirking as the provost squirmed.

The provost swallowed hard. "We are still reeling from the…the apparent murder of our dean."

"Dean-elect, I think is the right word." Steinlauf tolerated no imprecision.

"Yes, yes, it is." The provost's blood ran cold at the indifference. "I guess that's right. Dean-elect."

"Well, as tragic as her death is, we don't have time to wallow. We need leadership, and I assume Andy is eager to get to Ann Arbor."

"He is, Ruben. But it isn't exactly a crisis. We can manage

for a bit. Give us a few weeks, okay? We need to deal with this situation, to grieve. The first black dean of a South Side law school gunned down on the lake shore isn't exactly a public relations coup. We have to get things under control first, then I suspect we'll have an interim dean and another national search." The provost couldn't believe he had to explain this. His frustration showed through. "A few months at least, I suspect."

"Dean-elect. And I get it. You've got some bullshit you have to deal with first. Sure. Fine. I'm not saying we don't shed a tear for the lady. Do what you have to do, then pick him. Got it?" Steinlauf rose and walked over to the window that looked out over the Quad. A campus that sparkled as never before and was filled with top-notch students as never before in large part because of Steinlauf money. "These buildings, these grounds, look great, huh?" He drove home the point. "And I hear you haven't named the new medical school building." He turned on a dime and made eye contact with Valanov, whose pupils dilated and face tightened at the thought. Steinlauf liked playing both good cop and bad cop at the same time. The carrot was plump.

The look on Valanov's face said he was beaten—he'd been given an offer no sane person would refuse. It was a ticket to a successful tenure as provost, and then the presidency of a university. He could seal the deal here and now. Five. Hundred. Million. Dollars.

"We can't prejudge the process..." he sputtered.

Steinlauf wheeled on the balls of his feet. He cut him off, knowing that it was just his moral compass leading him astray.

"Fuck that, Uri. I don't give two hoots about the way you run things around here. I care about results. My investors don't care if I turn our companies around by using financial engineering, squeezing the unions, or dry humping them. They care about dollars. The rest?...Just talk."

"But..."

"No buts, Uri. He should have been the choice in the first place. With all due respect to the dead lady, of course. Never met her. Which is a mistake, by the way. Let's not make another one. Anyway, the guy is as solid as they come. *He* is the person who is going to continue our fundraising successes. Without him, I think they dry up considerably. If you know what I mean." Stick.

"What are you saying?"

"I'm not saying anything other than that gal wasn't the right pick."

Uri Valanov didn't get to be the provost of one of the world's great research universities by being obtuse. He could read between lines.

"I appreciate your input, Ruben. You know it matters a great deal. More than I can express."

Steinlauf cut him off again.

"Cut the crap. Is the guy the dean or not?" Steinlauf rubbed his hands like a surgeon washing up. "I'm eager to get this deal closed so I can move on to other things. He is the next dean of the Law School. Yes?" Another handful of beans dropped into his mouth.

"I'm not making any promises, Ruben, but you know I'll do what I can."

Steinlauf reached into his pocket and removed a cell phone. He looked at the number, then back up at the provost.

"I need to take this." He slid the phone into active mode and barked, "Give me a minute." He dropped the phone to his side, then said to the provost, "I know you will, Uri, I know you will. And for your sake, I hope it is enough."

Steinlauf turned heel, put the phone to his ear, and walked out of the provost's office.

"Matthew!" the provost screamed after Steinlauf got into the elevator. "Get me President Gottlieb."

Valanov slumped into his chair, letting his head fall back onto the soft leather. He closed his eyes and let out a big exhale. He gave himself just a moment, then sat forward, pushed the file of the Roman historian to one side, and got out a blank yellow pad. There was more pressing work to be done. He had to bury one dean and install another *tout de suite*. He was sure of one thing, no one was going to be happy at either event.

CHAPTER 12

"Who can tell me what the Supreme Court held in *Ex Parte Crow Dog*?" Professor Scott Miller slumped against the whiteboard in the front of the classroom. It was early in the morning and late in the semester. Eighteen sets of eyes looked away, and a few butts squirmed in their seats. No one wanted to hear their name. "Let's see," he scanned the seating chart with his index finger, "Ms. Woolridge, why don't you give it a shot. What happened in this case?"

She sat up with a snap, causing her phone to fall from her thigh, where she'd precariously balanced it to avoid detection. The phone crashed to the floor, sending an embarrassed laugh around the ring of students in Professor Miller's American Indian Law class..

"Um, well, that was a case…" She looked nervously at her textbook, scanning for the case. She was stalling.

"Let me help, Ms. Woolridge—a Lakota Sioux by the name of Crow Dog kills a chief named Spotted Tail. As punishment, the tribe makes Crow Dog give some blankets and horses to Spotted Tail's family. Following me so far?"

The student nodded diffidently.

"Now, the news gets out, slowly mind you, this is 1883. The settlers hear that the penalty for murder in Indian Country is a few blankets and some horses. The settlers in the Dakota

Territories are outraged. If the penalty for killing were so small, wouldn't the Lakota start killing them too? They think these Lakota are savages, and this result just confirms it. They need to be civilized, they argue—Crow Dog must hang! That's what *civilized* people do to murderers." His condescending tone got a nervous laugh. Miller knew his job was not just conveying information. With kids these days, it was more like infotainment.

"So, the feds arrest and try Mr. Crow Dog, and sentence him to hang by his neck until dead. Crow Dog appeals all the way to the Supreme Court. What does the Supreme Court say, Ms. Woolridge?"

Flipping frantically in her casebook, the student heard a friendly whisper from her right—"The Court held that federal law didn't apply on the reservation." Jane from Wisconsin had her back.

"The Court held that federal law didn't apply on the reservation," she repeated, loud enough for Professor Miller to hear this time.

"Well, that's not exactly right, but it's a start. Welcome to the conversation, Ms. Woolridge."

She smiled nervously. "I guess..." More stalling.

"What were the key assumptions that made the Court conclude that there was no role for the feds here?"

"That Crow Dog had already been punished by the tribe?" she trailed off at the end, so that the professor could barely hear her.

"Speak up, Ms. Wooldridge. *Fill this room with your intelligence.*" He did his best impression of Professor Kingsfield from the movie *The Paper Chase*, but the reference and his patrician accent were lost on the students. He thought he was being witty and culturally informed; they thought he was being a tool.

More confidently this time, Ms. Woolridge went on, "The tribe had already meted out justice, and who is the federal government to say whether it was too much or too little?" She could feel the improvement.

"Good. Better." He walked toward her, smiling. He buttoned his corduroy blazer and approached her slowly. "Where a tribe engages in a criminal process, the Court believes that process should be respected. Yes, yes?" He looked from one end of the room to the other.

There were nods, but the room was not exactly electric. Behind these laptop screens, Miller knew shopping and poker and worse was probably going on.

Professor Miller went on: "Think of it this way. Replace the tribe in this case with the State of Illinois. If Crow Dog were in Illinois and did this horrible thing, and the state tried him, would the federal government really not respect that punishment? After all, doesn't Illinois have strong incentives to get the level of punishment right?" One hundred eighty fingers typed furiously.

A hand went up. It was attached to Sandy Blasius, notorious gunner.

"What about if the penalty were too harsh in the opinion of the federal government? Can't the feds prohibit 'cruel and unusual' punishments? If the Bill of Rights applies, they can't let Crow Dog be tortured. Right? The Eighth Amendment prohibits that." Miller nodded. "And if that is true, then why not allow a floor on the punishments that can be given out too? We might expect the federal government to set the boundaries of acceptable punishment for states and tribes—not above a certain amount, and not below a certain amount—and thus this case is really just about where those boundaries are."

There were moments of actual pride in teaching, and this was one of them. It was a good point. But, along with the pride, Miller felt a stab of disappointment—it was a point *he* wanted to make. This was Miller's little show, not Blasius's or anyone else's. And the ringmaster doesn't like it when someone else puts on the top hat and grabs the microphone.

"Are there any limiting principles on this power?...Back to you, Ms. Woolridge." He wanted to have one over on the students, and he was afraid Blasius would steal his thunder again. She paused, searching again or hoping for a whisper. *Sandy, help me.* She tried telepathy.

The professor looked up, but then caught sight of the clock in the back of the room. "Well, you're saved by the bell, Ms. Woolridge. Let's pick up there next time."

The students shuffled and started packing up their bags. Over the noise, Professor Miller shouted, "We'll start off with that question—under what condition would the Supreme Court admit there is a role for federal criminal law on Indian Reservations? And then, back to the case of Crow Dog. What happens after he was released? How'd Congress respond to the Court's smack down? See you then."

The students filed out, chatting about the latest episode of *The Bachelor* and the Cubs' chances in the playoffs, not the sovereignty of tribes or theories of optimal allocation of criminal jurisdiction, as Professor Miller hoped. He packed up his briefcase—an old Hartman box his dad bequeathed him—wiped the board clean for the next class, and filed out behind them.

Head down, eyes on his Twitter feed, Scott ran headlong into the dean's assistant.

"Oooh, sorry, Jeremy." He dropped his phone, which clattered along the hallway. Scott reached for it, fearing a crack or worse. When he flipped it over and found it intact and functional, his sense of relief was irrationally big. In that instant he vowed to become less reliant on his phone, but before he got it into his pocket, he checked his email and the score of the White Sox game. He forgot entirely about Jeremy, who eyed him as the professor looked up again.

"Professor Miller, I'm sorry to bother you, but Dean Saland would like to see you."

The tone was disconcerting. Tenured professors didn't get called into the principal's office the way high school losers did. Miller prided himself on not having a boss. Or, at least one that didn't do this kind of thing. Tenured professors were not employees but islands in a chain, ringed together only loosely by bits of submerged coral and rock unobservable to outsiders.

"Sure, I'll just drop my stuff off..."

"I think you should come now," the assistant insisted, then turned and walked as if to say, *follow me, now*!

The few hours after a lecture was usually when Scott shut down his brain, or at least put it in neutral. It was time to watch Netflix or daydream about the new Tesla model. But the command to report to the dean sent Scott's normally squishy, post-lecture brain into overdrive. He ran through his recent social media posts, public speeches, and comments at faculty lunches searching for something that might have offended. There were plenty of shoe leather sandwiches—they were the specialty of his house—but none recently that seemed to rise to the level of decanal concern. But, then again, he thought, in an age when speakers were routinely drummed off campuses for running afoul of the thought police, anything was possible. He followed Jeremy at a safe distance, the dread rising up in him like water filling a tub.

The dean's assistant led him to the faculty lounge. The Workshop, as it was known, was a blank space tucked into a corner off the main reading room of the Kushnir Family Law Library. On that day, it was filled with a dozen small tables and forty-eight identical, and extremely uncomfortable, chairs of a modern design. The Workshop served two roles: it was where, every Thursday at twenty minutes past noon, the faculty presented their latest research to each other and, on occasion, as it was this Monday, where the faculty discussed matters of administration. The Works-in-Progress talks were blood-sport, famous across the academy; on the other hand, faculty meetings were when trivialities of administration were discussed in the most rigid and high-sounding tones. It was as if the Roman Coliseum were used for both gladiatorial bouts and an insurance seminar.

Two hours before the planned faculty meeting, it was an empty space where Scott Miller sat nervously for ten minutes awaiting his fate. The dean strode in triumphantly. He was not tall or particularly good-looking, nor was he well-dressed. But he exuded confidence and competence. He put people at ease, whether they were high rollers or stressed-out 1Ls.

"Scott!"

Hearing his name called, Professor Miller looked up from his phone and, on seeing the dean, rose to his feet.

"Dean Saland," Scott whimpered, holding out his hand reluctantly.

"Have a seat, Scott, I've got some news."

The dean pulled up a chair and eyed the professor.

"Whatever it is, Dean, I didn't do it," Scott tried to defuse the situation with a lame joke that was just true enough.

"I'm afraid this time you did. You did it, Scott. You did it."

CHAPTER 13

Dean Scott Miller turned the brass handle of the door to his new office. Although he'd been in the Dean's Suite many times, he'd never noticed the door handle before. But today he was going to notice everything. Today was a day to stop and savor a door handle. The handle was round, but a bit out of shape from dents accumulated over the years. It was the color of over-creamed coffee and had what appeared to be the head of an animal, maybe a sheep or goat, on the flat side. The significance of this was totally lost on him.

"Can I help you, Dean?" his assistant asked, as he stood frozen, bent slightly at the waist, his head cocked to one side.

"Oh, sorry Jeremy, I...I just never noticed this before." He stood up tall and pointed at the handle with his index finger. He felt like a kid caught sneaking around in his dad's desk.

"You have a ten o'clock with the associate dean for administration, an eleven with the associate dean for admissions, and lunch with the provost. This afternoon—"

Scott cut him off. "This is in my calendar?"

"Yes, it's all there. I just thought..."

"I'm all set, Jeremy. Thanks for your thoroughness."

"Okay," Jeremy whimpered. He'd hoped to make a good impression.

"One more thing. Tell Mike Church in the Environmental

Law Clinic I'd like to see him."

"Now?"

"Now. Everything else can wait."

Scott opened the door and walked into his new office. Jeremy shouted after him.

"Remember, tonight, dinner with Mr. Steinlauf."

"Got it. Thanks," he said without looking back.

He shut the door with the sole of his shoe and walked into the center of the room. It wasn't an impressive space, except for the square footage. The carpet, an industrial gray set in square pieces that gave the appearance of parquet, was worn in places and not inspired to begin with. There was a simple wooden desk of unknown provenance and a side table that didn't match. Bookshelves lined three walls, but they were empty. In fact, there was nothing in the room, except a slim brass desk lamp with a dangle chain. On the other wall, a set of floor-to-ceiling windows looked out over a lush garden of evergreens ringed with walking paths and benches that normally contained students, their noses in red casebooks. But not on this day. The rain fell in sheets. The dark skies did not fit his mood, but the rain pounding the glass made a rhythm that sounded like a drummer announcing the new king. At least that was what Scott Miller, newly minted dean of the Rockefeller Law School, thought.

Scott sat down at his desk and placed a few mementos around. It was his desk. The desk he wanted since he was a student at Rockefeller. It mattered not a whiff to him that the way he got it was unorthodox. Everyone expected another national search. A search that would have found another black woman to replace Jante. When instead his name was announced just weeks after her death, everyone was shocked at the speed and at the choice. Not surprised that it was Scott per se—he was smart and capable, outgoing and had good judgment—but that his race and gender were not exactly what was called for under the circumstances. But Scott wasn't going to let whispers and rumors and racism ruin this day. He pulled his laptop out of his messenger bag.

Time to get to work. He fired up the computer and opened Word. He started to type out some notes for his budget meeting, when a knock came at the door.

"Come!" he shouted. That would be his entrance command, he decided in the moment after he said it. Or, should he say "Enter," or the more benign, "Come in"? He decided to decide later.

"Your majesty," Bruce Michels, his closest friend on the faculty, put his right foot forward and bowed deeply in the Elizabethan style, pretending to remove a hat and drag it down nearly to the ground.

"Cut the shit, Bruce. Get over here." Scott jumped up and jogged around his desk and over into Bruce's arms. They embraced. As they did, Bruce turned his head slightly to the right and breathed him in.

"Love you, man."

"Love you too." Scott said it without thinking it meant anything more than a high five or a bro hug, but he suspected that Bruce meant it in other ways too.

"So, this is the big time, huh?" Bruce said, stepping back from the embrace.

"Yes, welcome to my lair."

"Indeed. So, how's the first day? I see you're all moved in."

"Funny. I just got here. Beth and I went out to breakfast to celebrate. I don't think we've gone out to breakfast alone in like ten years. It was decadent, to just sit and eat pancakes and linger over coffee and the *Times*."

Scott pulled a picture of Beth—the red hair that had first caused him to notice her dancing on her shoulders—out of his briefcase and set it on his desk.

"Sounds nice. I just got done trying to explain cost-benefit analysis to a bunch of kids who majored in French poetry and modern dance before they got here. Fun times."

"Yeah, *U.S. News* rankings have made us all whores for statistics—a four-point in basket weaving is better than a three-point-five in chemical engineering. The world is nuts."

"So are you going to, you know—" he waved his arms around, "—do something about it?"

"Who, me?"

"You are *the dean*. Of one of the best law schools on the planet. If not you, then who?"

"It's my first day, buddy, give me time to at least get unpacked before I try to fix legal education. Okay?"

"It's a deal."

"Then, I'll turn to solving the problems of racial subordination in the country. Okay?"

"Yeah, you get on that." They shared a laugh, although they both knew it wasn't a funny matter.

"So, what can I do for you?" Scott was all business. He had a tight schedule, and he meant to impress on his first day.

"Oh, so that's how it's going to be then. I see..."

"Don't do that, Bruce. I've got—I'm in a new role here, and I've got to play the part."

"Okay. I get it. Good call."

Bruce looked over at the rain-soaked glass. He watched streams of water cascade down the glass like balls in a Pachinko machine. Without turning back to Scott, who was now typing away on his laptop, Bruce mused, "I wonder if they have any leads. Have you heard anything?"

"About what?" Scott kept typing out questions he had for one of his assistant deans.

Bruce turned back and stared at his friend, or rather the top of his curly head.

"The murder, silly. *Jante's murder*. You know, your predecessor who was murdered in a public toilet in broad daylight. Hello?" He saw Scott look up and stare back at him. "Do you know if they have any leads? What is the status of the investigation?"

"How would I know?" Scott was surprised.

"How would you know? You're the dean. She was a colleague. She was supposed to be sitting here. The robes you wore at your induction ceremony were borrowed—they were hers. You aren't interested? You aren't inserting yourself in this investigation?"

"Look, the eight hundred souls in this building are my responsibility, and I have to tend to them. Make sure they have the best experience possible. I'm sad, obviously, but I don't see how it has anything to do with me."

"Are you mad? *The souls in this building*?" he said in a mock British accent. "Are you Captain Jack Aubrey now! Come on." He shook his head. "The *people* in this building, students and faculty and staff, are broken apart by this. Did you know that the Black Law Student Association is planning a march to the provost's office to demand an inquiry by the University?" He was short of breath.

"Are you serious?"

"Wake up, Scott. There are people that aren't happy a black woman dean—the first black woman dean of a top school—was murdered before she could take office. This is like a Martin Luther King moment for our black students. Do you not see that?" Bruce stood and walked over to the empty bookshelves. He rubbed his finger along an edge, eyed it, then wiped the dust onto his pant leg.

"What do they think happened?" Scott was genuinely stumped. "It was a robbery or a rape or something random like that. Happens all the time around here."

"She was jogging, Scott. She didn't have anything on her, and they found her phone in a pool of her blood. Her diamond studs were in her ears. As for the rape, I'm told by my source in the CPD that she wasn't raped." Scotts eyes were wide. "This was an assassination."

"Hold on, Bruce..." He could hardly get the word out. "Assassination? That's quite a claim."

"I believe it."

"Why are you so interested in this? Who's your source in the police department? As a matter of fact, why do you even have one?"

Scott was getting tired of the conversation. If there were people who needed soothing, he'd say the right things. He made a note to meet with the head of BLSA. But that he'd get involved in the case seemed like madness.

"It is quite a claim. But I believe it." Bruce walked back toward the windows.

Scott finally caught up.

"They don't think I had…they don't suspect *me*, do they?" Scott felt his blood coagulate in his veins.

"I don't know, Scott. I don't know. There are rumors."

"Rumors? What fucking rumors? What is this!" he whispered, but his gesticulating knocked over a glass tchotchke he got from a term serving on the Navajo Appeals Court. The shattering brought Jeremy to the door.

"Is…is everything okay, Dean?" Jeremy's balding head peeked around the corner of the door frame.

"Yeah. Nothing but love and intellectual combat in this room." The assistant nodded. "Shut the door, please."

"Okay. Professor Church is here to see you."

"Give me a minute. Give us a minute. Tell Mike I'll be right with him."

The two men sized each other up, circling the room like prize fighters. Scott found himself by the windows now, looking out at the rain too.

"You were about to accuse me of murder. Or, rather, murder for hire. I assume you don't think I pulled the trigger." He mocked his dear friend. Or, was he now becoming his dear rival, or worse?

"Of course, I don't think you pulled the trigger. To answer your question about why I'm interested, I'm interested because I know how much you wanted this job. You told me every time we—"

"Shut up, Bruce. That was a long time ago. I don't…" The dean trailed off, head spinning.

"You had the most to gain, Scott. Who else would benefit

from her—"

"Stop right there, Bruce. Seriously. I have no fucking clue who..." he gulped. Nothing was going to ruin this day, but this was going to ruin this day. "Look, you've known me for, what, fifteen years? Have I done anything in that time, any fucking thing, that makes you think I'm capable of...of...murder?" Scott grabbed his friend by the bicep and turned him toward him.

"No." It came out as a whimper.

"Well, I'm telling you, on Beth's life and the lives of my kids, I had nothing to do with this."

"Well, if that's the case, you've got some work to do. Convincing me is one thing, convincing them—" he motioned through the door of the office and out toward the classrooms and offices of the Law School, "—is going to be a lot harder."

"Thanks, Bruce. Now I see it. You weren't accusing me, just getting the message across." Scott hoped this was true.

"Sure, Scott."

They shook hands. Bruce walked out of the office, and Scott flopped back into his chair from the standing position. He had a problem to solve and time was of the essence. But first he had another problem that needed to be solved, and it was waiting in the anteroom.

"Jeremy," he shouted. A few seconds later, the door opened and he appeared.

"Yes, boss?"

"Send in Mike Church."

CHAPTER 14

The Courtroom of the Rockefeller Law School was a small amphitheater tucked into the basement below a much larger auditorium. When used as an actual courtroom—for the annual student moot court competition and, on occasion, for a sitting of the Navajo Supreme Court—the three black, high-back leather chairs set on a small pedestal, were used by judges. On this day, they were empty. So was the jury box set off to the left of the judges' dais and the tables and chairs reserved for the attorneys. Microphones were off. Gavels sat askance, unused. In the center of the room, where a lawyer would have paced and gesticulated while making an opening argument or questioning a witness, Dean Scott Miller stood at a podium facing the audience. About fifty students, alumni, staff, and a few local residents were in attendance for the annual Curran Lecture on Human Rights.

"Good afternoon and welcome!" the dean brought the room to attention. "And Happy Halloween." He'd thought about wearing a costume—Halloween was an irrationally big deal in the Miller house—but his assistant talked him out of it. Irony had long been killed and buried in lime on university campuses, and Scott Miller, a white male known for an occasional social media faux pas, was not the guy to resurrect it. A pinstripe suit, a costume of sorts in academia, was a smarter choice, Jeremy told him. He'd only been in the job for two months—there was no reason to push the boundary.

Hearing the program starting, a few students looked up from their phones tucked between their knees under cover of the seatbacks in front of them. There was a smattering of applause from the locals. They froze when they realized that they'd clapped at the wrong time, like newbies at the symphony clapping between the third and fourth movements of Beethoven's Fifth. The dean smiled at their eagerness.

"It is an honor to introduce our speaker for the day," he said, pressing ahead. "Andre de Lesseps is the Wallace Family Professor of Law at the Yale Law School. Professor de Lesseps is a distinguished scholar and prolific writer on the history of human rights, especially on the embodiment of human rights principles in written constitutions. In his work on the constitutions of Africa, he has shown..." The introduction stopped mid-sentence, like it jumped the tracks. The dean's eyes seemed to burst out of his face, and the blood ran to his vital organs.

The students looked up from their phones and everyone seemed to cock their head to the side slightly at the same time. Scott Miller was typically the color of Wonder Bread, but somehow, he'd turned even whiter. After a few seconds, soft whispers turned into a murmur and then into a commotion, as the dean stood open-mouthed. Then, zombielike, he raised a finger and pointed toward the back of the room. The point was not intended to draw the attention of the audience; it was a threat aimed over the heads of the crowd. But turn they did. As he held it, like a gun pointed into the distance, the look on his face was a blend of shock and rage, growing angrier by the second.

The audience turned their heads around to the left in unison, as if they were part of a choreographed routine. Standing in the back, two students held aloft an off-white bed sheet. The word "MURDER" was painted in a deep red paint, the letters dripping and drying in clumps. Or, the dean hoped it was paint. The commotion turned into a roar.

"Mur...der...mur...der...mur...der," the students intoned

rhythmically. It was low at first, so that only those in the back row could hear them. But they raised their volume steadily. As they did, a few students close by joined in, although most did so surreptitiously, using the person in front of them or a raised hand to hide their mouth from the dean. Participation in the chant cascaded down the rows like ripples in a pond, eventually reaching the front of the room in a crescendo. The few faculty present—tenured faculty couldn't be compelled to do much so attendance at these events was always sparse to the point of embarrassment—winced, while the locals were flabbergasted at the scene.

The students' message, for all its flashy and inflammatory rhetoric, was ambiguous. Was it a specific or a general accusation? Those who threw the stone and watched the waves propagate likely had a strong view on this question. They didn't voice it; they just kept a slow roll going. The more people that joined, however, the clearer the message became. The crowd turned back to the dean, who'd dropped his finger and stood at the podium, his shoulders slumped and his face twisted like he'd had a stroke.

The students chanted. He figured that some were chanting as an act of rebellion, some because they believed the person responsible for Jante's murder was in the room, and some because the guy next to them was chanting. A mob is rarely true for this reason. And this was quickly becoming a mob.

The dean tried a few times to bring order, but his body mic wasn't powerful enough to overcome the collective voices accusing him of murder or, at least, callous indifference to a murderer at large. The world he'd so carefully constructed in his first several weeks and that'd he'd imagined he'd inhabit for years to come seemed to be slipping from his grasp. It was time to regroup, to do damage control. He'd done nothing wrong, but he didn't have time to feel sorry for himself, and this wasn't the time to make his case. He was unprepared for battle and he was on enemy territory. Dean Miller sounded the retreat: he gathered his papers and walked directly to the exit. Up the stairs, through the chants, rows of audience members turning to watch him as he walked by.

During the three-hundred-yard walk from the Courtroom to the Dean's Suite, he avoided eye contact with anyone. It was out of character, and several of the students he passed turned after he did and raised an eyebrow. When he reached his office, he felt faint.

"No calls, Jeremy," he barked as he lurched into his office, locking the door behind him. Collapsed in his chair, he allowed himself a moment of pity. He felt the tears welling up and thought for a minute about reaching for the wastebasket. But the feeling passed. Time to solve the problem. Obviously, he hadn't pulled the trigger, since he was bed with Beth at the time it happened—his alibi was ironclad. Could he prove that he didn't hire the hit man to kill her, if that is what happened? How do you prove a negative? It was a classic legal problem Professor Miller presented to his students all the time. Now he was living in it.

The phone on his desk was no good to him—who would he call? His best friend had basically accused him of murder already, and the two hadn't spoken since. There were no confidants on a faculty, only spies and subordinates. His parents were both dead, but they would have been useless in this situation when they were alive. His mother would have told him not to worry, that everything would work out for him, as it always had; his dad would have told him to just fire everyone and replace them, like "Reagan did with the air traffic controllers." Scott would have just smiled and said, "Great idea, Dad."

There was a PR firm on retainer, but that was risky too. There was no more central node in the modern world of tweet-talking than a public relations professional. Scott was still new and hadn't yet earned the loyal service of his underlings. If he was viewed as vulnerable, and that was surely the case now, his staff might deploy against him in favor of a rival. *Bruce!* The thought poked him like a tack on his seat. "He wouldn't," Scott said aloud. "He couldn't." Bruce had wanted the job too. Suddenly, he felt as alone as he ever had, friendless and besieged.

His only hope, he thought, was to find Jante's real killer. It was an easy solution, but impossible. *How could he do that?* He was a professor of American Indian Law, and, if he were honest, not a particularly great one at that. He'd never been a prosecutor. Heck, he never even sat for the bar exam. It was straight from a clerkship on the Supreme Court to the Ivory Tower. These were not exactly the best training grounds for private dicks.

Jeremy peeked his head in through a crack in the outer door.

"Boss?"

"Yes, Jeremy. What is it?" He couldn't hide the annoyance in his voice.

"There is someone who's been waiting to see you."

"Who?" The surprise in his voice was laced with more annoyance. "Where?"

"I've got her in the lounge drinking a cup of coffee. I told her you were at an event. She insisted on staying."

"Who is it, Jeremy?"

Looking down at a Post-it note, Jeremy said in a whisper, "Detective Dunlay. Chicago Police." The words came out like an accusation or an embarrassing secret being revealed.

The dean closed his eyes and felt the blood rush out of his face.

"Send her in." Resignation. "Wait, give me a minute."

It hit him. Looking around his office—her former office, it hit him. Not Jante's former office, for she never sat a day in this chair, but the dean that they didn't talk about anymore. The dean that had to be taken down from the wall in the Workshop where portraits of all the former deans, save one, hung. The dean that never was. When he thought of her, the one that let the demons into Rockefeller Law, he figured it out. Or, rather, figured out who could figure it out. The dean knew exactly who to call.

CHAPTER 15

Royce Johnson steered his dead brother's faded blue Volvo 850 wagon onto South Chicago Beach Drive and headed north. A pedestrian half waved at him before catching herself. Everyone in and around the university recognized the wagon with its charming rust spots and fraying "Reagan/Bush '84" bumper sticker. People waved before they could make the connection that the car's owner was gone. Apparently, some parts of the brain worked faster and better than others, a fact Royce knew every investigator used to their advantage.

The destination was Cornell Field, a vast expanse of baseball diamonds and open space on the land side of Lake Shore Drive at 47th Street. The fields were home to the South Side Fire, the top youth soccer team in the city. He was betting the target of his first beat as an off-the-record PI would be there.

All the parking spots along the narrow road were filled by local residents home after work and parents staying for practice. Frustrated, he eased the Volvo in next to a dumpster by the loading dock for a nearby apartment tower. The stink penetrated the rust-thinned Swedish steel, but the view of the field was unobstructed and plenty of other cars were double-parked nearby. Parents who couldn't find parking watched practice from a distance, listening to the radio or flipping through their phones. Hazards on, he reached onto the passenger seat and grabbed a Nikon D5 with a five-hundred-millimeter telephoto lens. Alex's D5.

Looking through the lens, feeling the weight of the camera, Royce couldn't help think of Alex. Think of his hands manipulating the dials, his eyes scanning the players for the perfect shot. Think of him sharing the shots with the kids—*Look at this one!*—he could practically hear Alex and he could definitely see his smile. The thought sapped his strength. He lowered the lens. But there was no escaping the ghost of his brother. Royce was in his car, in his neighborhood, living in his house, and drinking his booze. The wrappers for his fireballs littered the foot well of the passenger side. Every step he took, Alex was with him like hiccups that won't go away. It wasn't just a reminder of Alex—Royce was living Alex's sort of life.

Royce raised the Nikon. He preferred his Mossberg. But it was in a federal warehouse somewhere with the rest of his weapons. As an ex-con, the Nikon would have to do. Plus, he was there to record, not take anyone into custody.

The autofocus brought his subject into view, even from nearly a hundred yards away. She was dressed for a fundraiser, not a windy fall day on the lakefront. Widening the frame, the audience for her figure-enhancing blouse came into focus as well. Akeem Bailey danced on his toes, as he shouted instructions at the lines of red-and-white clad kids weaving in and out of mini traffic cones set in a serpentine pattern on the field. The reason she was attracted to him was obvious—carved physique and features, topped off by two-toned dreadlocks that swirled elegantly skyward, ending in a bun that seemed to defy gravity. Juggling a ball with his feet without looking, he was the definition of youthful male virility. The exact opposite of the sixty-year-old chair of the Department of Classics, who was his rival for the affections of Royce's target.

Snap, snap, snap. The Nikon clicked and recorded. She rubbed against him, flicked her hair, and bent down unnaturally often. Nothing compromising or even particularly noticeable to the tiger moms and dads cheering from the sidelines. Royce knew better. As he watched, David Attenborough narrated—*The female moves closer, signaling her interest.* He had recorded her for just short of a month, and the findings were clear in his mind, if not yet on film. Flipping to video, the flirtations could be brought even more to life. Then, Royce's pocket buzzed.

"This is Royce," he whispered, even though no one else could hear him even if he shouted.

"Agent Johnson?"

"Who is this?" Before the caller could answer, he added, "And I'm not an agent anymore."

"Sorry about that, *Mister* Johnson."

The camera back on the passenger seat, he slumped down, knees up on the faded brown steering wheel.

"What can I do for you? I'm a bit busy at the moment."

"I'm sorry to bother you. My name is Scott Miller. I'm the dean of Rockefeller Law School."

"How'd you get my number?" He'd been a cinder dick for only a month or so, still working his first case.

"Professor Musgrove gave it to me."

"Well, as a matter of fact—"

"I need your help." It was a plea from a trapped animal.

"What kind of help?" Royce was intrigued. Word travels fast.

"The kind you gave Alex."

The hook was set.

"You knew Alex?"

"We worked together for nearly two decades. He was my friend. I miss him every day." Anyone would have heard the sincerity.

"Me too," Royce chirped, "me too. But what do you mean, what I did for Alex?"

"I hear him in your voice, and I know what you did for him. For all of us really."

"I just did what any big brother would do, and it was for Alex, no one else. The rest was, well, just icing on the cake."

"That's some icing, Mr. Johnson. You made history. You reshaped American politics forever. You should be proud."

"My brother is dead, Dean Miller. I don't care about the Supreme Court or politics. I care that the people who killed him are being brought to justice. Some have, some haven't. There is more work to be done."

"Okay. I get it."

"So, let's cut the shit. Why are you calling me?" His eyes went back to the soccer practice.

"I need your help. I'm desperate. And Alex told me that whenever he was desperate, he could always count on—"

Royce cut him off, growing weary of his sentimentality. "How can I help?" He rotated the bracelet on his arm—Alex's silver bracelet cuff, the one with the bear claw motif that the head of the Navajo Tribal Council gave Alex for his work with the tribe.

"Well, I'm sure you saw that our dean was murdered in June."

"I did, but what does that have to do with you?" He was intrigued. "You didn't do it, did you?" Royce said half joking.

"No. No I didn't. But, I'm not sure how to say this, but I think that some people...well, there are rumors." He sounded like he couldn't even believe it.

"And where do I come in, Dean?"

"I need you to find the killer. To clear my name. I won't be able to be an effective dean under this dark cloud of suspicion."

"I can see why you and Alex were friends. A flair for the dramatic. Nice." He took a sip from a White Sox water bottle stuffed between the seats in a cup holder two sizes too small. "Aren't the cops working the case? Why do you think you need me?"

"The investigation stalled. No leads, no clues. Whoever did this was a pro. It wasn't a robbery or...well, you know. I'm not sure it is a cold case just yet, but the detective I talked to a few weeks ago told me they are 'cautiously optimistic.' From her tone, I guessed they are stumped."

"Well, these cases—"

"Then, today, one of them came to see me." His voice cracked.

"Who?"

"The police. A detective. Dunlay, I think. I was flustered. She…she seemed to be doing more than asking questions. I'm worried."

"You did have motive."

Royce meant it to be a blow to the chest. Meant it to provoke a response.

The dean breathed and took a long pause. "I didn't kill her."

"I think you should leave it to the cops, Dean. Really. This isn't my business and I'm retired from finding people who murder professors at the Rockefeller Law School. But can I offer you a piece of advice?"

"Sure." The dean sounded disappointed.

"You'd better practice your story." Royce tested him.

"I can't leave it to the police. Please!"

This was the first believable thing he said.

"You think I can find what they can't, huh?"

"Well, isn't that what you did? Find what the Chicago PD couldn't find? What no one else could have possibly found?" Royce heard the cry for help.

"Even a blind squirrel, as they say."

"I'm pretty sure it wasn't luck. I know every detail. My predecessor, the president, the chief justice, because of what you did. We know about you. What you are *capable of*. We all know, Mr. Johnson."

"Call me Royce, please."

"Okay. Will you help me, Royce? Will you help me?"

"I can't. I can't be involved in an ongoing investigation—I'd lose my license." He was trying to talk himself out of it.

"If you say so, but you aren't a private investigator, right? So, you have no license to lose."

"Hmmm."

"In fact, Royce, it seems you have nothing to lose, other than a chance to be the hero. Again."

"I could go back to jail—I'm a convicted felon, Dean."

"I heard something about that." The dean giggled. "This isn't legal advice, but as long as you don't do anything illegal, you'll be okay. There is nothing wrong with asking questions—this is still America."

"Last time I checked." Royce chuckled at his own joke. He was coming around to liking Dean Miller.

"So, you'll do it? You'll help me? Why don't you come by the house? You can meet my wife, Beth, and our kids. I think you like Beth—and I know she'll be grateful for your help."

"Look, I'll think about it. No promises. Give me twenty-four hours." Royce had already made up his mind. He'd do it for Alex. Again.

"Thanks." The relief was palpable, even over the phone.

CHAPTER 16

The fence looked different. Bare-topped and rusty in spots a few months ago, now it was ringed with concertina wire and cameras on fifty-foot intervals, some pointing in toward the property and some toward the street. Even from Benson Street, Church could see that the fence also now ran along the shoreline, preventing access for kayakers who might have run aground or who brought clipboard-wielding 2Ls. This wasn't about keeping the neighbor kids out and limiting liability. This was about him. There would be no more covert landings. The field trips were over. *Someone saw me.* Instinctively, he looked over his shoulders. But the street was bare; he was alone with thoughts of who might be looking at him through the cameras. They wouldn't just be playing defense but soon going on offense as well. Panic welled up in his throat.

As he eyed the new signs announcing a new development of commercial, mixed-use, and residential space coming soon—several million square feet, private yacht club, and million-dollar homes—he realized the stakes were higher than he thought. The signage provided little detail as to what he was up against. It listed the dramatis personae of the Quayside Development: The Zhifu Construction Company, Inc.; K&S Partners, LLC; Patterson Design Build; and Patrick Doherty, Alderman for the Eleventh Ward. Google turned up little on any of these. No websites for

Zhifu or K&S or Patterson. *Beyond curious*. There were quite a few stories about Doherty. The nephew of the longtime mayor and grandnephew of the speaker of the Illinois House of Representatives, he was recently named one of the forty Illinois pols under forty to watch, according to *Crain's Chicago*. The Dauphin of Chicago. That the project had his support meant the climb to justice was taking on Everest-level proportions.

Realizing he had to get away quickly, Church flipped to the camera app on his phone and snapped some pictures of the sign and the site through the fence. He'd planned to take some additional measurements, maybe ask around the neighborhood to get a sense of the recent activity and maybe a bit of the site history. But his better judgment kicked in. No plan survives contact with the enemy, and he'd made first contact. He'd lost the element of surprise and didn't know anything about his opponent. Sun Tzu would not be pleased. It was time to retreat and regroup.

Seven minutes later, he was in an Uber, destination, the Illinois Institute of Technology. Time to check in with the samples he sent to Ben Edelman, professor of chemistry and former roommate of Church's in the famed "Kitchen Suite" at Princeton. Eight boys—they were not yet men—with the only working kitchen in the undergrad dorms was a recipe for chaos, but also lifelong friendship. There were the near fires, as well as the mess and the rats and the occasional "chemistry" experiment gone horribly wrong. But it was when they hooked up hoses to the faucet and made a water slide out of the internal staircase that ran out into the Quad that their fame was secured. Twenty-five years later, everyone that was there that night, and most of their class was, still talked about increasingly scantily clad undergrads propelling down the stairs on cafeteria trays. Going to see Ben always made him smile at the thought. He could count on Ben.

The Uber was a tin can—an Altima or a Hyundai—but when he fell back into the velour seat, it felt like an M1 Abrams tank. Safe and sound. As the distance between them and the vacant site increased, he relaxed. His path to tenure, to fame, to endowment money for his clinic, was all the sudden much more difficult than he thought, but as they merged on to the Stevenson Expressway headed back toward the lake and the city, he no longer feared for his life. The adrenaline retreated like waves going out to sea. The relief became sleep, his head flopped forward, chin to chest, drool forming in the corner of his mouth.

"Mister. Mister!" The driver wrenched his head around. "We're here."

Church awoke with a sniff and a hard squeeze of his eyes, closing them and then opening them wider. Wiping the drool with his sleeve, he looked up, disorientated. Asleep for hours, it seemed, but it had only been minutes. Fight or flight, and he chose flight. For now. He swallowed hard and sat up, ready for some good news. Then, the fear surged back, and with it the adrenaline, coming back in like the tide.

The building they'd stopped in front of, at the corner of 31st and State Street, was gutted by fire. A fire that had been extinguished only recently, it seemed. Yellow tape was strung around light poles and poplar trees that ringed the three-story, modernist building, still smoldering from the center of its roof like a venting volcano. Windows were shattered and the entire east-facing wall had collapsed. The smell—an acrid mix of chemicals and smoke and musty dampness—overwhelmed Church as he alighted the Uber, mouth agape. He was in a war zone.

"What happened?" he sputtered to an IIT police officer resting on the front fender of a squad car. The officer was watching a crew sweeping debris into piles, ironically smoking the end of a cigarette.

"Fire. Last night. Whole place is gone," he said nonchalantly, without taking his eyes off the scene or the butt out of his mouth.

"Did...Was anyone inside when it happened?"

"Not sure yet. It started late, I heard. Maybe some folks were in there. Can't be sure. Some of these eggheads keep crazy hours."

Church walked away in the direction of nowhere. Ben, or

what was left of him, might be in there, and the officer's casual attitude didn't fit the scene. He needed to get away. A few steps from the corner, he stopped mid-stride and watched the front door of the building. The glass on all sides, full-story plate-glass windows, was shattered, bits and fragments dangling like stalactites from the steel frame of the casing. No one was going in or out, and wood was being put up to cover the holes, presumably made by firefighters or perhaps blown out by what must have been the intense heat of a fire fueled by volatile chemicals.

This was the home to the IIT Chemistry Department, so the samples sent to Ben were likely consumed in the conflagration. Perhaps they'd been analyzed, the results making it out of the building and up into the cloud before the flames came. Even this, however, depended on Ben having made it out alive. If he didn't, they might as well have not either, since Church would have no way of accessing them. He hated himself for even speculating instead of just dreading what had happened to his old friend.

Ben picked up on the third ring. He was shaken, scared.

"Ben, it's Mike. Are you okay? What happened? I'm at your office. What's going on?" The words spewed out of him, spraying like the hoses he could hear behind him dousing the carbon-black embers of Ben's office.

"I'm okay. Just a bit frightened. I easily could have been at the lab when this happened." His tone flat, his attitude resigned. "I sleep on my office couch with some regularity, waiting for results or if I'm just too tired to bike home. I could have been..."

"Thank God. Whew!" the relief overwhelmed Church. He choked back a tear. "Where are you?"

"I mean, it went up, with the chemicals and all. Just a tinder box. So much lost."

"I'm coming to you. Where are you?...Ben? Are you still there?"

"Still here. I think I've got to go lie down."

"Sure, sure, of course. Can I bring you something? Can I do anything?"

"I'm good. I mean, I'm not good. Far from it. But I'm good for now. Thanks, man."

Church could feel him about to hang up but interjected loudly before he could.

"Hey, one more thing! The samples I sent to you...should have been delivered." His voice trailed off. He tried to hide his hope. And his indifference to Ben's plight and his own selfishness.

"What about them?"

"I just wanted to...They're part of a big fish I've got on the line." Church took a deep breath. He regretted asking, but it was too late. "I just didn't know if you'd gotten to it yet or not. I assume they were lost in the fire."

"Yeah." He was eager to move on. "They are ashes like everything else in my office and my lab. I'm sorry if that means you lost something too."

"Again, I'm sorry to bring it up, Ben. It's just." A deep sigh. "Never mind. I'm glad you're okay. I was really worried when we pulled up and saw. I hope by sending them to you I didn't..." The last line slipped out. He tried to catch it, fumbling after a wine glass falling from a table, but there was no stopping the words from hitting their target.

"Didn't what?" Irritation mixed with fear.

"Never mind. Really. Thanks anyway."

"No, what do you hope you didn't?" His voice grinded.

"It's just. Well. The samples relate to a potential case I'm working on, and now I'm worried there may be some connection. I swear, when I sent them I had no idea—"

Ben cut him off. "What'd you do! Are you saying the fire was on purpose? Targeting me?" Panic shouted through the receiver.

"No, I'm not saying that. I don't know. I just...Can we talk about this in person?"

"Listen, I've known you a long time, Mike. We've been through a lot. I know you wouldn't do anything to hurt me. Not on purpose. But if you're mixed up in something here, something that almost killed me, something that may have killed people, mixed up with someone who would blow up a building to destroy some chemical samples, then the last fucking thing I want is for you to come see me. You see that, right?"

"Yeah, yeah, of course. I just...I don't know what to do."

"I know what I've got to do. I've got to rebuild my professional life. A life that was, it seems, accidentally destroyed by one of my oldest friends. I just can't give you more. I'm sorry."

Church closed his eyes and breathed deeply. He was adrift. A monster had been awoken, and he had no idea what it was, where it was, or what it was capable of. But it was capable of a lot. That was clear. He wanted to rewind, to call the Spill Line and not worry about the Quayside Development ever again. But that was impossible. He couldn't stop worrying about it, because *it* was worrying about him.

"I'm the one who's sorry, Ben. If I could do it all over, if I could go back and start over—"

"We're good." A silent grenade detonated between them. "Now, I'm going to sleep."

"Thanks, Ben. Honestly..."

"We're good."

"Good." Church moved to hang up.

"Hey, Mike."

"Yeah."

"The other day I was thinking."

"Be careful with that."

"Hardy har har...I was thinking about that night we destroyed your computer when the office under the stairs flooded. Remember that? When we made the waterslide down the stairs into the hot tub we made out of a kiddie pool...when you thought you lost everything? Your senior thesis, all your files. It made me smile." He sounded like he was trying to rebuild the damage done to the friendship, now decades old. That could be rebuilt far easier than the department building.

"This is called salt in the wounds, Ben."

"The fuse of karma is sometimes quite long, eh? Good thing

you had your files all backed up."

"Yeah, good thing. Thanks, Ben. Have a good rest."

Church breathed a sigh of relief. He didn't know why his friend was playing coy—maybe he saw someone following him or found a listening device in his office or just had a sense after his friend asked him an unusual favor—but the coded message was received. His evidence was secure. The samples were lost, but the data about what they were was safe. Somewhere, Dr. Ben Edelman had proof about the truth at Bubbly Creek.

CHAPTER 17

The Glasgow Inn served the best fish and chips in Chicago. There was no dispute about that. Alex said so, and he was usually right about everything. Especially when it came to his favorite food. Royce preferred a rare steak and a twice-baked potato, extra bacon, extra sour cream, and chives. Most importantly, washed down with an Old Grand-Dad, his bourbon of choice. But he chose this place, an out-of-the-way bar hell and gone from Rockefeller and its environs, to meet up with Professor Paul Lewis. And when at the Glasgow, fish and chips was what you had.

When Royce pushed through the revolving door keeping out the Chicago wind, he felt his brother's presence. The smell of fried fish, the coats-of-arms on the walls, and the wooden-plank floor slightly sticky from beer reminded him of Alex. This was his place. It was also the perfect place to interrogate a law professor—dark, remote from campus, and, most importantly, patronized by cops and steelworkers, people who were decidedly not law students.

Some asking around the Law School led him to Professor Lewis, an allegedly dissenting member of the search committee that originally gave the deanship to Jante Turner. Royce knew it was him as soon as the professor walked in. Gray three-piece suit, striped tie, he looked as comfortable as a sailor on shore leave walking into a tax conference. Royce signaled him with a raised index finger and a knowing nod.

"Are you Royce?"

"Yeah, have a seat. Drink?"

To a bystander, it had all the appearances of the start of a bad Tinder meetup. Lewis looked as nervous as if it were. Location set the mood, a reason Royce chose the location and thus the mood.

"What are you drinking?" the professor eyed Royce's glass.

"Bourbon. I think. Could be brown food coloring in grain alcohol."

The waitress sauntered over. Her look told him the customers didn't tip well.

"Guinness, please." She walked away without saying anything. Professor Lewis shook his head.

"So, you said it was a matter of life and death, and that somehow this involved your brother. He was a good guy, by the way. That whole escapade, what a tragedy."

"Yeah, that's one word for it."

"I assume you didn't ask me here to talk about that."

"Definitely not."

"So, what can I do for you? I've come a long way." The professor scanned his surroundings with regret.

"The dean, the one that was murdered, was she your first choice?"

"I'm sorry, why is this your business?"

The answer was focused and tight. Royce remeasured him. Royce took a sip of his bourbon. He wasn't steeling himself, but rather raising the dramatic tension.

"I'm investigating her murder. I'm starting with motive, which is always a good place to start. I think whoever killed her might have done so to prevent her being dean." The professor crinkled his face, causing deep creases to form around his eyes. "The identity of other candidates might be instructive in that regard."

"We don't discuss these matters outside of the Law School. In fact, it isn't something we've really discussed outside of the search committee. And, as you probably know, I've already talked to the police."

The Guinness arrived, and a good bit remained in Lewis's substantial moustache after he took a big gulp. He slurped with an exaggerated noise. He was apparently skilled in the art of mood setting as well.

"My client is interested in helping the police catch the killer. I told my client to leave it to the professionals, but this person has reason to believe that the cops are missing something."

"May I ask—"

"I'd love to tell you, but client confidentiality and all that. I'm sure as an attorney you understand."

"I do. Of course. But is your client Scott?"

"As I said, I can't say. But why do you think that?"

"It's quite a fuss around the Law School. The scene in the Courtroom. I just figured, with the timing..."

"Like I said, I'm not at liberty to say, but you can imagine there are a lot of people interested in getting an answer to the question. Can you help me?"

He took another long sip of beer, and another loud suck of the foam out of his stash. His walrus ancestors would have been proud.

"I'm not sure what you want, Mr. Johnson. I don't know who killed Jante. If I did, don't you think I would have told the police?"

"People have all sorts of reasons for not talking to the police. Not sharing their speculations with them. If there is only a ten percent chance someone did it, you might not want to sic the cops on them. But in my world, ten percent is a good lead. I can run it down without anyone getting wind of it. And, who knows, it might be the first step in a ten-step chain that leads me to the killer. At this point, any information is valuable information."

"I don't know anything about this. Really." The answer was a laser beam, showing Professor Lewis had no interest in mollifying his interrogator, which his body language suggested was how he increasingly felt about Royce.

"That's my job, Professor. To figure it out. I just want to know who you think might have had a reason to kill her. Is there someone you suspect when you think of the murder, but you wouldn't want to tell the cops for any reason?"

"Well, Scott, naturally."

It was an obvious point but made little sense. If Scott did kill for power, why hire Royce?

"Interesting." Royce eyed him carefully.

"That's why he's the subject of all these rumors. He stood to benefit the most—he was our second choice, and, after all, got the job when it became available."

So much for the confidentiality of the process. Royce smiled inside.

"Why did you pick Jante over him?" Royce downed his bourbon for emphasis. He signaled the waitress for another.

"The answer is as plain as her face, Mr. Johnson. Do I need to spell it out for you?" Lewis squirmed against the vinyl of the booth bench.

"Because she's black?" Royce was genuinely surprised. Affirmative action was not unknown in the Bureau, but it was usually reserved for positions below the top. And it was surprising that Rockefeller would choose their leader on such flimsy grounds.

"Of course because she's black. Don't get me wrong. She is smart, capable, and will be...would have been...a good dean. But the tiebreaker was what she looked like, where she came from, what she overcame. From Englewood to Rockefeller, that's something. It's also just the way of the world, I'm afraid."

"Very interesting."

"But Scott wouldn't do this. Not in a million years." He backtracked, though Royce couldn't tell whether he was covering for a friend or just trying to appropriately calibrate his point.

"Why so certain?" Royce drained the second bourbon.

"I've known him a long time. You just know."

"But sometimes, you don't." It was a knowing comment made through downward-glancing eyes. "You know what I mean?"

"Well..." Royce could tell the professor wasn't used to losing arguments.

"Do you know his favorite sexual position?" Royce couldn't hide his delight at the look on the prudish professor's face.

"Excuse me? What does that have to do with it?" Lewis's Irish cheeks, reddening already from the alcohol, burst into flames. Royce knew right away that Professor Lewis was not kinky in bed.

"You don't know nearly as much as you think about Scott Miller, that's all I'm saying. We all have secrets—how we like to fuck, what we do when no one is watching, what we would do if we were certain we could get away with it. Or, maybe in this case, what we'd do if getting our dream job depended on it. I don't think knowing a guy at work can tell us what that guy would do if his life depended on it. It just doesn't. Maybe his life depended on him getting that deanship."

"Perhaps."

"Would you kill someone, Professor?"

"What kind of question is that?" He half stood up in his seat, an indignant tone unmistakable in his voice. "You aren't suggesting—"

"I'm not suggesting anything. Please, sit down. I'm merely trying to make a point. I think you would, and I think you are lying to yourself if you think you would never, ever kill someone." The look on his face was a mix of confusion and concern. "Self-defense of you and yours. That might justify killing someone else. Imagine a home invasion—would you kill someone about to rape your wife? How about war—would you kill to defend your country from invasion? How about if a murder could net you a hundred million dollars, and you knew you'd get away with it? We could play philosophy professor all day, but you see the point."

"I'm not certain I do. I wouldn't kill someone over a job."

"I think you might, under the right circumstances, but that's not my claim. Whether you would starve first or kill first isn't my question. It is whether Scott Miller would. I think you'd kill if you needed to survive. I'm only saying that some of us will kill for a lot less than that. And, heck, for all we know, Scott Miller's survival, as he thinks about it, might have depended on it." The professor nodded along. "Maybe that pretty wife of his was going to leave him if he didn't get the gig. Who knows?"

"Okay, maybe, but I firmly doubt it. I'm a pretty good judge of character, and this seems waaaay out of character for Scott."

Another beer and another bourbon arrived. The waitress set the check on the table, then disappeared again in a flash, her mood not improved.

"Fair enough. Who then? Who else beside him would want him to be dean?"

"We are on dangerous ground."

"Dangerous? Like murder. Don't be coy, Professor. I get the sense there's something you aren't telling me."

"Let's walk." The Guinness disappeared in two gargantuan gulps, and Lewis set the glass down on the table with a thump. "I assume you've got these." He stood, put on his camel-hair overcoat, and headed out into the night.

Royce put three twenties on the table, and chased out after him, arming into Alex's North Face puffer as he went.

"Why the cloak-and-dagger?" he said when he caught up.

"The father-in-law."

"Whose father-in-law?" Royce slipped as he chased after Lewis, who was nearly jogging at this point. He turned to look at Royce, still lagging behind.

"Scott's. Scott's father-in-law. I don't have any evidence or know exactly what motive he'd have, other than having his daughter be married to the dean, but he's a bad dude."

"Bad dude?"

"I've said enough already. I'm out of my element here, Agent Johnson." He stopped and faced his pursuer. They were standing in front of a sushi taco truck, a line of drunken twentysomethings cueing for the latest trend. "I'm more comfortable interpreting revenue rulings and running regressions on tax data. I…I'm not into this."

"You've been helpful, and I'm grateful. Can you just tell me why? Why did you mention him?"

"Look into him. You figure it out. I don't know if he is involved. Honestly, I don't. I do know about the tax avoidance schemes he perfected. At Treasury, I was on the other side of these deals. He is creative, smart, and a devil. No one gets to be worth as much as he is worth by being a nice guy. By following the rules. I'm not saying he pulled the trigger or paid the guy who did or whatever. But if you ask me whether Max Klepp is capable of doing it, the answer is yes. A thousand times yes."

"Seems like a stretch, but I'll look into it." Royce made a mental note: Max Klepp, taxes, devil.

"Do that. Please. But, if he is behind this, I doubt your client is going to be very happy with what you find."

With that, Professor Paul Lewis turned the corner and disappeared into the night.

Client. The word stuck in his mind. As an FBI agent, his client had been the United States or justice or some abstraction he'd never thought about. Let right be done, was his motto. In government, he was representing the people, and the people as a whole always wanted the truth. Did Scott Miller, the accidental dean of the Rockefeller Law School and his second paying client, want the truth? Would he have hired him otherwise? Sure, Royce was duped in his last case in the Bureau, but only for a bit. He eventually cracked the case of the murder of Professor Alex Johnson, and the butler definitely didn't do it. If Dean Miller did do it and hired Royce to pin it on a patsy, did he really think he could set a better trap than Bob Gerhardt, the FBI, and the other bastards who set Royce up last time? Or, perhaps the dean was unaware of the service his father-in-law had done for him. A chill went down Royce's spine. But it could have been the chill of wind curling down Clark Street. Whoever it was that killed Jante Turner, he was sure of one thing, they were going down. Client or not.

CHAPTER 18

Royce turned off the Skokie Highway at Kennedy Road. Thirty miles north of the city, he was in the suburb of Lake Forest. Founded in 1857 as a stop on the way from Milwaukee to Chicago, it became a redoubt for the city's titans of industry at the turn of the century, when immigrants, socialists, and other untouchables began to transform the city's neighborhoods. Millions fleeing oppression in the American South or in Europe came to the Midwest and remade Chicago's many neighborhoods, like the one where Alex had lived and Scott Miller now lived. Home to about twenty thousand people, about ninety-five percent of whom were white and one hundred percent of whom were wealthy, Lake Forest looked now as it did before the masses came. It was wooded, beautiful, clean, peaceful, and just far enough from the grit and the grime. It was a land of mansions surrounded by land, of country clubs and high teas, and of perfectly manicured sidewalks in front of quaint shops. Max Klepp fit right in.

The Klepps came to America from Alsace, the region that, from the time of Charlemagne's death until World War II, couldn't decide whether it was in France or Germany. One of Max Klepp's great relations—a cooper from the Black Forest—married Clarice DeLangie, a Huguenot girl from near the border with Flanders, when he moved to Strasbourg in the 1650s. They didn't last long, chased out of France because of their heretical religious views in piously Catholic France. Some of the family made it only as far as the Netherlands, but others went further. The American Klepps came ashore in New York just forty years later, settling in the town of New Rochelle on the northern shore of the Long Island Sound. Klepp branches thrived in that area for generations, working in various trades, fighting for King then country, and buying up land and influence. Klepps still prosper in Westchester County and in towns radiating out, up the coast of Connecticut and down into Manhattan. The Max branch of the tree went west in search of independence and adventure in the 1850s, just as Chicago became a thing. His great-grandfather, the ninth of nine, was never going to amount to anything, Max's great-great-grandfather never tired of telling anyone who would listen, even his son. Determined to prove him wrong, he came to Chicago on a four-day train ride with nothing but a few nickels in his pocket and a Bible written in curlicue French that he stole from the house before he left in the middle of the night. Work was easy to find in Chicago in those days, especially in the stockyards burgeoning on the city's South Side. Tales of how awful the work in the slaughterhouses were still told by the Klepps to this day. Max could recount the smells and sounds of life being turned into calories as if he had been there. But, after three decades of pushing intestines and offal with a broom, a determined man could get his son a job at a desk in those same stockyards, pushing paper around instead. Then with some hard work and a fair bit of luck, that man could get his son into Rockefeller University, and with some more hard work and a little bit more luck, that man's son could live in the house that Royce was going to break into that morning.

Royce hung a quick left onto South Ridge Road, and then an immediate right into a dirt turnabout. He killed the lights of his rental car and pulled onto the grass behind a stand of large oak trees. The car wasn't visible from any street. It would be safe this time of day. Grabbing his duffle bag from the backseat, he zipped his black overcoat and put on a black wool cap. He unscrewed the license plates and put them in his bag. It was enough to raise the costs of a search for a bored but lazy patrolman. It wouldn't stop a hero, but most cops weren't heroes.

He headed out west across an empty field. He'd picked a moonless night, and as he ran slouched over at the waist, he was confident his movements were undetected. Google Maps told him it was about a thousand feet from where he'd parked the Jeep to the grove of trees that stood in Max Klepp's backyard. His route would be longer. He hugged the tree line on the eastern side of the field, headed south toward a small, almost perfectly round lake that stood at its southern end. It was surrounded by trees and large shrubs, and he planned to use these as cover as he made his way east to west across the open space. In under five minutes, he was prone inside the trees that separated Scott's father-in-law's yard from the field.

Reaching into the duffle, he pulled out a pair of relatively low-tech night-vision goggles he'd bought on eBay. "Vlad17" from the Ukraine said they were military issue, but as Royce looked through them, he realized you get what you pay for, which, in his current state, wasn't much. They were sufficient for his purposes—merely scouting the scene.

The backyard was empty, as one would expect at five a.m. on a Wednesday. There were light standards on the tennis court and around the pool, but they were out. A children's playset with swings, a slide, and a little fort stood in one corner. *For the grandchildren.* He had to bury empathy. It was dead weight for any investigator. Behind the playset, a large rectangular pool, empty this time of year. He waited. Let his heart rate and breathing slow. Let the scene settle in around him. All was quiet and still. He army-crawled forward, his duffle slung over one shoulder. He felt his Mossberg, slung over his other shoulder. But it wasn't there. Another phantom limb. Without it, he felt naked. And afraid.

Staying close to the trees on the east side of the property, he maneuvered his way past the tennis court and behind a large evergreen bush at one short end of the pool. Again, he paused for minutes, letting things settle, inside and outside his body. The house appeared empty, no lights were on. He had an hour to kill. Surveilling the house and Max's movements for the past few days, he learned their maid arrived every day precisely at 6:30 a.m. She picked up Klepp's copy of the *Financial Times* and *Wall Street Journal*, then keyed into the front door. This triggered an alarm, which she then disarmed with an eight-digit code punched into a keypad in the foyer. That was the weakness in fortress Klepp.

There were too many combinations for the code to be guessed in the fifteen seconds before the alarm contacted the police, but thankfully, there was a defect inherent in the system—the sensor in the door sent a radio signal to the control system, alerting it about an entry. Like every home security system, the one at 7 Reilly Lane did not encrypt these signals or require the system to authenticate them. The best burglar's tools were sometimes made of bytes.

Royce learned this while working a burglary ring in the tony Pittsburgh suburb of Sewickley a few years back. The paintings and jewelry and artifacts boosted from the big stone mansions made their way across state and national lines, meaning the feds took an interest. When the Federal BI got them—Royce always got them—a low-level jacker turned over their strategies and equipment, including something called a USRP N210. Resembling a large block of white cheddar cheese, the N210 was a software-defined radio. When hooked up to a laptop, the N201 allowed a user to receive radio signals, and then, when routed through that laptop, to process the signal and play it back over the airway to the receiver at the source of the original transmission. In lay terms, it was a way to listen in on unencrypted radio signals, and thus hack a security system that involved transmitting over the airwaves. With two thousand dollars borrowed from Claire—no questions asked, but a solemn promise given that it was to be used for good—he'd bought one, and it was now in his black duffle.

Royce moved twenty feet closer to the house, finding a semicircle of rhododendron that hid an air conditioning unit. He huddled up and waited, crushing hand warming packs he'd bought at Costco, and sliding them into his shirt, pants, and combat boots. While he waited, he pulled out his laptop—or, rather, Alex's old laptop—and connected the N210 with a one-gigabit ethernet cable. Booted up, he waited.

The maid was a few minutes late, but the sneak worked just as planned. When she opened the front door, the connection between a pad on the door and one on the door frame broke, sending a signal to the unit's brain in the basement. This activated an alarm on a fifteen-second delay. The maid stepped into the foyer, set down her bag, and entered the eight-digit code to disarm the alarm. The keypad in turn sent the code via wireless radio signal to the main unit, which, upon receiving the proper code, disabled the alarm. It was at this point when Royce, with the help of the N210, intercepted the content of the radio signal. Although the technology was a bit more sophisticated, it was akin to intercepting a note passed in gym class.

Klepp's alarm code was stored in the laptop and ready to be spat back to the alarm system on Royce's command. Forty-five minutes later, right on schedule, a black Suburban pulled into the driveway, then departed shortly thereafter. The Klepps were headed downtown; Max to his office, his wife to her daily ritual of a workout, shopping, beauty treatments, and a lingering lunch. Duffle packed and slung back over his shoulder, Royce waited just ten minutes more for the maid to exit the side door with the family dog—a Weimaraner named Bernadotte—for his daily exercise at the park. He had between thirty and forty minutes before she returned. It was a sunny morning, so he bet on the latter.

Royce leapt from concealment, picked the lock on the rear door of the house—a simple Yale Teton lock he'd picked dozens of times—and disarmed the alarm using the code he'd swiped from midair. He simply pressed Enter and the code transmitted from his laptop to the alarm control panel. It dinged a welcome in return.

The layout of the house was unfamiliar, so he moved quickly from room to room looking for Klepp's lair. He found it, set off from the rest of the first floor by a large set of French doors. The space was impressive. About a thousand square feet, it was surrounded on three sides by floor-to-ceiling bookshelves stuffed with volumes, old, new, and ancient. Another wall was spotted with art—he preferred Dutch painters it seemed, and a few antique maps. Royce took a seat behind the expansive oak desk and settled back into Klepp's high-back leather desk chair. It was a command position.

The desk was tidy, but not fastidious. There was no computer, which made Royce feel like a time traveler, not a burglar. Piles of papers were stacked on every inch of the desk. Leafing through manila folder after manila folder, there were no clues. Real estate deals, investments in manufacturing companies, service on various boards of directors, and on and on. It was quite a portfolio. Even Royce was impressed.

Klepp's bank statements for the prior several years were stacked neatly in a folder. Photographing them all would take too long, so Royce found June, the month of Jante's murder, then worked backwards. The numbers were staggering. He did a double take, trying not to let the envy in. But there was a lot to be envious of—trips, jewelry, fancy dinners, chauffeurs, security details, club memberships, boat docking and maintenance fees, caretakers for at least two separate homes, it went on and on and on. Skimming through them, looking for something particular but not obvious, he felt like a kid sneaking into his dad's collection of *Playboy* magazines. He took quick shots of May, April, March, February, and January. Nothing jumped out at a glance. He put them back neatly and moved on.

Frustrated, he leaned back in the chair. Ornaments and artifacts abounded, but nothing suggesting a devious mind or someone capable of ordering a murder. The drawers were locked, but accessible to even a moderately talented picker like Royce. Stuffed with power cords, office supplies, and miscellaneous desk detritus, this was strike two. A quick check of his watch—less than ten minutes left. He couldn't cut it close. Getting caught meant violating his parole, and that meant returning to Petersburg.

Pacing around the open space between the burgundy leather sofas set perpendicular to the desk and the far wall, Royce noticed a map of Chicago set in among what might very well have been paintings by Rembrandt or a Brueghel or Kalf. It wasn't an antique or covered in glass. It wasn't especially interesting or appealing the way old maps can sometimes be. It wasn't beautiful. It was remarkable for its ordinariness. As if someone took a AAA fold-out map, glued it to a foam board, and put a frame around it. In the Louvre. It was even marked up. Circled roughly in a red Sharpie, an area on the south side was labeled in what Royce guessed was Klepp's hand. It read "Bubbly Creek Development."

He moved closer, inspecting the map and the markings. Stuck into the corner of the frame, a small black-and-white photograph, yellowed and tattered. It was a tin plate picture, probably a hundred years old. Royce pulled it out and looked into the eyes of the man, clad in thick overalls and resting on the handle of a large industrial broom, surrounded by animal pens and machines of all varieties. It wasn't Max Klepp, but Royce could see him in those eyes. He could see Max's success in that broom. Something special was happening there on Bubbly Creek. It wasn't much, but it was all he had to go on, and experience taught him that much often masqueraded as not much.

Back at Klepp's desk, Royce flipped through the folders and piles of paper. A few down from the top, he found a folder labeled "Quayside/Bubbly Creek." Inside, there were maps, diagrams, architectural drawings, contracts, and Excel sheets of cost estimates and projected cash flows. At the bottom right corner of one grid sheet, the number "$2.65 B" was circled in a bold hand—a red Sharpie. The note read "Is this the base case?"

Each document captured with a push of a button on Royce's phone—spying sure was easier with a smartphone—he took one more riffle through the documents on the desk. That amount of money was definitely worth killing over, but there was no discernable connection between the project and Jante Turner or the Rockefeller Law School. Frustrated but out of time, Royce reordered the desk and went out the way he came. Five minutes before Bernadotte bounded in through the front door, he was out the back, then through the bushes, across the field, and back to the Jeep, which was unmolested and right where he left it. Ten minutes after that, plates reattached, Royce was headed back to the city to return the car. As he turned back out toward Route 41, he heard sirens and watched three squad cars zoom past. Everything went perfectly, except for the most important thing. Sure, he hadn't been caught and wasn't going down again for B&E, but the investigation was no further along. Jante's killer remained a mystery.

CHAPTER 19

Aliza Kahan sat at a semicircle desk surrounded by over a dozen large screens in the basement of her Chicago townhouse. Tall—just over six feet—and fit, with short hair left over from her armed forces days, Aliza made everyone take a second look. One of the first women to serve in Shayetet 13, the Israeli equivalent of the Navy SEALs, there were still two Hamas bullets in her left leg. She felt them on rainy mornings and when she did Bharadvaja's twist at her seven a.m. daily yoga class. But if one were to keep score—and Aliza was always keeping score—she was winning. Dozens and dozens of enemy fighters had bullets in them that she put there, most in tight groupings in vital organs. None of them were doing yoga on Devon Avenue or anything else for that matter. With so many confirmed kills to her name, she had more than earned the respect of her male counterparts. In the field, she wasn't exactly one of the guys, but they found her to be reliable in the field and approachable despite her beauty.

The daughter of a general lionized for his role in Israeli's founding-era battles, she rose quickly through the ranks. Aliza didn't volunteer but came into camo like millions of the children of Israel—through compulsory service. Most women chose non-combat roles, but Kahan was a dead-eye with an M-16, was as strong as the average male soldier, and had a penchant for violence. Plus, she was smarter than almost anyone, exhibiting grace under fire and a preternatural instinct for battlefield strategy. Her commanders saw these things in her before she knew they were there, and they pushed her to be what she was born to be—a leader of people in combat. After six years of killing for Theodor Herzl's vision, she took these leadership skills to the Mossad, the Israeli version of the CIA, and distinguished herself with her courage and ability to predict how situations were going to unfold. Kahan was always a step ahead of the enemy and her own team. But fifteen years of skirting through alleys in Lebanon and the Occupied Territories in the West Bank on a government salary were enough. America and a fortune in private security contracting beckoned.

She ran her security business out of a modest home in Chicago's Rogers Park neighborhood, unbeknownst to her neighbors, who knew her as a fitness instructor and life coach. As Royce Johnson made his way around Max Klepp's home office, Aliza caught a glimpse out of the corner of her eye. She pressed the up arrow key on a computer causing one of the cameras to zoom in on a man seated at the desk of her client, Max Klepp. Her firm—Haganah, Inc.—didn't work directly for Klepp, but rather was hired through various offshore companies he and his partners used for developments around the world. This particular contract—to install cameras throughout his home and office, as well as several work locations, and have them monitored by former Israeli Defense Force special-ops troops—was with K&S Partners, LLC.

Kahan noted another development on another screen for another client, but Mr. Klepp was not to be trifled with and a client she couldn't lose. She pressed a button on the other console, and alerted an associate to handle it, whatever it was. She needed to focus on what was happening at Max's house. Reaching for the phone, her heart beat in her throat.

"Mr. Klepp." Her voice calm and full of confidence.

"What is it, Aliza? You caught me in the middle of a—"

"Someone is in your office on Reilly, sir."

"What! Who?"

"A single. Adult male. Maybe fifty. Not sure how he got access, but the alarm didn't trigger. He took note of the map on the wall and is taking shots of some documents from your desk." She paused but heard nothing. "I had to make sure he was unauthorized before I called it in." Factual and direct. Just like giving a sit rep from Gaza.

"Did you…?"

"The police are on the way."

"Do you think he's a threat?"

"Not sure who he is or what this is, but it definitely wasn't a burglary. Maybe corporate espionage?"

"What should we do?"

"We could let the Lake Forest PD handle this, if they get their butts in gear, or we could send in a team."

"I'm not looking for equivocation. I want a recommendation."

"If the police get there in time, which I doubt based on my experience with them, we can work behind the scenes to find out. If not, I'll send someone."

"Good. There is no margin for error. I'm close to a deal that is going to generate generational wealth, Ms. Kahan. I don't know who this person is, but we have to make sure they are neutralized. Is that clear?"

"Got it. You can count on me, Mr. Klepp."

The word "neutralized" stuck in her brain like popcorn in her teeth. She didn't like killing, even though she was really good at it. Her father served in the El Arish armored division under General Tal during the Six-Day War, and he had killed so much Kahan believed it turned him to stone. Even though Aliza relished her time serving the cause of Jewish nationalism, every time she pulled the trigger, she felt a little bit more of her flesh harden. Daughters are supposed to be better than their fathers, even though Kahan knew that most just become them in one way or another. She could feel the inevitable creeping closer.

Aliza hung up the phone and looked back at her monitor. The man was gone and nowhere on her internal or external monitors of the Klepp property—the local cops were still a few minutes out. It was time for Plan B.

Plan B was named Ivan Olej. A veteran of countless missions for Kahan over the years—IDF, Mossad, and Haganah—he was the only person she trusted with her life.

Aliza adjusted her headset and barked a series of commands in an amalgam of Hebrew and English her team affectionately called "Hebrish." On the other end, Olej did a U-turn in his Ford Focus RS, and headed north toward Lake Forest, eyes peeled for…well, a man driving and acting in a way that after ten years doing this he would recognize but couldn't describe to anyone else.

Ten minutes later, he thought he saw him. But when he radioed in the license plate to Kahan, she reported back that the car belonged to a Lake Forest dentist, an unlikely prowler. Klepp's cabinets held no secrets for someone who scraped plaque all day. Frustrated, Olej slowed his Ford but stayed in the left lane headed north, hoping to catch a glimpse over the Jersey barrier separating him from the man he knew was headed south toward the city. At a stoplight on the divided highway, just as it was about to turn into a freeway headed into the city, a Jeep Cherokee caught his eye. The man behind the wheel was in his fifties, wearing a plain baseball cap. He had that look. Like he was running from something, but not in a hurry. It was him. Like people who could identify the sex of a baby chicken—hens were kept, roosters were discarded—Olej could do it but couldn't tell you how. There was no doubt this time, it was him.

"Budget, rented at Balbo and Wabash," Aliza responded when Olej read her the license plate.

"On it, Manhig."

Olej did a U-turn in the lot of a Potbelly sandwich shop and moved forward in traffic to come up behind the Jeep. As he did, he reached for his hip and the Jericho 941 that was always there. The weight and feel of it there on his right side reassured him. There was little chance he'd need it, even if matters came to that, since Aliza preferred anything to gunshots, but knowing that it was always right there just in case, made his heart rate slow.

The twenty miles back toward downtown passed uneventfully. Olej kept his distance but with every dashed yellow line he put behind him, he became more confident this was his man. When the Jeep turned down Wabash Street, he was certain. Target acquired.

Slowing as he approached the entrance, Olej saw the gray Jeep pull into the drop-off area of the Budget Rent-a-Car. The car return was in a parking garage in a squat, three-story red brick building at the foot of new, glittery, high-rise condo buildings. The old gradually giving way to the new, as Chicago urbanized all over again. The city was molting. He stopped in a loading zone on the other side of the street, watching the entrance to the Budget office with a mini uniocular scope.

A few minutes later, his heart skipped a beat. The most famous FBI agent since Elliot Ness emerged onto Wabash Street, folded a rental receipt into his pocket, and headed south on foot. At least he thought it was him. The face looked different somehow. Like it had thinned and then fattened and then thinned again. The eyes sunken and sadder somehow. The lively spirit of the face he saw on television pretty much nonstop for weeks replaced by...well, he couldn't be sure after just a quick glance. But Agent Royce Johnson looked different. There was no doubt about that.

Olej stayed put, having the advantage of surprise and speed, plus good sight lines down the barely trafficked street. He pressed the button on his two-way, but then released it without checking in with Aliza. As tempting as it was to report the possibility, he could already hear the response: verify and report back.

After giving his prey a few hundred yards, Olej followed,

easing the Focus along in traffic, using only a few dozen of its three hundred fifty horses. The man, clad in black from head to toe, walked easily and seemingly unaware of the tail. If it was the former Agent Johnson, his skills had atrophied in prison. A zebra with a limp.

Where is he going? Ahead, at the intersection of Cermack Road, there was a CTA Green line stop. The man turned right when he got to Cermack, headed that way. There were plenty of parking lots, as they were within the orbit of the vast convention center known as McCormick Place. Olej found a surface lot, assuring easy exit, handed the keys to an attendant, took a ticket, and headed off to the L stop. He'd lost sight of the target but took a calculated risk that he was taking the Green line south toward Rockefeller, where Royce's brother had lived and where he'd made his fame. After a decade of this, it was two plus two.

He found him standing on the southbound platform as expected. He'd changed into jeans and a Bears hoodie. *Maybe he isn't as out of shape as I thought.* But the switch didn't fool Olej. The train approached. He watched from a few yards away, taking note of his body language, what he was carrying, whether there were any bulges in his clothes. An investigator investigating an investigator. Of course, no one would have noticed this—it was just two guys standing on a train platform.

They boarded, one car away from each other. Olej could see his profile through the narrow rectangular windows separating the cars, even though they were marked with age and streaks of graffiti. It was him, there was no doubt. The face was possibly him. What gave it away was the attempted evasion through a clothing quick change. By trying to hide, he'd given himself away. It was time to report.

Olej took out his phone and messaged Aliza.

Ivan: Tracking. CTA GL. Likely Agent Royce Johnson.

Aliza: ?

Ivan: Yup.

Aliza: Stay on him. Shit.

***

Kahan put down her phone and called up the footage from Klepp's house that morning. She watched the man's movements. Calm and focused—he was looking for something but Aliza could tell by the way he sat at the desk and combed through the files that the man wasn't sure what he was looking for. At one point as he moved from the desk toward the bookshelf, where the surveillance camera was hidden in the base of the bust of the Roman orator Cicero, his face came into focus. Aliza froze the image, then zoomed in. The resolution was grainy and the edges distorted. Had she not been clued in by Ivan, she would never have identified him. But knowing it was him, she could see that it was him. She stroked the outline of his face with the tip of her index finger.

"What are you doing there, Agent Johnson?"

She could feel her adrenaline surge, and with it, a bit more of her flesh turning to stone.

CHAPTER 20

The take-home pay of an unmarried assistant clinical professor of law at Rockefeller was enough to rent a sizeable loft apartment in the South Loop neighborhood. Mike Church did just this. Just a few years ago, this neighborhood, between downtown and Hyde Park right along the lake, would have been characterized as "God's country," if God were really into light industrial. But the mayor's ambitious revitalization plan had transformed it into a hot residential area in just under a decade. High-rise apartments sprouted like crocuses, interspersed with old manufacturing buildings that had been converted into restaurants, karate dojos, coffee shops, performance spaces, and everything else demanded by recent Big 10 graduates in search of a city experience. Professor Church's building was the former home of an industrial bakery. A six-story brick building topped by four large water towers, it occupied an entire city block just across from Soldier Field.

As his Uber approached, the façade of the old bakery and the faded paint logo of the Stanislavski Baking Company on the side of the building brought him a sense of comfort—home. In there, among his collection of Kachina dolls, plopped into his Eames chair, was where he could work out the next steps. Ben's cryptic story at the end of their phone conversation told him the data from his samples survived the fire—it was backed up in the cloud, just like his computer files had been backed up on floppy disks he kept in a plastic storage case that had insulated them from the cascade of water caused by the flood from the waterslide on the stairs above his dorm room office. The evidence was safe, but the case was not yet made. And the fire at the chemistry lab was proof that making it would be the hardest thing he'd ever attempted. *They were willing to destroy and to kill to stop me.* The thought sent a chill down his spine and out to the tip of every nerve.

Church pulled his keys from his backpack as he alighted the Uber and walked toward the front door of his building while fishing for the front door key.

"Professor Church," came a voice from behind.

Jumpy from the fire, Church wheeled like a pudgy, middle-aged man facing his sensei at his first karate class. He saw his across-the-hall neighbor holding the end of a leash, while her bulldog, Roger, peed against a sapling in a small patch of dirt surrounded by sidewalk.

"Oh, hello, Phyllis. I didn't...you surprised me."

"Sorry about that, dear." She squatted down with a baggie inverted over her hand and picked up Roger's poop. She tied it off and held it in her outstretched hand while she spoke. "I didn't mean to frighten you." Phyllis stepped toward him as the Uber sped off. Although she looked fifty, Church believed she was pushing seventy. Work had been done. But he knew Phyllis as a sincere and gentle woman, always quick with a compliment and generous with baked goods, casseroles, and gossip.

"No, not at all. I've just had a rough day. I'm a bit on edge about some goings-on at work. Faculty politics and such." He turned back toward the door, reaching out with the large square key. He felt her come up behind him.

"Someone was here looking for you. Just a few minutes ago when we came out for our walk, Roger and me."

Before he turned, Church swallowed. "Really? Did they...did you get a name?"

"Everything okay, sweetie?" She switched the bag of poop

into her left hand, holding it along with the leash, and reached out and put her right hand on his bicep, stroking it gently. "How about a nice hot cup of tea?"

"I'm fine, thanks. You are too kind, Phyllis." He pulled his arm away gently. "Now, did my visitor leave a name?"

"No. I asked and they said you'd know who it was and what it was regarding. I got the impression they thought you were expecting them. The man seemed surprised you weren't here."

"Well, like I said, it's been one of those days." They shared a smile. "Could you describe him?"

"Medium height, dark hair. Cubs hat. Seemed like he works out a lot. I figured he was a friend—he was about your age."

"A Cubs fan—I could never be friends with a Cubs fan." Another shared smile. Church set his allegiance with the South Side Sox when he moved to Chicago and took a job defending South Siders against environmental injustice.

"Right, I knew that about you. Not much into sports, but I do know about the cross-town rivalry. Funny that."

"Sorry, the description leaves me wanting. Well, I guess he'll be back in touch." Church went to walk away, but she stopped him.

"No need for that, sweetheart, he left you a note."

"Oh, great." It wasn't. "Where did he leave it?"

"I said I'd take it for him, but he said it was important that you got it and he...well, he didn't trust me, I guess." She seemed disappointed that a total stranger wouldn't trust her. But Mike Church knew why.

"So, where is it? What did he do with it?"

"We put it in your mailbox—remember you gave me a key the last time you went away for a...Guatemala, wasn't it?"

Indeed it was. The mention of it transported him to the top of the pyramids of Tikal and Palenque. A longtime lover of pre-Columbian art and amateur historian of Mayan settlements in the Guatemalan highlands, Church had spent the best three weeks of his life trekking in the jungles and ascending the stony temples. His kindly neighbor Phyllis kept an eye on his succulents and dealt with his mail.

"Great. Thanks, Phyllis. I know I can always count on you."

"What about that tea, deary?"

"A raincheck. I better get that note and get to the bottom of this. Plus, I've got to put the finishing touches on a brief."

"Always working. Find time for the flowers, will ya?"

"It's a deal. And I'll come by for tea another time."

"Good."

Church keyed into his building and then into the tin mailbox with the number 12 on it. Reaching inside, he found a stack of junk mail and catalogs and solicitations. Environmental waste subsidized by taxpayers. It boiled his blood every time. We lose billions to deliver advertisements for corporations, and most of it ends up right in the landfill. *Disgusting*, he thought as he reached for the plain envelope with no stamp and no writing on the outside. Church held it between his fingers for a long moment. It was thin and contained only paper, he was certain. There was no bomb. The thought was ridiculous, but then again, he'd just come from a building that he was pretty sure was obliterated by the same people who put this in his mailbox.

Church went to open it, then remembered the spate of anthrax-laden letters that had paralyzed Washington a few years back. He stopped and stared, twisting and bending it with care. He felt Phyllis's eyes on him, so he looked over his left shoulder, and there she was standing on the street, holding Roger's leash and gawking at him through the windows of the apartment foyer. Church nodded. Then, tore open the envelope.

There was no powder, no explosion. Just a plain white piece of paper. There were no markings, other than the words: "Proverbs 26:17" typed in Courier twelve-point font. The aesthete in him was revolted by the choice of font, but he put that aside. He turned it over and examined it. Held it up to the light. All the while, Phyllis watched and Roger panted.

Church was not versant in Biblical references. The unknown

message frightened him, not just because it was religious. He suspected Phyllis might be able to help him decode it—he saw her headed to worship every Sunday morning when he collected his *New York Times* on the stoop—but he worried what the passage might say and that Phyllis would jump to conclusions and tell everyone she knew about her professor neighbor who did this or that. *No, better to keep this to myself.* Only he and Google would know what it said. Church smiled at Phyllis and waved goodbye.

He climbed the six flights up to his loft, missing every other step as he pumped his arms and let his fear turn ever so briefly to cardiac motivation. Once inside, he poured himself a filtered water from his Brita and pulled up a chair in front of his computer workstation. He opened a private window, typed "Proverbs 26:17" into the Google search bar, and hit Enter. The first hit was BibleHub.

Church clicked. The page listed dozens of translations of the text of this line from Proverbs in Hebrew and English and Aramaic, from Bibles new and ancient. He clicked on the entry for the King James Bible: "He that passeth by, and meddleth with strife not belonging to him, is like one that taketh a dog by the ears." Thrown off by the eth's, he looked down and saw a translation that summarized the threat perfectly: "Interfering in someone else's business is as foolish as yanking a dog's ears."

Church closed his laptop, and all his screens went black. He had yanked the ear of a Rottweiler, and it knew where he lived. Time for a new strategy. They were probably outside watching him right now. The thought made him vomit right on his keyboard. Reaching for a towel, he realized it didn't matter. Church threw his laptop, a change of clothes, a toothbrush, and his passport in a backpack and headed for the fire escape.

CHAPTER 21

Two stories tall and two buildings deep, Schaller's Pump was surrounded by vacant lots making it stand out like a prairie dog's head peeking out of a hole. "The Pump" as it was known among White Sox fans, Bridgeport locals, and the politicians who ate and drank there, was Chicago's oldest bar until it closed a few years back after one hundred thirty-six years of operation. The liquor license—granted in 1881, the city's sixth—still hung behind the bar, now caked in dust and bereft of elbows. The Pump was an institution. But when its long-time owner died at ninety, so did its property tax exemption. Within years, the tax man's pound of flesh killed it.

Max Klepp knew none of this history as his chauffeur-driven Suburban headed down Halsted Street south from the Loop toward 37th Street on a cloudless morning. The typical passenger driving out of the business district toward Schaller's felt their stomach turn and their mood sour. The land was flat, but the curve of poverty down Halsted Street was steep. Buildings crumbled, lots became vacant, chain-link fences started popping up like dandelions, and hope seemed to fade. But Max Klepp didn't see despair—he saw opportunity. He saw money. He saw hope, delivered in the form of concrete and steel and glass, in the form of shops and restaurants. Klepp the Capitalist saw fertile land in need of planting.

The two-car caravan of Suburbans pulled in front of the defunct bar with a screech. Klepp's driver came around and opened his door. The developer got out and turned three hundred sixty degrees, taking in possibilities. Across the street, a squat, two-story building was emblazoned with "11th Ward Democratic Party" carved into a concrete lintel. To the right and left and all around he saw shabby buildings and lots that begged to be developed. He could hear them calling his name.

The door to Schaller's Pump was boarded up, but as Klepp approached, it creaked open, and a thick-necked man with the haircut of a Marine and the brow of a Neanderthal motioned him in. The room was vacant and the scene cut straight from a zombie movie. Stray pint glasses lingered on the dusty bar, a few empty bottles lay askew on rickety shelves, and tin tiles hung from the ceiling like the skin flaking off of a Minnesota tourist on a Miami beach. The setting was perfect for what had to be done. He admired the director's choice.

"Over here," a high-pitched voice barked from the corner over Klepp's right shoulder.

Klepp wheeled in that direction and saw a thin man in his thirties underneath a two-hundred-dollar haircut and wrapped in a fifteen-hundred-dollar suit. Seated at a table cleaned of dust and detritus, he looked like a color character cut into a black-and-white movie.

"Mr. Doherty," Klepp said in a deep baritone, striding toward him, "Maximillian Klepp. A pleasure to meet you."

"Have a seat, Mr. Klepp. Can I call you Max?"

"Please. And you? Jimmy?"

"Alderman Doherty."

"Well, not for long, I hope. Let's me and you see if we can put a 'mayor' in front of that name, where it belongs. What d'ya say?"

"Let's not get ahead of ourselves, Max. Have seat. Share a drink with me. Bourbon?"

The alderman slid the only other clean glass in the place

across toward Max, popped the top off a bottle of Blanton's and poured four fingers for his guest.

"To Quayside," Max said as he raised his glass.

"To Chicago," the alderman intoned, downing his in a gulp.

"Here, here," Klepp responded as he sipped. Then, he quickly added, "Why the Pump? You aren't going to murder me, are you? 'Cause this would be a great place for a murder." He smiled but wasn't exactly happy to be there.

"It seemed that this place—" the alderman motioned around the abandoned bar with broad gestures, "—the home of the old Chicago that has gone, would be the perfect place for our business...building the new Chicago."

"I think you've seen too many movies, Alderman." Klepp dripped with disdain.

"Perhaps. My uncle loves making me watch the classics. He showed me *Paths of Glory*, recently, you know, with Kirk Douglas..."

"Haven't seen it," Max responded diffidently.

"You should. It is a brilliant morality play."

"Mmm hmmm," Max grumbled, eager to get down to business.

"There's this French colonel, he's brave and a good leader. But when an impossible attack on a German fortification fails, the same generals that ordered him to do it want him to execute three soldiers, you know, as a lesson to others not to be cowards."

"Sounds like a real crowd pleaser, Alderman," Max mocked in an annoyed tone. "I'll be sure to watch it with the wife," Max lied. He never watched TV, except for the Masters golf tournament. When he wasn't busy trying to make money, which was nearly always, he relaxed by reading biographies and histories, a Davidoff Winston Churchill ablaze and stuck between his thick fingers.

"You'll like it, Max. Trust me."

"Well...down to business," Klepp said, reaching down and pulling a manila folder labeled "Quayside/Bubbly Creek" out of his briefcase. He set it on the table with care. It sat there for a moment, enough to impress the seriousness of its contents. Klepp opened it, and slid the paper inside across the table to the alderman. "This is the final punch list. We need these items cleared as soon as possible. I've got dozens of scrapers and dozers and concrete trucks, not to mention thousands of workers, many from your ward, waiting on this paperwork, Alderman. I am hemorrhaging here. We need this by the end of the week. Two at the outside." He tried to pump the brakes, but the urgency ran ahead of him.

Doherty picked up the paper gingerly and stared at it past the tip of his nose. Inspection complete, he let it fall to the table.

"This is quite a list—permits, zoning variances, environmental impact statements...you are making some ask here, Max." The words dripped from his mouth like melted wax off a candle. "Nothing gets built in this ward without my say."

Klepp knew this, having built hundreds of buildings in dozens of wards across the city over the past four decades. It was called "Aldermanic Privilege"—the veto every alderman had over every construction permit in their ward—and it was the wellspring of political power in Chicago. Pols had long said they wanted to get rid of the privilege, but these promises were not promises like Max's promises—they were slogans, cheap talk, or, as the Maxes of the world would call them, lies. Hoping alderman would vote to get rid of their privilege was like hoping fish would vote to get rid of water.

This was Klepp's first project on the South Side, but his palm greasing for north side projects was legendary in City Hall. More than a few politicians made a name for themselves by funding other candidates in other races with money given to them, one way or another, by Max Klepp. Little needed to be said of this. Both men knew it, and knew that they each knew it. But sometimes, maybe most times, making explicit what is implicit, advances the conversation.

"I know it is a big ask, Alderman, but you know these

buildings aren't temples to my ego—they are going to house your constituents, to provide jobs in construction and going forward for the people of your ward. But most importantly, when this new community is built along Bubbly Creek, the story of progress—environmental progress, social progress for the South Side—is one you will be asked to tell on every radio and TV show in the country. Why stand in the way of that?" Klepp took a long sip of his bourbon, not just because his speech dried his mouth, but because he needed the dilation of his blood vessels to keep his anger positive.

"That's a powerful point, Max, but it isn't the whole story. People these days just don't want new, they want some of the old. They also worry about developers getting rich with subsidies from taxpayers."

"That's bullshit and you know it, Jimmy!" Klepp raised up out of his chair, but then flopped back with a thud.

"Let's keep this civil, Max. I don't know it. I know that there are concerns about environmental impacts on the creek."

"Ha—that creek is a—"

"There are concerns about gentrification and pushing out families who have lived in this neighborhood for generations."

Max Klepp shook his head vigorously, not just because he thought these arguments were ridiculous—he knew they were just a front for the real ask.

"I'm not saying that I'm not going to make a buck on this, Alderman." Max quoted Adam Smith from memory. "'It is not from the benevolence of the butcher, the brewer, or the baker that we expect our dinner but from the regard to their own interest.' And I'm not saying things aren't going to change around here. Heck, that's a good thing. You are a progressive, aren't you, Alderman? You can't be a 'progressive' without 'progress.'"

"I am. I'm a progressive."

"Well, me too. I'm for change. I'm for development. For making the world better."

"We can—"

"I'm not done," Klepp cut him off. "Some people lose when things change. Taxes will go up around here, but that is your fault, not mine. I see blight, and I want to get rid of it. To build new things that give people hope. I just can't understand the human mind that wants to stand in the way of improving things."

"I think you are putting words in my mouth."

"Look, I've a meeting downtown in half an hour, Alderman. My bankers are tightening the noose because we haven't broken ground yet. I've got to go tell them that Mr. Would-Be-Mayor is getting cold feet. I've also got to tell them that development in this city, in places where it is desperately needed, is being held hostage by some hippies and 'community organizers' who are preying on people's insecurities for their own aggrandizement of power. I've got to tell them that we might need to find another person to help us lead the city into the future." Klepp stood on the word "future," buttoned his Armani sport coat, and turned to go.

"Wait, wait, Max. Let's not be hasty. I'm not saying no, I'm just asking for something that I can take back to my people so they can understand you are coming at this in good faith." The alderman stood and walked across to Max.

"Fuck your people, Jimmy. They are speedbumps. I hate speedbumps—they just make me late for where I'm going, with a good chance I'll get a coffee stain on my tie."

"Come on, Max. Meet me halfway here. Agree to an environmental quality report. Spend a few bucks of the millions you'll make on setting aside some wetlands. Pay a few people to do some good work. Hire a few of the right people to show you're a good guy. Throw a few million at some affordable housing. Something."

"Here's your something, Jimmy," he spat, his voice dripping with disdain. Klepp reached down and put a lawyer's litigation bag—a large rectangular briefcase that could hold a small child—on the table. "Take this to your people. Or, keep it yourself. I don't give a flying fuck. But, once you take it, I want my approvals by the end of the month."

The alderman looked over his shoulders, and seeing no one watching, clicked the brass latches and opened the bag. Neatly wrapped stacks of hundred-dollar bills filled it from top to bottom. One million dollars, at least. Jimmy Doherty swallowed involuntarily, and then raised his eyes to meet his new best friend.

"Oh, and one more thing, Alderman…"

"What's that, Mr. Klepp?"

"I want security redoubled at the site. I don't need protesters tying themselves to trees or pulling some stunt to derail this. We break ground in two weeks. Got it?"

The alderman smiled and nodded his head.

"Now," Klepp barked, "go fuck yourself."

Klepp walked out of the defunct bar, hopped into the back of his Suburban, and headed back toward the Loop.

CHAPTER 22

The waitress slid two coffee mugs across the booth at the back of the Medici restaurant. Scott Miller ignored his, focused instead on typing away on his phone. Royce took a big gulp, eyes on his client, trying to discern something about his character from his attitude, from his appearance. Maybe it was inherent in the nature of the business, but Royce wasn't sure if the work he was doing was really the work he was doing. All Royce knew was that he couldn't yet trust Miller.

"Sorry about that, Royce. Business."

"No worries."

The dean took a sip of his coffee, then added another cream and two more sugars.

"So, where are we? Anything to report?"

No need to mince words. Be direct. Raise the stakes. Throw the Hail Mary.

"Do the words 'Bubbly Creek' mean anything to you?"

A look of true shock was unmistakable in Miller's eyes. He lifted the thick porcelain mug to his lips and took an exaggerated sip.

"Yes, of course. It's a part of the Chicago River, I think. Where the stockyards used to be. Why? What's that have to do with Jante?"

"I'm not sure yet, but I think there may be a connection."

"What possible connection could there be? Was she somehow involved in something to do with Bubbly Creek?" The words all ran together.

"Again, I'm not sure. This is how the process works. Clues are not always obvious or something that can be explained. Clues often lead nowhere. The best ones often look like they will."

"But what made the connection?"

The waitress arrived to take their order, but the dean sent her away politely, begging for a few more minutes. He was gracious in his dismissal. Royce admired his style. He had a way with people that put them at ease and made them feel attended to and worthy. No doubt it made him an effective fundraiser and administrator. He suspected that the staff and alumni saw it and felt it too.

"Are you involved in anything at Bubbly Creek, Dean? Quayside. Does that mean anything to you?"

"Well, not directly, of course. But, Quayside, sure. That's a project my father-in-law is involved with. I don't know any details. Just that he's been working for a while to get a major project underway in that area. Riverfront commercial and residential. He's a big-time developer."

"I see." Royce already knew this. He played along.

"But what does this have to do with Jante? I'm afraid I'm lost."

"Perhaps nothing. Perhaps something."

"Hmm." Another long sip.

They ordered—pancakes for the dean; an egg-white omelet with spinach for Royce—and ate among sparse conversation. They eyed each other between bites, the dean making small talk to avoid the awkwardness of silence. As they finished up, Royce pressed the advantage again.

"If there is a connection between Rockefeller and Quayside, there could be motive in there somewhere."

"What motive? Motive for murder? You aren't suggesting my father-in-law—"

Royce cut him off. "I'm not suggesting anything." He paused and took a studious drink from his water glass. "Is there any connection?"

"I'm sure if we look hard enough and stretch our minds enough, we can find a connection between anything and almost anything else. I do it for a living. I meet alumni from every conceivable background, at all stages of life, and in countless different professions. My job is to find connections between them and the work the faculty does. I've linked oil men to feminist philosophers. So, if you're asking me if I can find some possible link between Bubbly Creek and my law school, the answer is yes. I'm a professional connection maker."

"That's cute. My question was: what's the connection? I think you're being evasive. And, frankly, it worries me."

"I apologize, Mr. Johnson. I promise, I wasn't being evasive. That wasn't my intent."

"Fine." A sip. "And the connection?"

"Off the record?" A whisper.

"Of course." *Here it comes.*

"A clinic of ours has been snooping around, trying to make out a case regarding alleged dumping of some kind at the site."

"That wasn't so hard—it sure didn't take a professional connection maker." Royce forked at his omelet.

"Look, I don't know the details of the clinic's investigation. Their work is confidential and not something that gets decanal attention. I no more supervise the clinics than I do the books or articles our faculty produce."

Royce saw his skepticism reflected back on the dean's face. He went on.

"I know this may come as a surprise to people outside of the academy, but the faculty, our clinicians, they don't work for me. I work for them. They have autonomy and independence. They call the shots, not me. I represent them to the outside world, to our stakeholders. I raise money to support them. But I don't know anything about what they're doing. And I'm fairly powerless to intervene in their work."

"Interesting." Royce took a twenty out of his wallet and set it on top of the bill, which the waitress left unobtrusively while they were engrossed in discussion.

"Even if...I don't see the link to Jante." The dean backtracked. "I don't know if Jante knew about Quayside or not. Even if she did, it would make no sense to kill her. Murder? Over some BS clinic case? I highly doubt it. Plus, even if the stakes warranted stopping the case, she had no power to influence any potential lawsuit."

Royce stood up. "Maybe it's a red herring. I've got to be thorough. You know?"

"Of course. Of course," the dean rose and put out his hand. "If there is anything I can do."

"I'll let you know."

"Great."

And, with that, the dean walked into the morning sun.

Royce sat back at the table and watched him leave, sashaying through the round tables of six and eight that were enjoying a lingering morning breakfast. It wasn't clear what Scott knew and what Scott didn't know. Royce was certain he was hiding something. It seemed the dean didn't yet trust him either. He couldn't yet say what role Scott Miller played, if any, in the death of his predecessor, but calling him a suspect in an investigation he himself instigated wouldn't be far off.

Across 57th Street, Ivan Olej sat in a Ford Transit van, eyes on the revolving door of the Medici, ears listening intently to the conversation between the dean and Agent Johnson. One of his crew was sitting in a nearby booth noshing on a bagel while holding a high-powered microphone hidden beneath his windbreaker. Olej scribbled notes in a composition book, but it was just to keep his hands busy. The conversation recorded in his mind, and he'd be able to relay it nearly word for word to Aliza.

When the conversation ended, Olej took off his headphones and raised a uniocular to peer out of a tinted window in the back of the van. He watched as the dean paused on the sidewalk, turned to scan the scene, then raised his phone and dialed a number. The dean paced as he talked, the expression on his face showing some distress. Olej couldn't hear what was being said until his man exited behind the dean and leaned up against the brick wall to light a cigarette. Earphones back on, Olej caught the last bit of one side of the call.

"...okay...that seems right. I appreciate it." Pause. "Thanks, honey."

The call ended, and the dean headed west toward campus.

The shit was about to hit the fan, and, like always, Olej was starting to think about how he could ensure he'd be on the right side of the fan when it did.

CHAPTER 23

Max Klepp was naked. He had the sauna at the Red Square Spa to himself. It wasn't because the Russian bath house on Division Street was empty that time of day, but rather because two armed guards stood watch, giving him the privacy the situation required. He poured another ladle of water over the glowing-hot rocks. The water vaporized instantaneously, setting off billows of steam. A dragon's breath of heat and moisture that wafted over his entire body. He breathed it in deeply. Prone on the wet wooden bench, bare as the day he came into the world, he felt deeply relaxed. The three shots of Pyat Ozer helped too.

The Red Square occupied a squat, two-and-a-half-story white stone building with faux Greek columns and frosted glass windows. It could have been a bank or maybe a casino in any number of Russian-speaking countries. Two red, quarter-sphere awnings and a series of high-profile security cameras welcomed visitors. Max Klepp was a regular. It was a welcome respite from the tony clubs that his type usually preferred. Here, he could mingle with plumbers and teachers, firefighters and steelworkers. These were his people, or, at least, he liked to think that they were. He wanted others to think this about him too, even though he arrived in a two-car caravan of chauffeur-driven Suburbans. Klepp spread the hundreds around liberally. He got great service, big smiles, and, when his guys showed up in something more than towels or when he wanted to meet with a woman in the male-only saunas, there were no questions.

Today was one of those days. The other thing about meetings at the Red Square sauna was that they had to be conducted in the nude, and he had his reasons for that, especially when it came to Aliza.

Aliza Kahan stepped into the sauna tentatively, even though she and Klepp had these meetings every few months.

"Max, it's me." The thick steam necessitated the introduction, although Frick and Frack at the door were sufficiently large and in charge to keep everyone else out. The two monsters nodded almost imperceptibly as Kahan dropped her towel and pushed into the fog. They stole a glance as she passed.

"Lie down," he said through the heat.

Klepp stared at the ceiling, unembarrassed by his stubby penis pointing up like a periscope. He felt Kahan's eyes on him. Sweat beads, spherical and translucent, formed at his temple, as if there were a tiny machine there manufacturing them, then fell in regular intervals, hitting the cedar planks of the bench with a plop. Kahan took a spot on the other side of the small room. They were perpendicular, feet nearly touching.

He used the sauna for his most important business—the birthday suits and the moisture ensured there would be no electronics of any kind. And some meetings weren't intended to be press conferences. Plus, seeing Aliza in the nude wasn't exactly a high price to pay.

"What can I do for you, Mr. Klepp?"

"My daughter. My fucking daughter!"

"Yes, what about her, sir?" she stumbled a bit, seemingly taken aback.

"I had to hear it from my fucking daughter." Klepp sat up with jerk, his belly fat forming an inflatable swimming ring around his otherwise thin body.

"I'm sorry, what did you hear from her? I'm a bit lost here."

"Royce Johnson. FBI superhero. Slayer of presidents and

Supreme Court judges. Royce *fucking* Johnson."

"Oh, right, well, I'm sorry this...I'm sorry you heard that way. We were just waiting to find out more. To see why he was in your house. Honestly, this was about making sure we weren't wasting your time and about bringing you an actionable recommendation."

"Spare me the crap, Aliza." He mispronounced her name, "A-Liza" instead of "A-Leeza," to irritate her. He knew that nothing pushed her buttons like that. Klepp stood up and walked over to the rocks. He filled a small bucket from a tap and poured the entire thing in one movement. When he was about ten, his father introduced him to the sauna game: the last to leave wins, and each person had a bucket of water to use however they wanted—to drink, to cool off, or, as Max just did, to raise the temperature to try to force a surrender. Max's dad deployed multiple strategies, and he consistently won. Then, when Max turned fourteen, he tried the kamikaze approach of dumping the entire bucket at once, betting he could withstand the intense blast a few seconds more. After that, Max always won. He tried that with Aliza. The rocks screamed. "He was in my house. My house! What the hell was he doing in my house!"

"We are still trying to figure that out."

"What am I paying you for?"

She went to answer, but he cut her off.

"Quayside. He was asking about Quayside!"

"We know—"

"You know? Fuck you!" Spit hit her in the face, but it just melted away with the sweat pouring off her.

She tried to talk him down. "We were at the diner. On 57th Street. We were listening. Ivan was there. Johnson hasn't left our sight since."

"Okay." This calmed the old man a bit. He was back on the bench, sitting on edge, his elbows forming deep dents in his thighs. "Do you think he knows about Church? About the samples? Where are we?"

"The samples were destroyed in the fire. We were confident that would happen, and the conversation between Church and Edelman confirmed it. We can have you listen to the tape."

"That won't be necessary. Where is the lawsuit? Am I going to be served?"

"We don't think so."

"I'm afraid that isn't enough. We were scheduled to break ground in two weeks. But it will be a few months before we can get this under control. I need to be sure before we sign the deal. That will offload some of our risk. I don't take risks like this, and I pay you to make sure there are no surprises."

"I understand."

"I don't think you do. This was a surprise."

"Church can't have much to go on, sir. We're following him, obviously, and listening to his phones. We think he's moved on. It's been a while. He received our message. Loud and clear. Also, we have eyes on the chemist as well, just in case."

"And the...dean?" The last word came as a hiss. "The dead one..."

"Your son-in-law hired Agent Johnson for that. We think it won't be a problem."

"And if it is?"

"We're ready." Her voice said, *We are always ready.*

Klepp rose to his feet and wiped his brow with a towel. He looked Aliza up and down. It was nothing he hadn't seen before, but beauty was made to be appreciated, he thought. And so he did. He wrapped another towel around his waist. His hand on the handle on the sauna's wooden door, he half turned in her direction.

"I'm not willing to risk it. Make it look good."

"Johnson?"

"Yes. Johnson."

He walked out. Frick, or perhaps it was Frack, put a plush white robe over his shoulders, then they walked down the hall toward the showers. Ten paces down the hall, Frack handed Klepp his phone. Two buttons later, his daughter, Beth, answered.

"Liebchen," he spat confidently, "I've taken care of it."

"Thanks, Daddy," she cooed.

CHAPTER 24

Alex's old Volvo wagon shimmied and squeaked as Royce navigated the potholed streets of the South Side on his way to Bubbly Creek. It was time to get a new car, but he had barely enough money for ramen and bourbon. Being on the trail of a killer didn't exactly leave free time for car shopping. No, for now, the good-ol' Freja would have to do.

Royce decided to go to the site of Max Klepp's development that he now surmised was the key to Jante Turner's murder. Walking the ground, seeing the place mattered. He wasn't sure why, but it did. In his decades of solving puzzles, it nearly always mattered. Not just because sometimes he found a shell casing or a syringe or another physical clue, but because...well, Royce couldn't say.

But on the way to Bubbly Creek, Royce had a stop to make. He headed north out of Hyde Park toward the neighborhood called Douglas, named after former Illinois senator Stephen A. Douglas. The "Little Giant," as he was known, still loomed in stone over the neighborhood from atop a fifty-foot pedestal. Douglas was the foremost advocate of popular sovereignty for new territories in the 1850s. He believed territories—on their way to being states—should be able to decide for themselves whether to be slave or free states. Before besting Abraham Lincoln in the 1858 election for US senator and then losing to

Lincoln as the Democratic nominee for president in 1860, Douglas bought the land that became the eponymous neighborhood. He bought one hundred sixty acres speculating that he'd succeed in bringing a terminus of the transcontinental railroad to Chicago, specifically the area around 35th Street and the lake—the neighborhood that now bore his name. The bet paid off—the railroad was built and Douglas's land became incredibly valuable. Awash in this wealth, he donated substantial portions to a new university on the site. Douglas's university rose but failed a few years later. Decades later it was reborn—several miles south—as Rockefeller University. The university where Royce's brother and Jante Turner worked before they died from assassins' bullets.

Today, the Douglas neighborhood, tucked along the lake between the blight of Bronzeville to the south and the newly hip South Loop neighborhood to the north, was betwixt and between. Gleaming new apartment buildings lived among tenements, public housing, and vacant lots strewn with garbage. A fancy grocery store was going up across from two bodegas. Glorious old houses cut into apartments were being restored while others were melting into the ground. It was in front of one of these dilapidated two-flats that Royce pulled up as the rain of the morning petered out into gray. He got out cautiously, scanning the streets. A middle-aged white guy wasn't exactly incognito in these parts, and what he was here to do he hoped no one would ever know.

Royce bounded up the concrete steps of the house, and knocked three times, as per the instructions the bartender at a dive bar down the street. He didn't give them to Royce, who looked like a cop, even after a year behind bars. Instead, Royce had given twenty dollars to a kid he found loitering in front of a liquor store, and asked him how to score. The kid asked the bartender, and then relayed the instructions. Standing there waiting, Royce hoped he wasn't being set up. He flinched, unsure of what was coming through the door.

A few seconds after his knock, a doggy door opened, and a

hand reached out. After looking over his shoulder, Royce put a brown bag full of two hundred dollars he'd borrowed from Claire into the hand. A few more seconds, and the bag reappeared. Back in his car, Royce peeked inside, saw the black tip of a revolver, and then closed the bag, put it under the driver's seat, and headed west down 35th Street toward Bubbly Creek. As he drove, he shook his head at how easy it was to get a gun. It took him less than an hour and cost less than a night out with Jenny.

The trip west on 35th Street cut a cross-section through Chicago's inglorious racial history. Between the lake and the Dan Ryan expressway, twenty blocks of agonizing poverty without a white face anywhere. During the "Great Migration," African-Americans from the south got off trains—on tracks laid in Douglas's time, eight decades earlier—here, and for reasons geographical, sociological, and racial, many didn't make it much further. There were times in the next century when it shined, but mostly it was the place you wanted to be from, not to be. The sad truth, however, was that if you were from here you lived here. The same could be said of the hollers of Appalachia, but color still made a difference in America, which made Douglas a special kind of hell.

Crossing the ten lanes of Dan Ryan—an artery of asphalt connecting Chicago to the south suburbs—changed everything. The home of the Chicago White Sox marked the change, giving way to blue-collar homes, small businesses, and a few parks and schools, populated with white faces. This was Doherty turf, and the hardscrabble faces of construction workers, city cops, barmen, down-and-out artists, mechanics, plumbers, carpenters, fire-fighters, teachers, pipe fitters, and high-end drifters reflected the Bridgeport neighborhood's long history of keeping blacks on the other side of the highway. Further on, the amount of Spanish on storefront signs increased, eventually becoming exclusive by the time Royce reached Racine Avenue. Hispanics were not so much on an island like the descendants of former slaves—they were "over there" around the corner, but not walled off by a ten-lane freeway.

Then, a burst of trees and a bridge over Bubbly Creek. There at the corner, a block-wide warehouse advertised itself as the home of the "Bridgeport Arts Center" and told hipsters that there were lofts with a water view inside.

Royce pulled Freja into an on-street parking space just short of the bridge across the creek. With a deep breath, he reached under the passenger seat and pulled the brown bag out with care—he didn't know if the revolver was loaded. Royce reached in like the bag was full of scorpions. The firearm was a grubby Armscor M200 revolver. It was unloaded, but the bag had a handful of .38 caliber bullets. Royce loaded the bullets, holding the pistol under the steering wheel out of sight. He'd seen more of these than any man should, including on two occasions pointed at him. He hated the gun. Hated the look. Hated the feel. Hated holding it. This particular gun had been used by the scumbags he'd spent his life chasing. Feeling it, seeing how it had never been cleaned, how the grip was cracked and how the muzzle corroded, knowing how it had been used, made him sick. But he needed it, and, being an ex-con, he had no other choice about how to get one. A justification that he realized in that moment was not unlike the ones used by the kids who'd used this particular piece to rob liquor stores and put lead into the bellies of dudes who'd wronged them.

Out on the bridge, scum gun tucked into his jeans, he took in the incongruity of the scene. Behind him, low-slung urban blah stretched out as far as he could see. There was low-rent commerce here and there, and a few flowers poking their heads out of grubby grass, but this wasn't anyone's postcard. No interesting buildings, no signs of history or the future. Then, as he turned back toward the creek, he saw a wide stream surrounded by flourishing trees lush with buds and leaves. He saw action—kayakers and even someone fishing, although he hoped just to catch and release. Open land fronted the river on both sides, and just a few steps down the slope, Royce felt transported.

He skirted along the shore just above the water line. He looked up at the Arts Center. The brick was spotty with stains where old advertisements of products long since forgotten used to hang. All of it was in desperate need of tuckpointing. But the defects were hidden beneath dozens of black iron fire escapes, like the metal cage on a hockey helmet covering pimply teenage faces. At ground level, there was a flat path about five feet wide with riprap going down to the water line for nearly two hundred yards. Royce used it to stroll amiably so as not to draw any attention. Then, the path ended. He found himself scrambling on the loose soil of a slope running from the Chicago Maritime Museum down to the creek. Using the trees as cover, he stumbled along, using his right hand to catch himself when he half fell.

The trees thickened. Royce felt them envelop him, giving cover and allowing him to relax. He felt for the six-shooter stuck in his waistband, and he cinched his belt. Two steps later, he felt his phone buzz. Pulling it out of his back pocket, he recognized the number—his PO. There was no choice. Even here. Even on his sneak toward Quayside. Royce sat on the muddy slope with a resigned flop.

"Royce Johnson," he half whispered.

"Mr. Johnson, this is Officer Cuthbert of the United States District Court." The voice was sure. "I'm checking in with you regarding your conditions of release and your probation. I'm your new PO. I'm taking over for Officer Gayed."

"Nice to meet you, Officer." Royce tried to sound sincere but he felt nothing but regret at how Alex had been murdered and Royce's five-years-to-retirement-on-a-fat-government-pension life had been derailed by politics. "I'm scheduled to meet in your office, what, next Tuesday?"

"Indeed. Tuesday at three. I'll see you then." He paused for a moment, pregnant with anticipation. "I'm just calling to make sure you are settling in okay with life outside of prison. Do you have work yet?"

Royce felt the revolver sticking into his hip.

"I'm still working with a startup in the health care industry." Claire had agreed to put him on the payroll of a company she'd founded with a few other doctors to develop better ways for hospitals to process and utilize the vast amounts of patient data they generated. She even got an Illinois tax break for hiring an ex-con. Royce logged into his work computer every day, sent a few emails to Claire with information she'd provided him in advance, and otherwise was free to do what he wanted. Most startups didn't have offices these days, making scams like this one almost fool proof.

"Great. We'll discuss that on Tuesday. Bring some proof of employment. Also, we'll being doing a drug test. In the meantime, stay out of trouble, okay?"

Royce grinned as he looked around at the scene.

"Will do. See you soon, Officer Cuthbert."

He ended the call, then breathed in deeply through his mouth. The scent of hyacinths mixed with a bit of wood smoke from a nearby backyard fire pit. It was like Proust's madeleine, transporting him instantly to his own backyard in Pittsburgh, with Jenny on the wicker loveseat beside him reading the newspaper, as he stoked the fire. Royce gulped, got to his feet, and headed north again along the shoreline.

After fifty yards, he found himself hugging closer to the waterline as the backyards of several houses stretched further down to the creek, lapping on bits of broken concrete and river rocks. At first they were modest remnants of the postwar attempts to revitalize this part of Bridgeport. Soon, however, the tan brick bungalows that were a signature of Chicago, from Skokie to south suburban Homewood-Flossmoor, gave way to faux chateaus with high fences, sport courts, and outdoor kitchens. The appeal of open land in this area became apparent. This wasn't the old wealth of Lake Forest, but money was money. And if what the tax professor told him about Max Klepp were true, money for him was everything.

Royce pulled the hood of his Steelers sweatshirt over his

head as he walked along the property line of the McMansions. If there were cameras, it would be best not to be seen. Especially since at this moment his computer was logged into work, and several emails he timed to be sent while he was away were scheduled. He hoped Officer Cuthbert wouldn't care so much about him, but after the hunt for Alex's killer, he was going to leave nothing to chance.

At the end of a high, wrought iron fence, there was a large clump of sassafras trees. Beyond, Royce saw the chain-link fence marking the boundary of the Quayside development. It was topped with razor wire and what looked like cameras pointed out in his direction. He was out of range and hidden pretty well, but caution was warranted. Down on one knee, he pulled pocket binoculars. The land beyond the fence was open to the horizon. Prime land. No wonder Klepp was willing to...well, Royce wasn't there yet, but he saw the reason for the interest.

The cameras stopped him from going further. Royce scrambled up the dirt shoulder, shielded from scrutiny by the sassafras trees. Up on flat ground, he found himself in an alley, with garages on both sides and basketball hoops getting some springtime use as Chicagoans emerged from their winter cocoons. He worked around to the front of the larger houses looking out on the creek and, facing them from across the street, the postwar bungalows looking like the scholarship kids at the prep school.

As he walked south back toward Freja, Royce noticed a young woman in a Rockefeller-green fleece on the porch of a particularly sad bungalow. She was holding a clipboard and had the appearance of an eager student or activist. Thirty steps, and Royce met her at the sidewalk.

"Hey, I'm trying to find the Chicago Maritime Museum," Royce lied. "Do you know where that is?"

"Sorry," the woman took him in, "I'm not from around here. I'm doing some research for a case I'm working on."

"Ahhh, thanks," Royce replied politely. He nodded toward her clipboard, "Political canvasing?"

"Oh," she said, looking down at it. "No, not collecting signatures. I guess this is a bit old fashioned. This is for notes." She smiled broadly. "I'm working on a project for a law school clinic—a case, something involving the creek over there." She motioned up and behind him with her chin.

"Rockefeller?" he asked.

"Ahh, yeah. How'd you—"

"The fuzzy." Royce pointed at the Rockefeller crest on her fleece.

"Right. Duh! Yeah, I go to the Law School. I'm working for the environmental clinic there."

"Interesting. I went to the Steinlauf Business School. Small world, eh?" Useful lies weren't lies in his line of work. They were part of the rules. At least they used to be. "Who runs the clinic—I have a few friends in the environmental game."

"Professor Church. He is amazing." The woman's eyes glittered. She reached under the clasp on the clipboard and handed Royce a business card.

"Thank you." He eyed it. *Mike Church, Associate Clinical Professor of Law.* Email and cell phone. Royce looked up at her. "What's your name? In case I cross paths with Mike, I want to be sure I tell him how you were out here working hard."

"Becca. Rebecca Goldman." Her face lit up with pride.

"Great. Keep up the good work."

Royce tucked the business card into his pocket and headed back to Alex's car. It wasn't a bullet casing or fingerprints, but he had a lead. Turning with a satisfied look on his face, he stopped in his tracks. A man was sitting in a Ford Focus, reading a copy of the *Chicago Sun Times*. Royce tried not to act surprised and concerned but was sure he didn't hide the fear. As he passed him, the White Sox game crackled on his radio through an open window. This was a tail, there was no doubt. Not just that—a tail that wanted to let Royce know he had one. Royce nodded, and the man, who looked the part, nodded back. The passenger seat was littered with fast-food wrappers, and, quite conspicuously, an

Israeli-made pistol. The game was on.

Royce quickened his pace. Looking over his shoulder, he saw that neither the man nor the Focus had budged. The muffled sound of the play-by-play wafted down the street. Royce turned, but didn't even catch eyes in the rearview mirror. Cool as Christmas. It made Royce shudder. In the distance, he saw Becca still going door-to-door. When he turned his torso back around, he felt the street piece dig into his side. It hit him—if the tail was on him since he left Hyde Park, which was almost surely the case, then the man saw him dealing through the doggy door. He knew he was armed with an illegal weapon, when even a legal one was forbidden. A call to the cops was all he needed to send Royce back to jail for violating his probation. Royce pulled the revolver carefully from his waistband and as he reached Freja, threw it into Bubbly Creek.

CHAPTER 25

The cell phone number on Mike Church's business card rang and rang. It didn't go to voicemail and he got no text message back. It just rang until Royce hung up, reminding him of the days before answering machines. The days when his body was full of hormones and he'd call Jenny's house wanting to know if she could come over to watch a movie, and the rings would echo for minutes around her empty house. Or, he hoped that was why she wasn't picking up.

Royce desperately needed to talk to Church—to warn him about the guy in the Ford Focus and the possibility that his work at Bubbly Creek might get him killed. Just like it got Jante killed. But the cell phone was a dead end. Literally. Time for another way.

In the days before Petersburg, Royce would have had a member of his squad pull the address linked to the cell phone. Verizon and AT&T were willful collaborators with the feds, especially when a call to the FCC could make their lives miserable in countless ways. But even heroes can be *persona non grata* with the feds if they don't follow the rules.

He could always call in a chit with his old partner, but Vasquez had climbed the ranks in the San Diego Field Office, which meant doing so would be much costlier than in the past. Bosses tended to play by the rules. Especially at the Bureau.

Even when they didn't before being bosses. And using federal resources to help ex-cons was not within the rules—it wasn't on any page in the FBI Domestic Investigations and Operations Guide. No, he needed to do this the old-fashioned way. Find the weakest link.

The security guard at the Law School directed him to the wing containing the offices of the various clinics run by and out of the school. Clinical faculty weren't exactly faculty, which explained why they were off alone in a remote part of the building. Royce had heard stories about the tensions. Practically minded clinicians were fighting to keep murderers off death row or to get free houses for the poor, while impractical professors were plumbing the depths of the market or the Constitution. Not until he had to be buzzed into the clinic space did Royce fully understand the wall between them.

"I'm looking for Professor Mike Church," Royce said with measured assuredness.

The woman at the front desk looked up at him indifferently.

"He's not here." She said it to her crossword puzzle.

"Do you know when he'll be back? I've got an urgent document for him." Royce held up a manila folder that he'd put an official-looking label on. "I really need to get this to him."

"Sorry, I don't know. I haven't seen him today."

"Ah, huh," Royce murmured.

"In fact—" she looked up at him, "—I haven't seen him for a while."

"Oh," Royce seemed surprised even though he wasn't. "How long, if you don't mind me asking? As I said," he added quickly before she could answer, "I have some extremely urgent documents pertaining to the case he is working on, and I need to get them to him as soon as humanly possible."

"I don't know. I'm not here every day. But I've heard rumors."

"Mmmm." He tried to sound moderately interested.

"Yeah, like he hasn't been seen in months. Some rumblings among his clinical students. You know, trying to get in touch with him about papers and the like. Grades, I guess."

"Right, right. Thanks." Royce turned to go. Then turned back. "One more thing. Do you know how I can get him this? It is kind of super important that he sees it."

"Just give it to me. I'll slip it under his door and send him an email that he has a package waiting."

"Thanks. But I'm afraid I have to give them to him personally—" Royce held up the envelope and patted it, "—you know, legal documents. My boss—pain in the ass—insists on it. Need a signature." Royce opened the folder and pointed to a "Sign Here" sticky he'd randomly affixed to a page full of gibberish formatted to look legal.

The receptionist nodded as if she'd been around lawyers for a while.

"Of course. Well, I'm not sure what I can do then."

Royce was ready. "Do you know where he lives? I could deliver them to his apartment. If he isn't here, he's probably there, right?"

"Maybe. But I can't—"

"I know, of course. But we work together on occasion, and I really have to get him these documents. It's urgent. He'd want you to tell me, I'm certain." Royce pulled Church's business card, the one Becca Goldman gave him, out of his pocket and handed it to the woman. "He gave me this."

She hesitated, looked Royce in the eyes for a long minute, then, after a quick search on her computer, scribbled an address on a Post-it note. She folded it and slid it across the half counter toward Royce. He took it with a smile. *The weakest link.*

Royce sat in Freja munching on a burrito watching the customers of the old Stanislavski Baking Company. Young women in yoga clothes, millennial metrosexual men with AirPods walking Jack Russells, the Amazon guy and the FedEx guy and the UberEats guy, coming and going. None of them, however, were Mike

Church. Royce had his picture pulled up on this phone from the Rockefeller Law web page. He wasn't remarkable looking, but from only thirty yards, Royce would recognize him, even if Church didn't really want to be recognized.

The stake lasted two days. Forty-eight, ass-numbing, garbage-food-eating, smell-producing hours later, there was no sign of Church. For a bit of it, Royce listened to the autobiography of Michael Collins—the guy who didn't walk on the moon with Neil and Buzz—on Audible. Collins described the ordeal of sitting in the tiny Gemini capsule for fourteen days. Royce empathized. But the astronauts had weightlessness. He was pretty sure this was worse.

Royce emerged from Freja and stretched like a moth emerging from a chrysalis. He walked toward the front door of the lofts, feeling the blood return to his limbs with a tingle. Once there, Royce bent down to pick up a newspaper stuffed inside an elongated blue plastic bag. Lingering for a few minutes, he rolled his eyes upward hoping someone on their way to work would swing the door open with vigor. It didn't take long.

A man in a chalkboard-colored suit pushed out into the morning and bounded off down the street with squirrel-like enthusiasm, giving Royce time to duck inside and catch the inner door just as it closed but just before it latched. He stepped into the foyer and found Church's name on the mailbox for Unit 12. The mailbox door bulged and at his feet, Royce saw a pile of mail addressed to Church. It appeared weeks and weeks of mail were unchecked.

Royce stepped over the mail, climbed several flights, and found Unit 12, seemingly no different from the outside than any other. Ear to Church's door, Royce's eyes were on the hallway to make sure he wasn't surprised. Nothing was stirring inside. He rapped on the door twice, then put his ear back, cupped with his hand. Nothing. Ready to chance it, Royce removed a lock pick from his pocket and went to work on the handle. Eyes still scanning for other residents, he picked the lock from muscle memory. Twenty seconds later, he was standing inside Church's apartment.

Church wasn't home, or if he was, he was lying dead somewhere under the stuff strewn everywhere. Royce stood motionless taking in the scene. Overturned couch, cushions cut open and their innards strewn around on the floor like bits of offal on the floor of an abattoir. A desk was on its side, a computer that used to sit on top was lying face down, surrounded by cords that looked like broken limbs. The refrigerator was open, its contents strewn on the Mexican-tile floor. Royce navigated the rooms like a solider traversing a minefield or a dad tiptoeing through a child's room strewn with Lego pieces.

The smell from the rotting food told Royce that Church had not been here in a long time. He covered his mouth with his hand as he wandered among the detritus of a life disrupted. Not looking for anything in particular, Royce kicked this and that with his boot. One thing he knew: the people who had turned the place over didn't find whatever it was they were looking for, either. Every corner of the place was tossed, which meant that unless the flash drive or case files or whatever was in the last possible place, they left empty-handed. If Church was alive, and that was a big if, he was still holding the key to Jante's murder.

Royce closed the refrigerator door, scooped the rotting food into a trash can, and put it in the hallway as he let himself out. As he did, he wondered why he was doing it. As he turned back toward the staircase, a voice from behind called out to him, "Hey buddy!" Royce turned casually, as if it were his apartment.

"Hey," he responded.

"We don't leave trash in the hallway here—there's a chute right there," the man, a stocky hipster with the beard of a Civil War general, pointed over Royce's shoulder as he walked toward him. "Who are you, by the way? Did that guy move out?"

Royce picked up the can, stinking like the back of a garbage truck on a summer afternoon in Phoenix.

"I'm a friend of Mike's. The guy who lives here."

The man ignored him, wincing as he passed on the way to the elevator.

Royce dumped the garbage down the chute, then waited until the elevator pinged. With a quick repick of the lock he stepped into Church's apartment to return the can. It was an act of order in a place of utter chaos, but Royce was like that. He also didn't need any additional attention on Church, and he'd learned a can in the hall did just that. Royce needed time to figure out his next step—he wanted to be the one to call this in, if that was the right move.

When he opened the door, he froze, the trash can tumbling to the floor as he reached instinctively for the revolver that was at the bottom of Bubbly Creek. Someone was headed out through the window onto the fire escape. The person heard the door open and lunged the last few feet out of the apartment. The sight startled Royce, who then wondered how in the world he missed the person—behind the shower curtain? Under the bed? In a closet? The thought sent a chill down his spine. He rolled awkwardly to his right, in the event that the shadow turned back toward him with violent intent. But the only pain coming to him was a stab in the side from the leg of an overturned table that he'd landed on.

After waiting a beat and seeing that what he assumed was a Klepp man had gone, Royce got to his feet and was out in the hallway, down the stairs, and out in the street in under a minute. He saw no one, not even the Ford Focus that he expected. Out of sight, but not out of mind. In fact, Royce couldn't think about anything else.

CHAPTER 26

Mike Church needed Becca Goldman. Not in the way that he knew that he imagined Becca wanted, but rather because if he was going to make out a case against the developers of Quayside, he was going to need access to the materials at the Rockefeller Law Library and the help of librarians and law students. His Westlaw account, which would have given him online access to all the legal material he needed, had been deactivated. At first, he thought it was just that he couldn't remember his password, but the reset didn't work. And when he called the reference attorneys for tech support, they referred him to an account manager for Rockefeller, who couldn't figure out what happened. Church suspected the worst. Hence the need for Becca.

A paper note left in Becca's mail folder in the hallway told her the meeting of her "Church group" was taking place at eight p.m. on Wednesday. He gave her an address. Church couldn't afford to email or call her, because he figured they were listening. He didn't risk going to the Law School either—they were definitely tailing him. He'd seen them. Or, at least he thought he did. He was taking no chances. The lawyer who lived in the apartment down the hall from his had a son applying to law school, and Mike used the chance to get in the good graces of a professor at a top school as a means of persuading him to put the envelope with the invitation in the folder of Student 6739. As he sat the bar at the Billy Goat Tavern, he hoped the boy could be trusted. Becca could read between the lines.

Becca pushed through the revolving door at 7:59 p.m.—always the eager beaver. She was smart enough and trustworthy. Church pulled the hood on his sweatshirt off his head and onto his shoulders, turning to let her notice him. Then he downed the last few inches of an Old Style in one gulp and raised his chin up to signal her. In a minute, she was on the greasy plastic stool beside him.

"What is this place?" she whispered, looking around at the assorted mix of jackhammer operators and pole climbers and sewer men hunched over "cheezeborgers" and drinking "Coke, not Pepsi" as the sign out front declared.

"A favorite. And out of the way." He raised his hood back up. "Try a burger, they're actually pretty good."

"I couldn't even find this place. I've been walking around searching for it for fifteen minutes." She signaled to the waitress and ordered what he was having.

The Billy Goat Tavern was on Lower Michigan Avenue, which only about one percent of visitors to Chicago and slightly more Chicagoans knew existed. Daniel Burnham, the architect responsible for Chicago the way Pierre L'Enfant was for DC, had the idea for a double-decker roadway along the Chicago River at the turn of the twentieth century. The idea was simple—make Chicago more beautiful by having trucks and boats and barges and other purveyors of dirty business ply their trade on ground level next to the river, while shoppers and strollers and businessmen moved about on the elevated streets above. The subterranean efficiency gave way to a dark and grimy and ignored world of delivery trucks and vagrants. It was the realm of the Morlocks, while the Eloi above strolled along The Magnificent Mile.

While Church waited, noshing on a burger, he imagined Becca holding her nose and steadying herself on her Manolos as she descended the metal staircase that led down from the Wrigley Building, then avoiding the homeless and puddles, unsure if they were water or urine. He was certain she'd be dressed up, either out of ambition or what he imagined might be her motive.

Squirming beside him, Church could tell she'd not yet figured out this was a tragedy, not a comedy. He whispered solemnly, setting the mood lights to deep blue.

"I need your help," he turned to her, his eyes screaming the urgency of the ask.

"Of course, Professor," she cocked her head to the side and exuded pure empathy, mixed with a look of desire.

"It's about our case. Bubbly Creek," he said the name so softly he could see her reading his lips to hear it. "I need you to pull together a case file—a trial-ready case file."

"Sure. I can pull the team together—"

"No," he bit. "Just you," the tone was more measured. "This has to be...well—" he turned away, took a sip of souring beer, and then slowly leaned toward her, "—discreet." The word dripped out.

Church saw the gleam in her eyes, which, he thought in that moment, were beautiful.

"You can count on me, Professor."

"Great." He breathed deeply. "I knew I could." Church put his hand on her shoulder.

"What's the case? Do we know what we are dealing with?"

"Quayside, our site, is sitting on an ocean of naptha and benzene and coal tar and other petroleum distillates."

"Naptha?"

"The byproduct of various refining operations that existed in that area from the late nineteenth century through the end of World War II. Rockefeller—the guy, not the college—built numerous facilities in Bridgeport and along the Chicago River. They brought in coal from the mines of southern Illinois and oil from fields in Ohio and Pennsylvania. At these sites, they produced natural gas from the coal and oil." He went full professor, forgetting for a moment he was hiding under a hoodie at a dive burger shop in the bowels of Chicago.

"Isn't natural gas cleaner?" She played the student well.

"We didn't know how to transport natural gas as we know it until the 1950s. Until then, most gas-powered lighting and so forth was produced through a chemical treatment of coal or oil. Basically, you turn coal or oil into gas by heating and treating it with toxic chemicals. The plants on Bubbly Creek lit up Chicago as it grew from nothing to a city of millions in a few decades. But back then development was all that mattered. They just dumped the byproducts into the ground, into the creek."

"Byproducts, like naptha?"

"Yes, naptha, which they hadn't yet figured out how to use for other purposes. Also, coal tar, aromatic and aliphatic hydrocarbons, and what they called, 'blue billy,' an especially nasty potion of cyanides and other noxious chemicals. Basically, a witch's brew of stuff that will kill you. You certainly don't want to live on top of it. It's a cancer volcano."

"And this is all under the plot of land that is about to become condos and shops and a park?"

"Yup." Church took a bite and chewed deliberately.

"Well." Becca smiled as if she'd found her calling. "This is exciting."

"That's a word for it."

"Can I ask you a question, Professor?"

"Of course. What?" It came out snippier than he intended.

"Why all the cloak-and-dagger? Why *this* place? The hoodie? Is there something you aren't telling me?"

He paused and smelled in the grease. The answer had been planned and worked over, but all that went out the window when she asked. *Planning is essential*, he remembered his dad telling him, quoting some old general, *but plans are useless*.

"There's...this...well, let me say it this way: when we file this case, it is going to be an earthquake. Powerful people are not going to be happy. So we need to be careful."

"Aren't you always causing the earth to move for powerful interests? I mean, why is this case any different? I haven't seen you at your office—I've come by several times."

"Dangerous is another one."

"Excuse me?"

"Another word for it. Dangerous. We need to be very careful."

"Yeah, when I went to the site the other day, I had a strange feeling…"

She stopped. The look on her face reflected back to Church the look on his face. Scared of the shock he saw, he turned to face the bartender and raised his hand to get another drink. Without looking back toward her, unable to stand her gaze, he admonished her.

"We can't go there. You *shouldn't* have gone there, Becca." He let a deep breath pour from his nostrils.

"You're scaring me, Professor. Why shouldn't I have gone? I was just doing some due diligence with the neighbors—you know, like you taught us." She sounded perplexed. But then, as she heard what she'd said, she was starting to connect the dots and see the picture form.

"They're following me, Becca. Well, at least I think they are. Maybe I'm paranoid. But I feel like I can't use my own computer or any of my other resources at the Law School. I'm living in a motel by Midway airport. That's why I need your help. There was a…a fire."

"Fire? Professor, what fire? What have you gotten me into?" She backed her stool away without standing up.

"They're probably following you." He sputtered, lobbing a warning at her.

"Who? Why would they follow me?" She looked over her shoulder instinctively. Before he could formulate a response, she talked on, working through the scene at Bubbly Creek and how it related to this in her mind. "A man came up to me."

"A man?"

"He asked me what I was doing. He seemed nice enough. I wasn't scared. Not as scared as I am now. I gave him your card."

"Did he threaten you?" His voice was tender, like a worried father.

"No. But, maybe I was just too blind to see it. I was obviously part of something that I had no clue about." Her voice trembled at the realization.

"I'm sorry, Ms. Goldman. I am truly sorry. If I had known, I wouldn't have gotten you involved in this." Church shook his head. "Can you forgive me?"

"Forgiving isn't really at the top of my agenda right now, Professor. Surviving is."

He let out a deep sigh, and she mimicked it, as one would sympathetically yawn.

"We need to leave town. I have a place…" He froze.

"I can't. I…"

"I have a place. Well, my family has a place. It's a cabin. In the North Woods. Wisconsin. Up near the Canadian border. It is remote and stocked and we can work there."

"I'd love to help you, Professor," she paused in case the opposite meaning of that phrase wasn't clear, "but don't know if I can just drop everything. Drop out of school and go to some rando cabin in the woods? I'm not sure I can do that. Do you understand why I don't think I can't—" another pause and a few blinks of her long eyelashes, "—as much as I want to help you."

"I guess you're right." He took a long drink from his pint glass. "So? What then?"

"I don't know, Professor. I just found out that I'm being stalked. That we're in jeopardy. I haven't even processed this yet. This isn't a cold call in one of your classes—I need some time to think. I need to talk to my parents."

"No!" He reached out and grabbed her wrist. She looked down it, pulling it away carefully. "Don't tell anyone. We have to keep this…you know…"

"Look, Professor Church, I'm not going to let this case ruin my life. I'm telling my parents. I'm involving the authorities. I don't really care what you say."

"You can go to the police if you want, Becca, but I doubt it will do you much good. There were a thousand shootings in this city last year—I don't think a law student claiming she's being threatened by mysterious forces is going to get their attention. Do you have any proof? What exactly will you tell them?"

"Why haven't you gone to the cops?"

"The same reason. What would I say? I can't prove anything. What I know and what I can convince others is true are two very different things." It was law school 101, and, for a moment, they could pretend they were in Classroom IV on a typical Monday morning, not plotting in a subterranean dive bar.

They drank in unison, thinking as they did.

"I'm not running away. They have nothing on me anyway," she said confidently.

"Look, at the least, I want you off the case. Drop out of the clinic tomorrow. Make it obvious—post something on Facebook about how you're sick of me. Tell everyone at school and around town. Maybe how hard I'm working you or something like that. Then, just go to your classes. Keep your head down. Hopefully that will buy us some time for me to figure out what to do."

"Okay, Professor. I'll do that."

"Good." They raised a glass to each other.

"Cheers" they said, looking into each other's eyes with hope laden with doubt.

"Oh, one more thing." Her burger arrived, and Church waited until the waiter went away to continue. "I need the files you have. Our notes. The original samples we took. Measurements. The pictures and the diagrams. Whatever is in the case files. Can you do that for me? Get those to me?"

"Sure. No problem. I have the banker's box at my apartment. It's got all the stuff. I can ask the others for their stuff too."

"Be careful, and indirect," he admonished.

"Will do. When do you need this?"

"Tomorrow. I'm leaving town. Headed to the cabin at nightfall. Meet me at the bar at Johnny's Ice House."

"The hockey rink?"

"Yeah, it's called the Stanley Club. On Madison. Meet me there at seven tomorrow."

"Sure thing."

She took a bite of her hamburger.

"Good. I think this will work. I'll go to the cabin, and figure out what to do about the research I need. Maybe get Westlaw back up and running. I can make this work." He didn't feel reassured by his own words.

"It might. Let's hope so." She eyed him sympathetically. "Why the ice rink?"

"No reason—I just tried to think of the last place they'd be looking for me."

A bar in an ice rink in a borderline neighborhood was indeed out of the way, but Church knew if they were watching, they'd be watching him there too. He suspected they were watching now, and figured that he was putting Becca at greater risk by meeting her. But he needed those files. He had no case without them. And, as bad as these bastards were, he doubted they'd kill someone like her. Not for money. No one would snuff out a life like hers for money. Or, at least he hoped, as he watched her walk out into the night.

CHAPTER 26

Twenty-four hours later, Mike Church sat at the end of the J-shaped bar at the Stanley Club nursing his third Bulleit rye. The plastic "Labatt" cup didn't even bother him at this point—his mind was on the door not the déclassé service. He checked his watch, then glanced at the door, hoping to see Becca push through. But she didn't. It opened and closed a hundred times with a screech in his mind, and each time he expected her smile and a present in a big cardboard banker's box for him. But every time he was disappointed.

Out of boredom and in search of any distraction, he stared too long at the waitress, her well-sculpted body stuffed into pale blue jeans that were a size or two too small. When he'd stared long enough, he watched the parents looking out the floor-to-ceiling windows of the bar at their prodigies a floor below, skating and stick handling. Church knew enough to know that none of these kids were headed to the NHL or even to a D-1 scholarship. He held this fact over the tiger moms and dads who moaned and who groaned, who leapt and gasped, as if they did. It was cold comfort for the disappointment he felt each time the door creaked and Becca wasn't there.

Church pulled out his cellphone, then looked over to the ice as a crowd of parents yelped at a peewee making a save. The shrieks were like Pavlov's bell—he turned without thinking. But it was nothing, so he found Goldman in his contacts and pressed dial. The phone went immediately to voicemail, and a recorded message told him that it was full. This was expected when he called his mom, who routinely let voicemails pile up undeleted in her phone, but shocking for a millennial. Messages were never ignored. It was like a golden retriever not fetching a stick.

A lump formed into a softball in his throat. He tried to dissolve it with the rye, but the Bulleit went down with a burning slide. He tapped the bar so Blue Jeans could pour him another. "Double," he mouthed. He rang again. And again. And again. Each time, the same response. A text went unanswered. And another. He tucked the phone back into his pocket and looked seriously at his rye. Swirled it, while images of Becca swirled too.

The parents for one game filed out and others filed in—the kids on the ice got older, probably bantams or midgets at this point, but the parents stayed the same age. Their enthusiasm was lower, however, as they likely understood the stakes on the ice better now that their children weren't getting calls from Boston University or Minnesota, Duluth. But still they came and still they watched and still they cheered. Church was struck by the triviality of their attention. He was waiting on a box of documents that could expose the biggest environmental crime in the city's history. He was waiting to find out if his student was alive or dead. They were exhilarated by a plastic puck going into a net. But then it dawned on him—their excitement was, while trivial, about family, about love, about achievement. All culture, from hockey to the Metropolitan Opera, was arbitrary. We all just need something to care about, to share. It didn't matter that sticks and ice and pucks and cross-checking penalties were completely silly. Hockey was as human and as important as what he was doing. He took another long drink.

"Hey, buddy," a deep baritone echoed from down the bar. "Over here."

Church looked up, jiggling like a bobble head, vision blurred.

"Me?" he slurred to no one.

"Yeah, you." The man, a thick slab of humanity in a Blackhawks T-shirt and topped with a growing-out buzz cut, stood from his stool and shuffled over toward Church. "I'm Dave." In Church's mind, the man's hand swayed like a steak hung from a string on the ceiling. He ignored it, knowing his chance of bringing his hand into contact with it was low.

"Mike. Nice to meet you. Can I buy you a drink?"

"No, thank you. In fact, why don't you skip the next one too? I think you've reached your quota." He said it loud enough so Blue Jeans could hear him. She looked over as he did, giving him a slight nod.

"I don't mean to be rude," Church spat, "but it's none of your business. I'm trying to drink my cares away. In fact, I think I'll have another. It's been that kind of day." He looked toward the bartender, but she avoided him. "Excuse me? Another," Church demanded. "And one for Doug too."

"The name is Dave." The man reached onto his belt retrieved a Chicago Police Department badge and placed it on the wooden bar with a thud. "Detective Dave Feinberg. My kid is a bantam. An '04. I've never seen you in the Stanley Club before. Do you have a kid who skates for the Jets?"

Church eyed the badge, then looked up at the officer.

"Nah, I'm supposed to be meeting a friend. No kids. Maybe someday." He pushed the plastic cup with a finger left of rye to arm's length and put a fifty-dollar bill on the bar. "I think it's time for me to go. Thanks for your help, Detective."

Bag retrieved, Church headed toward the door that Becca Goldman never came through. When he opened the door that led out to the rink, the cool of the air coming off the ice slapped him in the face, giving him the confidence he could get to his car and make it to the motel where he'd been staying. The two flights of stairs down to the street cast doubt on this prediction, but he made it to the landing and pushed out of the glass doors onto Madison Street.

Out on the street, he reached for his keys, ducking his head slightly to look into his pocket, since his fingers weren't doing the job he needed them to do. As he did, one of the glass windows behind him exploded. His senses and responses dulled by the ryes, Church stood frozen, trying to figure out what was going on. Before his mind worked it out, he was on the sidewalk, face pinned against the concrete by the weight of a large person who'd collapsed on top of him. Turning his head slightly to the side, he felt the burn of the sidewalk on his cheek. Out of the corner of his eye, he saw Detective Feinberg, his arms raised and held out, holding his service weapon, which was pointed out to the street. Church tried to wiggle free, but Feinberg's knee pressed firmly into the middle of his back.

Bang! Bang! Bang! Church saw the explosions burst from the tip of the detective's weapon. *Ratatatatatat!* The response came back. *Bang! Bang! Ratatatatat!* Call and response. The bullets whizzed and ricocheted, as Church tried to burrow through the cement to safety. Another bullet hit the glass behind them, showering them with bits of glass. There were screams and screeches of tires. More blasts from over there and right above him. Then, in an instant, the weight pressing into his back went limp, and Church felt Feinberg fall beside him on the sidewalk. A second later, Church heard the crunch of steel against steel, followed by an explosion. Then, nothing. There were no more shots, there were no more screams.

Church rolled onto this side so that he could face Feinberg. He wasn't moving, although Church was looking at his back. His savior wasn't saving him. Church wiggled over, grabbed the detective by the shoulder, and pulled him over so his back was flat on the sidewalk. As he did, Church saw that there were holes the size of quarters where Feinberg's face had been. It was black and sunk in. Unrecognizable. The person who had come to his aid in the bar, who had trailed him out of the bar to protect him from himself, and who had just saved his life was now just a pile of lifeless meat. Church vomited, then rolled back over onto his back. He tried to catch his breath, but he vomited again. It spewed up, then back down his throat. He gagged, then spit it all out on the sidewalk. It mixed with Feinberg's blood, which was now pooling beneath him and seeping into the concrete.

Church waited for a second, resigned to the possibility that Feinberg's fate awaited him too. Although hidden by the cars parked all along this side of Madison Street, he knew they offered little protection from the monsters that stoved in Feinberg's face. He knew that in a moment, a figure would appear on the sidewalk and put an end to Professor Church.

The moment passed, and then another. Church got to his knees and looked through the window of a Land Rover out into the street. On the other side of Madison, about twenty yards to his left, Church saw a Jeep Cherokee on its side, flipped over onto a parked car and smoking from under the hood. He stood up, shaky on his legs like a new-born foal. Church couldn't see what had happened to the people in the Jeep—he figured they were here for him, not Feinberg. They were incapacitated for a moment. A moment he needed to make his own.

Church reached into his pocket, fished out his keys, and stumbled toward his car. He wasn't waiting around to find out exactly what happened or who was who. The choice between fight or flight was clear, and he didn't care who was alive and who was dead. For a millisecond Church felt bad for Detective Feinberg, who he assumed had been trailing him out to his car to take his keys and call him an Uber. For another millisecond, he wondered if he had a family and thought about his fellow officers finding his body and working the mystery of his murder. But Church didn't have time for this. It would be a drive-by that missed its target. These were more common than bird song on West Madison Street.

Church fired up the ignition, hands shaking and mind swirling. Sirens screamed their arrival. Ten seconds later, he was racing toward the Eisenhower Expressway. The shock had counteracted his inebriation, giving him just enough focus to maintain his lane at a reasonable speed. Church tried to go with the flow, although he felt like ramming into the tractor trailer in front of him. If he didn't die, he'd find safety in the Cook County jail. When he thought of the scene back in front of the ice rink, he felt his right foot tense. But then he thought of his parents and how it would ruin them. And he thought of Becca. And the people who would be living on top of a toxic waste volcano. With the images of them in his mind, the people he could still save, he eased back.

When he was out of the city and finally heading north, he took a moment to think about how close he'd come to death and how he was now alone in the world. Up until that moment, it was still a game. Even after the fire at the chemistry building, it seemed like there was a way forward in which he'd still be the hero. But as he pushed the accelerator down and pressed north toward the cabin in the woods, he worried that he wouldn't even make it there alive. The thought nagged at him as he drove and drove, putting more miles between him and the scene. Between him and Bubbly Creek.

As he approached Janesville, just across the border into Wisconsin, the gas gauge read empty and his bladder read full. Church pulled into a Shell station and swiped his card. He eyeballed the others filling up, and he wished desperately to trade places with them, if just for a moment. To be worry free, to go back to their ranch house, pop a beer, and watch *Game of Thrones*. He envied them in their simplicity.

Car full and snacked up, he headed north again. When, after hours and hours, he finally sobered up and entered the dark and wooded realm of his childhood summers, he could still feel the panic. But now, in the world of his youth, the panic returned in the form he took when he was a kid. Of bears and snakes and boogey men lurking in the dark. The chill of the night air and the croaks of the frogs would normally have settled his blood pressure, but they just added to the dread of the scene. Even the familiar smells and sights of the cabin, the wood paneling, the smell of smoke, and the lap of the lake against the rocky shore offered no comfort. They merely reminded him of everything he had to lose if he couldn't figure a way out of the mess of Bubbly Creek.

CHAPTER 26

The outbound Green line train was late. Royce was headed back to Hyde Park, and he was using public transportation to make tracking him more difficult. With a moment to kill, Royce opened his phone and dialed his family. He was looking for his youngest, Siobhan. It was nearly her birthday, and he suspected the next few days might be so hectic that he'd forget. Already feeling like he was failing as a dad, he needed to start rebuilding his trust and his love with his daughters. Missing a birthday was not on the to-do list.

"Shivy-bivy," he cooed when Jenny passed her the phone.

"Hey, Daddy. I miss you."

"Miss you too, sweetie. I'm calling to wish you a happy, happy birthday."

"But it's not until Wednesday, Daaaad." The extra syllables dripped with annoyance. Thirteen.

"I know that. I was there the day you were born..."

"You've told me this story a million times."

"Come on, give your old man a break. Let me tell you again."

"Okay, make it fast, Dad. I'm meeting Maia."

Royce stood on the train platform, staring across at the passengers on the northbound side, all looking down at their phones. For a moment, he was transported out of this life and into the one he'd lived before.

"Your mom, she was in a lot of pain. I mean, not that you were causing it. It's just that sometimes—"

"I know about babies, Dad."

"Right, getting old on me. Anyway, we'd been at the hospital for about two hours, and they wanted to accelerate the process, so to speak. So, they gave your mom some medicine—Pitocin, I think—and sent us to bed. You know me, I hate hospitals. Worst night's sleep ever. A few hours later, your mom woke me up saying she was in pain. I told her I'd get the nurse. A groggy nurse came in and said, 'Let's take a look...' She lifted the cover draped over your mother. I was standing beside her, yawning. Trying to stretch out the knots from sleeping in a chair. The nurse—Sandy, I think—looks under there and screamed. Kind of a panicked yelp. Made me drop my coffee. She lunged for a giant red button on the wall. 'Doctor!' she yelled out the door. Then, she turned back to your mom. 'The baby's here!' Turning to me, she yelled, 'Grab a leg!' I did, and then you came out like a Nolan Ryan fastball. I caught one leg and the nurse caught the other. Greatest day ever. I mean, it was totally gross, but amazing too. I'm glad I was there to welcome you, to catch you, even though I'd have preferred to be in the waiting room with a scotch and a cigar. You know, like the old days."

"Well, I'm glad you were there, Daddy."

"Me too, kiddo."

Royce paced back and forth on the train platform as he talked. The pain of separation ate at him, a metastasizing tumor of regret and recrimination. He could feel the hurt, feel it growing inside him. It was just a matter of keeping it under control. But he wasn't sure whether these calls were the treatment or the disease. Claire always said that chemotherapy was the art of nearly killing patients to make them better. He hoped the pit in his stomach when he finished talking to his girls would someday be replaced by relationships he'd always taken for granted.

The platform was nearly empty, a few kids sitting on a bench at the far end, their heads wrapped in over-sized, neon-colored headphones. What looked like a homeless man huddled in the corner. Two women with shopping bags stood where they thought the train door would open. Royce scanned them briefly. No threats. He went back to the phone.

"Any of your sisters close by?"

"Nope." The clock was running out.

"What are you guys doing for your birthday?" He regretted the question as soon as he asked it. Better not to hear about the details—they'd make his regret more real.

"Mom's taking me to Nella."

"Nella?"

"My favorite...oh, right. It's a pizza place. You'd like it, Dad."

Royce gulped. It was like a punch.

"Well, you have a great time, sweetie."

"Thanks, Daddy. I love you."

"I..."

Royce felt the push, but initially thought it was just someone jostling past him. His first thought was that it was odd since the platform was hardly crowded. But as the contact increased and he stumbled forward, it dawned on him. He tried to turn to identify his attacker, but then quickly turned back toward the track as he felt himself falling forward. Preservation trumped investigation at that moment.

He landed with a thud, rolling onto his side. Fifty yards ahead, a CTA train barreled toward him, brakes screeching. He could see the conductor's face, a look of shock, of fear, of a career-defining moment etched in her face. Arms tense and extended, she was screaming, maybe at him. Injured but not incapacitated, Royce used his feet to push off the rail. He propelled himself backwards, like a backstroke swimmer launching off the starting blocks. Years of squats in the gym paying dividends. As his feet came over his head, he felt the train rush past and come to a flying stop. Faces at the windows looking out, but unable to see him, wedged as he was in the space between the train and the low wall that separated the two sides of the track.

Relief. Then pain. Searing, gut-wrenching pain. He reached around and felt a piece of metal wedged against his back. The adrenaline masked the pain, so it was the wetness on his hands that gave away the injury. A deep puncture wound. Looking at his hand, it was unmistakable. Deep red blood poured out of him. Unsure of who or what was waiting for him on the platform when the train pulled away, Royce decided not to stick around to find out. He sat forward, trying to do a sit-up. The steel bar, perhaps a loose piece of rebar, burned with an intensity he'd never imagined as it exited his body. The pain caused him to piss his pants.

He reached around and put his hand on the wound with as much strength as he could muster. Then he rolled over the half wall and onto the northbound track. A few people on that side of the track were now gathered in a semicircle watching, two on their phones, presumably calling for help. Royce crawled toward them, and then took two helping hands and somehow made it up onto the platform. He collapsed onto his back. Catching his breath, he looked over at the other side, and saw the train still there, blocking the view of those on the other side of the track. The northbound train arrived, shielding him further. But he had only minutes. He needed to get out of there.

He sat up against the urging of the good Samaritans. A gasp came from behind, as someone saw the blood seeping into his clothes and dripping onto the platform. There were screams and calls for help, people urging him to do this and that, talking to each other. But it was all white noise. His head was spinning and his ears were not working right. It was like someone pushed mute and slow motion at the same time on his remote control. The chaos of panicked commuters swirled around him, adding to his stress and pain.

Royce made it to one knee, and then to his feet. He accepted a towel from a woman who appeared to be on her way to the gym. He stuffed it into the space between his shirt and the wound, and secured it with his belt, cinched as tight as the pain would allow. The train on the other side was still standing, now empty of passengers. The person who pushed him wasn't visible. He still had a moment. A deep breath, the most painful of his life given what must have been several broken ribs, and he was gone, down the stairs and onto the street.

No doubt they'd be watching, so he ducked quickly into an alley, and then moved as fast as his injuries permitted through an open side door, into a storeroom, out through the front door of a Verizon store, and onto another busy street. His only hope was that they presumed he had been crushed by the train, and that they were back at the station waiting for the EMS to confirm it once the train had been moved. But that would be a while, as they waited on the CTA emergency response crew, as well as the first responders to get on scene.

He felt the stare of passersby, stumbling and bleeding and panting as he was, his pants dripping in urine and blood. Each step sent shocks of pain up his spine and out into his fingertips. He couldn't feel his lower extremities, but by some miracle, they still moved him along.

He ducked into a Starbucks on the corner and stumbled into the bathroom. It had a keypad, but just as he arrived, someone was coming out. He grabbed the door and pushed his way in.

Water into his mouth and all over his face made a huge difference. He sat on the toilet and caught his breath. Reaching back to the wound, he felt the towel soaked with blood. He repositioned it and tightened the belt to the last loop. Top priority was getting off his feet and slowing his heart rate to reduce the flow of blood. A hospital was out of the question. If Klepp drew half the water in this town that Royce suspected, he wouldn't be safe in a hospital bed, doped up on painkillers. He had to keep his wits and assess his injuries. If the steel bar punctured his kidney or bowel, then he'd have no choice but to find a hospital. If he could make it that long. Maybe he could get out of town, to Indiana or the suburbs. But, if it was just a puncture wound in the abdomen, as long as it wasn't the aorta, he figured he could manage. Stopping the bleeding was the top priority.

Opening his phone, he located himself on Google Maps, and then searched the nearby buildings for options. A Walgreens three doors down, and a "men's hotel" a block and half away. The start of a plan. Deep breath. Another splash of water, and he was back on the street.

Aisle five. He filled a plastic basket with supplies, dropped fifty on the counter, and ran out without ringing up the items. The cashier shouted after him, but there wasn't time for either of them to think much about it.

Royce calmed himself at the entrance to the Ewing Annex on South Clark Street. A simple white sign hung over the door, reading "Hotel: Men Only." There was a pawn shop on one side and a restaurant selling fried fish and shrimp on the other. It was a Russian nesting doll of poverty. The smell of grease and seafood turned his stomach, but he overcame the urge to vomit. He took a breath, buried the pain, and walked in.

The entry way was cluttered with signs, mismatched furniture, and disheveled people of all types. He fit right in. He limped as unobtrusively as possible up to the counter and rapped on the thick glass with his Penn State ring. A burly man in a plaid shirt and skinny necktie appeared, staring down his nose through cheaters at Royce.

"Can I help you?"

"I need…" he struggled to form the right words, the pain freezing his brain and disrupting the connection between it and his mouth. It hurt to talk. "I need a room, a bed, whatever you've got."

The clerk eyed him suspiciously. Nearly all the tenants were black and extremely poor, and Royce was obviously neither. Even in his state, he was no fit for the Ewing. But not asking questions was sort of why it existed and had so since the 1950s.

"You're in luck," the clerk said, looking down at a thick book, smudged and torn. "I've got one cube that just opened up."

"How much?" he blurted out between gasps.

"Twenty per day, a hundred per week, three fifty per month."

Royce put two crisp hundreds on the counter, and slid it under the thick glass partition. A key to room twenty-five came back. He took it, maneuvered his way through the crowded lobby, and headed to the stairs. It was on the second floor, but it was the only option. Royce paused on the first step gripping the handrail with his right hand with all the strength he could muster. Somehow, he lifted his left leg up, and then dragged his right leg, soaked with blood and barely functioning, up behind it. Then, fifteen more times. He'd climbed the one hundred twenty steps of the Pyramid of Coba in the August heat of the Yucatan. That was easy by comparison.

At the top of the steps, he turned right down an impossibly narrow hallway that reeked of urine and BO. The perfect combination to mask his scent. Halfway down on the left, a two and a broken five hung askance on a thin wooden door. The room, no bigger than six by nine, had a cot topped with paper-thin sheets and a pillow the size one gets on a low-budget airline. The walls of the room ran up to about four feet from the ceiling, and the cubical was topped with chicken wire. There was no time to even process the absurdity of it all. Royce kicked the door closed and collapsed on the bed. He reached into the Walgreens basket—*I walked out with the basket!*—and removed the bandages. Belt loosened, he pulled the towel away from the wound. The pain sent shivers over his entire body, and he vomited onto the floor. Working quickly, he poured an entire bottle of hydrogen peroxide down his back. He applied the largest of the bandages, and then wrapped a bandage around his waist as tightly as he could manage. Collapsing back on the cot like a building being demolished, he covered himself with the sheet and a wool-like blanket that was folded at the foot of the bed. He passed out. His last thought as he did was that he hoped he would wake up.

CHAPTER 27

He dreamt of Alex. Of Alex's pain, of his blood seeping out of his body, of his last thoughts and what they might have been, of his lost life. Royce knew that Alex felt no pain when Gerhardt's men put that bullet in his brain—that his death was instantaneous and that the pain was reserved for the ones he left behind. But this was a dream, and in his dreams, Alex could feel the life drip, drip, dripping out of him, just as he was certain Jante had. In Royce's fits and starts of deep sleep, Alex had time to imagine what he'd miss and how his loss would damage so many lives. Alex's pain welled up inside of him, and with every roll onto crushed ribs, every turn onto a badly bruised kidney, and every squish of the blood pooled against his bandage, Royce cringed in agony for Alex.

The sleep ended with a gasp. Royce sat up and vomited again onto the floor. He could hear some music coming from the cubicles around him and mumbling voices echoed throughout the Annex. But the odor was what woke him. Not the smell of homelessness or rancid fried food. That smell he'd smelled when he arrived, and he knew it still lingered. It wasn't that. It was the reek of death. He had smelled it many times, of course. There were corpses of varying states of decay seared into his memory, each with its own particular stink. Three days gone smelled different than ten days gone, and, on top of that, context mattered. A body left in a dumpster behind a Chinese restaurant reeked of death infused with garlic and five spice, while one abandoned in the desert of northern Mexico smelled indistinguishable from the lizards and antelope whose bodies were also known to be lying around in various states of decay. This smell was something else entirely. It wasn't just the smell of death as of dying. It was the smell of *him* dying. It was wet and fetid, an acrid odor of his insides rotting and putrefying that made his stomach do cartwheels. He wretched again, and in doing so felt the stab of pain in his lower back. He could feel the heat too.

Royce reached around and removed the bandage. Pulling it away from where it had been stuck for hours hurt like he was pulling a scab off his entire body. The bandage told a frightening story. Black with blood, as expected, but also covered with a yellowish-green ooze. He tried to bring it to his nose but pulled it back before it got within a foot. Infected. Badly, rottenly infected. There was no mirror in the room, but everything he needed to see was on that bandage. Death on its way to the party.

Another bottle of hydrogen peroxide down his back, but it wouldn't be enough. He pulled another large bandage from the Walgreens basket, and put it in place with a wince. He bit the tip of his tongue, while he wrapped the ace bandage around his waist. The simple task exhausted him, and he collapsed back on the cot. That's when he felt the sheets, soaked in sweat. A press of his forearm to his forehead confirmed the worst—a temperature that must be running at nearly one hundred four degrees. He was closer to death than he thought. There was no time to waste. He had to be treated.

He tried to sit up, but his broken ribs said no. They poked into his lungs and sent shots of pain radiating in all directions. He felt urine pool into his pants again and seep out into the sheets. He looked down past his chin and saw that the stain was tinged with blood. His kidneys. Bruised at least. Maybe worse. Time was of the essence. He tried to swing his legs around, but there was simply too much pain. He lay back in his blood, urine, sweat, and vomit. *Think*.

Claire! Even circling the drain, he had enough sense to remember Claire, the one woman you'd want on your side when death was approaching. Royce reached into his pocket and pulled out his phone. The screen was cracked and it was covered in some kind of fluid, but when he wiped it off, it worked. She answered on the second ring.

"Royce, I'm on service. This isn't a good time," she answered without giving him an entrée.

"Claire, I'm dying. I need you."

She'd never heard him like this, and it scared her. Royce was the rock, the stoic one, the one you could count on. He didn't need you, you needed him. Claire excused herself from a conversation with a nurse and stepped into a utility closet.

"What are you talking about? Where are you?" Her tone was a screaming whisper.

"I…they pushed me in front of a train. I'm hurt. Badly hurt. I'm at a hotel—more like a flophouse. The Ewing something. On Clark, or maybe Dearborn. I can't remember. Anyway, room twenty-five."

"How are you hurt? What do you mean, dying?"

"I got stabbed by something—maybe a piece of steel or a bit of the train. I'm not sure. It bled badly. I lost a lot of blood. Now its infected. I think I've got some broken ribs and I'm pissing blood. I've got a fever and sweats and it stinks to high heaven. Can you help me?"

"I can get an ambulance there in a few minutes."

"No! Claire, no ambulance!" Every bit of his energy went into the scream.

"What? Why? This isn't something to mess around with, Royce. We need to get you to the ER. ASAP."

"Claire, if I'm right about what I'm up against, I'm not sure I can trust the police. And I won't...be...safe...at...a...hospital..." His voice trailed off.

"Don't be silly, Royce. I'll bring you here. I'll protect you."

The other end was dead.

"Royce? Royce? Royce!"

Claire picked up her phone, ready to dial 9-1-1. Then she thought about Alex, and how Royce had been right about what he was up against. What they were all up against. His paranoid fantasies about the president and the FBI were true. She stopped dialing. Instead, she found her fellow, gave her instructions on several upcoming patients, and headed for the bridge that connected the children's hospital with the adult hospital across the street. She signed out her pager and texted a colleague that she had an emergency downtown that needed urgent attention. Coverage achieved, she quickened her pace. Two floors up, she found the adult ICU. She was on a mission. She was going to need supplies, and not ones dosed for kids. For the first time in her life, Claire was going to steal.

CHAPTER 28

Claire moved confidently down the corridors of the ICU, letting her eyes scan nurses' stations, carts, and patient rooms for what she was looking for. The white coat and hospital ID hung prominently around her neck next to her stethoscope, bought her not a second glance from anyone. She ducked into an empty exam room, shut the door, and rifled through the drawers. She filled her tote bag, a Glaser Designs beauty Alex bought her when she made full professor, with bandages, antiseptic ointments, iodine, a suture kit, needles, tubing, saline solution, and rubber gloves. As she was filling her bag, a nurse walked in, then stopped short, as if he were in the wrong room.

"I'm sorry, is this..." He peeked his head back and looked on the door. "Did you have this room?"

Scared to death, Claire turned calmly and stepped toward the nurse.

"Why can't we ever have supplies where we need them?!"

He moved forward to help, letting the door close behind him.

"What are you looking for?"

"I got it, I got it. I just had no sterile pads in my room. Ridiculous!" She pushed past him. "Thanks." *Whew.*

Moving on down the hall, she was still in search of what Royce really needed.

There! On an unattended cart outside of a patient's room,

there were several IV bags. Claire took out her phone and pretended to field a call from a colleague. She turned away from the cart, then backed slowly into it, as if distracted by the call. "Yes. That sounds right. Fifty milligrams...I see..." she spoke to no one. When her back made contact, she eased the Glaser down from her shoulder onto the cart, letting it come to rest such that the IV bags were between her hip and the tote. Without looking, she used her free hand to lift them up and drop them one at a time into her bag. No one was watching, or at least she thought so. *Let's hope they aren't just saline.* Someone was going to catch hell, but this was a matter of life and death. And the nurse could just make a quick run back to the pharmacy. Problem solved.

In the Uber on the way to the Ewing Annex—a quick Google search with the clues Royce gave her yielded only one possibility—she opened her bag to reveal its secrets. As she pulled things out, she felt like Mary Poppins, half expecting a floor lamp or X-ray machine to be hidden in its depths. There was a bag of saline with glucose, but also ampicillin, metronidazole, and gentamicin. A home run. She had what she needed. She just hoped it would be enough.

The Uber pulled up in front of the Annex, and Claire checked the address on her phone. She was afraid to get out of the car. Afraid of malingerers and the grime. Afraid she'd be mugged or worse in the time it took her to get inside. But mostly afraid of what awaited her in room twenty-five. She could see Royce dead in a pool of his own sweat and blood and piss and puss. It made her gulp.

But if she could tell parents that their child was going to die, that nothing could be done to stop death; if she could insert an inch-and-a-half needle into the spine of a baby to extract fluid; if she could attend funeral after funeral of patients who she'd come to love as her own, she could do this.

When she walked into the lobby, every eye turned toward her shapely and well-coifed frame. No one this beautiful or clean had ever crossed that threshold. And women, being banned from the place, were even more rare. Claire was the rarest.

"Ma'am," the clerk said with a surprised and condescending tone, "this is a men's hotel. I'm afraid we don't—"

"I'm not here for a room, thank you," Claire said politely. Bears and honey and all that. "A friend of mine is staying in room twenty-five, maybe checked in in the past day or two. He's hurt, and I'm his…well, his personal physician. I need to see him."

"Personal physician, eh? We don't have very many guests with their very own personal physicians. So, excuse me if I call bullshit on that one. Why are you really here?"

Claire held up her ID and opened the top of her bag, holding it up on an angle so that the clerk could see.

"Look, I don't know what kind of kinky sex you're into or drugs you think you're planning to do up there, but this place is not the place, sweetie. We might not look like much, but we are a clean place. If you know what I mean."

"It's Ernie, right?" She read the faded name tag through the glass.

"It is."

"Ernie, I am a doctor at the Rockefeller University Hospital. My brother-in-law is in room twenty-five. He was hurt; he came in bleeding profusely. You probably noticed. Now he has a serious infection. If I don't get up there now, he may die. Do you want a paying customer in that room or a dead body?"

The look on Ernie's face couldn't hide that he was flummoxed. It said he believed her, but also that he'd been wrong about believing people in the past.

"You've got thirty minutes." He buzzed her in.

Royce didn't answer her knocks or calls. The door appeared quite flimsy, so she pushed hard with her shoulder. She'd seen enough cop shows to have a bit of the technique and more than enough desire. It gave way, revealing her ex-brother-in-law in shock and near death.

"Royce! Royce!"

Claire stepped over to him, avoiding the vomit in her Jimmy Choos. The smell burned the lining of her nose. It made her gag. She touched his shoulder. He groaned his disagreement with being awoken. Rolling him onto his side, she felt his fever. It was in the danger zone. Ernie made a good decision.

She pulled off the bandage, causing whelps of pain. The wound was festering, a geyser of puss and sick. Claire put on gloves and emptied her Glaser onto the cot. She popped the top off the Povidone-iodine and opened the suture kit. With the scalpel, she tried to gently remove the puss that had hardened around the wound. The bleeding appeared to have stopped, at least externally, and that was a positive sign. But she wanted to clean the wound thoroughly, since it had been soaked in urine and who knows what else for the last day. With each gentle brush, Royce writhed in pain. Finally exposed enough, she poured the entire bottle of iodine on the hole, now gurgling with blood. A large wound patch went over it and the surrounding tissue for six inches in each direction. Claire taped the patch in place, and finally wrapped a large foam belt around his torso to put pressure on the wound. As she did, it was obvious he'd suffered kidney damage and a number of broken ribs. He urgently needed to be seen at an adult ER. This wouldn't be enough.

It had been a while since she'd inserted an IV—they had a full-time phlebotomist on staff to take care of that for the attendings—so she eyed Royce's vein like a three-foot putt to win the U.S. Open. It was something she should be able to do, wouldn't forgive herself if she couldn't do, but she was unsure whether she could actually do in that moment. The needle went in, no problem. Claire looped one of Royce's shoelaces through the top of IV bag and, standing on the edge of his cot, looped the other end through the chicken-wire roof. It repulsed and even amused her when she burst through the door, but now she thanked goodness for it.

Last step. She stripped the sheets, undressed Royce, and

covered him with her angora sweater. The doctoring had been done, but to recuperate, he needed more. She'd have to get him fresh linens, a comfortable pillow, some food and fluids. Claire wiped the floor with the dirty bedsheets and put them in her bag. It would need to be cleaned and disinfected too. Alex would understand.

The next day, Claire returned with a care package. Clothes, sheets, blankets, Gatorade, snacks, stuff to read, and Alex's old laptop. Ernie understood, even smiled a half smile at her. Royce was asleep when she arrived, but he opened his eyes when he heard her voice. She changed his dressing and IV bag. The fever broke, and the stink couldn't be detected in the hallway. Progress. Healing. Claire, the Healer.

"Claire, is that you?"

"It's me, Royce. I'm here to help you."

"Thank you. I..."

"Save your strength. I'll be back in a few hours. But, in the meantime, can you scoot to the side so I can put some bedding on the cot?"

Royce used all his strength to move to this side and then that side of the cot. When his head hit his pillow from home, she could see a sense of relaxation in his eyes. His breath was still labored and the pee on the floor was still laced with blood, but for the first time since Royce called, Claire let herself be optimistic.

"Claire, I need a favor."

"Anything. What do you need?"

"My wallet." He tried to point to the pile of clothes on the floor that used to be there, but that Claire had taken home to clean.

"I've got it, Roy. What do you need?"

"Business card."

Claire fished the wallet out of her bag. Inside, a few hundred dollars and a few credit cards were soaked in blood and other fluids. Stuck to one of the bills was a stained business card.

"Marcus Jones, Esquire. Who's that?" she asked just as he passed out.

CHAPTER 29

The Law Office of Marcus Jones was two sparse rooms above a bodega at the corner of 63rd Street and Martin Luther King, Jr. Drive. A once prosperous area—the Harlem of Chicago—the area now was pockmarked with vacant lots. The only commerce left was check-cashing shops, liquor stores, and off-label fast food establishments.

An outer room had a reception desk where a receptionist or a paralegal might sit, if it could be afforded. Gray metal filing cabinets left over from prior tenant—a bill collector who couldn't pay his bills—sat expectantly along one wall, and a Mr. Coffee circa 1985 gurgled on a card table on the other. A few folding chairs were arranged around a low coffee table, a copy of the *Chicago Tribune* and the *South Side Weekly* in a neat pile. The hope of clients hung in the air like rotting meat.

In the inner office, Marcus Jones sat at a long conference table stacked with papers and Redwells. A dozen cigarette butts, smashed at a wide variety of angles, lingered in a large ceramic ashtray his niece had made for him. When Claire walked in before her knock even registered, the lawyer's head was in his hands. Not out of deep thinking or frustration on how to approach a legal problem, but rather boredom. There were clients—evicted tenants, people denied disability, custody battles, petty crooks looking for a loophole—and there was some satisfaction in helping his people, but it wasn't the life he'd wanted. He got to wear a tie to something other than a funeral for a friend killed in a drive-by, which was more than he could say for most of his crew, but he should be wearing a thousand-dollar Italian suit, not one off the rack from Men's Wearhouse.

"Mr. Jones?"

He jerked his head up and smiled broadly. A potential client, and one that it was immediately clear could transport him sixty blocks north with the flick of a pen. A Montblanc probably.

"Yes, I'm Marcus Jones. How may I be of service to you?" He was out from behind the desk in an instant, striding confidently toward her with his hand outstretched.

"Claire Buc..." she caught herself. "Johnson. Claire Johnson."

It was a common enough name, but one could count the number of rich white women in this neighborhood in any month on one hand, and none had certainly made their way up the narrow flight of steps and down the unlit hallway to his office.

"I knew a Johnson once," Marcus quipped.

"He's my ex-brother-in-law. Or, if you mean...Alex, er, Professor Johnson, he was my husband. Ex-husband...I'm sorry. It's all been, uh, disorientating."

"Have a seat, Claire. May I call you Claire?"

"Yes, yes, of course. It's Dr. Buckley, actually, but Claire will do just fine."

"Okay, Claire. Disorientated is going around, it seems." Seated back behind his desk, Marcus motioned around the room. She followed his hands and his eyes. To the water stains in the corners of the popcorn ceiling, to the paint chips dangling like autumn leaves, to the linoleum floor and the large oval rug straight out of a '70s sitcom. "I had a job lined up at Sidney & Ellis. Making two hundred fifty thousand a year. Now I'm doing bail hearings for fifty bucks a pop. Pretty fucking disorientating."

"I'm truly sorry for you, Mr. Jones."

"Marcus."

"Okay, Marcus. I'm truly sorry for you. I lost the father to my children to those bastards, and one of them nearly killed me. We are all suffering in our own ways."

It was true, of course, but he didn't feel selfish in thinking that he was suffering the most. This rich lady had no idea what it took to get from where he came from to where he was going before it got snatched away. She'd leave here in a Range Rover and go back to her yoga classes and tea at the Ritz. He'd stop at the White Castle for some sliders and try not to get shot on the way to his dingy apartment. Then, another day of low-end ass-work for the bottom of a society he'd fought so hard to get away from.

"I'm sure we could spend the whole day wallowing in each other's miseries, but I've got clients to help and I assume you've got patients or whatever. So, can we cut to the chase? The stroll down memory lane is bumming me out. What can I do for you? I'm not exactly your kind of lawyer, am I?"

"Royce sent me. They tried to kill him."

"Gerhardt's guys? Damn."

"No. He's moved to Chicago and started taking some cases as a private investigator. You may have heard the dean at your old law school was murdered on the lake front."

"He's working that case?" Of course, Marcus had heard about it. You didn't have to be the former president of Rockefeller Law's BLSA Chapter to have followed the murder of the first African-American dean of a top law school.

"Indeed." Claire looked at her pager, but then clipped it back to her belt. "I don't know what he's uncovered or even if it is about that case, but someone pushed him in front of a CTA train."

"Damn."

"Almost killed him. He escaped by an inch, but he has suffered some serious internal injuries."

"That sounds like him. Motherfucking Superman."

"Yeah, he does have a knack for getting into and out of situations."

"That's one way to put it. Now, I don't want to sound heartless, but what does this have to do with me? He doesn't think I did it again, does he?" Marcus's smile gave away the joke. They shared a laugh. He could tell that Claire liked him.

"No, obviously not. I think he needs your help."

"And why would he think I'd help him? *Remember*? Plus, sounds like he needs a doctor, not a two-bit lawyer. Unless he needs a will—I'm getting good at those."

Claire reached into her purse and pulled out the business card. The blood and other bodily fluids had discolored it and made it brittle. She handed it across the table, and Marcus took it reluctantly.

Their eyes met, and Marcus swallowed hard. It was a turning point. These people had caused him no end of trouble and heartache, and he had no reason to believe things would be different this time. Plus, seeing Royce and going back would be too painful. There were too many bad memories. The chase down the alley with a bullet ricocheting past his face. The arrest that morning at his mother's house with the look on her face and the cries of his niece down the hall as the SWAT team kicked in their door. The time in lockup, the humiliation of the trial, the complete loss of whatever faith he had in the judicial system to sort right from wrong. Too many memories.

He fingered the card, looking at the dried blood like its patterns would reveal an answer. On the other side of the table, a desperate woman and an opportunity to do something other than trying to keep Mrs. Evers from being evicted. He wasn't sure how this was going to get him to Sidney & Ellis, one of the most prestigious law firms in the country, but if he let her walk out that door, he was sure it was never going to happen. Maybe Royce Johnson was his way out, his way back.

"Okay. I'll do it." Not for Royce, but despite him. But he'd keep that to himself.

CHAPTER 30

Stepping into the flophouse, Marcus reflexively buttoned his suitcoat. This was a thoroughbred walking into the glue factory. Out of the side of his eye, Marcus surveyed his fellow man—they were all men; all fallen and bereft of hope. Most were black like him. Most had come from where he had, and Marcus knew that a different step this way or that way, a seemingly insignificant choice to do this and not that, and he would have been right there with them. Or worse.

Royce was asleep, the pain of his wounds evident on his face. Marcus regarded him for a moment. The feelings were mixed. A bit of him wanted to grab a pillow and achieve his revenge. Another bit felt sorry for him. Just another dumb cracker who didn't know he was a dumb cracker. Then there was the bit that wanted to smack him in the face for all he'd done and not done. No part of him wanted to wake him up and ask him about their next moves in the Royce and Marcus show, but that was what he did.

"Marcus," Royce said through sleepy eyes. "I'm glad you are here." He tried to sit up a bit but gave up with a moan.

"I can't say it doesn't delight me to see you like this, Agent Johnson. I know that makes me a less than ideal moral being, but I accept the imperfection of man. It makes living life so much easier, and better. And, although I don't condone what these bastards did to you, I hope that when you're lying there you're thinking about what you almost did to me."

"Can't we let bygones be bygones?"

"Not fucking likely. I'm not sure why I'm here, actually."

"'Cause I need your help and you need something in your life other than doing welfare claims and tax foreclosures. Come on, Marcus. That's not you. You've got bigger—"

"You don't know me, man. Don't pretend to think you understand what makes me tick. You don't and won't."

"I knew you'd come. When I was dying, I handed your card to my sister-in-law. I knew you'd come when she asked you. And when I went to sleep last night, I knew I'd see you this morning. Even though I nearly got you killed. I knew you'd come. I think that means I know what winds you up." Royce smiled and eyeballed him.

"Well, I almost didn't."

"But you did."

"Yeah, I did. But that doesn't mean you know me. It was just a guess."

"Call it what you want. I'm just glad that you're on my team—you came. Whatever the reason."

"But I'm about to walk. Maybe I just came to tell you to fuck off. Which is really what you should do."

"Fair enough. What can I do to make you stay? I need you—I can barely lift my head off the pillow."

"I don't need you, Agent Johnson. I've never needed you."

They watched each other. The cards were played. It seemed to be a draw, which meant returning to the status quo. Marcus back to his life, and Royce to die from his suppurating wounds or a bullet in the head.

"That's too bad. But this isn't about me. It is about Jante. Don't do it for me. This is about her. Do it for her, despite me."

"I don't know this lady—why would I care more about her than about you?"

Royce pointed to a bag by the side of his cot. Claire had

retrieved his briefcase from Alex's house and brought it to him under strict instructions not to peek inside. But he told Marcus to do just that. Marcus picked up the bag and retrieved a manila folder. As he did, a set of pictures fell out, spreading out on the grimy floor of Royce's cubicle. Some fell picture-side down, but the ones that did not showed a gruesome scene. A woman strewn on a dirty bathroom floor, a large blood stain covering her chest, her face frozen in a surrealist expression. Marcus reached down and picked the other pictures off the floor. Leafing through them, he saw the heart-stopping juxtaposition of before and after that haunted every investigator—a faculty headshot of a beautiful black woman, smiling in front of a bookshelf and then that same face capturing the last moments of a life. He studied the pictures of the entry wound, just above her left breast, the toilet where she fell and hit her head, the blood-soaked floor and the drain that sent her life blood out to Lake Michigan. He swallowed, his own heart in his throat.

"A friend in the CPD got me those. She was like you, Marcus. A South Side girl. A comer."

Marcus rolled his eyes up from the photos and looked at Royce. Then, he couldn't help but look again—that base human instinct to see what shouldn't be seen.

"So?" he said, barely able to hide the cracks in his shell, widening by the moment.

"Look at her, Marcus. Look what they did to her. These are the same people who tried to do the same thing to you. To both of us."

"You're not saying—"

"No. This wasn't Gerhardt or anything political in that way. But even though it was different people, it was the same people."

"Are you suggesting I should risk my life for some dead lady just because she's black? That she's from my hood?"

"Yes. That is exactly what I'm saying."

Marcus admired the honesty. Matters of race and class and who owed what to whom weren't often spoken of in such blunt terms. And, if forced to do so, Marcus would admit that Royce had a point. The only way matters would improve for South Side kids like him was if the ones that could help did. Sure, Jante was dead and couldn't be helped much, but the next Jante, the next Marcus was out there, and raising the price on murdering them was a pretty noble calling.

"That makes us a racist. Again."

"If thinking you should do what you can to help people like yourself, to make things better for other kids, is racist, then I'm a racist. I call it giving back. I call it giving a shit. I call it a lot better than toiling away at some law firm. Not to mention—"

"Don't fuckin' mention it." Marcus hated that Royce knew of his state in the hierarchy of his chosen profession.

Marcus tucked the pictures inside the envelope and put them back in Royce's briefcase. He walked back and stood at the foot of Royce's cot. They eyed each other again—just as they did in the Walmart parking lot and in the FBI building in Chicago before that. Royce broke the silence.

"So, what do you say? Will you help? Help me, help Jante? Come on, partner."

Marcus let out a big sigh.

"Okay. I'll do it. But not for you, and only if you stop calling me partner."

Royce smiled with half his face, the other half twisted in pain. He moved to reach his hand out to shake, but then second-guessed it and lay back down.

"It's a deal, partner!"

CHAPTER 31

The pilot eased the Chicago Police Department's forty-four-foot Archangel Class SAFE boat alongside a smaller Hurricane yacht. The yacht had been headed out to Lake Michigan but had stalled along the north side of the river channel that cut through the skyscrapers of downtown. The pilot brought the boats within shouting distance, then idled its fifteen-hundred-horsepower engines.

"What's the problem?" the sergeant shouted over the gurgle of the engines. He waited, then tried again, up a notch. No response.

There was no one on the port side, and the sergeant couldn't see anyone in the pilot house either. He sighed.

"Skip, pull around," the sergeant commanded as he stepped carefully along the edge of the boat. There were only a few inches of space between the side of the boat and the door to the cabin, so he turned sideways, hugging the wall with his butt. As he came around to the front of the boat, he grabbed a gaffer pole, and thrust it out toward the yacht bobbing in the morning tide.

When the boats were alongside, the sergeant jumped aboard, his right shoulder tensed in case he needed to reach for his service weapon.

"Chicago Police!" he shouted. "Anyone onboard?"

"Over here," a man's voice whelped.

The sergeant could tell it came from down near the waterline. He quickened his pace and bounded across the decking. When he came around on that side, he saw a single individual on his knees, torso thrust over the side, looking down at the water. The man wasn't barfing, which was the most common sight the sergeant saw on these waters from people in this position. The next most common reason was a man-overboard, but he wasn't holding anything or flailing around in rescue mode either.

"What's the matter?" the officer asked, stopping short, ready for anything. "You really shouldn't be stopping in the channel during the morning rush."

The man turned on his knees to look at the sergeant, who was standing at a tense half-turn.

"You'd better see this. I was just about to call it in." He breathed out of his nose loudly, as he got to his feet.

"Are you alone on the boat, sir?" the sergeant asked.

"Yes, yes. Get over here." His voice was urgent and a little scared.

The sergeant lumbered over, steadying himself on the handrails. He was in no rush. He'd seen it all. Looking over the side, he saw a person floating face down. It appeared to be a woman—dress, long hair. But it was risky to assume these days. The body was clearly lifeless, so the sergeant stood and stared. She appeared to be young, and not in the water long—her body wasn't bloated or discolored. This was fresh. He'd seen this before. He'd seen it all.

He looked up to the shore. The boats were floating ten feet off the shore directly in front of the Centennial Fountain. The sergeant knew about the fountain. Down off Michigan Avenue and hidden away at the side of the river, it was a spot where illicit things happened—drug deals, solicitation, and the occasional OD. But he also knew because his great-grandfather—or was it his great-great-grandfather?—had been a sand hog on the project that reversed the flow of the Chicago River, an achievement that the fountain commemorated.

The sergeant was not a detective, but the story he was a part of seemed straightforward. After a night of drinking, the woman, and maybe a friend, made their way down to the fountain to watch it cascade down to the river. She strolled along the edge and lost her balance. Heels, drink, the allure of the edge. Maybe a selfie gone wrong. It was a combination he'd seen become fatal more times than he'd like to recount. People were drawn to water, to cliffs, to danger.

Grabbing a push pole from the deck, the officer reached into the water and flipped the body over. It was indeed a young woman, and she had been in the water just a few hours he reckoned. Her eyes were closed, but her mouth was frozen in a last gasp. She'd struggled for her last breath, and it was there for the men on the boat to see. Even though he'd seen it all, the sergeant was embarrassed to see it. The moment belonged to her, and the voyeurism of it unsettled him, just like when the boys took him to a strip club to celebrate getting his stripes.

"Dispatch, I've got an eleven-forty-four," the sergeant said in a formal tone into his radio. "In the water by Centennial Fountain."

Just as he released the talk button, the fountain threw a giant arc of water over their heads and both boats, reaching all the way across to the other shore. It did this on the hour every hour for ten minutes. Reflexively, the sergeant checked his watch—seven on the nose. The water fell like rain on them, the drops making the water around the victim dance. Her body bobbed among the drops aimlessly, not reacting to the moment. All joy extinguished in her, whoever she was. Turning away, and finding cover under the awning of the boat, the officer reported the details to dispatch. He then sat down with the man who'd found the body and took a statement. By the time the ambulance and land units arrived on the scene, the sergeant was back aboard the Archangel, which was now tied to the shore. The body of the woman, who he'd learn soon enough was a student from New

York studying law at the university, still bobbing in the water, secured to the boat with a line like a fish.

Checking his email the next morning, Royce Johnson opened his daily Google alert for mentions of Rockefeller University. Prone on his cot, he could still feel the rebar poking into his back and reverberating through his torso and out of the top of his head. Just navigating around the screen with the trackpad on his computer made him want to wretch. He wished for a medically induced coma, but there was no time to sleep the way he needed. In fact, he was sure that if he slept too long in this place, he wouldn't wake up, either from what he'd catch or from what they'd do to him if they found him.

Thankfully, after a quick scan, a distraction appeared. A story caught his eye and quickened his pulse. He clicked and read:

Chicago—Becca Goldman, 23, a student at Rockefeller Law School, was found dead floating in the Chicago River yesterday. Her body was discovered near the Centennial Fountain by a fisherman who was headed out to Lake Michigan early Wednesday morning. He alerted authorities, who were able to identify the body based on a student ID recovered at the scene. Authorities indicate that the incident is being investigated as an accident. Preliminary toxicology results showed the presence of drugs in her system. Police Spokesperson Michael Fitzpatrick said that the police believe she accidentally fell into the water while walking along the Riverwalk…

Royce read on, but what captivated him was not the story of her youth and how she came to Chicago or her parents' grief, but the photo that accompanied the article. There was no mistake—this was the woman he'd seen at the Bubbly Creek site going door-to-door. The woman who'd given him Mike Church's business card. The wholesome do-gooder who was taking a school project seriously. By all accounts, a good person who unknowingly stepped in front of a Mack truck.

Convinced that the woman's death was not an accident and that it was somehow related to Jante's murder, Royce texted Marcus—*Be careful.* For now, he'd leave it that.

CHAPTER 32

Marcus drove straight through. The Chequamegon-Nicolet National Forest, five and half hours due north of Chicago in the North Woods region of Wisconsin. Somewhere in the woods was a middle-aged law professor who they needed to crack the case. Marcus was on his way to find him. To motivate him to action and to bring him back into the fold. Time was of the essence, he was told, so he didn't even stop to pee. A used Gatorade bottle sufficed.

Prone on his cot at the Ewing Annex, Royce gave him the address of a cabin in the town of Three Lakes. His instructions were simple: find Mike Church and get him in touch with Royce. Numerous calls and texts to the clinician over the past forty-eight hours went unanswered, and the attempt on Royce's life made the public unveiling of the lawsuit even more urgent. The case and the link to Jante Turner's murder were not yet completely clear to Marcus, but the assignment intrigued him. He'd never been north of Milwaukee, and it was exhilarating to just get out of the city.

The Impala could be linked to him directly, and he didn't know who was watching. Marcus rented a Nissan Maxima at O'Hare using a bogus ID and a credit card that a fixer in his neighborhood got him for five hundred dollars. "Take no chances; trust no one," Royce told him. It seemed overly dramatic, but he did say it from just this side of death, the bad guys having pushed him in front of a train. *Better safe than dead.* Plus, the cloak-and-dagger made him feel, well, different than sitting behind a desk filing out Medicaid disability forms.

Turning left on State Route 32, headed west toward Spirit Lake, Marcus was in awe. The area's twenty-eight interconnected lakes—the largest chain of freshwater lakes in the world—created a landscape out of a fantasy movie. Spits of land gave way to vast tracks of water. Around every corner a new angle revealed vistas he'd only seen on TV. This was the land of water sprites and forest trolls in his mind, even though the three thousand or so people who called it home were just typical Cheeseheads—beer-loving, Packers-cheering, fishing enthusiasts with a high tolerance for low temperatures in winter and bug bites in summer.

He passed the Sunset Grill, propped out on the edge of Big Stone Lake, and for a moment thought about stopping in for a drink. He needed one. But a guy like him in a place like that? Not so much. It would have been the scene at the Dexter Lake Club in *Animal House*, only in reverse. The country and western band would have dead stopped when a black guy in a White Sox hat fell into the place. He pressed on. The sooner he found Church and reached Royce, the better. A thousand feet later, Waze told him to turn left, even though there was barely a road. It was more of an ATV or snowmobile trail, but he put his faith in Israeli technology.

The cabin was about what he expected. Thirty by fifteen or so, made of logs, and connected by a long dock to Spirit Lake. He eased the Maxima down the stubby gravel driveway that ended in a small shed that could have served as the garage for a car no bigger than a Prius. He killed the lights. The sun was setting. Hidden in among the thick forest, the cabin was already cloaked in darkness. There were no lights on in the cabin, and despite the cold, no smoke came from the stone chimney that protruded out of the roof like a pipe out of a sailor's mouth.

Fear. He hadn't felt it in a while, and that was a good thing.

But after the past few months, this was a good thing, too. Marcus reached into the glove compartment and pulled out his weapon—a Smith & Wesson .45. Feeling its weight and power, he was alive. He tucked it into his belt and headed toward the front door of the cabin. Church wasn't expecting anyone and seeing him—a strange black man—coming towards the door, might cause Church to do something stupid. Marcus played it cool. He walked carefully down the flagstone path that connected the driveway to the cabin's front porch. His right hand in grabbing distance of the wooden handle of his piece at all times. He called out, "Mike! Mike Church! I'm a friend of Royce Johnson. I'm here to help." As he said it, he realized this was exactly what someone sent to kill him would say. Marcus put his hands up, like he was turning himself in, to show his benign intent. He expected a gunshot at any second. His pulse pounded in his teeth.

No movement. The air and the water were still, and nothing even creaked in the cabin. Cicadas sang. On the front porch, Marcus craned his neck to look through the window, while keeping his torso safely behind the log walls. There were no lights on inside and no sign of life. If this was where Church were staying, he didn't appear to be home. *Maybe he's down at the Sunset Grill*, he thought, tasting the vodka on his lips and feeling the hunger pangs in his stomach as he did. That would be the next stop. The burger appeared in his mind's eye.

A rap at the door went unanswered, so Marcus worked his way around back. A canoe bobbed in the water, clanking against the dock, but otherwise the place seemed abandoned. The rear door—a glass slider—was unlocked and even slightly ajar. In he went, cautiously but calling loudly, the Smith & Wesson a finger's reach away. No one responded.

Marcus had never been in a cabin in the woods. He'd seen them in shows on the old Sylvania his mom had propped precariously on one of those collapsible luggage stands you find in hotels. He was expecting Perk's Pine Lodge from the movie *The*

Great Outdoors, and that's basically what he got. A large central room was roofed by thick timber beams, dominated by a fireplace constructed of huge glacial boulders. Above the ratty plaid sofas hung hunting trophies of deer, a fish bigger than Marcus thought possible, and even a bear head. Taking in the scene, Marcus imagined the people who came to places like these, who relaxed and felt at home here. He wanted to jump out of his skin.

Then he saw him. Just feet at first, protruding out beyond the edge of a sofa set perpendicular to the fireplace. The feet, clad in white socks, were set at ninety degrees from each other. Even from a distance, in the dark, he could tell they were not attached to a living person. Marcus had never seen a dead body, but the person these feet belonged to was unmistakably dead.

Approaching slowly, looking into the kitchen and down the hall as he went, the rest of Mike Church came into view gradually. First his shins and thighs, then his chest, not moving up and down as it should, and finally his head, thrown back and matted with dried blood. Next to his head, a fireplace poker, also covered in blood. Actually, Marcus had no idea what Church looked like, so he couldn't be sure it was him, but he had the appearance of a law professor, not a professional killer. And this was the cabin where he was supposed to be. Odds were Marcus was too late. Or, rather, he'd arrived at exactly the right time. If he'd been there when they came for the professor, maybe he'd be lying there beside him, his brain bashed in as well. He checked the man's pulse, but it was a formality.

Marcus walked to the kitchen, found a bottle of Irish whiskey and a glass, and headed back to the couch. He poured himself three fingers and downed it in a gulp. He'd studied hard and stayed as far from the gangbangers as possible his whole life so that he didn't end up in a room with a dead guy. And now here he was. For a moment, he wondered about destinies and allowed himself to feel self-pity, but then he put the cork back in the bottle and got to work. He snapped some photos with his phone and texted them to Royce. Then, he searched the cabin for Church's laptop. The place was clean. Nothing except some clothes and toiletries. Everything else, including his wallet, watch, and anything of value was gone. Even the TV, likely a tube, was missing from its spot on an IKEA table in the corner. A robbery gone wrong, the Three Lakes PD would say. There was no doubt about that. The murder weapon on the carpet proved it wasn't done by pros. The pros who did do it would count on the local cops to not think two steps ahead. In the event they did, the place was clean.

Marcus wiped his prints off the door handle and ran a wet cloth along all the surfaces he might have touched. He took the whiskey and the glass with him, throwing them into Crystal Lake on his way out of town. Back in the driver's seat after he watched them sink, his phone rang. It was Royce.

"Marcus?"

"He's dead, man. What the hell? You sent me to a fucking ambush."

"Are you okay?"

"Definitely not. I just saw a dead guy. I'm lucky I didn't walk in on them bashing his head in. He was still warm. Could have been me there next to him."

"Thank goodness it wasn't."

"Spare me. What's next? Am I just supposed to drive back to Chicago with the image of that dead white boy in my head the whole time?"

"What choice do you have, partner?"

"Don't partner me, motherfucker. I agreed to help you, that don't make us partners."

"Okay. Relax. I appreciate your help. There are at least three people they've killed, and one more they tried to kill. I doubt they'll think twice about killing more."

"And I'm supposed to 'relax'...Come on. I'm as relaxed as you were that day you chased me down the alley behind my mom's house. Nice and reeeeelaxed."

"Did anyone see you?"

"How the fuck do I know? These motherfuckers probably got drones and shit. I'm gonna be on the evening news up here. First brother ever to set foot in these woods gets lynched for a murder he didn't commit. Sound familiar?"

"Look, if they wanted you dead, you'd be dead. And they wouldn't rely on Barney Fife to do it. Just get back here. Return the car, then get back to the Annex. Make sure you aren't followed. We'll regroup."

"Why are you still there, man? Aren't you on the mend?"

"They don't know I'm here. I'm staying put until we have a plan. Oh, and speaking of that, I need a favor."

"Another favor that's going to get my black ass killed?"

"No, this one is going to protect us both. Trust me."

"Not fucking likely."

CHAPTER 33

Marcus stormed into Royce's room at the Annex, ready to let loose on Royce for almost getting him killed. But the scene made him wince. A putrid smell of rotting flesh and body odor filled the air. Royce lay on his cot, his face frozen in the anguish of a death mask, as he slept. It was almost enough to make him feel sorry. Almost.

"Ahem!" Marcus grunted.

He watched Royce struggle to wake, like he was swimming up toward the surface through a pool of pudding. After a few minutes, his eyes were open enough for Marcus to look into them and see the pain, but also the hope.

"Thank you for coming," he squeaked.

"What have you gotten me into?" Marcus said firmly. "They killed that guy."

"They probably would have killed you had you not stopped for fried chicken every two hundred miles on the way up there."

Marcus breathed out deeply through his lips. He figured Royce was just being playful—in the worst way possible.

"I'm going to let your racist comments alone just because they are trying to kill us."

"Oh, chicken is racist now?"

"You damn right saying I'm stopping for chicken is...ah, never mind. Nope, not gonna."

Marcus could hear Royce smile.

"Ever see *48 Hours*, you know, Murphy and Nolte?"

"Listen, old man, here's some advice, let's keep this professional. Okay? I don't need a friend. I've got plenty of friends, and they don't try to send me up into moose country to get my head bashed in with an andiron."

"Deal. Not friends."

"Agreed."

"What you got for me?" Royce's smile suggested he was enjoying himself too much, and it made Marcus seethe. "Did you get me what I put on my Christmas list?" Royce asked.

"I'm a regular fucking black Santa Claus."

He handed Royce a duffle bag, weighty with prizes. Opening it revealed a shotgun, not his Mossberg but something serviceable, a Glock 9 mm, and a smorgasbord of ammunition. Then, Marcus reached back and handed him a brown bag, stained with grease.

"Al's Beef! You may not be my partner, but you do love me. I won't let you deny it."

"Keep tellin' yourself that, white boy. You're a cop, and I've never loved, will never love, a cop. It's just in my DNA."

"Not a cop."

"Okay, G-man."

"Not one of those either."

Marcus groaned. "Close enough."

Royce was fingering the weapons, checking their actions and appearing to imagine putting them to use.

"Not really, but we'll have to agree to disagree. Partners have to do that all the time."

"We aren't fucking partners!" Marcus was past irritated.

"You brought me lunch. You went street shopping for me. You drove to *Wisconsin* for me. I think we are partners."

"Look, I'm—"

"You can go, Marcus. There's the door. More of a fence gate than a door, really. But walk out of it and leave me for dead. You'll never hear the name Royce Johnson again."

Marcus stood still, eyeing him.

"Okay, partners then. You don't have to like me. Heck, I don't like you. But you need me. We need each other. This is the big time, Marcus. We're hunting killers. Bad people. People who will murder and destroy lives to get their way, to preserve the status quo. You and me, we're the heroes. The good guys. The ones who will do things to help people who can't, for whatever reason, help themselves. Something tells me that's why you went to law school in the first place. Not to fill out forms or get guys off DUIs. I can't offer you a seven-figure salary. But what I can offer you is the chance to make a difference. A big fucking difference."

Royce paused and they looked into each other's eyes.

"Well, I'm still standing here, motherfucker. What's next?"

CHAPTER 34

Royce's instructions were simple—*Know the victim.* He said it in his plain-spoken way. Marcus admired the point. It was true and, once said, obvious. Lots of good points were. Although to a man as smart as Marcus, the implication of his advice was clear, Royce went on: *The victim is the key to every murder. After all, they are the victim, and the murderer chose them for a reason. Figuring out what it is about them that made them the choice out of all the people on the planet is the nut.* It sounded to Marcus like a bad speech. Like something Royce had heard in a grainy video in a stuffy conference room at Quantico, had written down in a composition book in a fit of overzealousness, and then had repeated to everyone and anyone who would listen from that day to this one. But Marcus put the awkwardness aside and decided to get to know Jante.

A bit of googling, and Marcus found Jante's family, or, rather, her mom. Like too many South Side kids, Jante had just one parent. Two was better, there was no doubt. More money, more love, more hands on deck, more perspectives on the world. Marcus would no sooner run down a single mom than literally run one down with his Impala, but if he were telling the entire truth, he'd wish there were no such thing as a single mom. Sure, one was better than two if the second of the two were an alcoholic, a crackhead, a banger. But second-best wasn't good enough for kids like Marcus and Jante. Kids needed the first best.

Jante's mother lived in Pill Hill, a middle-class neighborhood about thirty blocks from the Rockefeller Law School. It was just a few miles south, but no one from that far south made it that far north. No one except the two of them, that is. Jante and Marcus—the two that scaled that flat mountain and made it to Rockefeller. Yes, he'd come from Bronzeville, which was to Pill Hill what Pill Hill was to the Gold Coast, but their stories were more or less the same except for the street names and a few other changes. Changes that were apparent as Marcus headed south on Jeffrey Street deep into the heart of what his sociologist friends called structural racism. To them, the apartment blocks and low-slung bungalows interspersed with check-cashing shops, fried fish joints, and dives advertising "cut-rate liquor," were evidence that the decks were stacked against black America. But even here, among the vacant lots and half-empty arts centers, won so optimistically by alderman and "community leaders," Marcus saw progress and hope. Black people could make it out. He was proof, even if he got spat back.

Further south, around 95th Street, Marcus passed under Interstate 90, known locally as the "Dan Ryan." The name struck him as he did, even though he'd been on it a million times. It was the hunt he was on that made him curious now. He had no idea who Mr. Ryan was, and he didn't really care to know. The only value in knowing something like this was to impress someone at a cocktail party, and Marcus had long given up trying to wow the kind of people who would care about something like that. In fact, he suspected that the days of naming things after dead white guys no one had ever heard of, were coming to an end. They could name them after dead black guys or dead women instead, but he suspected that that might be too controversial, since it would likely be viewed as a statement. Naming freeways after numbers, like they did in California, would be cleaner. "The 90." It had a cool ring. No one could be put out by "The 90."

Whatever it was called, the freeway divided worlds. The world he'd just come through was his. A White Castle here, a public housing block there, people loitering about on a weekday afternoon everywhere, a ball game on a crooked court with chain nets. Then, after passing under a hundred yards of concrete overpass, urban suburbia. The world of taxpayers, not tax-takers. Neighborhood restaurants replaced the fast-food joints. There were florists and banks. A bar method place. The apartments shrunk to two-flats and tan brick bungalows. At midmorning, the streets were deserted, like they were shooting a zombie movie.

Marcus felt his stomach turn over. It was involuntary. He wasn't used to middle-class streets and they were, he wasn't ashamed to admit, way better. No one had ever been accidently clipped in a drive-by in Pill Hill. Perhaps then his recoil was in his DNA, encoded in his Gs and As and Ts and Cs by decades of fear experienced by his ancestors. Crossing under "The 90" into Pill Hill or across "The 94" into Bridgeport meant a brick in the face or through the window, a cross burned in the yard, a chase, or worse. If enough of your ancestors had their cortisol levels spiked when they crossed, the lesson was transmitted, even if no one ever shared it with you. Freeways in Chicago were like electric fences, marking territory and stinging anyone who crossed that wasn't supposed to. Except when they were used to keep out instead of keep in.

Marcus let the Waze app guide him, as he took in the scene of Pill Hill. The one-story houses weren't fancy but they were mansions when you lived in a dilapidated high-rise on the other side of The 90. The lawns were green and the evergreens in front sculpted like tree versions of poodles. As the Impala lumbered by, Marcus could see Mike and Carol Brady inside, yelling at Jan—always at Jan. The whole ten square blocks of Pill Hill seemed frozen in the 1970s. Once an island of affluence, Pill Hill was teetering. Doctors who worked at a nearby hospital built ranches and split levels there in the 1950s, and for a few decades it was a place a doctor, white, black, or otherwise, would have lived. The few square blocks were actually a hill, rising a few hundred feet up from the key-shaped Calumet shipping canal that was cut into the shore at the southern tip of Lake Michigan. Doctors on a hill. Hence the name.

The house at 9211 Clyde Avenue seemed sad. Marcus eyed its unkempt exterior—the grass a bit too high, the bushes untrimmed, the driveway split by a large, grass-filled crack—as he took a drag on a cigarette. Public records told him Jante bought her mom the house, just around the time when she got tenure at Stanford. Plucked from the projects and dropped in Pill Hill, it must have seemed like she'd won the lottery. But now, the house seemed to be crumbling around her. The brick needed tuckpointing. The gutter hung a foot down from the edge of the roof at one end, a small maple bud struggling skyward peeked its leaves above the edge. The window casings were in desperate need of paint. Yet Marcus knew that the real scars and the place where the real renovation needed to be done, was on the inside. He got out of his car, stubbed out the cigarette with his shoe, and walked up to the door to find out how deep the scars actually were. Maybe he could plumb them and find the clue that could help seal them up. And, in doing so, put a bit of putty in his own cracks.

She answered the door casually, eyes bleary, from tears or booze or lack of sleep, he couldn't tell.

"Ma'am, my name is Marcus Jones. I'm a friend of Jante's. I came to pay my respects."

The woman eyed him, unable to respond quickly and seemingly unsure about whether to believe him.

"Marcus? I don't remember Jante ever talking about a Marcus. How'd you know my baby?"

"I was a student at Rockefeller."

She eyed him skeptically, her arm held firmly across the door frame, a *do-not-enter* look all over her.

"Mmm-hmm," she breathed, as she wiped her teeth with her tongue.

"I want to find out who killed her. The police are, well, they're not putting the resources into this that they would if this was a kid from the suburbs is all I'm sayin'." Marcus's eyes pleaded.

"I've got to be at the dialysis center in half an hour, Mr. Jones, but you can come in for a moment."

Marcus noted her slim figure and her white clothes and shoes—a nurse or aid, he surmised, not a patient.

As he crossed the threshold, the screams of children surprised him. They came into view, one trailing the other, hairbrush raised and eyes ablaze.

"Chantel, you don't hit your brother!" the woman shouted, then turned back toward Marcus. "These are my babies. And, now that my Jante is gone, my responsibility." She yelled at them down the hall, "Come in here and eat. We are leaving in fifteen minutes, and you ain't leavin' this house without food in your belly. You hear me!"

Marcus sidestepped a pile of Legos. "If you're busy, ma'am, I can come back."

"No, it always like this 'round here. Come on in, make yourself at home."

Marcus took stock of the living room as he followed Jante's mother into the kitchen. Photos and memorabilia of Jante made the house look like a shrine. Jante in pigtails holding an award; looking skyward in a ballet costume, her long legs forming graceful lines that seemed to stretch her from floor to ceiling; smiling proudly in academic robes. The sadness welled up in Marcus. He bit his upper lip with his bottom teeth and exhaled.

"Do you know what happened to her?" Marcus asked, as he pulled out a chair and sat down at the breakfast nook table, strewn with the morning's dishes. Then, catching the abruptness of it, added, "I mean, sometimes people know things without being able to prove them or know the details."

She poured him tea into a Stanford Law mug.

"Child," she said as she sat slowly into a chair beside him, "I can't but for the life of me think of anyone or any reason. She never hurt no one, my baby." She shook her head and sighed deeply, "Mercy. Lord, have mercy."

"I'm devastated for you and for the children and for everyone who she touched, ma'am. But I want to give her justice. I want to see that the people who did this—"

"Did you know she had a scholarship to study dance in New York?" It was involuntary—just a random fact about her child, who had been destroyed and left to bleed out on bathroom floor. If Marcus had come a few minutes later, it no doubt would have been some other fact, just what she was thinking at the time, the wheel of Jante spinning in her mind. "Turned it down to go to law school. She was always so practical—thinking about what was realistic and what made sense for her family. She supported us all. Bought me this house. Helped her brothers for a while until…" She trailed off. Her gaze on the wall behind Marcus, the corners of her mouth drooping like a melting ice cream cone.

"I knew she was a dancer." It wasn't exactly a lie—Marcus had seen the photos and the medals and the awards in the woman's living room on the way into the kitchen. "And everyone at the Law School spoke of her generosity." He fiddled with his mug.

Silence fell over the table, and Marcus saw tears in the woman's eyes. He met them, but she didn't look back. After a moment, she stood up and walked over to the refrigerator. Retrieving two brown lunch bags, she set them on the table and called for Jante's kids. They bounded around the corner and collapsed into their grandmother's arms. The embrace lasted unnaturally long, and Marcus looked away, overcome with pain at what he was watching. It was something not to be watched. When the kids retreated and could be heard gathering their stuff for the day, Marcus looked back and saw her standing in the center of the kitchen, frozen.

She didn't move as he approached her. Inching closer, Marcus noticed she shifted from heel to toe, and she was murmuring something.

"Mrs. Turner," he called. "Are you okay?" Marcus reached out for her elbow.

"Chantel, come here. Let me do your hair," the woman walked back toward the kitchen table, and pulled out a chair for her granddaughter.

The girl, Marcus guessed about nine, took a seat with a bounce. She pulled a graphic novel from her backpack and opened it to a dog-eared page about halfway through. Handing her grandmother a unicorn-shaped hairbrush over her shoulder, she kept reading intently. The woman took her granddaughter's hair in her hands, and moved the brush through it with long, sweeping strokes. Marcus felt voyeuristic, but he was transfixed. The woman's fingers, bent and misshapen like gnarled tree branches, held the bright pink brush delicately, flinging it and flicking it through the girl's hair with ease. After a moment, the sound of a low hum rose up from behind the girl, whose eyes were set on the page. The humming turned from a murmur into a melody, and then a song, although one that Marcus could not identify. All of the sudden, he was nine himself, in the Baptist church on Cottage Grove, across from the Fairplay, bouncing on his own grandmother's lap while she sang hymns to Jesus. The grief of losing her, and of seeing her across from him in the body of Jante's mother, imagining the grief she'd felt in losing some of her own, overwhelmed him. He wiped a tear surreptitiously. Then, went back to the scene he was sure he'd never forget.

Jante's mother sang her song, her work song. She brushed and twisted and tied her granddaughter's hair until she was transformed into a close facsimile of Jante that Marcus had seen on the mantle in the living room. And then, in an instant, it was over. She tapped her granddaughter on the shoulder. The brush and graphic novel went into the backpack, and Jante's daughter bounded for the front door. Her grandmother reached to pat her on the head, but she was gone too fast. She held her gaze on the spot where the girl had been for a long minute, so long that Marcus had to turn away. As he did, she snapped out of her funk, picked up her keys from the counter, stepped around the table, and headed after her granddaughter. Then, she turned back to him.

"Thank you for coming by," she whispered.

A dead end. She was broken. There was nothing Marcus could do that would glue her back together. Not even solving the case. But it didn't dull his desire. Justice had to be done, one way or the other. He decided to try one last time.

"Ma'am," he said, as they stood on the brick front landing, pots empty of geraniums on all sides, "do you have anyone else I can talk to? Anyone who might help me find out who did that horrible thing to your daughter?" He turned toward her, grasping her forearm gently and turning her a few degrees in his direction.

"Wait for me!" she shouted at the children, running toward a twenty-year-old Honda Accord. Then, softer and more reflective of her mood, she addressed Marcus: "Tanisha." The word was not so much a clue as it was a plea. A plea to let her be, to let her get her grandchildren to school, and to let her get to her distraction—helping patients whose kidneys had died. The look in her eyes suggested that she was going to continue to live out of duty and an obligation toward Jante. To carry on her life through her grandchildren, rather than because there was anything left for herself. Somehow, he sensed, the ripeness of life had gone just a bit past that moment when that particular fruit achieved its maximum sweetness. As he heard the word "Tanisha," he wondered why Jante's mother couldn't savor the lives standing on her crumbling concrete driveway, make them the sweetness, if not the ambition, of her remaining time. But, as she went on to explain that Tanisha was Jante's best friend and that she worked at the Madam C.J. Walker School, down the hill and east on 93rd Street, under the Skyway and bordering on the Calumet River and shipping canal, he realized he was in no position to criticize her. The murder of her baby must have sucked all the joy from the world, as one of her grandchildren might suck all the helium from a balloon, leaving her, as them, in an altered state of being. But unlike how the effects of helium on the vocal cords fade fast, he doubted in that moment that her altered state ever would go away.

"Thank you, Mrs. Turner," he said. Then added, "Bless you." It felt forced to him but she seemed to appreciate the sentiment. She reached out and hugged him. It was if she were apologizing for being so distraught and overwhelmed as to be unhelpful, but was grateful for his work. Over her shoulder, Marcus eyed Jante's children staring at him, as they embraced. They didn't seem to remark the sight of their grandmother hugging a stranger. Their world was so full of oddities and things they couldn't understand these days, Marcus figured. He patted the woman on the back, then headed to the Impala parked out on Chappel Avenue. When he got to the driver's side door, he looked over the roof of the car, and saw the woman tucking her grandchildren into their seatbelts. He got in and did the same, the value of human life never more apparent.

CHAPTER 35

Marcus headed east toward the lake, down out of the relatively rarified air of Pill Hill and toward the Calumet Shipping Canal. As he did, he wondered about Jante's kids, about what would become of them, and about how a bullet in a bathroom sent them hurling through space, spinning on an entirely unstable axis. They tumbled and twisted in his mind as Brady Bunch Land quickly gave way to public housing, vacant lots, and retail behind thick plexiglass and rusty iron bars. Then, as he passed under The Chicago Skyway, the poverty and teetering capitalism gave way to blight. Docks that once unloaded iron ore and coal and coke were grown over with weeds. Their planks hung down like the docks were dipping their toes into the water to test the temperature. Individual smokestacks stood alone; the buildings that gave them purpose, crumbled. Moving further east, he saw the six-hundred-acre footprint of the giant U.S. Steel plant. There, twenty thousand employees once used nineteen furnaces and twelve rolling mills to turn Minnesota iron and Illinois coal into the steel for Studebakers and Fords and Chevrolets. Now, the ghosts of these machines, and of men, were all that remained. Marcus's grandfather scrubbed the floors in the administrative building at the South Works, as they were known, before the union men ran him out for being willing to work hard for less money than they thought right. And for looking like he did.

Somewhere among the fossils of machines and the scrub grass peeking up through the cracked concrete, his ghost wandered. Marcus felt his presence. It was fleeting, and then Jante's ghost appeared in his mind, urging him on.

He found the Walker school on a block littered with tumbleweeds of empty chip bags and orange soda cans. The building looked like it had been taken straight off the set of *Grease*—but this Rydell High had aged worse than John Travolta. The cornices were crumbling and gaps wide enough to house birds pockmarked the entire front façade. Flag poles out front clanked flagless in the morning breeze, as if a coup were under way and the rebels, having stormed the place, had not yet gotten their act together to raise the new standard. Either that, or the person in charge of the flag just didn't care anymore.

Tanisha Dunbar was as easy to find as the school. Marcus walked past an inattentive guard, then asked the first kid he saw in the hall where her classroom was. Two rights and a left later, he peered through a narrow window in the door at a bright-eyed woman with a Shaft-era afro pacing in front of a room of about forty distracted children. Marcus watched. There was no sound, but he could tell she was passionate. The name "Crispus Attucks" on the chalkboard, scripted with a graceful touch, told him they were studying the American Revolution. Stevie Wonder's song, "Black Man" rang in Marcus's head: "First man to die for the flag we now hold high was a black man." In his mind's eye, Marcus could see his mother dancing in her house coat on the braided wool rug in their apartment on 69th Street, singing along about the black man and the red man to Stevie's psychedelic rhythm. He got lost in the feelings of those days, when he didn't know what he knew now, when the roaches were amusement and the boxed Kraft mac and cheese was a treat to be savored. But it didn't last long. Jante poked him again.

Back in the moment, Marcus checked his watch. Coming up on ten a.m. He leaned his back on the cinder-block wall, and waited for the bell. For a second, he was fourteen again, tensed like a runner waiting for the starting gun. It came, and he watched the children file out. They were more subdued and orderly than they were in his school back in the day. Marcus felt a small bit of hope for the future. On the drive to Wisconsin a few days before, he'd heard the rapper Common was proposing a massive new development on the South Works site—residential, commercial, a recording and film center. The South Side was rising. But how long would it take? Would it bring folks like him along, or banish them to Gary, a bit further down the coast? These thoughts were a distraction, but he sensed they were the broth in which Jante's murder happened.

"Ms. Dunbar?" he said, his voice unthreatening.

"Yes?" she answered, then, turned away and, patting a young girl in pigtails on the shoulder said, "See you tomorrow, Tamika." She looked back at Marcus, a perturbed look on her face. "Who are you?" It was curt. "I've only a few minutes for a cigarette."

"I'll walk with you." Marcus tried to defuse the situation. They started to walk together down the dim corridor, lined with lockers, dented from years of kids banging other kids into them for their lunch money or just because. "My name is Marcus Jones. I'm a friend of Jante's. Was a friend, that is."

She stopped, turned on her heel, and glared at him. Then she walked on.

"Jante never mentioned a Marcus to me." She studied him, from his closely shaven head to his shiny Nikes. "I'm pretty sure she would have mentioned *you*." She smiled, admiringly.

"I was a student of hers at Rockefeller. I'm working—"

"Friend." She paused. "Student." She scrunched her face, then tilted it to one side, raising an eyebrow in a way that Marcus suspected her students had seen countless times. "Why do I feel like you aren't being entirely forthcoming with me, Mr. Jones, was it?"

"Yes, Marcus. Call me Marcus." He put out his hand.

"Who are you, really, Marcus? Because, like I said before, I have just a few minutes before I need to prepare for my next class. Pardon me for saying so, these kids matter a lot more to me than you do."

"Look, I'm sorry to bother you. I know this is a hard time for Jante's friends and family. I just sat with her mother and met her children. Mrs. Turner sent me here, to talk to you. She thought maybe you could help me?"

"Help you? Help you, how?" She pushed through a door as she talked, turning the corner with Marcus trailing. He let the question hang in the air like in a cartoon thought balloon. They ducked behind a dumpster onto a gravel patch out of sight of the students, and she pulled out a Newport menthol. Marcus pulled out a lighter and lit the tip, as she studied him carefully through a breath of smoke.

"I'm trying to find out who killed her, and I was thinking you might be able to give me a place to start." He refused her outstretched hand offering him a cigarette.

"I talked to the police already, Mr. Jones." The return to formality bit. "I've talked to them more times than I'd like to recount. At times, I felt like a suspect." She blew smoke through her nose. "I don't need to tell you how that feels—white cops coming here and treating us like Jante's murder is on our hands somehow."

Marcus knew how it felt. And that she knew, and that she'd say it, made him admire her right away. He wished he'd been her student. He thought of her and Jante together, seeing right away why they were friends and imagining the chemistry between them. In another moment, he'd ask for her number. See if she wanted to go with him to the Bud Billiken Parade. But not here. Not now. Not talking about whether she had any leads on the assassination of her best friend.

"I know," he whispered.

"I just can't imagine anyone would want to kill Jante." The teacher drew in another drag of smoke. "I've known her since nursery school. She was a peacemaker, not a troublemaker. Trust me—" she motioned toward the school, "—I know the difference."

"I'm so sorry," Marcus padded the comment with empathy. "I'm also sorry to bother you on your break."

Reminded, she checked her watch, took a furtive drag, then stubbed out the butt with her heel. Even the way she did that—aggressive and elegant at the same time—made Marcus's heart flutter.

"I better get back. World cultures." She smirked. "These kids could use some."

"Okay. I'm sorry to bother you." He admired her, as he trailed behind her. "This isn't a great place for a school," he mentioned as they turned the corner and headed back toward the classroom. They both turned and looked east toward the slag piles and petcoke ash heaps that marred the pristine coast of the lake like chicken-pox scabs.

"You don't have steel mills and refineries in Lincoln Park?" She jabbed him in the arm.

"Proud South Sider," Marcus quipped back.

"I know." She smiled at him in that way that men loved to be smiled at. "And you know that companies dump this shit where the poor folk and the black folk live. They know no one will listen to *our* complaints."

"I hear that," Marcus intoned. He held the door for her, and they walked back into the crowded corridors of Walker High. The cliques and out groups were apparent as they walked the halls, even though he didn't know any of these kids. It made him thankful he wasn't back in school.

"You know Jante was going to take that on as dean?"

Marcus stopped in his tracks. "What? The slag piles?"

"Yeah, and environmental racism more generally. Sue the BP refinery in Whiting. Go after Mittal and U.S. Steel for all the cancer piles they left us. She came up on these streets, even though her mama lives up on the Hill now. Jante played in those slag piles out there—we used to ride them on cafeteria trays like we were in the Olympics—like in that *Cool Runnings* movie." She let herself smile for an instant, then feeling the guilt of it, drew it back in.

"That might make her a target, right? I mean, taking on the polluters. What's at stake, billions?"

"Mmhmm." She pushed into her classroom, where a few kids milled about, sitting on desks and twisting their hair. Marcus followed. "Jante was killed for being good, not bad."

"I mean, someone might," he dropped to a whisper, "kill for that."

"No doubt. But I don't know if that's what happened. I mean, she hadn't even taken over yet. I don't think her mission was public knowledge."

"How'd you know?" Marcus asked gently. He knew the answer, but he wanted to hear her say it.

"I knew because we talked every day." She bit her lip, the loss all over her face. "I remember Jante telling me she had a project in the works already, something on a creek, and that they were going to do big things." She shook her head. "Jante was always going to do big things."

The bell rang. Tanisha Dunbar, on whom Marcus now had a serious crush, gave him a sideways glance, then flipped her chin up as if to say, *Time for you to go*. And it was. Time to go back to Royce and tell him about the possibility that wanting to help clean up the South Side of Chicago, that wanting to give the future Jantes a brighter future, got Jante a slug in her heart. But, first, a stop at the university to find out more about the goings on at the environmental clinic, or what was left of it.

CHAPTER 36

When Marcus walked back through Griffin Gate onto the Rockefeller campus, he felt the same way he did when he was a pawn in his parents' divorce. On those weekends when it was his father's turn to have him, and when the judge said it was okay, he took the nineteen bus to Garfield Park and walked across the threshold of his dad's two-room apartment. Deep in the pit of his stomach, a mix of anxiety, rage, regret, love, and home. To be nostalgic and revolted by a place at the same time splits the mind like a wedge splits a log. After the sledgehammer's first hit, the two halves are still connected by straining fibers, but the fissure that has opened can never be closed. Try as it might, the log will never be the same. With enough strikes, the pieces become their own whole. But, if the lumberjack hits just once or twice, depending on the size and resistance of the wood, the log will remain two and one at the same time.

So it is in the mind. In some patients, the corpus callosum, the connector between the right and left hemispheres of the brain, can be severed. The result is a person with, in effect, two brains. These people walk among us, but don't necessarily stand out. They behave normally, as if their brains figure out how to work together to make their one body do its best to get around in the world. But, if the two parts of the brain are exposed to different stimuli, then a quite different result emerges. The split-brain person becomes two people battling for possession of the same body. The consequence can be a type of schizophrenia—a Siamese twin living inside you choosing for you and sending you off to places you don't want to go.

Marcus's corpus callosum was intact, but his traumatic childhood severed it, as if a neurosurgeon had split it with a scalpel. A dad who used drugs and was thrown out gave Marcus two highly dysfunctional worlds to inhabit. His mother was a God-fearing taxpayer. She bought him new clothes at Kohl's every year and there was always just enough food on his plate, but try as she might, she could never balance all she had to. They existed right at the poverty line, skimming along it year to year like a water bug bouncing on the surface of the water, unable to get more than an inch into the air. Physics and biology just wouldn't let it happen, or, in her case, racism and history and...well, a whole lot of things, Marcus thought.

His mom served her kids and God, in that order, and nothing else. His father's passion was crack. This meant that even when he was clean enough to have Marcus for a few days, his apartment was like an alien planet—dark, desolate, and bereft of creature comforts. The curiosity of a new place made the experience interesting, but one wanted to leave quickly. There was so much to see and experience that was different from his Mom's world, but his oxygen tanks wouldn't last long on Planet Dad. Marcus admired his dad's muscular physique, his way with words, and the charm that exuded from every move he made and every smile he flashed. But he hated his selfish ways and his lies. He wanted to be his father, and the thought made Marcus hate himself. The paradox, which Marcus thought had died when they buried Lamar in a cheap casket that nearly bankrupted the family, came back as he strolled into the Law School again. The two halves of Marcus now split again.

"Excuse me," he said gently as he approached an African-American female student chewing on a bagel and highlighting in a red casebook. "Can I ask you a question?" Marcus chose what he thought was the target of least resistance.

She smiled at him, motioning to an empty chair.

"I'm a graduate of the Law School, a few years ago, and I wanted to ask you about Dean Turner."

The student gulped and narrowed her eyes at him.

"I don't know anything about what happened." She sounded defensive, but Marcus suspected it was just discomfort at the subject.

"No, no. I'm not…I'm merely interested in finding out more about her. I know she wasn't here long, but I figured some of the students here got to know her. Got a sense of the woman. Did you know her?"

"Of course I did."

"Right, of course. It was about time to have a black…er…woman, right?" It came out wrong. She eyed him suspiciously. "I've got a client that is interested in getting to the bottom of her murder. I'm just trying to see if there is anything obvious the cops missed. And I figured the people here might—"

"You aren't suggesting someone here murdered her, are you? Maybe Dean Miller?"

Marcus made a mental note that a student just accused the current dean of offing the former dean-to-be to a total stranger.

"I'm not suggesting anything, just wondering. I'm Marcus by the way."

"Dominique. Nice to meet you. But I've got to run to class."

It was 2:40 p.m. and Marcus knew there were no classes coming up—he had gone here, regardless of what Dominique thought. But he understood why she wanted to be away from him. Marcus pushed the chair out and stood up. "I'm sorry to bother you. Good luck with—" he turned his head sideways and bent over to read the header of the casebook, "—Criminal Procedure." He flashed a smile and was gone.

A few other conversations with students rushing here and there were equally unhelpful. Students who had her for class or got to know her during the dean-search process spoke of her charm and brilliance. No one could think of a reason anyone would want to kill her. Other than wanting her job. A few mentioned Scott Miller again. Marcus could tell that they'd been questioned before, whether it was by the police or university officials. Their answers were not so much practiced as routine. A mine without a vein, as the other investigators no doubt found. Frustrated, Marcus bought a coffee at the Law School café, and took a seat at an unoccupied table. He checked his messages, punting the nonurgent matters to a paralegal he'd hired while pretending to be a PI. He checked the sports scores and rolled through Twitter. As he finished his last swirl of coffee and thought about his next move, a voice behind said something in soft tones. Marcus turned.

"Excuse me."

"Yes? Can I help you?" Marcus asked.

"I heard you were asking about Dean Turner."

"Yeah, that's right." Marcus motioned to an empty seat, putting his phone in his pocket. "Sit down. I'm Marcus. What's your name?"

"I'd rather not, I mean, I'd rather just tell you what I've got to tell you and then move on down the road, if that is okay."

The man was as typical a Rockefeller Law student as one could imagine. Nerdier than the average law student at other schools, which was already pretty nerdy. Thin, pasty, and somewhat aloof, clad in khaki pants and a polo shirt that was too big around the neck, revealing a white undershirt. He was headed for a life of tax appeals and conference calls and sex once a month. Marcus pitied him. Or, at least half of his brain did. He was also going to be retired at fifty-five and would never want for anything.

"Sure, we'll keep this on the down low. What do you know about Jante?" Marcus tried to familiarize and humanize her. But what came next made the preface unnecessary.

"Dean Turner came to us as a savior. I mean, not really. But for the progressive students here, having a woman dean, and also an African-American dean from the South Side, was just such a monumental thing. I know it seems like it wouldn't matter much, but the pictures of twenty-odd white male deans staring at you in the admin wing was just depressing for so many of us. Not because any of them were bad per se. I mean, maybe they were, maybe they weren't. But that wall of white was like a four-hundred-year slap in the face. We finally did it."

Marcus nodded along, familiar as he was with all of this, having felt the same thing himself. The lawyer in him wanted to mention that there was a woman dean once. She had conspired with the president of the United States to sentence Marcus the death penalty for a murder he didn't commit in order to swing the balance of the Supreme Court. She wanted to please those same progressive students he spoke of. But he let it slide. The student went on.

"And she was amazing. Bold and smart and funny and kind and full of empathy and vision for how to make things better. Then, boom. Well, her murder was not just a tremendous personal loss for us. It was also a realization that progress of a certain kind has enemies. Powerful enemies. Don't you dare try to make things better for black folk and working-class people. The powers that be won't abide it."

"Tragic," Marcus said. "But you didn't seek me out to tell me this. I mean, everyone knows this." The student scowled a bit. "Don't get me wrong. I'm not belittling the feelings. I'm just sayin'—"

"Well, I don't know anything for sure, but there was one thing I wanted to tell you that I've never told anyone."

"Why not?" Marcus needed to know this to set the stage.

"I'm not sure. I guess I was afraid. I've carried it around with me, wanting to tell the police or…or someone. But I was worried about a false report or maybe sending the investigation down a rabbit hole."

"Understandable…" Marcus leaned in.

"When I heard you were working with someone on a private

investigation, I just figured it might be a way to run it down without, you know, causing too much trouble in case it turns out to be nothing."

"Look," Marcuse intoned his deepest baritone, "you did the right thing. Distracting the police with a rumor is always a risk, and I can definitely inquire about this without causing too much trouble. What do you know? What did you see?"

"It was a confrontation, an argument of some sort between Dean Turner and an alumnus."

"What kind of argument?"

"The guy is a big donor—he funds a generous scholarship program for top students called the Steinlauf Scholars. I'm one of them. This guy does stuff with us. Dinners. Finds us mentors. Hangs out with us. He is a tough guy, real Horatio Alger story. But also I found him to be very generous, not just with his money but with his time. You can see why I was reluctant to—"

"Right, Steinlauf," Marcus said it like he was writing it down. "What happened?"

"It was a bit before seven in the morning. I get here early so I can snag a free parking space on the street. I like to get my reading done in peace. I was sitting in the corner over there—" he turned ninety degrees and pointed to a couch out of the line of sight of the hall that ran through the center of the atrium, "—when I saw Dean Turner walk in. She wasn't dean yet, but she had that way about her. She was striding toward the administration wing. Anyway, Mr. Steinlauf—he makes us call him that—comes up behind her and he puts his hand on her shoulder. I just happened to look up and see it happen. It looked like he wheeled her around like a top. The look on her face was pure shock."

Marcus took a sip out of his empty coffee cup. As the conversation intensified, he thought of a line from one of his favorite poems: *The mind is its own place, and in itself can make a heaven of hell, a hell of heaven.* All the while the earnest law student talked, Marcus could feel himself wrestling the demon inside, using all his strength to make this new life he was living some kind of paradise. He felt the investigator's tingle. There was hope.

"What happened next?"

"I couldn't hear them. I was too far away. But at first it seemed like a normal conversation. I just figured he was talking to her about the scholarship program or funding something else. The guy donates a lot all over campus. So I went back to my reading for the day. A few minutes later, I looked back up, and she had lost her smile. Her face was...I'd say, concerned. Then, after she said something to him that he mustn't have liked, he got animated and I heard their voices, loud enough to make me take note, but not loud enough to hear. Then, she turned and stormed away."

"Interesting." Marcus thanked him, then asked, "Anything else you remember?"

"Nah, that's it."

"Did you ever tell anyone or get to the bottom of what happened?"

"Not really. I'm not a gossip, you know. Kind of keep to myself. And, like I said, I didn't want to start any rumors. I mean, the guy is paying for me to go here, and it was probably nothing."

"Yup. Most likely. But I'll look into it. And this conversation never happened. Your story is safe with me. Okay?"

"Thanks, I appreciate it." He got up and walked away.

Marcus sprung from his seat. He couldn't wait to tell Royce.

CHAPTER 37

Ruben Steinlauf stepped out of his chauffeured Maybach, pulled his French cuffs out from his tuxedo jacket, buttoned up, and strode into the Four Seasons with purpose. A tourist from Wisconsin or Iowa walking along Delaware Place at that moment would have giggled at the sight. Steinlauf looked like a penguin, not just because of the tux, but because of his short, muscular frame, the slight waddle of his duck-foot gait, and beak-like effect created by his close-set eyes and sharp nose. But this was a killer whale in a penguin's suit.

Steinlauf waddled confidently passed the registration table—he wasn't wearing a name tag or getting a bidding paddle for the live auction. Paying a million for a few tickets to a Blackhawks game would be unseemly, and he didn't write checks smaller than that. His donations came via wire transfer from the Caymans.

The annual "Inspirations Ball" benefited the Rockefeller University Preparatory School, the private school of choice for the faculty, for a few local kids sufficient to make the school less than all white, and for Chicago's intellectually minded millionaires. The Burnham Ballroom of the Four Seasons featured a giant rotating Rubik's Cube and thumped with the music of Michael Jackson, Cyndi Lauper, and Duran Duran. Normally corduroy-clad professors and their spouses were decked out in double-layered polo shirts, parachute pants, and big hair befitting the

'80s theme of the evening. Steinlauf was the only one in a tux, but that was how he liked it. The king wearing purple robes, while his attendants and toadies circled him in brown rags.

He took a glass of white wine that tasted like off-brand grape juice from a silver tray, and made his way to the corner of the room. From there, he watched with amusement as people he otherwise respected made fools of themselves. He nursed his wine and munched on a bowl of carrots and celery. His kids had graduated from U-Prep decades ago, but he was still one of the biggest donors to the school. He wasn't here to contribute but to make a withdrawal. The mayor sent his kids to U-Prep, and so did most of the other powerbrokers in the city. Steinlauf could get meetings with all of them, of course, but events like this provided a ruthlessly efficient way to rub elbows and twist arms without it seeming like he was rubbing elbows and twisting arms. Alcohol was always an equalizer.

He eyed the mayor and decided to cash in some of that philanthropy. Walking across the dance floor, dodging flailing philosophy professors and PhD post-docs like he was navigating a minefield, Steinlauf kept his beady eyes focused on the mayor. As he approached, a security guard stepped between them, but Steinlauf evaded him, ducking his shoulder slightly and sidestepping like a pass rusher for the Bears.

"Mr. Mayor, are you enjoying the evening?"

He saw the mayor's eyes flick away the security guard who was just about to grab Steinlauf by the arm.

"Ahh, Ruben, old buddy. I haven't seen you out on the dance floor. 'Take On Me' is a classic. Let's see your moves."

"I'm afraid the doctor told me my break dancing career is over. New hip and all."

"Well, it's our loss."

"Indeed." They sipped in unison, like a synchronized swimming team. "Can we talk in private, Your Honor?"

They walked away from various security personnel and hangers on. The two made an odd couple, with the mayor pushing six-four and sporting what could only be described as a Cosby sweater. They headed toward the bar, arm in arm.

"I'm worried about Quayside, Mr. Mayor. There are rumors that a lawsuit is imminent. The allegations are spurious, of course, but the blowback from litigation and the negative publicity would be very real, I fear."

"I, of course, have the fullest confidence in our processes, Ruben. I'm sure Max and Tony and their teams have complied with all the various rules and regulations. It is my understanding that things are proceeding apace, and that we are going to see a revitalization in Bridgeport very soon. This is a signature project for us. That's my home turf. My family has been there for six generations. Don't you worry."

The mayor tapped him on the shoulder reassuringly. Steinlauf felt patronized. He wanted to grab his arm, twist it behind his back, and throw the two-bit pol against the wall. But he just smiled. The mayor moved toward the bartender and ordered them drinks. Alone again next to an ice sculpture of what looked like Mr. T., Steinlauf pressed him.

"And the FBI man. What of him?"

"Ex-FBI man. I've been assured he isn't a problem. He has no authority, no jurisdiction. I'm not even sure he's still on the case, wherever he may be. There is also an APB out for him. Parole violation of some sort. The police commissioner tells me that they'll have him soon. We'll bring him back into the light and expose this sham for what it is. We obviously had nothing to do with Dean Turner's death. I'm not worried and neither should you be."

"I am worried, Mr. Mayor."

"Have a drink, Ruben. Bid on something in the silent auction. Overpay. The kids could use it."

The mayor walked away with the arrogance only political power can give you.

***

On the other side of the dance floor, Uri Valanov was getting sloshed. The Jell-O shots were going down far too easily, and ever since he'd been forced to pick a white man to replace a murdered black dean, he'd lost his appetite. There were other things on his mind too. Graduate students and adjunct professors were on the verge of a strike, having formed a union with the blessing of the National Labor Relations Board. Students were on edge too. The politics of free speech were being fought in pitched battles all over campus. Millennial students forever protected from insult by their helicopter parents bristled at even the idea of hearing something that might upset their worldview. Valanov, whose parents had survived the Soviet Gulag, had exactly zero tolerance for any of this silliness, but he had to bow to the realities of running a modern university. Millennial snowflakes were the paying customers, and the customers were always right. The sign over the counter at his father's electronics shop in Cleveland said as much. But all of it paled in comparison with being mixed up in whatever his money-spigot was mixed up in.

He saw Steinlauf in his patented alpha-male pose—hands on his hips, groin thrust forward—when the disco ball illuminated his corner of the dance floor. Being confronted was not Steinlauf's thing, but two more slurps of Jell-O made Valanov forget. He headed that way, crossing the dance floor, weaving between a classics professor being all grabby with a female grad student and one of his assistant provosts standing rigidly, moving his arms like he was robot whose battery was nearly drained.

"Ruben! It's Uri!" The words slurred despite his deliberately telling them not to.

"Mr. Provost. A fun evening, wouldn't you say? And a good cause to boot."

"I don't know about that. Spoiled fucking rich kids, if you ask me."

"That is certainly one point of view. What can I do for you, Uri?" Steinlauf took him by the arm and manhandled him over to the side of the room where the caterers were starting to set out dessert.

"You can start by telling me what the fuck is going on, Ruben. You won't answer my calls. You won't take my meetings. What the fuck!"

"First of all, lower your voice." Steinlauf growled. He narrowed his eyes, focusing in on the bridge of Valanov's nose, like he was taking aim. "Second, I'm a busy man with multiple businesses to run. I don't work for you, Uri. And, believe it or not, this university is not my top priority. I give you my leftovers—my leftover money and my leftover time. That's where you fall. Understand?"

"Oh, I understand all right. When you need something from me—like your boy, Scott Miller, to be dean—I'm supposed to deliver, no questions asked. But when I need something from you, I'm supposed to get in line behind everyone else. Is that how it's going to be?"

"Exactly. I'm glad we understand each other. Now, if you'll excuse me..."

"Hold on a minute."

Valanov grabbed him by the elbow as he started to walk away. Steinlauf wheeled on a dime, eyes full of rage.

"Get your hands off of me, Uri. Now!"

"Did you kill her?"

Rockefeller University's biggest donor grabbed its provost by the shoulder and walked him like a dog on a leash into the men's room of the Four Seasons. He handed the bathroom attendant a hundred-dollar bill from a stack cinched tight with a gold money clip.

"No one comes in. Yes?"

"Yes, sir," the man said. He tucked the bill into his breast pocket, his month made. He stepped outside.

"Now, where were we, Mr. Provost? Ah, yes, you were accusing me of murder."

Valanov was up against the counter. He could feel moisture from around the sink seeping into his acid-washed jeans. Steinlauf was giving him his version of "The Treatment." Lyndon Johnson used his size to loom over and intimidate his targets; Steinlauf, nearly a foot shorter than the provost, used his tenacity.

"I…I…I…"

"Spit it out, you pathetic fuck. What were you saying?"

"I was just asking a question. I wasn't accusing you." Valanov squirmed away from the vanity and pulled an embroidered towel off a rack by the side of the sink.

"It felt like an accusation. I'm not a lawyer anymore, but that's how I took it. You can see that, right?"

"When you came to my office, you asked me for Scott, and now I find out that…well, one of my clinicians is missing, and there are rumors about a lawsuit targeting a development you—"

"Articulate and thoughtful, Uri. It's a lethal combination. I see our beloved university is in good hands."

Steinlauf moved over to the row of sinks, picked up a comb and ran it through his hair. He poured some mouthwash into a tiny paper cup, and rinsed, all the while admiring his tanned face in the mirror.

"Listen, let me be crystal clear. I didn't kill anyone. I didn't order the murder of anyone. I don't know about any murders or killing. I had no role in whatever happened to that woman. Either directly or indirectly. Got it?" Before Valanov could answer, he went on. "I took advantage of a situation. That is what I do. I find opportunities, and I pounce on them. Like a fucking panther. When she died, it gave me an opening. Put a guy in their who might be able to make certain things happen for me. A friend. We all need friends in important positions." He'd been talking to him in the mirror. Then, he turned to look him in the eye: "How do you think you got your job, Uri?"

"What about Klepp? Is he behind it?" It was a whisper, even though the attendant was earning his hundred.

"Of course not. Think about it, Uri. Klepp is a lot of things, but he is logical. Smart. Tactical. Would you kill her if you were a devious, money-grubbing bastard like Max Klepp?"

"Are you asking me this? Seriously?"

"Yes. Would you kill her to save your project?"

"As Max Klepp?"

"Yes."

"No, I wouldn't kill her."

"Why? There's a lot of money at stake, and, after all, you *are* Max Klepp. As ruthless a motherfucker as there is."

"Because the dean doesn't typically wield that kind of power. Even if she could squeeze Church, he could resist. I bet people think deans have way more power than they do. And, in any event, Church could always just take the case and do it himself. Quit the clinic and become a crusader. The case would make him famous. Rich too. Or, just rat to the feds."

"Exactly. And if you know this, Max knows this, because that is what he does. He knows stuff that people like him aren't supposed to know."

"Okay, so why'd you push for Scott?"

"Potential benefit at no cost. Maybe the dean can do something to help, even if just a bit. A roadblock here, a PR win there. Once the project is going, it's an avalanche going downhill. What makes the difference between what I did and what you think I did is all on the cost side. In one case—where you commit murder—you get a new dean that might help but are risking the death penalty. In the other case—where you just take advantage of a murder someone else committed—you get the same benefit but you're just calling in a minor favor. That's your job, by the way, to do favors for me."

"Hmmm. I guess..."

"Look, Scott Miller is a sensible guy. As I told you in that meeting, he should have been your first choice, not some environmental nutjob, affirmative-action case on high heels. I think the Law School is better off with him at the helm, even if he does nothing about Quayside. If he did do something to derail that frivolous case, it would have just been icing. But people don't kill for icing. They kill for the cake. If you really care about finding out who did it, you need to find the cake."

Valanov felt better, but somehow he suspected he wasn't getting the full story.

"Are you done here, Uri? They're playing '99 Luftballons.' I love that song." The sarcasm and disdain dripped off his chin.

Steinlauf pushed past him and disappeared into the ballroom. Before the bathroom door swung closed, Valanov saw him reach for his phone.

"Max," Steinlauf spat into his phone.

"Ruben, my friend. Did you dance with the mayor?" It was all business.

"I asked him to dance to 'Total Eclipse of the Heart,' you know, the one by Bonnie Tyler, but he demurred. Said the change of pace half-way through makes that song undanceable. Or words to that effect."

"That's too bad. I always thought he was more creative than that."

"Mmmm." Steinlauf waited, but he knew what Max was going to do. At this point, they were Astaire and Rogers.

"I guess that leaves us no choice."

"No, it doesn't."

"I'll take care of it." It was resigned but confident.

"Wait one sec. The mayor did say that he'd dance with me at our next opportunity—that's in twenty-four hours. He hopes that there's a jazz band instead."

"I see. Well, let's give him one more chance. If he doesn't have you on his dance card after tomorrow, I'll do it. I'll dance with you, old buddy."

"It's a date."

Steinlauf hung up. He breathed deeply through his nose, then out the same way. Determined despite the deep hole they were digging, he stepped into the Maybach that was waiting for him. It sped away into the night, Frank Sinatra cooing at him while he swirled a Laphroaig that was waiting for him on the center console.

CHAPTER 38

Aliza Kahan walked out of the Jerusalem Bakery carrying a challah loaf for her family's Shabbat dinner. She held up her hand and looked down the length of Skokie Boulevard, her hand with her palm facing her—two fingers between the sun and the horizon meant dinner needed to start in about thirty minutes. She had just enough time to drive home, bless the challah, and say the kiddush. Named after her great grandmother, who died manning a barricade during the Warsaw ghetto uprising during Nazi occupation, Aliza took her name and her religion seriously. But they were the same thing in her mind. Every time she didn't use a light switch or get in a car or do work during Sabbath, she did it to honor her namesake and the millions like her who perished in Nazi ovens and pogroms across the Pale of Settlement. God had no place in her universe, only good and evil.

As she reached for her key fob to unlock her Cadillac CTS-V, a windowless Mercedes Sprinter van pulled up blocking her path across the street. She stood in the middle of the road dumbfounded. The sliding door opened and her biggest client, Max Klepp, looked out at her from the captain's chair on the other side behind the driver.

"Get in. Leave the challah."

Kahan dropped the loaf involuntarily and stepped into the van. Years of military hierarchy and client service, which were one and the same in her mind, triggered in her sympathetic nervous system. They sped away before the door even closed.

"Have a seat," Klepp said motioning to the bench in the rear. It was occupied by what appeared to be two sumo wrestlers in matching red Adidas track suits. She squeezed between them. Klepp spun his chair around to face the three of them. Aliza tried to hide her look of fear and discomfort, but it leaked out, as if she was trying to hold back a hose with tissue paper.

"What's going on, Mr. Klepp? I'm going to be late. I'm shomer Shabbos."

"I don't care what you are or where you have to be. What I need you for takes priority over whatever you were going to do with that loaf of bread. Okay?"

One didn't need a decade as an Israeli spy to know a rhetorical question when they heard one. Kahan nodded anyway.

"Good, we understand each other. Now, why did I just snatch you from the sidewalk in Skokie in broad daylight?"

"I was asking myself that question."

"Royce Johnson, Aliza, Royce Johnson. He's my question. Where is he? You promised me. We were there, naked in the Red Square. I said get rid of him, you said, 'Yes, sir, no problem.' Remember that?...What happened?"

"Is this all necessary?" She looked to her left and right, then moved to get up. The men to her right and left linked their arms in front of her chest and threw her back into her seat.

"It is. Sadly, it is. I need to know what's going on. I told you to take care of a problem. The reason I pay you a hundred thousand dollars a month is so that I don't have problems. Up to now, you've been very effective at making my problems go away. But you didn't make Royce Johnson go away. I need to know why not."

"We tried to—"

"Whatever you tried, failed. I don't accept failure. You know that about me. It's one of my best qualities. The reason I've kept you around is because you've never failed me. Until now."

The veiled threat made Kahan squirm. For a moment, she wondered if this was how it ended. Not with a bag over her head in a cinder-block hut in the Sinai, not from a sniper in West Beirut, but strangled in a van in Skokie, Illinois.

"It was a choice. It nearly worked, and there was no blowback at all. No cops, no press. Our guys—or, your other guys—took care of that. We had it under control. Millimeters is all we are talking about. A few millimeters and he's—"

"Horseshoes and hand grenades. Really, I don't care. I want him taken care of."

"We can definitely do that, but I don't understand why all this drama is necessary." Her eyes threw darts at the sumo wrestlers. "I mean, this is all a giant cliché, Max. The van, the giants. Clichés."

"I care about results. I've trusted you, Aliza. If I can't do that anymore, I'm going to have to use Tony's boys."

"Are they On Leong or Hip Sing?"

"Hip what?"

"Never mind."

"Look, I don't want to. They don't have your grace, your intelligence. But they also don't have your scruples."

Kahan had had enough. She was bored and she didn't like anyone questioning her methods. She lunged forward, causing the twins to put their arms up. She was ready with a set of handcuffs that were always with her and that she'd moved from her pocket into her hand while Klepp was monologuing. She snapped the cuffs into place, binding the twins together before they knew what was happening. Then, she ducked her head under the bridge their interlocking arms made, rose up with a jump, and threw both her hands back at their throats with as much force as she could muster. She hit the vagus nerve on both with a karate chop. Perfectly placed, both men fell forward, gasping for breath. Kahan rolled forward, landing at the feet of Max Klepp. The van was stopped at a light, so the driver wheeled around when hearing the commotion.

"Mr. Klepp!" he signaled his willingness to intervene.

"It's okay, Roger. Everything is under control." Then, turning to Kahan, on her knees in front of him. "You've proved your point. Now, sit up, and let's plot the way forward. I don't believe in the past, just the future. I need to know our future. What's it going to be?" He put out his hand.

Kahan didn't take it but sat up in the other captain's chair. She swiveled around to face Klepp, noticing his former guards, still slumped on the floor of the van.

"I'll take care of it. Keep Tony out of this. I'm saying this not just for my benefit but for yours. These meat-bags aren't nearly as good as you think, and their methods are as refined as their fashion sense."

The look on his face said that he didn't disagree. She knew they were a last resort, and his smile revealed his delight that it was one that he wouldn't have to deploy.

"Okay. Get on it." Then, to the driver, Klepp spat, "Pull over, Roger."

"Hold on. There's a problem I want to discuss, and I have a question before I leave."

"There always are."

"The problem is finding him. Ivan's been looking for him, and we haven't found him." Resigned tones were unusual for Kahan. "I remain confident, but even the cops are striking out. He must have had help. We suspect the sister-in-law, so we're following her now too. So far…well, so bad."

"*Your* problem. You have a month. That's my answer. One hundred Gs. That's my solution."

"I just figured you'd have—"

"Your problem. Solve it. I have my own problems."

"Okay."

"And the question…"

"Well, while I'm willing to do this no questions asked…You know that, right?" Klepp nodded. "But I don't understand why he needs to be taken care of." Kahan blanched.

"Are you being deliberately obtuse? It starts with Q and ends with side."

"Well, you see—"

"I can't have this project sidelined for years and spend hundreds of millions of dollars to clean up a mess I didn't make. It's pretty fucking simple."

"No, no, no, I get that. I mean, it's just, we've taken care of the lawyer, we've taken care of the samples and the data. The chemist, we've seized all his files and computers from his home as well. We are watching him, but there is nothing he's got anyway. We have it all. They don't have access to the site. The IEPA isn't a problem. The mayor or the alderman or whomever you've got on your books took care of that. The old foundation is gone, and I saw them pouring the new slab the other day. Plus, my guess is that Agent Johnson is far gone, clinging to life in a hole somewhere. Even if he has a miraculous recovery and comes back guns blazing, his investigation of that woman isn't going to lead him to us. We had nothing to do with it. So, I guess I just don't see the loose end that requires us to risk so much in order to kill Royce Johnson. I mean, it's not some nobody law professor who won't be missed. I haven't even seen a news story about Church. It's like the guy never existed. This will be...this will be front-page news. By the way, you should have clued me in about Wisconsin. Tony's boys don't exactly do good work." She couldn't resist the dig.

"Hang on, Roger. Put the hazards on. I need a moment."

He turned toward Aliza, reached forward, and held her at the elbow.

"When I was about eight or nine, my grandfather asked me to scrub the floor of his butcher shop. Have you ever seen the floor of a slaughterhouse?" He didn't wait for an answer. "I resisted, obviously, seeing the blood and the scraps of flesh and fat and sinew mixed with the dirt and grime of the outside coming in. My friends were playing baseball or riding their bikes, reading comics. Kid stuff. I wanted to be with them. Anything but being on my hands and knees, face to face with the grim realities of using animal protein for nourishment. It was just all a bit too much. So, I asked my father, 'Why?' It was the bravest thing I'd ever done up to that point in my life. Maybe since. He put his cleaver into a large block of wood with a thump. It was aimed at my chest and that is where I felt it hit. He stared at me for a long time. Must have been a minute or longer. I could feel him, the weight of him pressing down on me, overwhelming my ability to resist. He wasn't going to answer, at least verbally. He just stared at me, fingers dancing on the wooden handle of that meat axe. 'I mean, don't you have someone who's job this is?' I filled the dead air like a fool. He let his stare linger for another moment, then picked up his cleaver, prying it out of the hole it created in the wood. He went back to carving up a dead animal on his table. I watched him take it apart with ruthless efficiency and precision. As I stood there watching, I felt like he was dressing me. We never spoke again about the episode. And you better fucking believe that I scrubbed that floor. You could have performed open-heart surgery on that floor when I was done with it."

"I understand. But—"

"No buts. You are right, Aliza. The project is full steam ahead, and there is very little Royce Johnson can do to stop it. But he might be able to find out who killed Jante Turner, and I won't let it happen. I'd spend every penny I've ever earned to make sure that doesn't happen."

The message and her assignment were clear. It made no sense to her, but it was clear. The door to the van swung open, and Aliza Kahan stepped out into the twilight. Her mind was on the challah and her family, sitting around the Shabbat table waiting for her to join them in song and prayer and blessings to welcome in the Sabbath. But it was also on Royce Johnson and how she was going to find him and kill him. It was either him or Max Klepp. The thought of doing either made her gulp.

CHAPTER 39

The chicken-wire cage felt more and more like prison every day. But, with his infection under control after several visits from Claire, he was nearly back to fighting shape. His ribs still ached and he felt stabs of pain with every deep breath and every pee he took. Claire told him with a few more days of rest, he'd be back on his feet. After he'd worked all the IV antibiotics through his system, he insisted that Claire stay away. They, whoever *they* were, were smart. They'd eventually put two and two together and link his survival to the only doctor he could trust. Marcus, on the other hand, was his ace in the hole. As far as they were concerned, Marcus had an anti-connection to Royce. Plus, a young black man could move a lot less noticeably on South Clark Street and into and out of the Annex than Claire walking around on thousand-dollar shoes.

Royce took a few laps around the second floor of the Annex, and since the pain was not enough to make him puke, or maybe just puke a little bit, he knew it was time to go home. Time to find Jante's killer. He texted Claire, and when the Uber pulled up in front of Alex's old house, she was standing at the door holding a mylar balloon. Originally it said "Get Well Soon" in curlicue letters, but she'd crossed out "Well" with a black Sharpie, and replaced it with "Jante's Killer." She knew him well. Seeing it, he smiled broadly enough to make his ribs hurt.

"Thanks, Claire." He reached forward and kissed her cheek, feeling alive, or at least not circling the drain of death, for the first time in a long time.

She embraced him, then handed him her iPhone, already dialing Jenny. Royce had avoided calling her, only sending cryptic texts for days. He desperately needed to hear her voice, to see his kids' smiles, but he resisted until he'd come out on the other side. Royce took the phone and wandered through the foyer of Alex's house, over to the spot where his brother had fallen and spent his last seconds. Pacing like a tiger that walked the same concrete pad for years, he told his wife a G-rated version of where he'd been. He knew she was used to getting little from him, whether it was by rule or his own personal code. Unsurprisingly, her concern was more what the endgame was—she hadn't even known of his predicament, and now that it was over, she focused on the bigger picture problems. Royce sensed that her patience was approaching its breaking point.

Phone in his outstretched hand, Royce walked into the kitchen where Claire was unloading the last of the groceries she'd bought to stock the fridge. She took a bottle of Red Stripe from a six-pack on the top shelf and handed it to him. Another in her hand, they clinked bottle necks and swigged in silence. He said a loving goodbye, then turned to Claire.

"Thanks for all of this." He smiled in between sips. "I can't ever repay you for saving my life."

"All in a day's work." She giggled. "Now, I've got to get back to the hospital, but before I do, what's your plan? I'd hate to see you get killed and have all these groceries go to waste." She paused, seeming to notice his indecision. "You do have a plan, don't you? I mean, you're a sitting duck here, aren't you? Right?" Her tone was that of a woman who planned her vacations in fifteen-minute increments.

"Well, not exactly. I've been focused on not dying. It is harder work than it looks." Royce realized this fell awkwardly on the ears of an oncologist who was around dying people every day.

"Any ideas?"

"That's a joke, right? When I see a problem, I have two solutions: irradiating it or throwing just enough poison at it so that the chemicals kill the problem and not the host. I don't know a thing about...whatever it is that's happening to you. I assume radiation or chemotherapy won't help."

"If I can find the people who put me in that flophouse, the people who killed Jante, I'd love to expose them to some serious doses of radiation. But you're right, we need something else for now." He took a long sip, letting the hops tingle the inside of his mouth and the cold of the beer swirl down his throat and into his belly. "I see two choices," he announced while smacking his lips. "I need to make it more difficult for them to kill me. I can either defend myself, which means hiring some muscle, or make it costlier to murder me."

"What do you mean?" Claire said as she folded the canvas shopping bags and set them on the end of the kitchen counter.

"I could tell the world where I am, what I'm involved in. Go public. Make the costs of them murdering me a national story and a high-profile investigation. I could hide in plain sight."

Claire nodded, but expressed her doubts. "Seems risky. But I'll leave it to you. Why not do both? I mean, go public and hire some security? Chemo and radiation on the same tumor."

"A good idea, sis. A good idea."

They hugged, she handed him the keys to her house, and headed back to the hospital. When she was gone, Royce opened the fridge, finding it populated with the foods an oncologist would want you to eat rather than the foods most people, especially a man imprisoned in a federal facility and a flophouse for most of the last thirteen months, would want to eat. He pulled out a carrot with the green stems still attached and munched on it without even peeling it.

Muscle didn't come cheap and could attract attention, but he knew who would know how to get him some on the cheap and with the minimum amount of attention. A quick text to Marcus to meet him at Alex's house was the first step in shoring up the fort. He'd ask Claire for some money to pay for them. But later. He didn't want to ask for too much all at once. Then, he searched on LinkedIn for a woman Alex dated briefly after he got a divorce from Claire. A reporter for the local NBC affiliate. When he got her email address from Alex's account, he fired off a lead for her on a story that would make her day.

The plan in motion, Royce cracked another beer and retreated to the second-floor den. He flicked on the TV and sat back on the couch. The whir of NASCAR and the alcohol in his veins sent him off to sleep in under thirty seconds, the beer falling out of his hand and spilling all over a Turkish rug Alex brought back for Claire from a conference in Istanbul.

The next afternoon, Royce stood on Alex's stoop and told the world, friends and enemies alike, where he was and what he was doing. He spoke haltingly of his brother's murder, his time in jail, and, then more confidently, what he was doing in Chicago. Alex's old friend stared up at him past false eyelashes and held a puffy microphone with an NBC logo at his mouth. The whole thing was over in less than five minutes. Royce set out a marker that he was on the case of Jante's killer and suggested that he was getting close.

The bait was set. Or, rather, the anti-bait. Royce figured that whoever was trying to kill him already knew or could easily find out where he was, especially now that he was out of the Annex. The presser would make coming after him that much more difficult, Royce having put a target on his chest and said to the world, "Come and get it." But he had texted Marcus to round up some men just in case. Men who would willingly shoot whatever they were told to shoot at.

When the interview concluded, polite goodbyes and thank-yous were exchanged, and then Royce sealed himself inside and waited for Marcus's men to arrive. As he walked past the place where Royce long thought Marcus shot his brother, the irony was not lost on him. He closed his eyes and shook his head, hoping this time everything would be different.

CHAPTER 40

"Ruben Steinlauf," Marcus blurted, as he pushed past Royce into the entryway of Alex's house. He stopped short, then added, "So, this is where I killed him, huh?"

"Too soon, too soon."

"It's been nearly two years..."

"It will never not be too soon, Marcus." He walked past him into the kitchen. When Marcus pulled up a stool at the soapstone island, Royce pushed a Red Stripe toward him. "Now, who's Ruben Stein...what was it?"

"Steinlauf. Billionaire. Into everything, land development, light manufacturing, commodities, private equity. A bit of shipping and oil. Probably weapons. You name it and he's into it. Anything that will turn one dollar into two."

"And what does he have to do with us? Did he kill Jante?" Royce took a long sip from the squat bottle.

"I don't know that yet, and I doubt he shot her himself, but is he involved in some way? Yup, I'm pretty sure he is. I don't know how or why, but I suspect it has something to do with Bubbly Creek."

"Interesting." They took multiple sips in silence. Royce got some celery out of the refrigerator—a Claire special—and set it out. They munched like rabbits. After a few moments, Royce summed up what they were both thinking. "Jante was unwilling to shut down Mike Church's case at Bubbly Creek." He speculated, as if he were summing up the case to a jury during closing arguments. "She was even going to put the university muscle behind it. So, Steinlauf had her killed."

"Something like that, yes, that's what I was piecing together."

"What's the connection with Max?"

"They're probably golfing buddies."

"Ha! I wouldn't doubt it. I'll Google it," Royce said, while reaching for another piece of celery. "Steinlauf is definitely connected to the university. I've seen his name all over the place, and we have a student on a Steinlauf Scholarship alleging bad blood with the dean. If we can put Steinlauf in bed with Max, the picture starts to look complete."

Marcus didn't miss a chance to show his smarts. "The developers—Max, Ruben, whomever else—are afraid of an environmental lawsuit that will derail their plans. They want to install a Quisling as dean in order to put sand in the gears of justice." Feeling himself go full Baptist-preacher-on-Easter-Sunday, Marcus downshifted the rhetoric. "When they didn't get their way, when instead they got a stranger—and not just any stranger but a black woman from the South Side who'd experienced environmental injustice and wanted to use her new position to do something about it—well, they just put a slug in her heart to give their man a chance."

Royce tagged in. "And, given the influence Steinlauf has on campus, he probably put the screws to the administration to make them pick Scott Miller." Royce took a satisfied swig of beer.

"Do you think Scott knew or was he a patsy? Did he know what Klepp and Steinlauf were up to?"

"You know, partner, at this point, nothing would surprise me. Scott doesn't seem like a killer to me—more of a patsy. But remember that time when I got you sent to death row?" Royce giggled like he was recounting a practical joke from their youth. Marcus grimaced. "I think we shouldn't yet take Scott off the list."

"Agreed." They clinked beers again, then each finished them off with a gulp.

"Another?" Royce asked playfully.

"Sure. I think better when I'm buzzed."

Royce walked to the fridge and retrieved two more Red Stripes. As he handed one to Marcus, he threw out a theory: "Maybe Scott had Jante killed as a way of pleasing his father-in-law. You know, do him a solid that the old man would have to repay?"

"Kill Jante so he could be dean?" Marcus played along, wanting to see where it led.

"Maybe. Or maybe just to help on the Bubbly Creek project."

"Arranging a hit to suck up to the in-laws is a bit farfetched, don't you think? I mean, I'm not married, but...Hey, you are married, Royce—would you off the head of the FBI to make your wife's dad happy?"

Royce smiled. "I don't work for the FBI anymore. But I see your point. I'm just throwing out ideas. I wouldn't have thought a president would have killed a law professor and tried to pin it on a law student to get a pedophile onto the Supreme Court either." He paused and smiled a toothy smile. "Just sayin'." They enjoyed the moment as much as two men with their history could. "Plus, if enough money is at stake—if my father-in-law would lose everything if I didn't, I just might. I mean, who am I to say. People are capable of things they can't even possibly imagine under the right circumstances. Do you think those Argentinian soccer players woke up that morning and thought they'd be cannibals?"

Marcus's eyes flared. "I'm sure I've got no idea what you are talking about, man. Cannibals? Soccer? Huh? You know me, I'm an NFL guy. The real football. Anyway, I see the point."

"So, we keep Scott in our sights, but our focus is on Steinlauf and Klepp. We agree?"

"Yes. Now, what's our next move? I mean, we've come a long way, but I still feel like we haven't proved anything. We don't have any idea who killed Jante and Mike."

"And that Becca Goldman girl." Royce threw in as an afterthought.

Marcus threw his head back in surprise.

"What? Becca who? What are you talkin' 'bout?"

"Oh yeah, I forgot to tell you about that."

"Damn straight you did. They killed someone else? Damn."

Royce told the story of the woman he met at Quayside, the connection with Mike Church, and the story he read about her body floating in the Chicago River from an apparent overdose and accident.

"So that's three people these two old bastards have killed, and they tried to kill you."

"We don't know that," Royce said.

"Which one?"

"Me. We don't know it was them that pushed me in front of that train."

"True, I guess. There are lots of people that want you dead. Maybe it was me," Marcus joked.

"Ha, ha. But, seriously, it could have been one of Gerhardt's boys. Revenge is not unfamiliar to those guys."

Marcus sighed. "I'm having a hard time keeping up with one group of killers after us, let alone two. For now, maybe we ignore the demons of your past and focus on the demons of your present."

"Deal. But, as I see it, it is *our* present."

"So, what are we up against here, Royce?" A note of fear was evident in his question, despite his attempt to hide it.

"I suspect it's more than two old guys. Good old Statler and Waldorf aren't killing law students or tracking environmentalists to the woods in Wisconsin—they've got professional help. Heck, maybe even the cops."

"Slow down there, Skippy. First, who are Statler and Waldorf?"

"The old guys from *The Muppets*. You know, the theater critics?"

Marcus shook his head. "You a damn fool, and old. What am I going to do?" Marcus blew out a large breath through his lips. "Where was I? Oh, yeah, are you saying that the Chicago Police are working on this? I mean, that's a whole 'nother level."

"Again, I'm just saying we can't take anything for granted. We're on our own here, and we need to assume that everyone is against us unless they prove otherwise. The cops, the feds. I trust no one. Not anymore."

The doorbell rang, as if on cue. Marcus immediately strode toward the front door.

"Well, we aren't entirely on our own."

"Who's at the door?" Royce asked.

"The cavalry. The mother fuckin' cavalry."

Royce turned the corner as Marcus welcomed five men into his brother's living room. They looked as threatening as five average men could look. Not particularly fit or large, they ranged in age from about twenty to about fifty. They were cooks and garbage men and accountants. Not killers. But when they set down their duffle bags on the old heart-of-pine floors that Alex was so proud of and took out an arsenal that looked like it could defend Fort Saint Elmo in Malta, Royce felt secure for the first time since that rebar punctured his gut.

"Welcome to our redoubt, gentlemen. I'm grateful for your service. Make yourselves at home. What's mine is yours. Food, drink, whatever."

"Why don't you give them a tour, Royce? Show them where they can shit and sleep and such."

"Good idea. While I'm doing that, I have a suggestion for you. We will set up defense here in the unlikely event our Muppet friends get frisky—why don't you go on offense?"

"What do you mean?" Marcus asked, eagerly.

"Steinlauf. Track him. Confront him. He's an old man. Intimidate him. Outsmart him. You are good at that. Both, actually."

Marcus smiled.

Royce watched him smile. He knew Marcus well enough at

this point to know that he wasn't smiling so much at the compliment, but at the feeling he had that he'd made the right decision about what to be when he grew up.

Grabbing a semi-automatic pistol from the duffle bag, Royce felt the weight in his hand and the security of hearing a bullet chamber.

CHAPTER 41

Royce provided the address. Marcus wasn't sure how. *That's just what FBI agents do, even ex-agents.* When he was a runner on the South and West sides, Marcus always wondered how the cops were so effective when every cop he knew was an idiot. He now got it. No individual agent was that powerful, but if you thought of the collection of agents working together, they were superheroes. Their superpower was the ability to be anywhere at any time, to know almost anything, and to deploy vast resources around the globe in an instant. If one thought of an agent as a cell in a larger organism instead of a stand-alone individual, then that organism, that beast called the FBI, or, even better, the federal government, is Superman. Each cell, just a bit part of the whole, had the powers of the whole. Even ex-cells, apparently.

From a bench in Washington Park, Marcus looked across Dearborn Street toward a three-story mansion surrounded on three sides by gleaming glass apartment buildings. The dark sandstone—quarried from Lake Superior in 1888, Google told him—gave the appearance of a Medieval fortress, or a prison from the movies. Another search told Marcus it was on the market a few years back for nearly thirty million. A perfect lair for Ruben Steinlauf.

Marcus turned the pages of the *New York Times*, eyeing the driveway leading out onto Delaware Place. He could hear the

Impala, idling a few feet away on Dearborn Street, ready for pursuit. His watch said 9:15 a.m. Maybe Steinlauf was a night owl. Or, perhaps, Royce was wrong. Even Superman was wrong sometimes.

Fifteen minutes later, a Lincoln Navigator edged out into traffic, and headed east toward the lake. Seeing a stream of red taillights ahead of them, Marcus took his time. He slid into his Impala and put the *Times* onto the passenger seat. His eyes on the Navigator, he pulled his Smith & Wesson from his waistband and put it under the paper. In under thirty seconds, he was in pursuit.

The SUV's first stop was a deli. The driver, an athletic-looking forty something with the shape of an inverted triangle, got out, went inside, and came back with a brown bag inside of a minute. The scene made Marcus's stomach growl. Lox and bagel, he imagined.

The slow-speed chase through the packed streets of the Loop went on for about twenty minutes. It ended at a modernist, steel-framed skyscraper that could have been in any city in the world, and yet was quintessentially Chicago for anyone with a passing familiarity of architectural history. Marcus parked in a thirty-minute loading zone while he watched the SUV disappear into a subterranean parking garage. This wasn't going to be easy.

Marcus waited with the hazards on, but after an hour, he realized this wasn't a viable long-term strategy. Plus, he had to pee. After dropping the car off in a local garage and emptying his bladder in the bathroom of a Starbucks, Marcus found a low retaining wall holding elaborate landscaping near the entrance to Steinlauf's office. He took a seat and pulled a paperback book—a Louis L'Amour he'd grabbed from the lobby of the Annex.

The wait was interminable. After an hour, and not loving the story of his book, Marcus started to fidget. After two, his butt ached, and he started to worry that a black man reading a Western in front of a downtown office building was going to start drawing attention. The one lesson every black kid on the South Side learned early and often was not to draw attention in the Loop. The cops were one thing, but every office had private security, and they were even more dangerous than the cops. Less trained, less regulated, less talented. More trouble. Especially since he was sitting on private property with an illegal firearm hidden beneath his shirt.

Just as he felt the fear of being watched, of being judged, Marcus saw Steinlauf spit out of a revolving door, followed by a leggy assistant barely keeping up in high heels and a tight skirt. Marcus shot his eyes down to a shootout on the page, trying to seem inconspicuous. He read a line or three out of context. After they passed, Marcus waited a beat, then walked behind them at a distance. The entire six blocks to a restaurant while Steinlauf spoke on his cell phone while his assistant half ran to keep up with him. He ate a salad and drank tea across from a young-looking man that Marcus guessed was a politician.

Marcus grabbed a burrito from a Chipotle across the street and sat on a stool at the window with a view of the entrance to the restaurant. This was going nowhere. Steinlauf might have been conspiring at his lunch, but without listening equipment or a confederate, Marcus wouldn't know. Whatever he was doing in his office or in that black SUV or in his mansion on Dearborn Street was a total mystery. *I suck at this.*

Except Marcus never let himself suck at anything. In college, Marcus taught himself how to play the Chinese game, Go. He got pretty good. But when a kid from Andover beat Marcus by more stones than he cared to remember, and put him down by telling Marcus to practice up for the next time, he realized he sucked. He took the insult to heart, spending the next few months doing little else. When they played again the next semester, Marcus didn't suck anymore—he won handily, then congratulated his victim on a game well played. In his mind, he thought, *Not well played enough*, but his mama raised him better than that.

He'd sucked at Go, and then got good. He still sucked at

this. No plan crystalized in his mind as he turned the possibilities over while chewing on his burrito, but when Steinlauf shook hands with his lunch date and headed back toward his office, Marcus knew just what he was going to do. Doing it, however, was another thing altogether.

Marcus trailed them on the walk back to the office, waiting for the right time to pounce. The pistol dug into his hip, and he knew it could be a liability if things went sideways. But this was the moment. He wasn't going back to Royce empty-handed.

"Mr. Steinlauf," he shouted from about five feet behind Steinlauf's assistant, who was, as usual, trailing a few feet behind her boss.

Steinlauf turned, suspicious, expecting to ignore whomever it was. His assistant spun a hundred eighty degrees on a dime, prepared to be the left tackle protecting her quarterback's blindside.

"Mr. Steinlauf," Marcus said again in a softer voice. "It's Marcus. Marcus Jones. I was a Steinlauf Scholar."

The look on Steinlauf's face relaxed on connecting a black face with those last two words—*one of mine*, the look on his face said. He stopped, and in a moment, Marcus was standing in front of him. Marcus stretched out his hand and smiled as wide as his nerves would allow.

"Marcus Jones," he said confidently. "I just wanted to thank you for all you did for me. I couldn't have gotten to where I am had you not put me through Rockefeller Law, and opened all sorts of doors for me. I am forever in your debt, Mr. Steinlauf."

"You are welcome, young man," Steinlauf replied proudly. "It was my pleasure. I came from nothing too, you know? Worked my way up from the bottom, but I caught a few breaks here and there. I'm happy to have designed a break for you and folks like you."

The old Marcus, the one who read everything by Ta-Nehisi Coates and had a poster of Tommie Smith and John Carlos at the '68 Mexico City Olympics hanging in his dorm room, would have responded: *Folks like me? Who exactly are "Folks like me," you racist old cracker?!* But this Marcus, the one who had partnered with a racially obtuse former FBI agent to catch a killer, bit his tongue. He was too pleased that his plan had worked and didn't want to jeopardize it. He bet Steinlauf would be too proud to admit he'd never met Marcus before, too racist to differentiate between the black men he'd helped, or too aloof to have ever paid his scholars any mind at all. Turns out, he was correct, although he didn't know which explanation provided the opening.

"Can I buy you a drink, Mr. Steinlauf?" Marcus asked, as he reached and put his hand on Steinlauf's shoulder.

"I don't drink during the day, and I do need to get back to work. But it was great meeting you." He made a half turn to go, but Marcus turned him slightly with his hand.

"Please—I insist. Let's get an iced tea or a coffee. Not only do I need to tell you the ways in which you have helped me, but I have an idea I want to run by you."

Steinlauf eyed him with the suspicious glare of someone who was constantly being pitched business ideas. But Marcus saw in there an opening. He pressed his advantage.

"You promised us that you would always be our mentor—remember that? The speech you gave us, about the importance of mentors and the way they helped you over the years, stuck with me. I know it is an imposition, but it won't take but a minute. Please? I really could use a mentor. Just someone to react. I promise I won't ask you to invest." It was a risk mentioning a speech, but he was sure Steinlauf had said that or something like it. In Steinlauf's eyes, he saw it pay off.

"Sure. I've got—" he looked up at his assistant who mouthed him the answer, "—fifteen minutes."

"Great." Marcus turned around and looked at the options. "How about there?" he said, pointing to a bar that looked like it had been there since the founding of the city.

They walked together, Marcus making small talk as they did.

They found a booth at the back and ordered two iced teas. Delaying until they arrived, Marcus wove a tale of a career in private equity, doing due diligence on a Canadian tire manufacturer and an oil and gas company in Oklahoma. Then, when the waiter delivered their drinks and retreated to the bar, he had his moment.

"Do you remember me, Mr. Steinlauf?" he asked pointedly.

"Of course. It's really great to see you again." Marcus knew he was lying, or, more accurately, being polite and assuming good faith.

"Well, that is surprising. I was never a Steinlauf Scholar."

Steinlauf narrowed his eyes and furrowed his brow.

"I'm sorry, I don't understand." He looked over his shoulder to make sure he wasn't part of something, to make sure he was safe. But the threat was under the table.

"I've got a loaded gun under the table." Marcus tapped the table from underneath. "It is pointed right at your balls."

Steinlauf rolled his eyes nonchalantly.

"If you want money, I don't have any on me. And, this isn't exactly, you know, a place where I feel threatened. If you shoot me here of all places, the cops will have you in a minute."

"You don't think I planned this? You think I'm stupid? Well, I'm not. I know every exit from this place, and I've got four routes planned out down to the cracks on the sidewalks," Marcus lied. "I'll be in the wind before you bleed out. So, don't try me."

"Okay," the response was cool, "whomever you are. What do you want from me? Like I said, I've a meeting that I have to get to in a few minutes, and I frankly don't have time to waste on some kind of amateur shakedown." He took a sip of tea and stared at Marcus. "I've been threatened by thugs a whole lot tougher than the likes of you."

"Why'd you kill her?"

"What! Who? Who are you talking about? I didn't kill anyone." He leaned in.

"Jante Turner. Dean at Rockefeller. Why'd you kill her?"

"Dean-elect. And, what are you—brother? Boyfriend?"

"Just a concerned citizen."

"Right? Okay," he said in a mocking tone. "I had nothing to do with her death. I met her once. I had no dealings with her. I had no grudge against her. Why would I kill a law professor?" He blew his breath out in an exaggerated way, and it sounded like air coming out of a balloon.

"Bubbly Creek," Marcus spat. He saw the recognition in Steinlauf's eyes.

"What about it?"

"Your development. I hear it's sitting on a toxic waste dump. I know Mike Church was going to expose it. You killed Jante when she wouldn't shut the investigation down, so you could install your real estate partner's son-in-law as dean. Then, when Mike Church went rogue, you killed him. You're currently working your way through his clinic students, taking them out as well. Does this all sound about right?"

A slight smile formed in the corner of Steinlauf's mouth. "You think you know more than you know, Mr.…well, whatever your name really is."

"Jones. Marcus Jones."

"Right—Mr. Jones. I repeat, I didn't kill Ms. Turner. Now, can I go?" Steinlauf rose slightly, but Marcus reached forward and put the tip of the pistol into his leg. His eyes set to menace.

"Sit down!" he barked. Steinlauf complied with a sigh. "Are you saying you didn't have a hand in appointing Dean Miller? That this had nothing to do with Bubbly Creek? 'Cause if that is what you are saying—"

"I didn't say that, Mr. Jones." His tone was condescendingly professorial. "You asked me whether I had a hand in the murder of Ms. Turner. I emphatically did not."

"More iced tea?" the waiter asked, surprising them both.

"No thanks," Marcus said. He wondered whether the waiter heard their conversation, and, if he did, he could see how Marcus's awkward position at the table suggested he was holding the other man at gunpoint. But he walked away nonchalantly.

Turning back to Steinlauf, Marcus continued his interrogation.

"So, you did push for the university to make Miller dean?"

"That I did do." Steinlauf leaned back and puffed out his chest.

"Why?"

"Because I could. Because I wanted to. Do you know who I am, Mr. Jones? I get to do what I want to do. A billion dollars does that."

"I know how the world works, unfortunately. I read about public choice economics in law school..."

"So you did go to Rockefeller. Well, you've certainly seen my largess all over campus. The buildings with my name on them is all you need to know about this situation."

"I never doubted what you could do, Mr. Steinlauf. The question I asked is why you did what you did. Why Scott Miller?"

Steinlauf checked his watch. Then he took a long sip of tea, munching on a piece of ice at the end.

"I'm going to go now, Mr. Jones. And I'm certain you aren't going to shoot me. But I will answer your question, so you'll stop bothering me. I pushed for Scott as dean because the enviro-wackos in a law school clinic were trying to derail a valuable urban development of an impoverished area because of bogus claims about environmental racism or some such horseshit. My life has been dedicated to building things and making things better for people. The Quayside project is no different. We are taking a big risk building something like that on the South Side. I will do whatever I can within the law to make sure it works to make the community better off. And, although I know it's obscene these days, among the Antifa and Bolsheviks on campus, make a few bucks for me and mine. So, when Dean Turner was murdered, I saw an opportunity. If I install a friend in that position, maybe he can help me out. Call off the attack dogs. Or at least tighten the leash a bit. There's nothing wrong with a little nepotism. This is still America, right?"

"A student told me he saw you arguing with Dean Turner..." Marcus tried his last trump card.

"We weren't arguing. I told you I met her once. That was the once. I was trying to tell her that her campaign of environmental justice mumbo jumbo was misguided. All these lawsuits and attacks on companies that are trying to bring development and jobs to poor areas are counterproductive. They lead to underinvestment. I was trying to tell her to support development, not hide behind bogus theories of gentrification or some such crap. You can't complain about dilapidation, and then expect investment. The real world doesn't give out stuff for free. She needed to hear that."

"So you didn't threaten her?"

"We might have raised our voices, but that was because we both felt passionately about our positions. That's it. Now, can I go, please? I have things to do, and I'm frankly goddamn sick and tired of having you point a gun at me."

"I know you're involved in this. Somehow. Even if you didn't kill Jante, you took advantage of her death. And that sickens me. You also conveniently didn't mention Church or that Goldman girl. I find your silence interesting."

"You can find whatever you want interesting. I find animal fornication and ballroom dancing interesting, but I sure as shit didn't bring them up to you. We are done." Steinlauf slammed his iced tea on the table.

"I know where you live. I know where you work. When I find out how you are involved in this, I'll come for you, Mr. Steinlauf. When you aren't ready, I'll be there."

He stood up and put a hundred-dollar bill on the table.

"Look, I appreciate your passion. I do. I don't know why you care so much about this lady, but I admire the zeal. You seem like a smart kid. Why don't you put that to work on something, well, something more productive for your people?"

Marcus wanted to shoot him right there and take the consequences. Whether he had a role in killing Jante or not. But he pulled the Smith & Wesson back and tucked it under his shirt.

"Fuck you," he spat. "You racist prick."

"Good luck, Mr. Jones. I'm sure I'll be seeing you around."

Steinlauf walked away. Marcus turned over his right shoulder and watched him go.

Out on the street, Steinlauf put on his sunglasses and asked his assistant to dial the police commissioner's personal phone. She dialed the number, then handed him the phone. He stopped in the middle of the street to talk.

"Jimmy," he said with authority, "I need a favor."

CHAPTER 42

Three days later, Marcus and Royce sat at Alex's kitchen table trying to figure out how to prove what they knew to be true. There was a Rockefeller University adage that he'd seen on T-shirts worn by undergrads that seemed apt: "If the facts don't fit the theory, change the facts." It was attributed, some say wrongly, to Einstein. But to Marcus, and he was pretty sure to Royce as well, it didn't matter. Whoever said it, he liked how it fit what they were up to. Marcus was pretty certain about their theory, but the facts they had didn't support it. Time to change the facts. And quick. The security detail Marcus scared up was running a thousand dollars a day, and Jenny's calls were now as regular as the tides.

Marcus had taped a large piece of white poster board to a wall in Alex's kitchen, and, as he'd seen on *The Wire*, started to draw an org chart of the conspiracy they were facing. When Royce looked at him and it askance, Royce assured him he'd never done such a thing in all his decades in the Bureau, and, in any event, whatever the Muppets were up to, it didn't rank an org chart.

"So," Marcus filled the air as he paced around the kitchen, "we've got connections between Max and Ruben, between Ruben and Valanov, the provost, and between Max and Scott, the new dean."

Royce's mouth started to form a response but before he could utter anything, the doorbell rang.

"Mar-cus!" a voice boomed from the other room a second later.

Marcus hadn't ordered anything and he surely wasn't expecting any visitors. But the guard at the front door hadn't sounded an alarm, so he relaxed a smidge.

"I'll get it," Royce said.

His partner already was headed toward the foyer. Marcus trailed behind cautiously. When he turned the corner, he saw Royce standing in the door frame, a member of his crew who went by "Deep Dish" standing behind him, a sawed-off shotgun aimed at the middle of the front door. Royce was speaking in normal tones and after a few moments, reached out his hand. Then, the door closed, and he turned back toward Marcus, who was standing expectantly. As Royce walked toward him, Deep Dish stepped to the door and looked through the peephole. Then, he lowered the shotgun, and leaned against the entry room wall.

"Just a couple of Jehovah's Witnesses." Royce grinned, trying not to give up the lie. Deep Dish belly laughed.

"Ain't no Jehovah's Witnesses," he cried.

Marcus stood with his hands on his hips, asking who.

"It was Steinlauf. Or, rather, his minions. Apparently, his honor seeks an audience with us."

"Seriously?"

"Seriously."

"Hmm," Marcus grunted. "That's unexpected. What did they say?"

The two of the them walked toward the dining room.

"Where'd you get these guys?" Royce whispered as they walked. "They aren't exactly Rockefeller men, if you know what I mean."

"Not all great men are Rockefeller men, Royce." Marcus ignored the question. *Or walk with Kings—nor lose the common touch*, he could hear the poet sing to him as he did.

"Ford Focus on the other side of the street," Sarge called out.

Another of Marcus's crew—called that because he made sergeant first class in his exactly twenty years in the Army—was sitting in the bay window that looked out onto the tree-lined street. An AR-15 sat across his lap. He called after them as they made their way into the dining room. Marcus turned and looked out over the living room furniture at the street.

"What do you make of it, Sarge?" he asked.

"Just sittin' there for about ten minutes. Driver at the wheel, lookin' at his phone. I'm on it."

"Thanks. Keep me posted. Maybe get a plate and see if your friend...what's his name?...can run it?"

"Roger, wilco," Sarge barked.

Royce turned back to Marcus.

"Where were we? What was I saying?"

"You weren't answering my question about these guys."

"Forget that. What you were about to do was to tell me what Steinlauf's goons said," Marcus said with a note of exasperation.

"Right—apparently our boy Steinlauf cracked the case?" Royce said as he took a seat.

Marcus moved around the table toward the globe bar. He pulled two glasses out, filled them with ice, and haphazardly topped them off with scotch. He slid one toward Royce and took a seat across from him.

"Which case? Our case? The one where Steinlauf did it? Did he admit it?"

"They didn't say. They only said that Steinlauf has information about who killed Jante. He wants to do a deal."

"Ha! A deal? Bullshit. This is a trap."

"Obviously."

They drank in unison.

"Why didn't he just take us out? I mean, why deal with us? What can we offer him?"

"Maybe I was persuasive? Or scary, even? I am black." They

shared a small laugh, which cracked the tension a bit. "But, I mean, we are a threat to him. No doubt you've been less than your normal superhero self, but I'm a lot better than Robin. You should have seen me collar that fucker and get him to admit what he did to get Scott the deanship."

"I'm sure you were a…" A metaphor failed to materialize. "Look, however convincing you were, Steinlauf denied involvement. Now, a couple of days later, he claims to know who's done it. I doubt it. I've been doing this for a lot of years—no way he cracked this nut that fast. No way."

"Maybe he knew all along."

"Huh?"

"Maybe Steinlauf didn't crack the case. Maybe he didn't do it but knew who did. He's just giving us what he's always known."

"Hmmm. Or maybe he's selling us Florida swampland."

"So what do we do?"

"He wants us to come to the Ferris wheel at Navy Pier at noon, the day after tomorrow," Royce said.

"Let's do it."

Royce guffawed. "Not likely."

"Why? They said he'd be willing to talk with us, but out in the open. A public place where there won't be any funny business."

"You don't have to be General Patton to know to fight on your terrain, not theirs. We set meeting locations, not the bad guys. No way I'm walking into that. Nope. Not going to happen." Royce stood up and walked toward the kitchen. Marcus hurried after him.

"I get it. But it was a take-it-or-leave-it. Risky or not, it seems like we have to see what he has to offer. If he gives us a lead, we can bring in Jante's killer. We can be heroes. And, better yet, you and me can be even."

"If you want to die a hero, Marcus, I'm not going to get in your way. Heck, I'll even help you."

Marcus smiled. “All right! That’s my man. Fucking Superman. I love it.”

They shook hands involuntarily. Then Marcus continued.

“So, what do we have to do?”

“I don’t know yet. We need the layout of Navy Pier and then I need to see the place in person. And we are going to need a plan. A couple actually. And friends. More of your friends.”

Marcus nodded. He had friends, all types.

“But, first, we need some liquid courage.” Royce opened the fridge and pulled out two more Red Stripes. He popped them, then slid one across to Marcus. They clinked.

“Here’s to suicide,” Royce cheers’d.

“To fucking heroes,” Marcus added.

Just then, the bell rang again. They both jumped. Deep Dish answered, then called for Royce. A few minutes later, Royce appeared back in the living room holding a large FedEx box.

“Thank goodness,” Marcus exhaled. “I thought it was—”

“Nah, just a package from—” Royce looked at the return address, “—a Ben Edelman.”

CHAPTER 43

George Ferris, Jr. came to Chicago from Pittsburgh in the summer of 1892. It was hot, but his mind was on making history, not the sweat pooling in his heavy cotton shirt as he toured the South Side near the newly founded Rockefeller University. The organizers of the World's Columbian Exposition of 1893 were looking to outdo the monument Gustave Eiffel built for the Paris Exposition of 1889. Ferris proposed a giant rotating wheel that would carry passengers over two hundred fifty feet into the air in sixty-person cars. Originally told it wouldn't work and that it was too risky for the Exposition, Ferris persevered, and the "Chicago Wheel" opened for business on June 21, 1893. Situated on the Midway Plaisance in Hyde Park, just down the street from Alex's house, the wheel carried nearly forty thousand passengers per day for fifty cents a ride, making it one of the smashing successes of the Exposition.

Royce Johnson knew this history—every Pittsburgher knew about its famous son and the eponymous wheel that now thrilled people all around the world—but as he approached the Centennial Wheel at just before noon the next day, he was thinking of surviving and nothing else. Situated on Chicago's Navy Pier, a thirty-three-hundred-foot-long hang nail sticking out in Lake Michigan, the wheel was the perfect place for an ambush. On any given day, it was bustling with nearly thirty thousand visitors who provided cover and a crowd for an assassin to disappear into. When he walked the pier the day before, he learned there were a substantial number of public and private security guards on hand, as well as countless video surveillance cameras to record what happened. But the rent-a-cops were, well, rent-a-cops, and the cameras were far from state of the art, and there were obvious dead spots. On the other hand, the wheel itself offered eight minutes of privacy, as it rose above the pier and then came around again, something that Royce suspected was the reason Steinlauf chose it.

Royce wore a bright orange Chicago Bears baseball cap. For his entrance, he chose the tree-lined promenade along the water instead of the large brick pavilion in the middle of the pier that was a visitor's typical entry point. The openness of the walkway offered him more escape options, although he realized that was optimistic—inside or outside, he was easy prey. As he walked between the tourists queueing for the harbor cruises to his right and those waiting to get into Harry Caray's Tavern on the land side, he felt like everyone was watching him.

A bit further on, around a corner and through some tall shade trees, the wheel came into view. The bottom half obscured by a low gray building housing a few more ways for businesses to separate tourists from their money. A set of stairs led up through a tunnel-like opening in the wall of the building. Royce looked around before he bounded up the stairs. They were enclosed on three sides, so when he emerged on the raised platform, the visual impact took his breath away. Spinning silently in the bright, midday sky, the sight of the wheel would have normally delighted him—the size and grace, rotating endlessly—but under the circumstances it looked like a saw blade ready to cut him to pieces. He froze. Turning around, he took a step back toward the entrance. Although he knew the path back, its woven bricks ultimately led nowhere. The realization hit him after just a few strides. Whatever future he had was ahead, not behind.

The wheel was surrounded by low circus tents and a few carnival rides. Families milled around, noshing on churros and corn dogs. Laughter and a few delighted screams echoed off the walls of the low glass buildings of the pier surrounding the wheel. He pressed forward, weaving through the crowds.

He saw Ruben Steinlauf standing on the low retaining wall of a planter at the base of the wheel. Royce exhaled and then strode purposefully toward him. As he approached, his mouth went dry and he felt his palms sweat. It was like a first date, but with the risk of death thrown in.

"Mr. Steinlauf," Royce sputtered. "I'm Royce Johnson."

"So, you're the fucker causing me so much trouble." Steinlauf stepped forward and shook his hand. Two men standing like guard dogs lurched forward as he did, keeping an even distance between Steinlauf and them.

"I'm the fucker," Royce jabbed, as he glanced over his shoulders with the side of his eyes.

The guard dogs moved around and stood beside Royce. The smaller of the two—Chinese or Mongolian, Royce thought—patted him down as inconspicuously as possible. When he was done, and suspecting Johnson wasn't packing, he nodded to Steinlauf.

"Well, follow me, fucker." The man turned and headed toward the small set of stairs leading up to the spot where there was a break in the fence around the base of the wheel and passengers got in and out. Royce followed. A few paces on, they cut to the front of the line, over the howls of a few dads further back. Steinlauf dismissed them with the wave of his hand, and with a nod to the attendant he'd greased earlier, stepped toward an empty gondola. The attendant acknowledged him with a return nod. He held up his hand and let four families board ahead of them. As the fifth approached, he signaled to Steinlauf, and they all stepped into an empty gondola. The door closed, and the four of them rose up alone.

"We don't have much time."

"Eight minutes, in fact," Royce snapped back.

"Indeed." His eyes showed Royce that he appreciated someone who was prepared.

As the doors to the gondola closed and they started off with a jerk, Royce took the initiative.

"What's the deal, Ruben? I assume we're here to negotiate, not to enjoy the views."

"You have two options, Agent Johnson. First, walk away. Go home to your wife and kids."

One of the guard dogs handed Steinlauf a manila folder. He took out some photos and handed them to Royce. They were of Jenny and the girls. Swimming in the lake, sitting on the porch, toasting s'mores at their cabin in the woods. Royce swallowed hard but tried to hide it. He leafed through the pictures quickly. He wanted to savor them, to know every detail of what his girls had been up to, but he was unable to look at them for long. There were also shots of what he guessed were Marcus's mom and a child that he assumed belonged to—well, he wasn't sure. But it was small and cute and fragile. Royce shuddered. Steinlauf continued.

"Forget about me and Dean Turner and all the rest. Rockefeller University has been a nightmare for you and your family. It's time to move on. Go home. Open a restaurant or be a fly-fishing guide. Work in the fraud department for some credit card company. Herd sheep. Something. Anything. Just not this. I won't let you take this from me."

"Pass. What's the second option?" Royce steeled himself.

"I have these two rip you to shreds." He motioned to guard dogs with a nod of his head. "Do you like that one better?"

"Here, on this gondola? I doubt it. What are you going to do, drag my corpse out past the few thousand people between here and the street? Please. I thought you were a tough negotiator?"

"Not here, silly. Sometime. Couple of days. Maybe a week. These two take you when you're sleeping, maybe walking alone in your neighborhood—or, your brother's neighborhood, I should say. And then, when they've dissolved your body in acid and smashed your teeth to dust, they drive to Maryland and have their way with that pretty wife. Your daughters. I know I wouldn't want that if I were you. Maybe they rape them. Torture them. Who knows. These guys are unpredictable, and their culture doesn't respect life like ours does. Do you like those odds?"

The volcano rumbled inside of Royce. The mention of his family, of violating them, was too much for him. He reached under the seat and grabbed a taser that was duct taped under the seat. In a single motion, he raised it up and set two electrodes into the face of the guard dog over Steinlauf's right shoulder. The man convulsed into a pile on the floor of the gondola. Royce rolled off his bench to his right, keeping distance—and Steinlauf—between him and the second guard dog. It gave him time to reach into his cowboy boot and pull out a throwing knife. The knife was out of his hand in less than two seconds, landing in the guard dog's shoulder a second after that. As the man writhed in pain, Royce leapt to his feet and was on top of him. Three quick punches to the face, and the man was limp. He pulled the knife from his shoulder, and then turned toward Steinlauf.

"Sit tight," Royce spat.

He reached under the seat and pulled out a roll of duct tape, duct-taped to the underside. Steinlauf wasn't the only one who could grease the palms of a gondola attendant. The night before, Royce had visited the gondola and prepared car five for his rendezvous with Steinlauf. He wasn't sure if he was going to use the taser or the tape or the 9 mm handgun still taped underneath. But Royce always had plans, backup plans, and backup plans for his backup plans. His weekend trips to the hardware store had contingencies.

After he taped up the mouths and hands of the guard dogs, Royce took his seat across from Steinlauf, who was frozen in fear. Reaching under the seat, he pulled out the pistol, and brought it up, aiming center mass.

"Now that I've evened the odds," Royce said calmly, "why don't we restart our negotiation?" Steinlauf's eyes were wide. His voice mute. "I know you didn't invite me here to threaten me. I assume this was a test, and that I've passed."

"You have, Agent Johnson, you have." His voice was full of admiration, laced with surprise.

"Good. I have lost a step—a year behind bars will do that to a man—but I'm still better than anything you can throw at me. You or your buddy, Max." Royce lowered the weapon, sure that Steinlauf posed no threat. The guard dogs were coming to, but they were taped up, and the gondola was nearing the peak, giving him less than five minutes. Royce went on.

"So what's the real deal, Steinlauf? I assume you have information for me that you'll trade…"

The man across from him breathed in deeply, then reached into his pocket. He held out a flash drive, fingering it as he held it up in front of Royce.

"I know who killed Jante. This is proof."

Royce eyed the flash drive. He had half a mind to just take it. But it might have been another ruse. He needed to know what Steinlauf knew and what his role was in all this, not just take what might be an empty flash drive. Plus, Royce and Marcus needed a deal. Neither wanted to live his life looking over his shoulder, wondering if this was going to be the day.

Royce reached for the flash drive.

"Nah, nah. Not so fast. We haven't discussed what you do for me."

The ground was getting closer and the guard dogs were squirming. Royce raised the pistol center mass again.

"What do you want?" he growled.

"Leave Bubbly Creek alone. Walk away from that much. You should know, the two aren't connected. It's just a coincidence, as this will show." He held up the flash drive out of Royce's reach. "Jante's murder had nothing to do with our development. But don't just trust me, see for yourself." He moved it toward

Royce. "This is yours, if you just promise me that when you put her killer away, you drop the investigation into Bubbly Creek."

"What about Mike Church? What about Becca Goldman?" Royce asked, as he reached out for the flash drive, like he was grasping for a lifeline while drowning.

"I had nothing to do with those unfortunate deaths, of course, but they may indeed be related to Quayside, I'm sorry to say. But they aren't coming back, Royce, and the development is going to do wonderful things for lots of people on the South Side. I think we just have to say that their deaths, while shocking, were unavoidable. Collateral damage, sadly. But, hey, they weren't your case. Scott Miller hired you to find Jante's killer. Mission accomplished." He put the flash drive in Royce's hand. "Now, untie my men, put that pistol away, and let's get on with our lives."

The gondola was at around five o'clock on its rotation. Royce put the pistol in his waistband, and, down on his knees, took the duct tape off the guard dogs. As he did, their master talked them down from their revenge. As they sat back up onto the bench of the gondola, blood soaked the shirt of one, the other's eyes were red with rage. But, loyal soldiers, they took heed of Steinlauf's command.

As the gondola swung into position at the bottom of its arc, Royce looked right at Steinlauf.

"How do I know you'll keep your end of the bargain? How do I know this isn't blank? That you won't send your goons to kill me and my family?"

"You don't. I won't if you keep up your end. But, the sad fact, is you don't know. There is nothing I can do to reinforce my promise. I can't credibly commit, as your brother would have said in law and economics parlance. You'll just have to trust me." Royce smirked. "And, of course, I've got to trust you too. Not to go after Bubbly Creek. Not to screw me out of hundreds of millions of dollars. I think we have reason to trust each other, don't you?"

The door opened, and the guard dogs led the way. The blood-stained shirt got a few glances, but of the *I-can't-believe-that-guy-has-stains-on-his-shirt* variety, not the *Was-that-guy-stabbed?* variety. Steinlauf exited the gondola, then turned and faced Royce, who was exiting behind him. He reached out his hand, and Royce shook it.

"A deal well made, Agent Johnson. Now, go live your life."

Royce took back his hand. He started to speak, but before he could form a sentence, a shot rang out.

CHAPTER 44

The crack was unmistakable. High-caliber, long-range, and on-target. A piercing shriek, then the sound of lead impacting and spinning through flesh. Royce knew he hadn't been hit, so he fell to the ground and rolled to his right. Screams now flooded his ears in stereo. Everyone was running away from him. As he came around to his belly, he saw Ruben Steinlauf lying face down, his torso inside of the gondola and his legs out on the landing pad. Royce eyed him carefully. He wasn't moving. Whether or not he was the target, Royce suspected he was where the bullet ended up. Royce looked down at his shirt, and noticed that it was covered in blood, bits of skull, and clumps of flesh. He was wearing what had once been Steinlauf's brain and face.

Royce couldn't stick around to mourn. If he was the target and Steinlauf's head being in the way was a lucky break, he needed to move quickly into the crowds. Rolling back under the gondola for a bit of cover, Royce removed the 9 mm from his waistband, and army-crawled under the gondola and out on the other side. He took off sprinting toward the covered buildings of the pier.

Watching through a sniper scope, Aliza Kahan couldn't get a clean shot. The orange hat bobbed and weaved, blocked by the gondola, then metal bars and tents and outbuildings. In several seconds, he was out of sight. Kahan folded up the IWI DAN .338 sniper rifle and put it into a large backpack. As she did, she regretted the shot that spewed Steinlauf's brain all over Johnson's shirt. Part of her regret was because she was shooting for a double kill. It was timed and aimed perfectly, but something inside of Steinlauf's head sent the bullet tumbling off course. The other part of her regret was that something else was wrong. She'd killed before, more times than she wanted to remember. But when the corpses visited her in the night, their distorted faces shouting at her, she had an argument for them. A cool, rational argument about the why. What would she say to Ruben Steinlauf and to Royce Johnson when they came calling in the middle of the night? She had no idea, and it wasn't enough that Max Klepp said so. She wanted to hit undo but couldn't quite muster the strength to stop herself. She pulled out her phone, wishing it would be different. But when it wasn't, when she looked down from her perch on an abandoned floor of a new building under construction and still saw what used to be Max Klepp's business partner, she dialed her attack man stationed on the pier. Ivan Olej was waiting. She adjusted her headset and barked a series of commands in their own private code. Then Aliza fell back and let the tension of the moment fall into the floor. After fifteen seconds of concentrated breathing, she felt better. She picked up her backpack and headed down the stairs toward the pier, where she'd provide backup.

Ivan Olej had his orders. He dropped the soft pretzel he was eating and scanned the scene. Johnson wasn't in sight, but he'd heard the shot and saw the crowds running in all directions. Aliza told him that Johnson was among them, clad in a bright orange Bears hat. Olej pulled out his Jericho 941 and headed off in the direction his boss told him the target ran. Feeling the exhilaration of the chase, he was nagged by the oddness of the situation. Johnson was headed east, further out on the pier into the lake, where his options were fewer. And he'd marked himself with that hat in a way that made him easily identifiable. Two seemingly stupid moves from an otherwise savvy adversary. It didn't add up. But Olej chased like a dog after a stick. It was his nature to run toward the unknown.

After a few seconds of flat-out sprint, Olej saw him in the distance. Then, as quickly as he was acquired, he disappeared. Royce ducked through a side door into a low building. Olej slowed his pace, as he was now within easy range of the Jericho. Pausing at the door, he let his heart rate slow, then he walked in casually. It was a narrow arcade of shops, jammed with people. Immediately, the orange hat made sense. At least ten other people in eyeshot were wearing the same hat. *Smart.* Johnson, or more likely one of his confederates, had seeded the crowd with free hats, it seemed. A zebra among a herd of gazelles, he decided to better his odds by painting stripes on a few of them to blend in.

Olej walked quickstep past tourists, smiling faces and chins dripping with mustard and powdered sugar. Every male in a hat warranted a second look, but none were him. It was starting to look like a smarter plan than he realized at first. The fake zebras made ID'ing him tough, and if Johnson had scouted the pier in advance, which there was no doubt he had, there were countless ways of getting lost. There were too many doors to process—to the Shakespeare Theater, to parking garages, to a radio station, and to the USO. *Damn!*

But, standing amid the masses, he paused to think. He realized Royce would have to exit back to the city eventually. The neck of the pier was only a hundred yards or so. *Go back and wait for him to leave the pier.* He could get enough eyes on the exit to ensure they wouldn't miss him. Plus, he knew that Aliza was probably down off of her perch and waiting at the city-end of the pier as well. *Set the net, and wait for the prey to come to me*, he thought. Play the spider, not the tiger.

But then it dawned on him. Johnson knew this too. He

wasn't going back that way. Too risky. *But where? How will he get off the pier? The pier. Of course!* There was another exit off every pier. Through the tall glass windows of the building facing south, he saw the luxury yachts that ran tours of the lakefront bobbing alongside the pier. *A boat!* As the image of Johnson escaping on a boat out into the lake formed in his mind, his legs pushed him forward. He needed to beat Johnson to the end of the pier. That was the only way off. Both sides of the pier were inaccessible to private boats. On the south side, tour boats were docked from end to end. On the north side, the waters were restricted, since it was the location of the city's water filtration plant. Olej immediately deduced that the end of the pier was where his rendezvous would be waiting.

As he ran, the Dock Street shops gave way to a vast pavilion of towering ceilings and open space for meetings, conventions, and events. Olej saw no orange hats in the Festival Hall. No doubt Johnson had ditched the hat, and probably changed clothes in a bathroom. *Game on.*

Jericho holstered so as not to draw unwanted attention, Olej walked briskly through the airy space, eyes shifting right and left, but trying not to attract attention. The gunshots hadn't been heard out this far on the pier, but word traveled quickly. There were security guards and other pier officials escorting people this way and that, and the whine of sirens started to echo through the space. It was emptying out.

Finding himself more or less alone, Olej accelerated his pace to a brisk jog. The end of the pier was still a few hundred yards ahead, and he was increasingly certain that that was where Royce Johnson was going to make his escape. As he ran, he pulled out his phone and dialed his boss.

"Kahan," she answered matter of factly.

"Aliza, it's Ivan. I'm chasing Johnson through the convention space. He's headed to the end of the pier. I think he must have a boat waiting."

"Don't let him get away!" she barked. "He has the flash drive."

"Understood," Olej shouted back as he ran. "I need backup. Out on the water side."

"On it."

Click. She was gone.

Olej pressed on, hoping reinforcements were on the way. Either by sea or by air. Preferably both. He was up against a true adversary. Just as he thought that, Johnson came into view. Olej kneeled, raised the Jericho, and squeezed off a round.

CHAPTER 45

Royce didn't see Olej when he turned to look over his shoulder as he dodged his way through Festival Hall. Workers were setting up for the Annual Flower and Garden Show scheduled for the next week when the alerts to shelter in place came to their phones. Now they cowered behind empty earthenware pots and bags of topsoil. As he ran past, their eyes asked—*What are you doing?*—or begged him—*Get down!* One man in overalls tried to reach out and grab him to pull him to safety. Dodging and ignoring them, Royce raced toward the sets of doors at the far end of the pavilion, still fifty yards away. A duffle bag full of supplies he'd stashed in a false ceiling in a men's room during his prep visits to the pier bounced on his back as he ran.

He felt the sting in his arm before he heard the sound of the shot echo through the cavernous hall. The bullet ripped through the fleshy part of his bicep, sending him flying forward diving for cover. The sting was a thousand Novocain shots at once. It was Royce's first gunshot wound, and it couldn't have come at a worse time. His body was just nearly fully functional again after his puncture wound. This would be a biological setback. But, more importantly, getting clipped here meant jeopardizing his escape. He simply had to make it. His girls needed him. Marcus needed him. Jante needed him.

On the ground, he ducked behind a large planter, filled with tall evergreen trees. He reached for a nearby table, set out to receive flower displays, and ripped off a large tablecloth. Using the Helle Fjellkniven knife he'd used to stab one of the guard dogs, he cut off a few long strips, and wrapped them as tightly around his bicep as he could. The wound was near the surface, and it went clean through. It would bleed but it wouldn't kill him, the bullet having missed any major vessels. A lucky break.

But it was an expert shot from a long distance. He had to move. He could feel the blood pooling in the tablecloth bandages and dripping down his fingers, into little pools on the tile floor. His mind raced. Scanning his surroundings, he looked for any advantage. There weren't many options: a hose, a shovel, a bag of peat. Some flowering plants in plastic crates. Then he noticed a pallet of lime fertilizer. He reached up, exposing his arm to his pursuer, and pulled a bag of fertilizer off the top of the pile. Using his wounded arm as a guide, he wedged the bag between his body and his good arm, and then used all his strength to get it up on top of the planter. He pushed it over the side of the planter so that it was on the side of the shooter.

Then, he took the shotgun Marcus got for him out of his duffle bag, where it had been waiting patiently next to an energy bar, a first-aid kit, and a bottle of water. He wiggled himself a few feet away from the planter, exhaled three times in a row, and let a blast of buckshot loose into the bag. It exploded in a cloud of dust. Two more shots in rapid-fire succession left a large plume of lime smoke floating in the room between Royce and the shooter. Royce hoped the improvised smoke grenade would provide him enough of cover. He was out of other options.

Running low and in a serpentine path, he dodged pallets of shrubs and flowers, and ran past gardeners cowering under tables, even more afraid now than they were before. He heard their weeps and shudders as he bolted for the door. The pain from his arm radiated over his entire body, but his legs drove him on, unmoved by the tingling nerves that made him feel electrified. *The legs feed the wolf*, he could hear his father yelling, as he ran the stairs of his high school football stadium in his mind. *No son of mine will ever get tired at the end of the game.* Royce wrote a thank you note to his old man in his mind, but it was too late to be delivered.

At the end of the convention space, he slammed through a set of double doors, the panic bars serving the purpose of their design. A shot came in right after him, ripping a hole through the wood and careening harmlessly in the hallway. Then, in quick succession, more shots. Two, three, four. What sounded like a rifle and then a pistol. Royce thought for a moment that there were now two people shooting at him. Maybe more.

Ignoring the shots but hoping they were aimed at someone other than him, Royce ran as fast as he could, lungs burning and arm numb with searing pain. He burst through another set of panic doors and into the Grand Ballroom, the last building on the Pier.

The room was magnificent. Even someone, fleeing from two people who were trying to kill him and who was bleeding profusely from a gunshot, could appreciate the beauty of the building and the setting. The lake was visible for two hundred seventy degrees through giant windows in the dome. The space was bathed in light and the feel of the sea. Workers had been setting up for a wedding or a fundraiser, but they scattered as Royce burst in. The doors on all sides of the spherical dome were opened to the afternoon air, workers streamed out. Royce noticed the magnificent dome, ribbed with support beams running from the floor up to a point in the ceiling like lines of longitude converging at the pole. But half a second was too much.

He wove through the tables, across the dance floor, and out on the concourse with the frightened staff in under a minute. The florists and attendants and carpenters and caterers huddled by benches and behind trees and under delivery trucks. Royce found a position behind the cab of an eighteen-wheeler that was backed up to the rear of the ballroom, ready to unload tables and chairs for the event. He steadied his breathing and chambered another round into the shotgun. The door to the cab swung open with a pull, and he got into a prone position behind it, aiming up from the ground under the doorframe.

A minute that seemed like an hour passed. Then, a door to the ballroom opened slowly. All the workers had exited ahead of him, so Royce was confident it was one of his pursuers. He counted to three, then let another round of buckshot fly into the door to the pavilion. It swung back, now riddled with holes. As it traveled, he leapt to his feet and ran headlong for the end of the pier, about a hundred feet away. Counting out ten strides, he fell to one knee, spun around, and let three blasts loose in the direction of the doorways leading out from the ballroom to the concourse. Each shot caused a scream to rise up from the crowd of workers, hidden like Easter eggs among the planters, vehicles, and outbuildings on the concourse. The doors remained shut.

Running on, he thought about shooting another round over his shoulder, but he couldn't be sure there were no bystanders in the way. Royce pulled the duffle bag around to the front of his body, unzipped it, and put the shotgun inside. He tried to zip it back up as he ran, but the end of the pier was approaching quickly, and he couldn't quite get the angle or the leverage right. About half zipped, he hurled it off the end of the pier down toward the water below. Picking up speed, he reached the end of the pier, then jumped off the end headed for the lake, ten feet below. As he did, a shot rang off a flagpole at the water's edge. Another flew over his head, its unmistakable whiz sending shivers down his spine. *In the nick of time*, he thought, as he braced for impact.

CHAPTER 46

The landing buckled Royce's knee. As he fell, ten feet felt like a hundred. The mattress the captain set out in the rear deck where he expected Royce to land felt like concrete when he landed. Royce rolled onto his back, reached for the bag he'd thrown over first. The shotgun wasn't inside. Royce scanned the deck, and saw it a few feet away, up against a buoy. He rolled over twice and grabbed it, rounding a chamber in one motion. Aiming over the parapet wall of the pier, he let one round go, hoping it wouldn't find a target. Just a warning. Then, they were away.

The twin Volvo Penta IPS 500 diesels on the thirty-nine-foot Tiara fishing charter groaned. The nose of the boat to rise up out of the water. They left the pier behind in seconds. Two other nearly identical Tiaras peeled off the pier simultaneously, heading out in a pack. Royce took cover behind a large fish cooler, stuffed with ice, his shotgun aimed up at the pier. Several shapes appeared, looking over the edge and then out at them, but they hesitated, not knowing which boat to target. It was just enough time. Then, they were far enough away, moving at too high a speed and with too many evasive maneuvers for a clean shot.

For twenty-five hundred dollars, the captain, a South Side regular who'd run charters out of the 59th Street harbor for years and was indebted to Marcus in ways he wasn't willing to share, agreed to be at the end of the pier with his fleet ready to go at the appointed hour. They were told in no uncertain terms that the cargo was special and would attract attention, perhaps of the leaded variety. The captain merely grunted at the thought, happy to repay a bit of his debt and make some cash on the side. Getting to stick it to the mayor and the Chicago cops, whom he assumed were the bad guys in this play and would be in pursuit, was a bonus.

When they cleared the sea wall and passed the Chicago Harbor Lighthouse, the three charters headed off in different directions. One went northwest along the coast of Lincoln Park; one headed due east toward the town of Bridgman, Michigan, fifty miles away; and the final one, the one carrying Royce, turned southeast toward Gary, Indiana.

Royce let himself relax. Finding a boat to give chase and deploying it would take some time. As would a chopper. The police marine units were not out in force this early in the season, so even if they were mobilized, it would take a bit of time. He came up from behind the cooler and climbed the ladder up to the wheelhouse. Each step shot pain up his spine and into the base of his neck, but it was a welcome distraction from his arm, now dead with pain. The bandages were black with blood, but the pace of the bleeding seemed to be slowing. The captain was not into small talk, and he didn't want to know anything about what was happening. "The less you tell me, the better off we both will be. Now, get below and get ready." That was all he said during their entire voyage.

The Colored Comet—named after Jackie Robinson—hit its top speed of nearly thirty-five miles per hour as they approached Northerly Island. Royce caught himself admiring the majestic buildings of Chicago's Museum Campus—the Field Museum, the Shedd Aquarium, the Adler Planetarium, and Soldier Field. Alex loved taking his kids to see Chicago's cultural treasures, and the thought steeled Royce's spirit. As the more mundane buildings of the McCormick Place Convention Center came into view, his mind turned to his injuries and the task at hand. He stripped naked. Shivering on the mattress, he pulled out the first-aid kit from the duffle and went to work on his arm. Alcohol did its job, cleaning the wound and reinvigorating his spirit. He felt the tingles it created in every hair follicle. He wrapped the wound, still bleeding, with gauze and an ace bandage, as tight as possible. The leg and back, now aching as well, got a heavy dose of ibuprofen. It might make the bleeding a bit worse, but without it, he might not be able to go on. This was good as he could do on his own, bouncing on waves at thirty miles per hour.

Royce removed his Helle Fjellkniven and cut a large hole in the side of the mattress. He stuffed the old clothes, strips of blood-soaked tablecloth, and other evidence inside the mattress. He put in five twenty-pound weights for barbells that the captain had placed there on request inside the mattress as well. Each felt like moving a mountain. Using his good arm, he heaved the edge of the mattress up on the bulwark, and then, using his hip, moved the mattress into a position where a bump would send it afloat. As they passed Promontory Point and turned east, just offshore from where Jante Turner bled to death, he gave it a nudge. It disappeared in the wake of the boat, as they headed for their destination: the Edward F. Dunne Crib.

Built in 1909, the Dunne Crib was one of nine structures built to bring drinking water from Lake Michigan to Chicago. A pumping system and intake pipes beneath the crib carried fresh water from two miles offshore—where it was supposedly untainted by the pollution of the city—to water treatment facilities onshore. At the surface, the Dunne Crib was a hexagonal island of concrete about one hundred fifty feet across. A two-story building sat at the center. It housed the pumping equipment and a large fog light. Before the system was automated a few decades back, the building was home to several cribkeepers. There was a large kitchen and several bedrooms for them, as well as storage and a recreation space. The cribkeepers manned the pumps and the lighthouse, living out their days in isolation, the great city looming just out of reach. One of two still-active cribs, the Dunne Crib connected to an older crib via two large metal gantries. The other crib, known as the 68th Street Crib, was about fifteen feet away. It looked like the top third of a grain silo sticking out of the water. It now served mostly as a resting place for birds making the transit across the lake.

Naked and shivering on the deck, Royce saw the crib complex come into view. He put his pack, phone, wallet, keys, and other valuables into a waterproof bag he pulled from the duffle. He folded over the top and sealed it tight. He wrapped a plastic tie secured to the bag around his ankle and stepped to the edge of the boat. The stopwatch he'd started when they left the pier clicked over fifteen minutes. The Chicago Police Marine units, which he assumed were in pursuit, would be closing in. Or maybe Klepp's private army would quickly send up a chopper. Either way, giving them three fast-moving targets that could blend in with the other boat traffic on a clear and quiet afternoon would delay them, but not indefinitely. He gave himself twenty minutes. Tick tock.

"Get ready!" the captain shouted down over the roar of the Volvos.

They approached the cribs at top speed, then when they passed the cylindrical crib, the captain idled the engines, and turned sharply toward them. He slowed as they passed the edge of the Dunne Crib. Royce said a prayer, though he didn't believe in God, then jumped into the frigid water. The *Comet* disappeared in a roar and flurry of bubbles and waves. The captain turned east, headed out toward the center of the lake, where he'd put the boat on autopilot, clean the deck of any evidence Royce Johnson had been on board, then do some fishing.

The water stung, but he wasn't in it for long. Just a few paddles, and he found a rusty metal ladder dropped into the water. In moments, he was up on the concrete platform looking like a wounded sea creature struggling ashore, shivering and bleeding. The crib house was set back twenty feet from the edge, surrounded by a moat of large riprap. A concrete pathway connected the house to the outer concrete rim. Covered in gooseflesh, teeth chattering, Royce walked down the path, dragging the waterproof bag like a prisoner weighed down by a ball and chain. Every few steps, he looked up for signs that he'd been spotted by a helicopter. The bright blue sky was empty.

Halfway across the walkway, he reached down and grabbed a large diving bag he'd stashed at the crib a day earlier. He'd disabled the motion-sensing buoys that surrounded the crib—a post 9/11 precaution he'd learned about while working a terror case in Chicago years earlier. His muscles were in full revolt at this point, but he was able to muster just enough strength to get the bag onto his shoulder. Twenty more steps. At the large steel doors, Royce dropped the bag, removing bolt cutters and a wool blanket. Wrapping the blanket around his shoulders, he went to work on the thick chain secured by a padlock. He hadn't counted on a gunshot wound, which made working the cutter nearly impossible. Warmth and a bed and safety from spotters were on the other side, inches away, but there was no way to make it work. He needed shelter, now.

Dropping everything, he removed spare clothes and shoes from the bag, and quickly got dressed. The cutters and the blanket went back in, and he pushed the bag off the causeway and back onto the rocks a few feet below. Then, he ran down the path back to the edge of the crib. Sprinting as fast as he could, he made his way around the perimeter to the point between the two cribs, the lattice iron gantry overhead. On this side there was some idled equipment and scattered boards and junk. Royce picked up a piece of plywood and some heavy plastic sheeting that covered a small pump. He quickly set the wood on an angle against the side of the crib, and then used the black sheeting as camouflage. A makeshift lean-to would have to do for now. He had just minutes to get out of sight. It wasn't the Ritz, but it would hide him from any observers by air or by sea and would offer him a place to rest for a few minutes shielded from the elements. Let his wound rest and the painkillers take effect. Royce took a long drink of water and popped more meds. He changed the dressing on his wound, wrapping the bandage even tighter. Then, he lay back to let his body recover. He was asleep before his head hit the concrete wall of the crib.

A few hours later, he jumped up. Instinctively, the shotgun led the way. Eyes not yet open, he moved the shotgun in a one-hundred-eighty-degree arc, but there were only ghosts. The wind had turned the sheeting into a flapping sail, and he must have kicked out the base of the lean-to, since it was all more or less collapsed on top of him. It still provided protection from the sun and the bad guys, but how he was able to sleep was a mystery. Three energy bars and some water went down easily. Despite the circumstances, he felt refreshed.

Back at the front door, he tried again with the bolt cutters. His wounded arm still wasn't strong enough, so he used one arm and his other hip as leverage instead. Ten minutes of everything he could give finally paid off. The steel doors creaked open, years of rust falling away like snow. The interior of the crib was dank and cool. But it offered refuge. Royce quickly located one of the old bedrooms, set off the kitchen by a bathroom that was no longer serviceable. There was an old iron bed frame and some mismatched furniture. In a closet, he found some dirty linens, cardboard boxes, and miscellaneous junk. Home. At least for the next twelve hours, until, in the deep of the darkest part of the night, he'd get into the canoe he'd tied to the crib, and, gritting his teeth through the pain, row it into the Jackson Park Harbor, where Marcus would be waiting.

Royce piled the softest of the stuff onto the bed, covering it with some of the cardboard. Then he lay back and stared up at the ceiling, wet with moisture and paint chips hanging like stalactites. Counting them like sheep, he could feel sleep coming again. He reached into his pack and took out the shotgun. He put another round in the chamber, then rested it on his chest. His last thoughts were of the flash drive he felt in his pocket and the secrets that it contained.

CHAPTER 47

"It doesn't make any sense," Marcus said as he tended to the wound on Royce's bicep. Dabbing it with cotton balls drenched in alcohol, he repeated himself. "Why would Max have taken out Steinlauf? If Max had Jante killed, why would Steinlauf reveal this, since that would be the end of Quayside?"

"And if Max didn't have Jante killed, as Steinlauf told me, how would he know who did, let alone have proof?" Royce added.

"Maybe they were aiming for you and missed? Maybe Steinlauf set you up and was expecting the shot?"

"Anything is possible. But my guess is that Max, or whomever it was, can afford people who can hit a target with a well-scoped rifle. We were pretty easy targets."

Marcus finished cleaning the wound and applying a new bandage.

"All set," he said proudly. "Now, let's see what we've got here." He flipped the flash drive up into the air and caught it with a sweep of his right hand like he was trying to catch a fly.

They walked together into the kitchen and booted up a laptop on the counter. Marcus inserted the flash drive and opened its directory. There was one folder full of files—video files. He double clicked on the first one, then stepped back to watch it play.

The video appeared to be from a security camera surveilling

what appeared to be a lake-front jogging trail. Royce and Marcus turned toward each other, giving the other a knowing smile. This must be Park District footage of the area around where Jante Turner was murdered.

The videos covered the first six months of the year, most of which was irrelevant. Royce opened the day of the murder. Turner had been killed at around six a.m., so he started the recording at around 5:30 a.m. and let it run at three-times speed. As expected, there wasn't much to see. A few early-morning asphalt warriors, a guy walking his dog, and an occasional biker zooming in an out of the frame, their skin-tight, neon racing suits flashing on screen like luminescent bacteria in a ship's wake. The camera was set on a light pole on Lake Shore Drive, about thirty yards away from the running path. This meant that the figures were relatively small and vague, but general shapes and sizes were discernable.

Then she came into frame. Unmistakable in her blackness and her intensity. Even from this perspective, her power was compelling. Watching her, imagining her thoughts as she eased past the bathroom where she would die in minutes, Royce felt profoundly sad. Not that her life was ending, as he didn't know her from Eve. But that *a* life was ending. This life, right in front of him. His thoughts moved to Alex, as they always did. He was watching the grainy video of his brother's murder he'd watched in Gerhardt's broom closet, except this time, he could see his brother, sipping his coffee, reading the *Wall Street Journal*, and thinking about the tomorrows he'd never see. He could see the shot. The moment, the inflection between dreams and nothing.

Seeing her reenter the screen from the right side snapped Royce back to her murder. She stopped. He couldn't help but wish her on, shout at her to keep running. Maybe live another day. But the urging would be as effective as telling the cute co-ed not to go swimming alone at night in the horror movie. Jante Turner's fate was sealed by the screenwriter of her life.

Royce rewound. He didn't see the gunman, who must have

come in darkness, hours earlier. Then, after his work was done, he ran out the front door of the bathroom, straight down to the lakeshore. The building blocked his view from the camera for a bit, then a large hedge, and finally, the slope arcing down to the waterline. Once there, he must have moved in a direction that Royce could not see to places unknown. Smart. How he would have done it. Obviously a pro, although he knew that already. The gunman was a dead end. There would be no traces. He—Royce assumed with great confidence it was a he—would never be caught unless someone else made a mistake. The chain is only as strong as its weakest link, and it was very unlikely that whoever was hidden behind the concrete blocks and the mural of African-American heroes in that bathroom stall was weak. He'd waited for hours alone in the darkness of the bathroom and executed a perfect shot. Not weak.

Back to the day before. Nothing. Then the day before that and the day before that. They watched every day in May and then April and March, trying to identify any patterns. The same biker—a man clad in a neon yellow jersey and a blue bike helmet—appeared every morning at around 5:45 a.m., then came the heavy-set black man walking his poodle at around 5:50 a.m., and, before Jante Turner came into view between 6:05 a.m. and 6:10 a.m. every morning, an occasional jogger or walker. They weren't predictable, but they saw the same outlines. A day here, a missed week there, and then another appearance. But the three—the biker, the dog walker, and Jante—they were the regulars.

"Why didn't he give us the file we needed? Why make us look through all of these if he knows the one we need to see? Or is he just playing with us?" Marcus said, frustration filling his voice. He walked over and pulled a Red Stripe from the refrigerator, sliding one across the counter to Royce.

"Don't know. Maybe there's a reason he wants us to figure it out. We just need to keep looking. Either way, we'll know what happened on the pier."

By February, the path was mostly empty and even the regulars were gone. They played the same videos forward, running history in the way that would kill Jante Turner, not the way that brought her back to life. The second time through, Royce noticed something odd. Starting in early May, he saw a woman he hadn't seen before. She became a new regular, coming into the frame right after Turner left it. Usually by less than a minute or two. Like clockwork. Every day for about two weeks, and then, poof.

"That's odd," he said.

"Yeah, I noticed her too," Marcus replied. "Who is that?" He squinted and moved his face closer to the screen.

"Let's look back," Royce suggested.

They expanded the time frame. It meant a lot more work—boring, mind-numbing work—but it was like a gift from his arm and healing ribs to his brain. *Here, think about this instead of us.* Starting in March and going to the end of June, Royce and Marcus scanned the surveillance videos for any signs of the mystery woman. They took turns, as one went to the bathroom, to check the security on the perimeter, or to make some food. The woman didn't appear at any other times or any other days except for several weeks in May, always right after the dean-to-be passed in and out of the frame.

While Marcus was marinating some chicken breasts with his favorite jerk rub, Royce went back to one of these days in May. He paused as she entered the frame, and zoomed in. The quality was low, and as he made her bigger, it got worse. But some things were obvious. She had a long ponytail of what looked like red hair. Her clothes and poise also suggested she was well off. Also, not particularly athletic—she had the gait of a horse that had thrown a shoe. She looked like...

CHAPTER 48

Two months ago

"Dad!"

Beth Miller threw herself into a deep leather chair in her father's office on the sixty-fourth floor of the Hancock Building. He didn't look up from a sheaf of papers placed meticulously on his enormous oak desk. Max Klepp didn't have a computer at work either, and therefore the scene he was in could have been set in the 1950s or any decade since. As he liked it.

"What is it, Liebchen? I've got a busy calendar." His eyes still fixed on rows of figures and what appeared, to Beth, to be a map.

"It's Scott. He hired that FBI guy, the one who brought down the president."

This got the old man's attention.

"Hired him? To what end?"

"What end?! What end! To clear his name. To find the...the person who killed that bitch." Her pace was frantic.

He walked over to a credenza and meticulously poured himself a Pappy and his daughter a Żubrówka. The weighty crystal glass felt reassuring in her hand, and the cold vodka was an injection of calm. Klepp stood behind her, his hand on her shoulder.

"Okay, let's relax." He spoke as if she were ten. "Why is this a problem? And, bitch? Did you know her?"

"It should have been Scott, Daddy."

"Yeah, maybe. I'm...ah...I'm confused."

"Ambition. My ambition is his ambition. At least since I gave up my writing to raise the kids and go to the check-ups and be in the book clubs." She murmured it, as if to convince herself of something.

"Go back, sweetie. Why is this my problem? I assume that finding the killer and finding out that it isn't Scott is a good thing. It wasn't Scott, was it?" The look on his face suggested Klepp never entertained the possibility until he said it out loud just now.

"Of course, it wasn't Scott. He could never. He's too...He's got nothing to do with this, I'm positive."

"I wouldn't think so. He's flaccid as—"

"Dad!" She was that little girl again, her dad making fun of a New Trier mathlete she brought home for Easter dinner.

"Plus, if he did, why would he hire Johnson? I can see hiring some putz retired Chicago cop, but not this guy. No way you hire *this guy*."

"Right," her tone resigned, "Royce Johnson gets his man."

"So, I'm sorry, Liebchen. Isn't this a good thing? Isn't Scott operating under some kind of cloud? I mean, even if the students are nuts, which I assume they are, they are still important. If he can't satisfy them—"

"It was me, Daddy. It was me."

"What was you?"

"The murder. Jante Turner."

"What about her? I'm confused. What was you?"

"I did it."

"Did what?"

"I killed her. I got it for him. For us."

Klepp's laugh echoed off the walls of his expansive office. Back in his desk chair, he leaned so far back he almost toppled over.

"I never knew you were so proficient with a—"

"I didn't shoot her. I hired someone to shoot her." Her tone was dry ice.

"If you're trying to take the heat off of Scott, this isn't the way to do it. You'll both be accused."

"No, I really did it. I had her killed."

Max swallowed hard. "You did what?" It was a gasp at first, then the volume steadily dialed up. "You hired someone to kill your husband's boss?!"

"Yes. I had to. So that he could be the boss. So that the Millers would be on top. The ones that everyone talked about."

"Are you fucking kidding me! Why in the name of all that is good and holy would you do something so fucking stupid?!" He rose and put his hands flat on his desk as his voice rose to a crescendo.

"We were desperate. I wasn't satisfied."

"Satisfied?! Jesus, Mary, and Joseph. What are you talking about? You have everything."

"But it isn't enough."

Klepp shook his head, disgust pouring out of his eyes.

"How'd you find…how did you pay?"

"Finding is easier than you'd think. As for paying, it isn't that expensive really. Remember the money you gave me?"

"You told me it was for a bathroom…" he said, a bit of pity and sadness creeping into his voice. He sat on the edge of the desk, his shoulders slumped.

"I thought it would, you know, hide my tracks. That's why I asked for cash."

"What do you think they'll deduce when they see that kind of money moved out of my account in the months before the murder? A transaction labeled as for your benefit? Fuck!"

Klepp turned ninety degrees from his daughter and hurled the cut-crystal highball at the far wall. It exploded, fragments spraying everywhere, the residual bourbon leaving a stain on the wall.

"You stupid child, you've done more harm than you could possibly know. Do you know what you've done?"

Beth Miller shivered in fear. She often felt this way in the presence of the paterfamilias, whether it was about the B+ in Algebra, the birth control pills he found, or the time she wrecked his 911 Turbo and he had to fix the little problem about her blood-alcohol level. This time it was truly warranted, but it still scared her and stung.

"I'm sorry. I thought—"

"You didn't think. Not like I taught you. Not like a Klepp."

He turned his back to her.

She looked over his shoulder out over the blue lake stretching to the horizon and Michigan beyond. There were boaters, maybe even fathers and daughters, cutting their crafts through the water, feeling the wind and the power of the sail, basking in the afternoon sun.

"What are we going to do, Daddy?" She was sixteen again, begging him to talk to the police commissioner about an innocent mistake in which no one got hurt. Except this time, someone did get hurt.

"We? There is no we. This is your problem, not mine. You shat the bed—go sleep in it."

She felt abandoned, but not for long. She was too smart and he'd trained her too well.

"I know about the deal, I know about Quayside. This is *our* problem. Also, you just told me the bank statements will...I think this is something we are in together."

"If you know what you think you know about Quayside, why would you do something so risky, so stupid?"

"That job was Scott's. That bitch with her fake degrees and her skin-ticket to the promise land. It wasn't fair that Scott got passed over for her. The deanship was our way out. Out of our doldrums. Out of our financial mess. Her murder was our salvation. It's not my fault you pressured me to be a housewife, to stake my future on the shoulders of Scott Miller."

"What financial mess? Why didn't you ask me for help?"

"I couldn't," she whimpered pathetically.

"But you did." He spun toward her aggressively. "You did ask me for help. I paid for the goddamn hitman."

She ignored his rage, choosing instead to return to the original question.

"Scott was too proud. Too...I don't know. He would have gone crazy if you paid off our credit cards and the IRS."

"The IRS! My daughter owes money to the...Oh, good Lord. What a clusterfuck."

"We are three or four hundred thous—"

He cut her off.

"Scott is even more of a failure than I thought."

"Daddy...."

"I blame myself. I should have stopped you from marrying that schnook. I should have put my foot down. Like an idiot I bought into all that scrap about equality and true love, and now here I am. I was right, and now I'm fucked."

Max turned and faced his daughter, her body slumped in the high-back leather chair. She recognized the look in his eyes, as she'd seen it many times. He would help her. But he just stared at her. The silence between them expanded like a bubble, until the expectation of it ending overwhelmed her.

"Anyway, when she got it, when they picked someone less qualified just because of her race and her gender, and I saw her at a cocktail reception announcing it to public, I just couldn't take the thought of it. That was Scott's by right. He earned it. I couldn't just sit back and let them take it from us. It was ours! You told me to take what was mine. I was just doing what you taught me to do. To be a Klepp."

He turned his back to her again.

"Okay." He sighed deeply. Talking to the glass, to the city and the lake.

"What? Dad! What are we going to do?"

"Lower your voice, Liebchen." Max rose and came from

behind the desk toward his only child. He placed his hand on her shoulder and rubbed gently. “It’s going to be okay. Now, tell me again. I need all the details. Start at the beginning.”

CHAPTER 49

"Holy fuck! It's her. It's fucking her." Royce stood up and shouted toward Marcus.

"Who? What'd you find?" Marcus dropped a Ziploc bag full of chicken thighs and jerk marinade, its contents oozing out onto the counter. He made his way to the computer and looked over Royce's shoulder.

"It's her. Beth Miller. Beth Fucking Miller."

Royce had met Beth once, when he went to close the deal with Scott. Beth Miller was a woman that you remembered. She had served him iced tea with a smile that made him melt. She looked like lots of soccer moms, clad in yoga pants and an angora sweater hanging over her slender hips. The pants obviously weren't for exercise, as she stumbled around the kitchen like a baby giraffe. He sensed that discipline, not road miles, that kept her looking like she was eighteen. Royce was taken with her looks, but more with how she carried herself and what she said. Or, how she said. When she spoke it was in paragraphs full of interesting words and ideas. Even when engaged in small talk. He'd wondered in that moment what she was doing puttering around a kitchen. In this moment, he realized the kitchen was a cage.

Marcus squinted and leaned in further.

"Could be," he said hopefully. "I've seen pictures. But, it

could be any number of people. I mean, that is a big stretch, right?" Marcus turned and walked back toward his chicken.

Until that redhead jogged into frame, Royce suspected dean-to-be Turner was murdered to clear a path for the Quayside Development. The dean could stop it, he assumed, and when Jante refused, and, in fact, planned on doubling down, they installed someone—the son-in-law of the lead developer—to do it. But there were problems with his theory. Did a dean in fact have that power? Outside the ivory tower, there would be no doubt that a boss could squash an underling's work. But the more he learned about life inside that tower, the more he thought the dean worked for the faculty, not the other way around. Proof of this was that Max Klepp's son-in-law couldn't stop Mike Church and his quixotic quest to stop Quayside.

"I'll bet you dollars to doughnuts that's her. The ambitious wife gave up her chance to win the Booker Prize and bet all her appetite on a putz of a husband. The kids and the bridge groups and ladies' lunches aren't enough. The husband gets passed over. She decides to will her power through him. She murders the woman who stands in the way. Higher status level unlocked. It's a classic."

Marcus dropped a piece of chicken onto a cast-iron skillet.

"Or, maybe," Marcus speculated as he adjusted the sizzling chicken with a set of tongs, "the daughter of a big-time developer removes an impediment to his project by installing her husband as dean."

Royce saw the point and the ambiguity. Then added: "Or she killed two birds with one stone. Her husband is dean and her daddy is happy."

"She seems like the kind of person who'd have daddy issues," Marcus added as he turned the meat.

Royce stood up and went over to his briefcase. Leafing through his Moleskin notebook filled with the details of the case so far, he saw a note about the meeting with Professor Lewis over fish and chips, even though they never got to the fish or the chips. Lewis turned him onto Klepp as a potential suspect in the murder of Jante Turner. There was no doubt in the tax professor's mind that the real estate developer was behind the murders and arson and his own attempted murder. But the motive in his mind was Quayside, a deal that did in fact seem connected to Rockefeller Law School, but through Church, not Turner. If you were going to murder anyone to stop the lawsuit, you'd murder Church, not Turner. *So why murder Turner?*

Her death now seemed unconnected to Quayside. Church was eventually killed to clear a path to the hundreds of millions Klepp stood to make from the deal. That was now beyond doubt. They were willing to kill, and they knew Church was the key to stopping the lawsuit. Quayside and Turner were not connected in any way. The realization was a step forward, however, because it brought clarity to the investigative mind of Royce Johnson. Now, he could go back to the beginning and follow the clues looking for two paths to death, not just one.

Royce opened the photo app on his smartphone. He flipped to the morning he broke into Klepp's house. The Quayside map, the business plan and contracts for the deal, overviews of his office, and the bank statements, several pages for each month. Follow the money.

He flipped to January and started looking for outliers. There were routine five-figure exits and six- and even seven-figure entries. The money came, the money went. In bulk. It was a good thing for the rich and the powerful that financial transactions were private. If the masses, the so-called ninety-nine percent, saw the vast sums and the frivolities on which great wealth was squandered, they would come for Max Klepp and his ilk. The dekulakization of Lake Forest would be swift and bloody. That revolution would be televised.

Royce left the envy and the speculation about alternative future histories for another day. He needed to focus. There were monthly payments of many tens of thousands to American Express, something called Haganah, Inc., numerous Visa cards,

Barney's, and countless other businesses. They repeated regularly and consistently. Nothing suspicious, although he made a mental note to look up "Haganah," which sounded a discordant note.

Then, he noticed something unusual. It didn't set off alarm bells. Great clues rarely did. They were subtler than that. Camouflaged against the ocean floor with spots and shapes and textures to avoid the detection of predators. Predators like Royce. There was a large withdrawal on May 3rd. Fifty thousand dollars. To cash. No doubt Max Klepp could find lots of uses for that kind of money, but the timing was suspicious. Royce flipped to the pages where the checks and deposit/withdrawal slips were imaged in miniature. Scanning, he found the withdrawal. In the notes, a single word, "Beth."

CHAPTER 50

The students started arriving in significant numbers at 8:20 a.m. Sitting in a rental car and listening to NBA trade rumors on ESPN 1000, Royce watched them move in packs of two or three, laden with heavy backpacks and the stress of law school grades making their faces squinty. When a larger group of about ten moved past him, he got out of the car, grabbed his own backpack from the passenger seat, and joined in. No one would mistake him for a law student on close inspection, but he merely needed to blend in enough to make his way into the building, past inattentive security, and into the central lounge that separated the classroom wing from the administrative offices. There was only one way for the dean to get from his car to his office, and Royce planned to be there when he arrived.

Things hadn't changed much since the time Royce was there the day after his brother was murdered. Sydney, if he remembered his name, was gone, perhaps for good, but his replacement at the security desk put up even less of a fight. The pack of students walked right past, Royce trailing and blending in just enough. The guard didn't look up from his crossword puzzle. This place was no Fort Knox.

He found a leather chair with good sight lines of the entrances and exits, and pulled out Alex's old computer. He spun up the surveillance videos again and watched the key moments. He watched them as a parent might re-watch home movies—the goal that won the state championship or the solo in the middle school musical—on the eve of sending a kid off to college. He watched the morning of the murder—he saw the dean-to-be, full of life, jogging in and out of frame, then disappearing forever into that bathroom. Then, the shadow making his way down to the lakeshore and vanishing for good. Winding back to the weeks before, he watched Beth Miller stalking her prey. The woman who told him she had bad knees and wasn't a runner, jogging awkwardly. He was just killing time, or maybe boiling his blood for the confrontation that was coming. He knew every frame by heart.

The dean didn't see him, walking past aloofly, his briefcase in one hand and a Starbucks cup in the other. Royce shut the lid of the laptop, set it on a small marble side table, and rose to his feet.

"Dean Miller!"

Scott turned his head, and when he saw Royce remove his Rockefeller University ball cap and reveal himself, stopped and spun around.

"This is a surprise," he said, setting down his briefcase and extending his hand. "Good to see you. We don't have an appointment, do we?" He checked the calendar in his head, then said, "Come, come to my office. I'll figure out my schedule so we can talk."

"Let's do it here." Royce sat back in the chair and motioned to an empty seat next to him.

"Well, okay, if you want. My office is much more comfortable...and private."

Royce ignored him. Plopping into one of the chairs, he looked up at the dean expectantly. What he had to say was better said in public and on neutral ground. The dean carried his bag over, set it by the side of the chair, and took a long drink of his latte.

"So, what's up? News?"

"I know who killed Jante Turner."

The dean swallowed so hard his Adam's apple appeared to traverse his entire neck from shoulders to chin. A sense of relief and excitement came over his face. He moved to the edge of the seat, leaning forward so as to hear the words better.

Royce removed a plain manila folder from his bag. He rested it on the marble table between them, then put his right hand, palm down, fingers splayed out, on top with a thump. He looked up and made eye contact with the dean, letting the moment ferment.

"Who did it?" Scott reached for the folder, but Royce resisted.

"The identity of the person responsible is in here. Their picture. This person didn't do the shooting, I don't know who that is yet, but they definitely ordered the hit. I'm certain of it."

"Awesome work. Who is it?"

"First, before that, we have to discuss something."

The dean narrowed his eyes as if anticipating a shakedown. Alex always talked about the problem of renegotiation and commitment in contracting theory—he was like that—and Royce saw the same points being made in the dean's glare.

"What?" His impatience could be seen in the muscles tensing in his face and neck. He seemed ready to pounce.

"Well, let me put it this way, Dean, you might not want to know who did it."

"Of course, I do. Of course, I want to know who did it."

"In my experience, in my long experience with these things, that's not always true after people learn the truth. The situation you're in right now might seem unmanageable. You probably think knowing is going to solve everything. But it rarely does. It creates other problems. Every time. I'm just saying, be careful what you wish for." He tapped his fingers on the envelope. "I've got this, and you can ask me for it anytime. It's yours, actually. You paid for it." The dean reached for it again. Royce pressed his hand flat and hard. "But maybe, just maybe, you would prefer to think long and hard about who might have done this and whether you really want an answer to that question. Some questions are best unanswered."

"I have no idea what you're talking about, Mr. Johnson, but I'm not enjoying this. You're correct that the information in there is my property. I paid for it. Now, please, let me see it."

Royce sighed, then slide the folder over to him. The dean grabbed it like it was the last doughnut in the box. He pulled it up to his chest, looked up and made eye contact with Royce, then opened the folder.

"Is this a fucking joke?!" he spat, turning the picture of his wife, a nice shot from a recent charity ball, to face Royce. Several students turned to stare. The dean leaned forward, lowering his voice to a screaming whisper, his eyes full of rage. "I don't know what the point of this is but it's not going to work. My wife obviously had no role in Jante's murder, and for you to...to..."

Royce sat stone faced, staring at him as he worked up a lather, spraying bits of spittle across the table and Royce's legs. The dean waved the photograph accusingly at him.

"If one person other than us hears about this, so help me God, I will reign holy terror down on you. You'll have so many lawyers coming after you, you'll be nostalgic for that year you spent getting raped in prison." He let go, and the picture floated down to the table, landing facedown.

"She did it. I'm sorry about that, but it doesn't make it less true. I promise you, this isn't a game. I don't throw around accusations like this lightly. In fact, I have to be certain before I would. I'm certain." He paused and made eye contact. "Your wife killed Jante Turner."

Scott Miller rolled his eyes, then fell back into the chair, his shoulders landing with a thud on the seat back. In that moment, Royce saw the possibility in him that his wife did it, did it for him or for them, creep into his mind. Or perhaps the possibility always lived there, and it was the certainty that it was true that he saw come over his client.

An earnest-faced student strode by, "Good morning, Dean Miller!" she chirped like spring robin. The dean reflexively raised a hand in greeting, but it soon flopped back limply in his lap. He was an aging fighter, beaten and wounded, slumped in his corner. But there were no body men working his cuts or icing down the lumps that were forming. He was on his own.

"How do you know?" he asked in much less aggressive tones. Then, he tried to backtrack. "What's your evidence?"

Royce reached into his bag and pulled out a stack of photographs, printed on paper from Alex's home printer. Public options, be they CVS or FedEx Kinkos or Shutterfly, simply couldn't be trusted. He handed them to the dean, still slumped in his chair. He reached out and grabbed them with a limp hand.

"What am I looking at?"

"Screenshots from Park District surveillance cameras. There is Jante on the day she was murdered."

The dean closed his eyes.

"This is the killer..." Royce pointed at the shadowy figure running military style toward the shore.

"Okay, this is morbid and upsetting but I don't see where Beth—"

"The next set—" the dean flipped the page, "—shows a few weeks before. The picture on the top is Jante on her regular run, always passing the bathroom between 6:05 and 6:10, and then, here, returning after three laps around the Point about ten to twelve minutes later."

"And?"

"And, finally, here, for about two weeks in May—" Royce turned the page and pointed at the figure that he was certain was Beth Miller, "—here is your wife, following several minutes behind, tracking her, stalking her, learning about her routine. Learning so that she could provide that information to the man she hired."

The dean picked up the pictures and held them close to the tip of his nose. Royce watched his eyes squint and the realization wash over him like a tsunami, sweeping away everything. The waves crashed and the tide surged in, wiping out the life they had lived together, the life they were going to live together. In his eyes, the question was unmistakable, *Could she have really…done this?* He could see the sweat forming on his temples and could feel the dean's blood pressure dropping. The dean took a drink of his latte, while still holding the pictures inches from his face.

"I'm not sure that's her." It wasn't convincing.

"It's her. I'm sorry for you, but it's her." Royce clarified his empathy. He wasn't sorry for Beth Miller. She deserved it. Deserved what was coming to her. A ruined marriage. Maybe prison. But he was sorry for Scott, who Royce could tell had no role in this. Sitting in the parking lot, he wasn't sure whether he knew, whether he played a part. Nothing about him suggested killer or schemer, but Royce's instincts served him wrong in the past.

"How do you know? I mean, I admit it is a woman that more or less fits her description—her physique and hair are a match—but there must be hundreds of fit women who look like that from afar, running these paths on spring mornings." He set the pictures on the table and looked with hopeful eyes at Royce. It was a half-court shot at the buzzer.

"Look, I don't want to sound like the prosecutor here. You know it's true. And you know that I wouldn't accuse her based just on some grainy photographs. I've been at this for a long time, and this isn't the only piece of evidence I have." He tapped his bag with his hand. The dean eyed it like a Christmas package, waiting under a tree.

"What? What do you have?" The desperation made Royce sad. The whole episode made him profoundly sad.

"Financial footprints. I don't really want to show you them, because I don't want you to be implicated in what I've done. It wasn't exactly legal. And I frankly don't want to go back to jail. So, I'm going to keep that to myself, if that's okay." The dean's eyes were resigned. "But I don't need to show them to you anyway. I can see it in your eyes that you know I'm right. She had the motive. She had the opportunity. Someone like her was seen at the scene in a crucial period watching the victim. And…"

"And?"

"Well, her father."

"What about him?"

"You know, trees and apples, Scott."

Royce saw the irritation foaming up in his eyes.

"Look, my job is done. I don't take any pleasure in this. I wanted the killer to be someone that would save you, not one that would…well, do what this is going to do."

"You are just going to leave it at this? Are you fucking kidding me? Accuse my wife of murder and then just walk away!"

Royce stood up, put his bag on his shoulder.

"What would you have me do?" He looked down at him.

The dean rose and stood across from him. Eye to eye, they caught the attention of students moving in an out of classes, holding red casebooks open while they walked.

"Aren't you going to, I don't know, drive over to my house and arrest her?"

"I'm an ex-con, Dean. I don't even have a license as a private investigator. I broke the law multiple times to get what I got for you." He let that sink in again. "I'm not going to the police. My job was to find out who killed Jante Turner and to tell you who that was. I did that. I'm done. Next case."

As he said it, Royce realized the impact of what he had just said. It was true, though he didn't realize it until that moment. It wasn't about justice anymore. He wasn't sure what it was about exactly, but it wasn't justice. He was going to walk out the door and forget about Jante Turner and Beth Miller. Or maybe he wouldn't quite forget about them, but he was powerless to do anything about it. Meting out justice was going to be someone else's job. The thought made him fill with regret.

"You're not the Royce Johnson I've read about then, the

boundary-pushing, relentless crusader for truth, justice, and the American way."

"None of us are what they say about us." Royce said quietly.

"I don't believe you, Mr. Johnson." The dean reached down and picked up his briefcase. "I don't believe you for a second. My wife didn't kill Jante Turner or hire someone to do it. I know that's true. And you know what else is true? You aren't going to stop until you pin this on her and put her in jail. You're like the spawn of the Energizer Bunny and J. Edgar Hoover. You won't stop until you think you've saved the world. You're going to screw her like you screwed our former student. Haven't you ruined enough lives around here?" He picked up his Starbucks cup and tossed it into a nearby trashcan. "Well, listen up, our relationship is over. You're fired. Now, go fuck yourself."

He turned heel and walked deliberately toward the administration wing, nodding hello at several students as he went.

CHAPTER 51

He found Beth on her knees in the garden. The scene stole his breath. When they first met, at a party in Manhattan to celebrate the publication of a poem of hers in the *Paris Review*, his first glimpse was from behind—a ponytail of auburn hair dancing against the milky whiteness of her neck. When she turned toward him that first night, he nearly dropped his old-fashioned. It wasn't her striking beauty, although it was undeniable, but rather the intelligence in her eyes. She pulled him in like a star attracts a planet, although he felt more like a minor asteroid as he approached her—oddly shaped and pock-marked, hurling awkwardly toward her. Her gravity was undeniable, but his fear tried to propel him away. His destiny, and now hers, was sealed that night, as he had the courage to open his mouth and tell her how much he'd loved the poem he'd never read.

Standing on the back porch of the home they'd built together, looking out on the yard where he'd kicked more soccer balls and roasted more marshmallows and had more tickle fights than he could remember, he was as overcome with fear as on that first night. The fear wasn't of her—he'd never known her to hurt anyone until she murdered for him. And, after all, she had murdered *for him*. No, he had nothing to fear from her. Rather he was afraid *for her*. For both of them and for what was to happen. For their kids. So many lives ruined. Her life, his life.

Their lives were over as they knew them.

Why didn't she tell me? He was haunted by the question. But he knew the answer. She had not told him for a reason—she didn't want him to know. It wouldn't work if he knew and he never would have agreed had she asked his permission. Now that he knew, now that *Royce Johnson* knew, nothing could ever be the same again. He didn't believe Johnson would sit on the information. There was no way he wouldn't go to the police, and that meant they had to plan. To figure out a solution. There was always a solution. Time to work the problem.

But he lingered, watching her move the earth with her hands, planting bulbs he worried she'd never see come up. He yearned for the power to slow down time. He tried to control the moment, to let her live her good life a few more seconds. Until he revealed that her secret was now their secret, the world was one way, and, when he opened his mouth, to tell her the truth this time, the world would be entirely another. So, he lingered, preserving the Millers for as long as possible. Breathing in the air and hearing the twinkle of the wind chimes and the calls of the birds. Watching that auburn ponytail dance on the white neck for one last moment. Then, it was time.

"Hey, sweetie," he choked on the words. "I thought I'd come home for lunch. Surprise you."

She turned, her ponytail flinging around to the side. It was beguiling. His heart sank. The anxiety made his fingertips pulse.

"Be right up." Her smile, gleaming white teeth and lips he loved kissing more than anything in the world, was the last gasp of the old world. "What a treat!" she said to the ground, as she patted the earth on top of the bulb.

Scott walked in the kitchen and poured himself a drink. It was just after noon, but if any lunch called for a whiskey, it was this one.

Coming through the French doors, Beth dropped her gardening gloves on the side table and stepped to the sink.

"To what do I owe the honor, Dean Miller?" She scrubbed

furiously with lavender hand soap. The smell intoxicated him. He held back tears.

"I just thought I'd… We need to talk, Beth."

"Oooh, sounds serious. Can I change?"

"Just have a seat." He pulled out a chair at the kitchen table. She sat obediently, wiping her moist hands on three-hundred-dollar jeans. *Only Beth would garden in those.* The little charms he'd miss, if he didn't figure this out.

"Should I have a drink too?" she joked.

"I know who killed Jante Turner." It came out involuntarily.

"You do? Who?" The lie was completely convincing, even though he'd gotten quite good at detecting her lies over twenty-plus years of marriage. They'd been few and far between, and usually about trivial things like the cost of shoes or her personal trainers or the time she tried Botox and her eye drooped like she had a stroke. This one was a doozy, and yet she concealed it like a seasoned pro.

"Royce Johnson…"

"The FBI agent? He killed—"

"No, I just met with him. You know that I hired him to find the killer. To clear my name."

"Yes, I remember. I met him once. Remember, we had him in our kitchen for iced tea? Seemed nice enough. But I urged you not to get involved with him. Remember how much I begged you?"

"Well, he did an investigation."

"And? What did he find? You're killing me with the suspense." Not even a little crack. She was making this hard. *Why was she making this so damn hard?*

Scott turned away from her. It was too much. He walked over to the sink and turned on the cold tap. He let the water fall, hitting the stainless steel sink that was imported from Italy. The water sprayed in all directions. He tried to follow the droplets as they careened across the shiny surface.

"Scott? Earth to Scott?" she joked.

"I know what you did, Beth," he exhaled the words without articulating them. Still staring at the water hitting the sink, he continued, "I know you hired someone to kill her. I know it was you." He turned to look at her, but the sight hurt his eyes too much. He cast them down to the floor.

"What?! He said that? Are you kidding me? That's the best he could do? To pin it on the wife? Hilarious." The first crack, thin and small, formed in her armor. He saw it because he knew just where and how to look. He knew her defenses better than anyone.

"Beth, we don't have time for this game." He had to take charge, so he swallowed hard and stepped in her direction. The scene scared him like no other. Standing in front of the windows letting sunlight from the lake bathe their kitchen in warmth, she quivered. The crack was widening into a fissure, and he could see her coming apart. Her eyes, those brilliant, sparkling eyes that had drawn him in like a tractor beam, now glistened and drooped. "We need to get back on the same page. I need to know everything so that we can make a plan. Together, you and me."

"What can we do?" It was the whimper of an animal caught in a furrier's trap.

"I don't know, but we are both in this. There's no avoiding that. You've fucked us both, whether you wanted to or not. So, we need to work together, because no matter what happens we will share the same fate."

"I'll...I'll confess. I can take the rap. It was me. I did it. You can be free. You...You can—" she shuddered and lost her breath, "—you can raise the kids. They need you." She collapsed on the floor, the sobs overwhelming her at the thought of prison and her children, motherless, parentless. Orphans.

"Get a hold of yourself! We don't have time for this. Royce Johnson is probably on the way to the cops this minute. He's built a case. We need to find him and stop him somehow."

"What about the kids?" She looked up at him, desperation distorting her face beyond recognition.

"The kids will be fine. I'll have Peter and Jill take them for a bit. Don't worry about them."

"I mean, what happens to them when we go to jail?"

"We aren't going to jail, Beth. We can't. No way. We are stopping him."

"How? The kids!" she yelped.

"We need to focus on us right now. You know how when they do the safety briefings on airplanes they say to put on your mask before helping your children?" She nodded like he was making a good point. "Well, we need to take care of us first. If we do that, the kids will be fine."

"Are you mad? We can't stop him." She paused and took a deep breath. "I'll take the fall. Let me do it." She worked her way back to her feet. Straightening her blouse, she stood tall.

"Look, I appreciate the gesture. But be realistic. No one will believe it. Even if I wanted to take your offer, which I don't, it isn't going to work. No one will believe that I didn't know. I'll be in prison with you, for conspiracy or, at the very least, being an accessory after the fact. My life is over, same as yours. Unless we stop him."

"Stop him how?" Her entire face begged.

"I don't know how, but I've an idea who will. Trust me. It's what I do."

They embraced coolly, then walked together into the entry way to get their coats. They were headed downtown.

When the recording went dead, Royce pulled the earphone out of his ear. His arm throbbed. He had the evidence he needed. When Scott Miller left the lounge of the Law School, Royce remotely activated a microbug he put on the underside of an upper cabinet in the Millers' kitchen on the first day he met Scott to discuss the case. That day he met Beth and saw their perfect family in their perfect house on their perfect street. It was an old trick that had served him well over the years. The recording wouldn't be admissible, of course, but it would be enough to get the Chicago Police or the FBI interested in them. A bounce pass to the center, wide open under the net. It would be enough.

As for protecting himself, he could run. It wouldn't take long for the authorities to generate enough probable cause to arrest the Millers based on what Royce had collected so far. And once they were behind bars, the chance that any of Max Klepp's goon squad would come after him was nearly zero. Maybe he could go back home. Find Jenny and the girls and start to put things right. With the money the dean had paid him—he snickered at the thought—he could take some time and reenter the world a bit better this time. Less drinking, fewer corpses.

But it wasn't his nature. A sheep dog herds on instinct. Royce had once been at a party at the house of a colleague who had a border collie. After thirty minutes, a dozen or so of them were standing nearly on top of each other in the corner of the family room. Someone finally noticed, and they looked over and saw the dog, sitting proudly on his haunches, watching them. The thought of that episode, recalled deep from his memory box, came to mind, as he steered his car onto Lake Shore Drive. He had no more choice about what he was going to do than that border collie did. Plus, he had the upper hand. He knew what Scott Miller was going to do before Scott knew himself. And he was going to stop him and his wife from sowing any more destruction. That was what he did.

CHAPTER 52

"Royce, it's Scott Miller." The call came as predicted, but an hour later than Royce guessed.

"What can I do for you, Dean Miller?"

"Well, I've decided to work with you. On the—"

"I told you, I'm not working on anything. My work is done. It ended when I slid that folder across the table to you." He paused for effect, playing coy. "You do owe me twenty thousand to settle up, however. I'll take a cashier's check or PayPal. Do you do PayPal?"

"I know. I know you said that. But, well, I didn't believe you then and I don't believe you now."

"Believe what you want—"

"I went home, Royce. I confronted my wife. She...she went a bit crazy. I think she may hurt herself or me. She tried to attack me, but I ran out. I need your help."

"Help? Are you hiring me again?" He bit his tongue. "Because if you are, you've got to finish paying me for the last job first."

"I think she may be going to her father. I think he has...*people* to take care of these kinds of things. I'm afraid I'll be next. You will likely make the list too. I don't think we have a choice. Should we team up? I think they are capable of...bad stuff."

Royce smirked. *You have no idea*, he thought to himself,

feeling the pain in his kidney, in his bicep, and running down the length of his back.

"You think I'm in trouble?" Ex-Agent Johnson tried to hide his smile, lest it come across in his voice.

"I know it. Meet me. We can work out a plan. I think we need to partner up on this one, me and you. Will you do that? For me? To wrap up this case?"

"For the right price, sure. I told you at the school. My new MO is client service. For the right price, I'm your man. Where's the meet?"

CHAPTER 53

A Hyde Park institution since 1962, the Medici on 57th was where Claire launched Royce's career as a dick when she'd slid the name of the classics professor across to him. It was also where he'd met Scott to give his first update on the case of Jante Turner. There was a nice symmetry to the fact that Dean Miller chose it for what Royce suspected was the final showdown. With whom he couldn't be certain. But he knew at least one person who would be there waiting for him.

At two minutes to nine, Royce stepped into the entry way, ignoring the handwritten sign on the door saying the restaurant was closed due to a water leak. He removed his hat and sunglasses and bulky jacket, intended not to shield him from the elements but to disguise his appearance. He'd hope there wouldn't be the need to escape without his identity mattering, but he was prepared to do so if things went south. His backup plans had backup plans.

The host was not standing at the wooden podium in the narrow hallway as he'd seen in the past, and peeking down the hallway into the expansive dining room, open to second- and third-floor balconies, he saw few of the tables occupied. *So, it is a showdown.* A large man of Asian descent in a black Adidas track suit approached him purposefully. He put his hands on Royce's shoulders, then patted him down. Satisfied he wasn't carrying, he opened his hips and extended his arm toward tables in back.

Walking down the tunnel-like path to the dining room, past the kitchen on the left and a few two-person booths on the right, he couldn't help but feel he was on his way to meet his maker. Adrenaline coursed through his veins and his pulse quickened. As he stepped into the dining room, bathed in morning light from the skylights three stories up, he saw the actors in their places. At a round table to his left, another Asian gentleman in a matching track suit sat staring at him with fiery eyes. To his right, in a booth against the wall, two more Asian men, he guessed they were Chinese or maybe Korean, sat across from each other, one facing the front of the restaurant and the other the back. These men were leaner and were wearing jeans and leather jackets. The tattoo of a tiger crept up one of their necks. He didn't recognize any of them. Along the far wall, in the back corner at the large booth that families going to the Med for dinner coveted, sat Scott Miller, his wife, and Max Klepp. Royce looked down at his waist, wishing for his fanny pack.

"Over here, Royce," the dean motioned at him with a flapping arm. He couldn't help but be friendly. But Royce knew he was walking into a trap and that the friendly wave was a lure, like the fake worms a frogfish uses to attract its prey. Wiggle, wiggle.

He took a seat next to the dean, and across from Max and his daughter. The waitress, who seemed bewildered by the scene, came over to take their order. She wasn't in on it, he deduced.

"Four coffees," Max barked. Then, when she was out of earshot, turned to Royce with a glare that would melt steel. "So, Agent Johnson, what are we going to do?"

"What indeed, Mr. Klepp?" Royce threw it back at him with equal intensity.

"I'm prepared to make you a rich man before you walk out that door. *If* you walk out that door, I should say." He smiled in the corner of his mouth. Klepp slid an envelope across to Royce. "In there is a cashier's check for one million dollars. For the work you did to help my Beth. Let's call it a deal, what do you say?"

A busboy arrived to fill their water glasses. No one looked up at him, but as his arm reached across Royce to fill the dean's glass at the far end of the table, he noticed the dark black skin, and relaxed. He remembered the busboys from his two prior visits. They were all Hispanic.

"I don't know what you think is going to happen here, Klepp, but I'm walking out of here, and not with any of your or anyone else's money." He slid the envelope back and took a drink from his water glass. "Except for the dean, that is. He still owes me twenty grand." Another sip. "You know, for fingering your daughter in the murder of Jante Turner." He looked across at Beth. She pursed her lips at him.

"Daddy, are you going to let him—"

"Quiet, sweetie. Let me handle this." He patted her arm. Her hand was gripped around a fork as if she wanted to reach across and stab Royce in the eye with it. Turning to Royce, he continued, "We will get you your money, Agent Johnson. Don't you worry about that."

"Good. Bills, you know?"

"Now, back to the matter at hand, what do you think is going to happen here?"

"You tell me. Scott called this meeting. I didn't realize it was for you to bribe me. I thought we were going to discuss the case."

"What do you have on Quayside? I need that matter resolved to my satisfaction before we proceed any further."

"Max," his son-in-law interjected, "I thought we were here to talk about the scurrilous allegations about Beth?" The dean leaned into the table and raised his voice. But Royce could tell he wasn't used to confronting his father in law. It was half-hearted and not the confident Scott Miller he knew.

"And here I thought I was here for you to work with me to implicate your wife, Dean. That's what you told me on the phone," Royce quipped. "It seems we're all confused."

"Stop the games, Johnson. What did Edelman give you?"

"Who's Edelman?" The dean said in an exasperated voice. He realized he wasn't part of the same play as everyone else. He got the wrong script, or was at least on the wrong page.

Royce turned to face the dean.

"Oh, just some poor chemistry professor your father-in-law had murdered."

"What? What's happening?!" The dean's face was twisted with confusion and rage.

"Dad!" Beth yelped.

The waitress had impeccable timing. She arrived with the coffees. They were passed around but sat untouched.

"This has the danger of turning into an Abbott and Costello routine," Royce said. "Let me bring your kids up to speed here, Max. Should I start with when your guys, probably those two in the booth over there—" he mentioned over his shoulder, "—threw me in front of a train, or when they burned down the IIT Chemistry Department. Or, maybe we should start with the law professor with his head caved in by a fireplace poker in Wisconsin...Wait, I think the best place would be with the volcano of toxic waste that's under your big new development in Bridgeport. You know, the one you're trying to hide from everyone. Everyone except the mayor and Alderman What's-His-Nuts, of course, who are in on the whole thing. Yeah, that would be best. Start with your greed. It all flows from that. What do you think, Max?"

Max Klepp took a long sip of coffee, then put the oversized ceramic mug down with a thud. He smiled broadly at Royce and let out a belly laugh.

"You think you're so fucking smart. You've sold yourself quite a story there, Agent Johnson. I don't know what you think happened, but let me tell you what is going to happen. You're going to tell me what information you have on my project. If you don't, I'm going to introduce you to some of my friends. They don't do their work in cafes over coffee. Actually, they may use boiling liquids. I've never thought to ask them. But they get results. I was hoping we could avoid that. For your sake."

"What about Jante, Max? You don't care about that case? I'm surprised. You know Beth did it, right? With the fifty thousand you gave her. That makes both of you guilty of first-degree murder. Does Illinois still have the death penalty? Hmmm. Well, doesn't matter. Life is a long time to live in a cage. Take it from me. A year is an eternity in there. Dante's fucking *Inferno*."

Klepp had enough. He shimmied out of the booth and stood at the end of the table. He sneered down at Royce from the end of his Roman nose.

"I see." He sighed deeply. "If that's the way it has to be." Then, turning to the round table behind him, he motioned to one of men in the matching track suits. The other was presumably out front, shooing away any customers undeterred by the sign.

The giant stood up and walked over toward the table. Klepp motioned for the waitress.

"Miss! Miss, could we get some more coffee over here?" the goon shouted across the empty restaurant.

She approached, a pot of regular coffee in her left hand. As she leaned over the table to pour, the giant grabbed her with both arms, putting her into a headlock. The coffee pot fell the floor, sending glass and steaming coffee flying. Beth screamed, both from the shock and the burning liquid hitting her legs. Max stepped toward Royce.

"Tell me about where the information is or she dies." The tone was pure evil.

Royce looked across the restaurant at Marcus, standing at the bus station with a water pitcher. Deep Dish was behind him pretending to work the griddle. He shook his head slightly. It wasn't time. That morning, Marcus arrived early and stood at the back door. When the crew of busboys and kitchen staff—all of them immigrants from Central America making minimum wage—arrived, Marcus liberally passed out hundreds and replaced them with his team. His team was loyal to Marcus in ways that people who were not raised in Englewood could never understand. The regular bussers and cooks hesitated briefly, worried what the manager would say, but Max had already cleared that barrier with his own cash or threats. Marcus had seen that deal happen, and he was a good salesman. The old crew walked away with smiles and flush with cash. The new crew stepped right in.

Royce doubted Max's resolve. "Look, Max." Royce raised his voice. "You don't have to do this. I don't know what you think killing this woman does, but it isn't going to help you. It's just another wasted life. It also violates the first rule of holes, Max—when you are in one, stop digging."

The waitress wiggled like a deer being constricted by a python. Her torso was stationary, but her legs flapped around, smacking the sides of the booth and the legs of her would-be murderer.

"You've made your choice, Agent Johnson," Max spat.

He turned toward the waitress and bobbed his head slightly. With that, the giant put his hands around her neck, and twisted sharply. The kicking stopped instantly, sending a shock wave through the entire restaurant. The man dropped his arms to his side, and the waitress's lifeless body flopped to the floor. Then he reached down, grabbed her by the arms, and dragged her to the center of the room. Max Klepp stepped into the spot where she had been standing and put his hands flat on the table.

"It's show time. What's it going to be? Am I going to have to kill someone else?"

Royce noticed that the men seated at the booth had stood up and assumed positions on the perimeter. The other giant at the front of the restaurant had moved into the dining room, bringing with him at gunpoint two busboys and the cook from the kitchen. Everyone was assembled in the open dining room, the body of the waitress at the center of them.

Royce made eye contact with Marcus. He blinked three times, the signal to move into position.

"First, you didn't kill anyone. Your goon did. Probably because you don't have the guts. Or the strength. Second, I don't know why you think I'd be moved by her death. I don't know her. She's nothing to me." Royce lied. He was buying time. Another body wasn't part of the plan. A failure he'd live with forever.

Marcus moved toward the table. Royce knew he had a sawed-off shotgun hidden under his white bus boy coat. Klepp's team had searched each of them that morning, and they'd searched the kitchen and dining areas for weapons. But they didn't check behind the wood in the pizza oven or under the beans in a large pot on the stovetop, where Marcus, the other busser, and the cook, friends since he was a kid, hid them earlier that morning. Royce doubted the men could be counted on, but Marcus assured him that they'd been in tougher scraps and that they would do anything for each other.

"You're leaving me no choice here." Max said.

"Nor me, Max," Royce raised his voice, then threw his coffee toward Max's face, ducking under the table as he did.

On cue, Marcus and his team removed their weapons. Marcus put a round of buckshot into the back of the man who had murdered the waitress. Deep Dish spun and put a .45 round into the chest of the other giant in the tracksuit. The man tumbled backward, sending a round from his 9 mm into the ceiling of the restaurant as he did. The Sarge, posing as a cook, rolled to his right, aiming his TEC-9 submachine gun at his targets, now sprinting away toward the front of the restaurant, where they hoped to find a covered firing position. Rounds hit one in the leg. He dove forward, a head-first slide into the chairs of a nearby table. The other of Klepp's men dove behind a thick wooden half wall and shouted at his fallen friend in Chinese. Writhing in pain, gripping his leg with one hand and shooting back at the cook with the other, he shouted that he was okay.

Royce tackled Klepp, who was clutching his face from the second-degree burns. A few punches to the face, and Klepp was disabled.

Marcus made his way around to the busboy station and took cover behind the stand-up soda machine. The other busboy was prone behind a thick wooden table he'd tipped over and made into a shield. The cook let loose a few rounds, then scrambled back behind the table with the busboy.

"Give up!" Marcus shouted at no one in particular.

Back at the booth, Beth was screaming at the top of her lungs, crumpled on the faux leather seat of the booth. Scott was under the table, where Royce had been until he leapt out and tackled Max Klepp. Royce surveyed the scene. Klepp's body men were down, but not dead yet. The other two members of his team were in strong, covered positions. At least one was wounded, and with limited mobility.

Royce asked for covering fire, and his team let loose a thundering barrage. He ran toward the overturned table, reaching down to grab a pistol from one of Klepp's apes, who was able to put up only mild resistance to the pilfering. Sliding along the floor, Royce's team finally assembled behind the table. From that position, Royce signaled to Marcus to move along the far wall toward the left flank of the wounded man. He instructed Sarge to, on his mark, run perpendicular to the other far wall, and move behind the tables to the right flank of the other fire position.

"On three," he whispered to them. "One, two..."

Royce jumped up and let loose ten rounds from a Steyr M. They burst coffee pots and glasses on the half wall, ricocheting into the kitchen and around the dining room. They were causing quite a racket, and he figured the clock was ticking quickly before the cops arrived on scene. And none of them wanted to be there when that happened.

Royce peeked his head out, then dove back down as machine-gun fire exploded the top of the table. His team was in place. Deep breath.

"Now!"

They all fired at once, converging on the men from three sides. Bullets whizzed past Royce, who tumbled forward, firing as he rose back to the forward-facing position. The cook on his left let loose with the TEC-9, sending wooden fragments and eventually flesh and bone flying. His target managed to get off several rounds in his direction, one of which caught him in the shoulder. On his right, Marcus found a much easier target. The earlier shot to the leg must have hit an artery, because the man was nearly lifeless, raising his pistol half-heartedly. Marcus knew he was near death. He kicked the pistol away. It slid into the middle of the room.

"Are we clear, Marcus?" Royce shouted from his position behind an overturned table just feet from the men. He'd taken the risk, allowing his team to do what had to be done.

"Clear!" he shouted back.

"Sarge, you okay?"

"Clipped, but I'll make it."

Royce stood up. He turned and saw Max Klepp crawling toward the back of the restaurant. He raced over and leapt on top of him. Turning him over, he put his knee into his chest.

"I told you I was walking out of here, and without your bribes. You son of a bitch."

"You are a dead man. I promise you. If it is the last thing I do," Klepp slurred, hanging on to life by his fingers.

"The last thing you'll do is likely eat a lousy prison meal before they put a needle in your arm, you worthless piece of shit."

Royce let all his weight press into his chest. It shut him up. Klepp groaned under the weight, trying to wriggle free. Turning to Marcus, Royce barked, "Get your guys out of here. Get rid of the weapons. Make them disappear. I'll see you at the meet."

They'd arrived that morning in a windowless van that was still backed up at the rear entrance. The path to and from the restaurant scouted to be clear of cameras and witnesses. Hyde Park was the stone age as far as surveillance went. A sleepy college town in the midst of a big city. A clean escape was possible. But it had to be now. The police had to be nearby.

Royce reached down and grabbed Max, bringing him up to his feet. Beth was still screaming and the dean still cowered under the table.

"Is there anyone else, Max? Is this all you've got?" Royce didn't need another loose end. He also wanted to rub it in.

Max eyed him carefully, their faces inches apart. He spat in Royce's face, a large glob of spit hitting him in the cheek.

"Of course there are more. This is the B team. You've got no chance. As for who they are, you will find out soon enough." His tone mocked.

"We'll see about that, Max. We'll see about that. Good luck with this mess."

Royce turned to head toward the back exit when he heard the shot. Instinctively, he hit the ground. He hadn't been hit, but he didn't know if he was the target. He scrambled under a table and looked around to assess the situation. Max Klepp was facedown, a pool of blood forming around his head like a halo. Unsure whether Max was the target or the shot had missed, Royce hid beneath the table. The back door was twenty feet away. He could run for it but gave himself less than a fifty-fifty chance of making it under the circumstances.

"Stand up, Mr. Johnson!" the voice shouted from the second-floor balcony. There was additional seating around a balcony that overlooked the main dining room on the first floor. It had access to an outdoor patio on the second floor, closed for the season. The patio connected to the roofs of adjacent buildings and provided a ready entry and exit point to the restaurant for someone skilled in the arts.

Realizing the Chicago PD was likely going to be arriving any minute, Royce figured he had no other choice. He rose cautiously, exposing his hands, palms spread.

"I'm unarmed," he shouted back, looking up the balcony. Klepp was motionless, as were the body men. They'd all bled out. Beth and Scott were still frozen in terror in the booth. Screams were now whimpers.

***

Aliza Kahan aimed a Jericho pistol at his heart. She'd finally seen enough killing. She wasn't going to turn to stone like her father, but it took one last kill to ensure that. She wasn't going to let Max Klepp implicate her in his murderous schemes. Especially one to protect his daughter. She wasn't going to be responsible for the murder of that innocent women in the bathroom. And, more than anything, she hated to be dumped. Especially for inferior goods. When Klepp sent the Chinese to Wisconsin and to kill Becca, she'd had enough.

"You weren't here, Mr. Johnson. None of us were. Now, go!" With that, she walked out onto the patio, and was gone.

Royce walked over to the booth. He reached over and grabbed the water glass that he'd used. He put it in his pocket. It was the only thing that could definitively link him to the scene. He turned to go.

"Wait!" the dean screamed after him. "What about us?"

Royce stopped midstride.

"What about you?" he said with maximum indifference.

"You can't just leave us here. With this. What, what is going to happen? To us?"

"Good luck, Dean. You are going to need it." He turned to go, then stopped. Turning back toward the couple. "There's a million bucks in that envelope." He smiled at them, then left.

He rushed out the back door. In the alley, he reached into a dumpster and removed a duffle bag he'd placed there the night before. He could hear sirens approaching. Moving quickly between the buildings, he ducked through a chain-link fence that he'd cut open when he'd planned his exit. The back door of an apartment building made an easy pick on his rounds eight hours earlier, and he'd put a piece of sturdy tape on the lock to make sure he had easy access. Inside, he found a storage area under the stairs, where tenants put their bikes and other equipment. Changing into the clothes he'd stashed in the bag, he let his heart rate slow and the blood drain out of his face. After a moment of deep breathing, he was ready. He pulled a

White Sox cap on, put the water glass in the duffle, and walked out toward the front of the apartment. On the way, he picked up a *Wall Street Journal* in a plastic bag in the entry way. He took the paper out of the bag and opened it up. Looking at the front page, he opened the front door. A man on his way to work.

Out on the street, Royce beeped the key fob, and his Honda Accord rent-a-car responded. He sat in behind the steering wheel, found a jazz station, and steered down Dorchester Street headed toward Lake Shore Drive.

CHAPTER 54

One month later, the "Murders at the Med" had gone off the front page but were still at the front of everyone's mind. A waitress, the dean's father-in-law, and four members of the Hip Sing gang found dead in the popular restaurant, and no solid leads. Hyde Parkers had no choice but to go back to their lives, writing research papers, papering loans, pouring drinks. The manager of the Med had been held for questioning, but all she knew was that the man she now knew as Max Klepp had given her five thousand dollars to rent the restaurant for the morning. She saw nothing else. The regular busboys had vanished, and no one knew what happened to them. Whether they were involved or not, the police suspected they were undocumented aliens, and they had gone to their home countries out of fear. The police questioned the dean and his wife after finding their DNA at the scene. They told a fabulous tale about Royce Johnson and a team of African-American killers, but the detectives laughed it off. There was no link, no connection, and no evidence tying him to the scene. The dean had no answer as to why he would be there, or why his father-in-law was at the Med or how he was mixed up with Chinese gangsters.

Enough time had passed without anyone implicating him, so Royce went home. Over three weeks in a budget motel in northern Michigan had taken a toll on him. His beard was full and scraggly and he hadn't slept well, an eye always on the door. But after a week or so, he decided to make the time count. He'd lost at least twenty pounds from his daily ten-mile runs around the lake. *Moby Dick* was checked off the bucket list, and he'd spent many hours reconnecting with his girls by phone. He finally felt his top was starting to spin on center.

The For Sale sign in front of Alex's house took him by surprise, but it was auspicious timing. Claire had a sense for that kind of thing. She was on point, as usual. It was time for him to move on. Time to let Alex drift away to the recesses of his mind. Time to be fully Royce again.

He keyed into Alex's house for the first time in months. The mail filled the small entryway, and the house smelled of rotten food and must. He picked up the mail and set it on the table in the foyer, just steps from where his brother had been assassinated. Half expecting someone to be there for him too, he walked cautiously, like he was clearing the room. Seeing only the ghosts in his mind, Royce grabbed some of the letters from the top of the pile and retreated to the couch in the adjacent living room.

He'd checked his phone every day for news about Quayside or the investigation into the murder of Jante Turner, but nothing had broken yet. From a post office in Traverse City, he'd sent anonymous packages from the road to the Chicago Police, the Illinois State Police, and the FBI with the evidence he had on Beth. They would have to do their own investigation. The fruit he'd sent them had been poisoned by his illegal searches. Making a case against her, against them, would take time. Impatient as he was, he knew justice was coming for Beth and for Scott. It was as certain as the sun.

As for Quayside, Marcus had taken the case with the information he got from the chemist and that he pieced together from working with the clinic's other students. He passed it on to a friend at the firm that had rescinded his offer after he was implicated in Alex's death. The news would break any day.

"And, what about you?" Royce asked as they shared breakfast at a diner in Petoskey, Michigan a week earlier.

"I'll get the payday on this—a few percent maybe—and then…look for something else."

"They offered you a job?"

"They offered. I declined, *respectfully.*"

Marcus's smile consumed his entire face. Mission accomplished.

"So, it's back to helping people in the neighborhood then?" Royce took a bite of his French toast, eyes still on Marcus.

"I was thinking…"

"Always dangerous."

"Yeah." They shared a laugh. "I was thinking we make a good team."

"No, we don't. We almost got killed. All of us."

"*Almost*," Marcus emphasized.

"I guess we do." He looked at him through squinted eyes. "Are you sure you're up for this?"

"I'm sure…partner."

The shook hands over their breakfasts, then ate in silence. At the end of the meal, Marcus went to split the bill.

"On me." Royce pushed his money away. "This is for the Med."

"Hardly," Marcus scoffed. "You'll be paying that one back for years. When you save my life, we'll call it even."

They went their separate ways, planning to meet up in Chicago in a few weeks.

Collapsed into the comfy cushions of Alex's couch, Royce flipped through bills and solicitations. A pile of trash formed at his feet. Then, he noticed an off-white envelope with a return address of the Department of Justice in Washington. The name A.S. Fels was typed above the embossed address of Main Justice on Pennsylvania Avenue. Intrigued, he opened the envelope and removed a single piece of paper. The message was simple:

Dear Mr. Johnson,

Please contact me at your earliest convenience at the number above. It is a matter of great importance to you and to us.

A.S. Fels, Staff Attorney, U.S. Department of Justice.

Royce checked his watch. Ten-thirty-four a.m. eastern time. He dialed the number.

"Office of Presidential Pardons," the woman's voice said.

Royce smiled.

EPILOGUE

Beth Miller saw the blue lights flashing off her neighbor's windows as she went to answer the doorbell. The coffee in the Notre Dame mug sloshed and she swallowed hard. Every day she expected this moment to arrive. But with it here, she suddenly felt unprepared. The Tiger mom in her, the achiever and the planner who never left anything to chance, worried that there was something she should do before she opened the door to her fate. But scanning the entryway, noticing the lilies radiating perfectly from a Simon Pearce vase Scott had given her on their anniversary last year, the realization that there was nothing to do overwhelmed her. The mug went down on the polished table without a coaster. It would leave a ring but Beth knew there would be no one to notice.

In the time since the shootout, she hadn't slept or done much other than drink and fret. She'd sent her kids to live with Scott's sister and her dentist husband in Omaha. They'd be safe there. She hoped. Television was a salve, but only when wetted with bourbon and gin and vodka and tequila. Pills helped too. A steady dose of hydrocodone and cyclobenzaprine whited her out like a lake-effect snowstorm. Waiting was the worst part. She actually felt a sense of relief as she opened the door and saw the faces of three of Chicago's finest. They were all business.

"Mrs. Elizabeth Miller, you are under the arrest for the

murder of Jante Turner." They turned her around and slipped the metal cuffs over her delicate wrists. The diamond tennis bracelet her dad gave her on her wedding night, all twenty karats, was on her daughter's wrist in Nebraska.

The gunshot made them all jump. Even seasoned officers flinch when the metallic thud echoes unexpectedly. But only for an instant. The officer shoved Beth to the side and down to the ground, knee into her back. The other two officers pushed past them and headed into the home.

"Do you own a firearm, Mrs. Miller?" The officer now on top of her asked.

"My husband. It's my husband. He...he...It's okay. I think he is...dead."

"Mr. Mayor?" the mayor's staff secretary blurted over the intercom. "It's Cole Stanton from Sidney & Ellis. He's not in your calendar, but he says its urgent."

There was no answer.

"Mr. Mayor?" She looked up at Stanton, standing rod-straight in a dark suit, white shirt, and plain black tie, dressed for the occasion. "Mr. Mayor? Should I send him in?"

The door to the mayor's office swung open, and he stood in the frame, his sleeves rolled up to the elbow, his tie loosened and slightly ajar.

"Cole! To what do I owe the pleasure?" He strode across, smiling, arm outstretched.

Stanton shook his hand vigorously, letting his power show. The mayor felt the intention in his balls.

"Come, let's talk." He led the way, closing the door and begging off his appointments for the next hour and asking for coffee for two.

When the mayor was back around behind his desk, Stanton reached down to his rectangular black catalog case, flipped the brass locks, and withdrew a Redwell folder. Holding it close to his chest, he eyed the mayor. His eyes were on the folder.

Stanton extended his arms and placed the folder on the large oak desk. He sat back, and let it sit between them, out of reach of them both.

"What's this, Cole? A donation to my reelection campaign?" The mayor tried to break the tension. He reached for the folder reluctantly.

Stanton sat forward, reaching out toward the folder. They both gripped it loosely, ready to pull it to their side.

"This is a complaint we are prepared to file in the Northern District of Illinois pursuant to the Resource Conservation and Recovery Act alleging a significant and imminently dangerous toxic waste spill beneath the Quayside development in Bridgeport."

The mayor swallowed hard. "What does this have to do with me?"

"Everything." Cole Stanton eyed him, knowing these moments came along once in a career, if you were incredibly lucky.

The mayor opened the folder. He pulled out the complaint and set it to the side. Flipping the folder over, its contents spilled onto his desk. Pictures. Dozens and dozens. He flipped through them—pictures of chemicals, of law students at the Quayside site, of burned-out buildings, of a corpse in a Wisconsin cabin, of gaping wounds and blood-soaked bandages on the floor of a flophouse, of Becca's bloated corpse, of the bloody floor of the Medici...he stopped, and his eyes rose up to meet Stanton's. A broad smile covered Stanton's face, one eye closed slightly and a boyish smirk he couldn't hide.

The mayor leaned back in his chair and put his hands behind his head. "What do you want, Cole? I'll give you anything you want."

"I'm counting on it."

M. TODD HENDERSON was the biggest baby born in Tennessee in 1970. A professor at the University of Chicago, he is mostly renowned as being the tallest law professor on Earth. He's also written dozens of books and articles on business law and regulation. Prior to becoming an academic, he worked as a designer of dams, a judicial clerk, a Supreme Court lawyer, and a management consultant. A graduate of Princeton and the University of Chicago, he lives in the Hyde Park neighborhood of Chicago with his wife and three children.

On the following pages are a few more great titles from the Down & Out Books publishing family.

For a complete list of books and to sign up for our newsletter, go to DownAndOutBooks.com.

Madness of the Q
A Sam Teagarden Thriller
Gray Basnight

Down & Out Books
December 2020
978-1-64396-088-3

Humble math professor Sam Teagarden is plunged into a global crisis of religious bloodshed sparked by discovery of the Q Document, an ancient parchment uncovered in northern Israel.

Allied with American agents, he soon finds himself alone, trying to save the maximum number of lives while struggling against an international gauntlet of paranoia and blind religious zealotry.

Mickey Finn: 21st Century Noir Vol. 1
Michael Bracken, editor

Down & Out Books
December 2020
978-1-64396-158-3

Mickey Finn: 21st Century Noir is a crime-fiction cocktail that will knock readers into a literary stupor.

Twenty contributors push hard against the boundaries of crime fiction, driving their work into places short crime fiction doesn't often go, into a world where the mean streets seem gentrified by comparison and happy endings are the exception rather than the rule.

All Due Respect 2020
Chris Rhatigan & David Nemeth, editors

All Due Respect, an imprint of
Down & Out Books
November 2020
978-1-64396-165-1

Twelve short stories from the top writers in crime fiction today.

Featuring the work of Stephen D. Rogers, Tom Leins, Michael Pool, Andrew Davie, Sharon Diane King, Preston Lang, Jay Butkowski, Steven Berry, Craig Francis Coates, Bobby Mathews, Michael Penncavage, and BV Lawson.

White Trash and Dirty Dingoes
Jason Parent

Shotgun Honey, an imprint of
Down & Out Books
July 2020
978-1-64396-101-9

Gordon thought he'd found the girl of his dreams. But women like Sarah are tough to hang on to.

When she causes the disappearance of a mob boss's priceless Chihuahua, she disappears herself, and the odds Gordon will see his lover again shrivel like nuts in a polar plunge.

With both money and love lost, he's going to have to kill some SOBs to get them back.